HAPPY EVER AFTER FOR THE CORNISH MIDWIFE

JO BARTLETT

Boldwood

First published in Great Britain in 2023 by Boldwood Books Ltd.

Copyright © Jo Bartlett, 2023

Cover Design by Head Design

Cover photography: Shutterstock and Adobe Stock

Every effort has been made to obtain the necessary permissions with reference to copyright material, both illustrative and quoted. We apologise for any omissions in this respect and will be pleased to make the appropriate acknowledgements in any future edition.

A CIP catalogue record for this book is available from the British Library.

Paperback ISBN 978-1-80483-916-4

Large Print ISBN 978-1-80483-912-6

Hardback ISBN 978-1-80483-911-9

Ebook ISBN 978-1-80483-909-6

Kindle ISBN 978-1-80483-910-2

Audio CD ISBN 978-1-80483-917-1

MP3 CD ISBN 978-1-80483-914-0

Digital audio download ISBN 978-1-80483-908-9

Boldwood Books Ltd
23 Bowerdean Street
London SW6 3TN
www.boldwoodbooks.com

This novel is about sisterhood of all kinds. As such, it's dedicated both to my sister, Sam, and to Den, the sister of my good friend, Kerry.

For Sam, my sister, my friend, with much love. From tiny tears to grown up ones and all the laughs in between, always by my side xx

For Dennamac, Maccy, Den, lovely sis. Miss you always – forever in my heart and thoughts. Love you xx

1

'Imagine being told that you can't have the one thing you've always wanted.' The training facilitator looked across the room and Meg deliberately didn't make eye contact. She could imagine it far too easily, except that she'd had the one thing she'd always wanted and it had been taken away from her.

'That's what infertility is like for so many people.' The facilitator was still scanning the room, and even with her head dipped slightly, Meg could see lots of people nodding, including Jess, who was sitting on her right. Jess had first-hand experience of the pain of infertility and she'd been open about it with Meg since she'd joined the midwifery unit as a part-time receptionist. Meg did two days at the unit and two days at the GP surgery, fitting in her studies to become a counsellor around both jobs. It was Jess who'd suggested she come along to the endometriosis awareness training and Meg had jumped at the chance. Anything that helped her to understand the challenges people were going through was a positive, but this issue was close to home for Meg too.

'What if there was something you could do that might give you the chance of having a baby after all, even if the timing wasn't right?' The facilitator clicked through to the next slide. 'That's often a predicament faced by young women diagnosed with more severe cases of endometriosis.'

Meg leant closer to Jess. 'They've told Tilly not to leave it too long, but she's nowhere near ready to have a baby.' She whispered the words to her friend, who shot her a sympathetic look in return. Meg had shared enough in the past for Jess to know why this was such a dilemma for her daughter. Tilly was twenty-three and had just completed the second part of her solicitor's qualifying exam and had started her two years' qualifying practice with a small law firm in Port Tremellien. She should be thinking about how to make the most of her twenties and build her career, not choosing whether to gamble with her fertility. Tilly's boyfriend, Ed, was a nice enough lad, but he was only a couple of years ahead of her in training for the same career. It seemed far too early for them to have to decide whether they wanted a link to each other for the rest of their lives.

'For me, it wasn't just the issue of decreasing infertility.' The facilitator shook her head. 'I knew I couldn't have the treatment that was most likely to reduce my pain until I'd decided my family was complete. Facing the prospect of getting pregnant or risking infertility when you're only in your twenties is hard enough, but agreeing to have a hysterectomy at a very early age is arguably even harder. I know it was for me.'

Jess scribbled something on the pad she was holding. She'd been involved in running an infertility support group in Port Agnes for over three years and it was so in demand that GP surgeries from across the region had made contact to see if some of their patients could attend. With the need for support growing, Jess had asked Meg if she'd be willing to help out and it had seemed like the perfect role to help her develop her counselling skills. She was already volunteering for a bereavement charity, but that wasn't what she wanted to do forever. Meg had spent the last ten years being defined by bereavement and making a career out of that had never been part of her plan.

There was a murmur of agreement from around the room at the facilitator's words. The audience were all professionals involved in supporting patients with infertility and the last segment of the day focused on endometriosis. Willingly choosing to undergo a hysterectomy at a young age probably seemed unimaginable to most of the people in the room, but not Meg. She'd witnessed her daughter in so much pain from her endometriosis that if someone had offered Tilly the solution there and then, she'd probably have taken it just to stop the agony. But Meg knew that her daughter also wanted a family more than anything; a chance to get back what they'd once had, until fate and a freak accident had stolen it from them. Sometimes she'd dream the accident had never happened, and the raw grief would hit her all over again the moment she woke up. If Tilly added to their family, it wouldn't fill the void, but if grief was love with nowhere to go, there'd be a tsunami of love waiting for that baby to arrive. Just the thought of someone new coming into their lives made Meg's eyes sting, but she couldn't work out if the threatened tears were the good kind or the bad.

'As a GP, I think that's something I need to bear in mind.' A woman to the left of Meg directed her response to the facilitator. 'It's easy for me to tell a young woman with a more severe case of endometriosis that she needs to consider her fertility sooner rather than later, if she wants to give herself the best chance of having a child naturally, but I can never fully understand what other factors might be involved in deciding whether or not to try for a baby.'

'Absolutely; it's not the black-and-white decision that some health care providers present it as.' The facilitator smiled. 'That's something for us all to think about over the next coffee break.

When we come back, we'll be doing small group work to see if we can come up with some ideas on how to talk to women with endometriosis and other infertility issues, which take into account what those other factors might be.'

Meg turned to Jess, as everyone started to head towards the trestle table at the back of the room, ready to swoop on the drinks and biscuits that had been set out for the break. 'Thank you so much for swinging it for me to come to this.'

'No problem at all. If we get the funding to start running some counselling sessions at the surgery, all of this is really going to help. Not to mention how important this is to you personally.' Jess touched her arm. She was such a force of nature and Meg would bet her last pound on Jess getting the project off the ground. The GP surgery and midwifery unit were increasingly working in partnership with each other and they'd identified a huge need to extend the mental health support for patients using both services. Meg had been working at the unit for a year and had only attended eight infertility support group sessions so far. But Jess had shared from the start how worried she was about the emotional impact of infertility on some of the members and she was incredibly honest about how her own infertility had affected her, so it had been easy for Meg to share what Tilly was going through.

'I've got to admit it's made me think.' Meg tucked a strand of chestnut brown hair behind her ear. She'd been adamant that Tilly shouldn't panic and rush into motherhood when she'd brought up the prospect just after she'd got her exam results, but she could see now that it wasn't as simple as that.

'Me too, I think training sessions like this are—' Jess stopped as Meg's phone started to buzz in her hand. 'Do you need to get that?'

'It's Tilly, but she knows not to ring me today.' Meg looked from the screen to Jess and back again, cold creeping up her spine for reasons that probably wouldn't occur to anyone else. It was just an unexpected phone call from her daughter and Tilly had probably forgotten all about the training. But ever since that day when Meg had been given the worst news imaginable, she didn't seem to be capable of expecting anything else and right now, it was like she was frozen to the spot.

'Her timing's spot on. We've got fifteen minutes before the next session, so you can take Tilly's call and I'll get us both a drink and some of those shortbread biscuits before all we're left with are oatcakes.'

'Thank you.' Meg's hand shook as she reached out to press the button to connect the call. Her heart was hammering, despite telling herself there was nothing to worry about. 'Hey, Tils. What's up?'

'Is that Mrs Sawyer?' The voice didn't belong to her daughter, it was male for a start, and Meg's racing heartbeat broke into a gallop. This couldn't be happening, not again.

Somehow she managed to mumble a response. 'Uh-huh.'

'Now don't worry.' His words had the opposite of their intended effect. She couldn't think of a single reason why a stranger would be calling her on Tilly's phone if there was nothing to worry about. 'But I'm ringing because Tilly collapsed at work.'

'Collapsed!' The word came out as a shriek and Meg was vaguely aware of people looking in her direction, but she didn't give a damn. She just needed to know that Tilly was alive.

'Sorry, I'm not putting this very well. It was probably more of a faint. She's awake and talking now, and she seems fine, but she won't let us call an ambulance. You're listed on Tilly's HR file as her next of kin and we thought maybe you could persuade her to get checked out properly.' The man cleared his throat. 'We don't want her driving home after this.'

'Don't let her move until I get there.' Meg wasn't going to waste time trying to talk sense into Tilly over the phone. She wanted to see her daughter with her own eyes and make sure she was okay. Once she got there, Meg would carry Tilly out and strap her into the car herself, like she was a toddler again, if she had to. She'd be going to hospital to get checked over whether she liked it or not.

'How long do you think you'll be? Tilly seems pretty determined that she's okay to drive.' The man on the other end of the phone sounded doubtful and something about his tone helped the tension in Meg's shoulders to relax. He wasn't worried about Tilly being okay, he was worried that they wouldn't be able to stop her leaving until Meg arrived. Nothing stood in Tilly's way when she'd made up her mind.

'I'll be twenty minutes at the most.' Meg caught Jess's eye. She'd explain everything later, but Tilly needed her. When that happened, there wasn't a single thing in the world that could stand in Meg's way either.

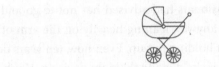

2

Jess had insisted on driving Meg to Port Tremellien, because Meg had been shaking so much. Despite the relief she'd felt at hearing that Tilly was being her usual feisty self, the adrenaline was still coursing through her veins as memories of a different day came flooding back. Except, that had started with two police officers standing on her doorstep, looking as if they wished they were anywhere else.

'I'm so sorry, but—' The young police sergeant had seemed to be speaking in slow motion, but a scream from somewhere stopped him in his tracks. Meg didn't even realise where the sound was coming from, until the female police officer put her arms around her. The next ten minutes or so were a blur of Meg begging the two police officers to admit that they might have got it wrong and that the bodies pulled from the rubble of the old house her husband, Darren, had been working on didn't belong to him or their teenage son. Seth had been so keen to earn extra money that he'd volunteered to help out in his father's construction business every school holiday. He should have been on the beach in Port Agnes, trying to get girls to notice him, like the rest of his friends from the local

high school, but instead – at just fifteen – he'd been pulled, grey
and lifeless from beneath a mountain of bricks that had left him
and his father no chance of survival.

The bargaining had started from the moment the police had
arrived on the doorstep. It wouldn't be them; it couldn't be. Meg
had even insisted on identifying her husband and son; there was
no way she'd have believed it if someone else had done it instead of
her. Some of the professionals had advised her not to go and see
Seth, but she'd gone in anyway, leaning heavily on the arm of her
mother, who was all but holding her up. Even now, ten years down
the line, she wasn't sure if she'd made the right decision. Her beautiful boy had looked so perfect in many ways and the coroner's
report had concluded that Darren had almost certainly tried to
shield his son when the wall started to collapse. It hadn't been
enough though, and both her husband and son had suffered fatal
blunt force injuries as a result of falling masonry. Meg had read the
report more times than she could count, but nothing changed the
verdict. Her only consolation was that it was likely to have been
very quick. She hated the thought that either of them would have
had time to have been scared, especially Seth. He was still her
baby, even at fifteen and almost six feet tall. To her he'd always be
the little boy who'd had nightmares about Power Rangers when
he'd been six or seven, and had crept into her bed for a cuddle
when he couldn't sleep. Looking down at him lying there, she'd
wanted to try and shake him awake, but nothing she could do
would bring him or Darren back.

It was in the months afterwards that she'd regretted seeing
them both, because it meant she'd forgotten how to picture them
as they were, before they were lying there in that room, with all the
life drained out of them. Darren and Seth had been so alike, their
sandy blond hair and ready smiles meaning they'd been mistaken
for brothers more than once. They'd both been taken far too early.

She and Darren had been launched into parenthood at a young age, but they'd taken to it better than she'd ever dared hope. Despite not planning for family life, Seth had been an easily contented baby, so it hadn't been a hard decision to try for a second baby a little more than a year afterwards. Tilly was born exactly nine days after her brother turned two and Meg had counted her blessings many times over the next thirteen years. She and Darren had grown together, instead of apart, and, as his small construction firm became more established, the money worries they'd had in their early days together had become a thing of the past. They'd had it all and had even seemed blessed with teenagers who weren't terminally embarrassed by their parents. The week before Darren and Seth died, they'd celebrated Tilly's thirteenth birthday. Everything had been right in the world, but in an instant it had gone more horribly wrong than Meg could ever have imagined.

For a long time, she hadn't been sure she would survive losing her boys and, if it hadn't been for Tilly, she probably wouldn't have. But somehow, they kept each other going. At first, it was all they could do to get through each day and Meg didn't plan anything beyond that. Thinking too far ahead just reminded her of what was missing from the future she'd always envisaged, but gradually that started to change. She needed to help Tilly make plans for her future. Time couldn't stand still, even if Meg had wanted it to, and eventually she'd realised she had to move forward too. Otherwise, when Tilly left home, she'd have nothing.

Having her own counselling had been a life raft for Meg, and she'd been three years into it when she'd started to think about training to counsel other people. Darren's life insurance had meant that Meg hadn't needed to work while Tilly was still at school, but she'd taken on a part-time job at the GP surgery to give her days some new meaning. Then, just before Tilly had left for uni, Meg had started studying online and now she had a psychotherapy degree and had started her counselling training.

On the seventh anniversary of the accident, during an evening at a friend's house where they'd drunk far too much wine, Meg had done something she'd never have dreamt of and set up an online dating profile. If the Chablis hadn't slipped down so easily, Meg wouldn't have agreed to it. The dating hadn't worked out quite as planned and she'd ended up bursting into tears on the first date she'd been on, but it had opened her mind to the possibility that she might be ready to meet someone. And now, here she was, over two and a half years into a relationship with a man who was born the same month she'd started secondary school. Her friends thought it was hilarious and teased her fairly relentlessly about her 'toy boy', but Johnnie had taken Meg completely by surprise.

She'd realised how much younger Johnnie was long before they'd started dating, but it had been part of what had made him feel safer than any of the profiles she'd matched with online. In her mind, the difference in their ages meant there was no chance of them falling in love or of it turning into anything serious. No one could ever replace Darren and she didn't want to try. Except, she hadn't reckoned on Johnnie turning out to be one of the best people she'd ever met. What he saw in Meg was a complete mystery. Eventually, he'd move on and want the life he'd be missing out on if he stayed with her. He'd be a great dad and she wouldn't stand in his way when he worked that out for himself. In the meantime, she was doing her best to try to enjoy it while it lasted and not rely on him too much, even though her first instinct after getting the call about Tilly had been to phone Johnnie for support. She was on dangerous ground, but it had already been too late by the time she'd realised it.

'She's going to be okay, isn't she?' Meg looked at Jess as she brought the car to a stop outside the offices where Tilly's law firm was based.

'Of course she is.' Jess gave her a reassuring smile and Meg took a deep breath. Everything was going to be okay; the worst had already happened a long time ago and no one could be that unlucky twice.

* * *

Jess, at barely five feet tall, was having trouble keeping up with Meg, who was at least eight inches taller and had stridden ahead once they'd reached the front door of Parton, Woodley and Thwaite. She could understand her friend's anxiety; anyone getting a phone call like that about someone they loved would worry. But after what had happened to Meg's husband and son, Jess couldn't even imagine how terrified she must be. It was why Jess had happily left the training early, despite spending weeks arranging it. She didn't want Meg driving with so much running through her head and Jess might be able to reassure her that a hospital visit wasn't necessary, or even help persuade Tilly that it was.

The receptionist ushered them through a door and Meg launched herself towards the young woman sitting on a sofa in what looked like a waiting area for clients.

'I'm so glad you're okay, sweetheart; that phone call nearly finished me off.'

'Oh Mum, you didn't have to drive all the way here!' Tilly had the same high cheek bones and dark brown eyes as her mother, but with long blonde hair closer to the colour of Jess's and in her elegant navy blue suit, she looked a picture of professionalism.

'Like I was going to sit around and wait after a call like that.' Meg shook her head. 'This is Jess, by the way; we were at the training together and she kindly drove me over.'

'Sorry you got dragged here unnecessarily too but thank you anyway. I've heard loads about you from Mum.' Tilly held out her hand and smiled.

'You too.' Jess shook the younger woman's hand. 'And it was no problem.'

'How are you feeling now? Still dizzy?' Meg reached up and put a hand on Tilly's forehead. 'You don't feel like you've got a temperature.'

'I'm fine. I got a bit lightheaded, that's all, and everyone panicked unnecessarily.' Tilly sighed. 'I just need a good night's sleep.'

'What you need is to get checked out properly young lady.' Meg's tone brooked no argument, but it didn't stop Tilly from shaking her head.

'I don't need to, Mum. I'm fine, I promise.'

'Are you a qualified doctor?' Meg raised her eyebrows. 'No, I thought not, so if you don't mind, I'd rather get the opinion of a professional than take your word for it.'

'Tell her it would be a waste of the doctor's time, Jess, and we've done enough of that over the years.' Tilly gave her a pleading look, but it was clearly going to take more than Jess's opinion to dissuade Meg. Luckily, she had an idea.

'Most fainting episodes are down to low blood pressure. I've got my bag in the car, so I can run a few tests to check your blood pressure, your heart rate and your oxygen levels, and if you're up for doing a urine sample, I can even check your blood sugar level, as that can make you feel faint too if it drops too low. If all of that's okay, then I'd say you'd be safe to make a follow-up appointment with your GP rather than an urgent one.'

'That's a plan I can live with.' Meg smiled, but Tilly was looking as if she might make a bolt for the door at any moment.

'Will the urine test show up anything else?'

'Like what?' Even as Jess said the words, she knew what Tilly was asking and a split second later it clicked for Meg too.

'Oh my God, are you pregnant?' She was waiting for the answer, but her daughter's face gave away the secret before she even spoke.

'I was going to tell you, but I wanted to wait until the right time.' Tilly looked at her mother and for a moment the whole world seemed to stop. Jess held her breath, hoping that however Meg reacted, she wouldn't say something she might end up regretting for a very long time.

'That's amazing, darling, congratulations.' The words coming out of Meg's mouth were the right ones, but her eyes were wide and, when she folded her daughter into her arms, she looked over Tilly's shoulder and caught Jess's eye. She was shocked but desperately trying not to show it and all Jess could do was nod, hoping that it would convey her belief that everything would turn out okay in the end. Jess had cared for enough women over the years to know that even the most surprising of pregnancies almost always worked out if the expectant mother wanted to go ahead. And she was as sure as she could be that Tilly's would too.

3

Jess had been worried about Meg ever since Tilly had announced her pregnancy. She'd texted her a few times and her friend's responses had said all the right things, but she had a nagging feeling they didn't tell the full story.

Jess was looking forward to seeing Meg in person to see for herself how her friend was coping with the news. When you'd lost part of your family, the way Meg had, change could have an unexpected consequence: guilt. Darren and Seth would never meet the new member of the family that was on the way. The baby represented a future that its uncle and grandfather would never be a part of and Jess knew Meg would be blindsided by that. It had been the same for Jess when she'd met her husband, Dexter, and, later on, when they'd adopted his stepson, Riley. The one person Jess had wanted to talk to about it all was her mother. But that choice had been taken away from Jess when she was still just a child herself.

Growing up in a series of foster homes, Jess understood better than anyone how important family was. That sense of belonging had disappeared when Jess's mother had died and she didn't even have any siblings to share her childhood memories with. It was why she was determined that Riley wouldn't grow up as an only child. Jess had been told there was no chance of her conceiving naturally and she was four rounds of IVF treatment down, with no baby to show for it. So she and Dexter were looking into another adoption. Riley's birth mother had died in a car accident and when his biological father had decided that parenting full time wasn't for him, it had fallen to Dexter to take on that role. Adopting again felt like a good fit for them, but the social workers had to be convinced that they'd come to terms with not having any biological children of their own, before they could be considered to adopt for a second time. And the truth was, Jess wasn't sure she was there yet.

All of that was why she could understand just how conflicted Meg might be. This new baby wouldn't replace Darren or Seth, but they'd eventually fill an empty space at the table. Most families weren't as complicated as hers or Meg's, so she needed her friend to know that it was okay to have mixed feelings and that she could share them with Jess if she wanted to.

'I think Anna's going to give us an update on the progress of merging services with the hospital today.' Toni, one of the other midwives, came into the staffroom carrying a tray laden with mugs of tea. Meg was behind her, carrying a second tray with two packets of biscuits and more mugs, which were filling the air with the unmistakeable scent of coffee.

'I know I'm the one nearing retirement.' Gwen, the oldest midwife on the team, narrowed her eyes. 'But you're looking older than me these days, Toni.'

'What, you mean all the excess baggage under my eyes? That's what you get when you've got two kids under the age of three.' Toni yawned, as if to emphasise her point. 'I don't know what's happened to the time since they announced we were finally getting a hospital in the Three Ports area, but I can't believe it's been nearly two years.'

'I didn't think there was any chance of it being finished before I retired, but who knows, I might even manage a handful of shifts before you lot pack me off with a tartan blanket, a case of haemorrhoid cream and a year's supply of Werther's Originals.' Gwen shook her head and Jess couldn't help laughing. Gwen might not be far off her seventieth birthday, but she was probably the youngest at heart of all the midwives and was infamous for her near-the-knuckle remarks that made everyone except Gwen squirm.

'I think we all know that your leaving gifts are more likely to be body glitter, vodka and underwear that could double up as dental floss.' Toni's words echoed what Jess was thinking, and Gwen clapped her hands together.

'You girls do know me after all!'

'Are you still planning to volunteer at the hospital after you retire?' Anna, who managed the unit, turned towards Gwen as she spoke.

'Yes, I'm all signed up to run the Friends of the Hospital shop on Wednesdays, but I might take on a few more shifts. I'm hoping I'll get the chance to see a bit more of Ella too; I still miss her so much.' Gwen sighed. 'I know she's only up the road, but if I'm missing her as much as I do, how am I going to cope without you lot?'

'I've got a feeling we'll see you all the time.' Jess gave Gwen's waist a squeeze. They'd all missed Ella since she'd retrained as a health visitor and started working out of the GP surgery. But with the unit working in partnership with local surgeries for more and more of their services, it meant they still got to see quite a lot of her. Gwen would always be welcomed back at the unit too, but Jess had no idea if her friend would find time to pop back in when it came to it. Gwen had more hobbies than the rest of them put together and she was already running belly dancing classes a couple of times a week in the Port Agnes community centre. She'd been talking about starting up pole dancing classes once she retired, but not even Gwen had been able to persuade the parish council to fit a row of poles at the back of the hall. Not yet anyway.

'I don't know about everyone else, but I'm desperate to hear what the plan is for working with the maternity team at the hospital. I just hope it's going to be okay.' Izzy, who'd started working at the unit three years before, exchanged a look with Jess.

There'd been a lot of rumour and guess work ever since the hospital had been given the go ahead, including a suggestion that the midwifery unit would be fully integrated with the hospital. There was desperate need for emergency maternity care in the area and it had already been confirmed that the hospital would have four operating rooms, mostly catering for day and planned surgery, with some emergency surgery cover for both obstetrics and trauma. The new hospital was taking over the services of the old cottage hospital, but the departments had been broadened out to include oncology and Macmillan nursing, renal and stroke units, and mental health services. It still wasn't going to be like one of the huge general hospitals in other parts of the country, but it would be amazing for a community that had been forced to rely on the hospital in Truro for any kind of urgent care. The plans Jess had seen for the Three Ports Hospital looked similar to some of the rural Scottish hospitals in terms of size and services. Many of those hospitals had a model of fully integrated maternity services, which potentially put the unit at risk. So Izzy wasn't the only one worrying about the prospect.

By the time the rest of the team had filed in, the buzz about what Anna might be going to share with the team had reached a dull roar. The meeting had been called before the unit opened for routine clinics, so Meg and the other receptionist, Gordon, who'd joined the unit at around the same time, had both come to the staffroom for the update too.

'So, come on then, Anna, are we going to be closed down? Because I'll go down on record as Port Agnes Midwifery Unit's shortest serving midwife if we do.' Emily, who'd started at the unit as a maternity care assistant but had recently completed her training to become a midwife, asked the question on everyone's minds.

'No.' Anna clearly didn't want to drag out the tension and it wasn't until the tightness eased from Jess's shoulders that she realised quite how worried she'd been. 'There will be some integration in the services, but the unit won't be closing and we'll still be able to offer home deliveries and the use of the birthing suite for our mums-to-be who don't need intervention. There will be opportunities for some staff to work across both sites and for newly qualified midwives like you, Emily, that could be a really good thing for extending your experience.'

'Are you trying to get rid of me?' Emily grinned.

'Not at all, but Bobby had already mentioned putting his name down for a split role if the opportunity came up and I just thought you might be interested in doing the same thing.' Anna turned towards Bobby, the only male midwife in the team, who also happened to be married to Toni. 'Are you still up for that?'

Bobby nodded. 'Absolutely; it'll be a great opportunity to widen my expertise, especially in terms of assisted deliveries.'

'What Bobby forgot to mention is that the real reason he's doing it is to get a break from me and the kids.' Toni rolled her eyes. 'We tossed a coin to see who'd get to put their name down first. A twelve-hour night shift on the wards sounds like a doddle compared to staying at home with the kids. One of you should have told me we were mad for having a second one so quickly.'

'You wouldn't have listened if we had.' Frankie, one of the other midwives, laughed. 'You have to find out for yourself what having your hands full really feels like.'

'And some of us got twins straight off the bat.' Anna had won the parenting top trumps, and Jess swallowed hard. She couldn't think of anything she wanted more than having her hands full. Riley needed her far less than he had done when they'd first come into one another's lives. He was eight now and already limiting the number of times she could kiss him goodbye at the school gate to one very quick kiss on the top of his head. She'd never got to hold him in her arms as a baby, but there had been another baby boy who'd felt like hers for a little while. Baby Teddy had been abandoned outside the front door to Jess's apartment and she'd fostered him until he'd been moved to an adoptive family. It would have been a life changing experience, even if it hadn't turned out that her ex-husband, Dom, was the baby's father. Riley had filled the gaping hole in her heart that had been left when she was forced to give Teddy up, but there was still an ache in the pit of her stomach to hold a baby in her arms and know that she didn't have to hand it over to its mother, because that would be her. Every time the IVF failed, she was more grateful than ever for the chance to be Riley's mum, but it couldn't completely take away the longing.

'Are you okay?' Nadia, another of the midwives, who was also Frankie's daughter, touched Jess's arm lightly, keeping her voice low. Like the others on the team, she knew Jess's story, but she was the only one standing close enough to reach out. Jess had a feeling that her expression was giving away the fact that she was struggling, and the skin on her face felt like it was suddenly too tight when she tried to smile.

'I'm fine.'

'Sometimes the rest of us take for granted how lucky we've been.' Nadia squeezed Jess's arm again, her voice too low for anyone else to hear, and Jess gave an almost imperceptible nod, not trusting herself to say anything else. She didn't blame her friends for taking parenthood for granted and the truth was, they probably didn't really. Anna had been through fertility treatment herself and they'd all been involved in midwifery for long enough to know that becoming a mother wasn't possible for everyone. But she didn't want to be that person – poor old Jess, the friend they couldn't grumble about the challenges of parenthood in front of, in case she suddenly burst into tears. She'd told Nadia she was fine and she was, she had to be.

'Is the completion date still December?' Jess needed a change of subject, even if she had to create it herself.

'Yes and they've appointed a hospital administrator already. She wants to meet with us to discuss a way forward for partnership working.' Anna looked around the room. 'I've got to admit, I did have a little cry when I got the email saying we weren't just being swallowed up by the hospital, because this place and this team has meant so much to me.'

'So they're definitely keeping the unit open?' Jess tried to keep her tone casual, but she couldn't bear the thought of the unit closing either. She wouldn't have got through the last few years without it. The idea that the place which had become a second home, and a second family to her, might no longer be there, wasn't one she could even contemplate.

'They are, but I don't know whether it'll be exactly the way it is now.' Anna let go of a long breath. 'But we'll still be here, looking after the women and their babies who need us. We have to see integration and partnership working as a positive, because it means we won't automatically have to send our higher risk patients straight to Truro for their care.'

'I'm really pleased to hear that the news is this good, but now I've got loads of protest plans I'll never have the chance to carry out.' Gwen had a twinkle in her eye and Jess hardly dared ask, but she knew she had to.

'You had protest plans?'

'Oh, lots of them, but I was going to start by kayaking naked around Sisters of Agnes Island. In fact, I was going to suggest we all did.'

'Someone would have harpooned me.' It was Frankie's turn to laugh. 'But don't let us stop you, Gwen. You'll have plenty of time for new hobbies when you retire.'

'Oh, I won't be wasting time kayaking, naked or otherwise. I'm going to be a magician's assistant.' Gwen was totally deadpan, but Jess was still waiting for the punch line when Toni spoke.

'You're going to be a what?'

'A magician's assistant.' She shrugged as if it was the most natural thing in the world. 'Barry's always enjoyed doing magic at home and we've finally got the time to take it further.'

'Oh my God, now I know you're serious.' Frankie's eyes widened. 'You're talking about Barry performing magic at home and not even turning it into an innuendo.'

'I'm deadly serious. We've already got a website.' Gwen grabbed her phone. 'It's Barry the Magic Man and the Great Gwendini. We're taking bookings for kids' magic shows, but there's also an adult version.'

'Okay, I definitely don't want to know what that involves.' Jess didn't even want to picture it.

'Oh no, not that sort of magic. Barry only performs that for me.' Gwen winked and Jess couldn't help laughing. The unit was going to be a very different place without her around. 'This is called mingle magic and it's an icebreaker for parties and corporate events. We just promise to get the party started, that's all.'

'Well, you've never let us down on that front and it's just one of the things I'm going to miss about you.' Anna exchanged a look with Jess, an unspoken understanding passing between them. Things were going to change at the unit, regardless of how the meeting with the hospital administrator went. It had been hard enough when Ella had left, but with some of the staff planning to split their time between the hospital and the unit, it was all going to be different very soon. Sometimes you didn't know what you had until it was gone, but, like Anna, Jess already knew she was going to miss moments like these when the whole team got together. So, for now, she was determined to make the most of the time they had left.

*　*　*

When the idea of the unit and the new hospital being integrated had first been raised, Anna had been keen to ensure the future of her team was protected. Part of that was to book some of the midwives who'd been in community midwifery the longest into refresher training. Jess, Toni and Bobby had also signed up to the NHS staff bank, to pick up some extra shifts at the hospital in Truro.

She was due to start a shift at the hospital two hours after the team meeting ended, but she wanted to catch up with Meg properly before she left.

'Are you okay?' Jess stood by the reception desk, where Meg was opening a box of leaflets. There were no patients yet, but the waiting area would start to fill up as the clinics got underway.

'I didn't sleep very well. Trying to work out how on earth Tilly and Ed are going to manage financially and whether I should think about downsizing to release some money from the house to give to them. It's all going to be hers eventually anyway, but I just can't bear the thought of selling the house.' As Meg looked at Jess, her eyes filled with tears. 'It's stupid, but part of me keeps thinking that Darren won't know where to find me if I move, and Seth would wonder where his room has gone. But it's not like they're ever coming back, is it? And Darren would have wanted me to make sure Tilly is okay. I'm just being selfish.'

'That's the last thing you're being. It must be tough facing another stage of your life and not being able to share that with Darren and Seth.' Jess was a hugger and even some of her friends, like Toni, who weren't big on displays of affection, had got used to that over the years. Luckily, Meg seemed to appreciate it as a show of support, even though they hadn't known each other as long.

'You should be a therapist, you know.' Meg sniffed. 'I kept crying last night, thinking that Darren won't even know he's going to be grandad, and Seth won't get to be the fun uncle I know he would have been. I didn't think anyone would understand that.'

'I've felt like it so many times since Mum died. I was so young when she died, and it feels like she's missed every big milestone in my life. Some of them were heart-breaking, but some I'm almost grateful she didn't have to see, like the mess my divorce turned into. But part of me still wishes she'd been there. I'm probably not explaining it properly.'

'You are. I know Darren would have been concerned about whether Tilly was rushing into this with Ed, just like I am. He fretted about the kids from the moment they were born and he'd have been worried sick about her for the whole nine months. It would have made him a nervous wreck and I would have hated seeing him like that, but I'd still have liked to share it with him. It doesn't make any sense, does it? But I know exactly what you mean.'

'And I can understand why you're worried, but I suppose you have to think about what the worst case scenario could have been for the choices Tilly was facing. She and Ed might not go the distance, and things might be tough financially either way, but she'll get through it. And I can almost guarantee you'll both think it's all been worth it, because you'll have the baby in your lives.' Jess held Meg's gaze. 'But if she decided not to have the baby now and discovered later on that the endometriosis had made her infertile, she might find herself filled with the sort of regret there's no way to get over.'

'I know you're right and I'm just glad she's okay. I was shocked that they were already trying, not to mention the fact it had worked, but the training was perfectly timed. It really opened me up to another point of view and you've helped me more than you'll ever know. I can see now that my "rules" for when Tilly is ready for a baby, with a mortgage and a marriage coming first, are just that: *my* rules. But I think Tilly is almost as shocked as I am, because she wasn't expecting it to happen quite this fast. They were playing Russian Roulette with contraception apparently.'

'What does that mean?'

'I didn't want any more details than what she told me to be honest.' Meg pulled a face. 'I know Tilly can't bear to think that her old mum might not be living like a nun any more and no one wants to think about their parents having a sex life. But it's no different when you're the parent. I want to pretend that Tilly and Ed's baby will be delivered by a stork. If I had to guess, I assume she means they don't always use contraception and I know she'd decided to come off the pill, to make sure it had completely left her system.'

'At the risk of sounding like Gwen, I suppose that's one way to make a box of condoms last.' Jess grinned, trying not to let her mind linger for too long on how easily some people found it to fall pregnant. She could play Russian Roulette with contraception for the rest of her life and still have absolutely no chance of falling pregnant. She had to believe there was another path meant for her. She just wished she could turn off the almost primal urge that came over her whenever she held a newborn in her arms, to have a baby of her own. She felt guilty when she looked at Riley for wanting that so much. It was just hormones with nowhere to go; it would pass. It had to.

'I just want everything to be okay. Even since Darren and Seth died I've found it much harder to believe that things will go right and I'm so worried about losing Tilly too.' There was a catch in Meg's voice, and Jess reached out to touch her arm.

'She's young and healthy, and the perfect age to have a child from a biological point of view. It's going to be fine.'

'It's not just the fear of losing her if something goes wrong. After the boys' accident, it was me and Tilly against the world. Since she met Ed, in her first year of uni, things have been different, but now she's going to have a family of her own and I'm scared of where that leaves me.'

'She's going to need you more than ever.' Jess had wanted to pick up the phone to her own mother a hundred times since Riley had come into her life. There'd been so many questions, from whether the rash he had looked more like measles or chicken pox, to whether it was normal for him to sometimes call her by his new teacher's name. But Jess's mother had been gone a long time. Thankfully she did have someone to turn to, though. Not long after he'd come back into Jess's life, her father had started a relationship with Frankie, who'd become like a second mum to Jess. If the IVF had worked, she'd have wanted every bit of support her father and Frankie could offer.

'I'm worried I won't know when to step in and when to step back.' Meg shook her head.

'Just talk to her. I'm sure you'll feel a hundred times better once you do and so will she.' Jess knew to her cost how wrong parents could get it, when they tried to second guess what they thought their children wanted. Her father, Guy, had got it into his head that she'd be better off without him, after her mother had died, but staying away was the worst possible thing he could have done.

'You're a wise woman, Jess, and I'm really glad I've got someone I can talk to about all of this. Tilly doesn't want anyone to know about the baby until she's a bit further along. Poor Johnnie, he'll probably run for the hills when he hears he's dating a soon-to-be grandmother!'

'You're not worried about that are you?' Jess looked at Meg, who was already laughing.

'I think he knows what he's getting into already, what with all the symptoms that seem to have hit me these last few months. I feel like an old woman some mornings and I thought I'd have at least another five years before I even had to think about the menopause, but now I'm not so sure. If Johnnie can put up with that, I don't think he'll mind dating a nana.'

'Sounds like he's got the makings of a keeper.'

'One day, he'll realise that being with me means sacrificing stuff he doesn't even know he wants yet. Maybe when Tilly's baby arrives, it'll be a stark reminder of what I can never give him.' Meg blew out her cheeks. 'But I try not to think too far ahead, because I know nothing's guaranteed. So if the flipping menopause will let me, I'm just going to try to keep enjoying things with Johnnie while they last.'

'I'm sure Gwen would have some advice for you on that front.' Jess couldn't help laughing at the look that crossed Meg's face.

'I dread to think!'

'Me too, but somehow I still want to hear it.' Jess touched her arm again. 'I'm glad you're feeling a bit better about it all, Meg, but you know where I am if you need me. I'd better head to Truro for my shift, otherwise I'm going to be late. See you later.'

'See you later and thanks for everything, it's really helped.'

'No problem at all.' Jess turned and headed for the door. She really was going to have to get going to make her shift in time and she wanted to be as ready as possible to work in the new hospital, if she had to, when the time came.

4

When Jess had completed her midwifery training, it had been community midwifery that had won her heart. As much as she'd enjoyed working in hospitals, there was no way to build the same sort of relationships you could in the community. But there was a lot more variety in the types of delivery that took place in a hospital setting and being able to care for high-risk patients was something she was looking forward to being able to do more of.

Arriving at the maternity ward in Truro, Jess was assigned the care of a woman called Krissy O'Brien, who was being induced at forty-two weeks. Induction wasn't something that was offered at the birthing unit, due to the increased risk of the patient needing an assisted delivery.

According to her notes, this was Krissy's first baby and Jacinda, one of the full-time midwives at the hospital, briefed Jess on Krissy's treatment so far. She'd already been at the hospital for forty-eight hours and had been given her second pessary to induce the labour, as well as a hormone drip to help speed up delivery now that the contractions had finally started. When Jess met her for the first time, it was clear Krissy was feeling even more nervous about the delivery than the average mother-to-be, not to mention being completely exhausted.

'Hi Krissy, I'm Jess and I'm going to be taking over from Jacinda.' Jess offered the other woman her most reassuring smile, but all Krissy could do was grimace.

'Got a contraction.' She gritted her teeth and Jess moved to the head of the bed so she could see the monitor and give Krissy as much support as she needed.

'Use the gas and air if you need it. That's good, take slow, deep breaths. You're doing really well and so is the baby.' The readings on the monitor offered the reassurance that Jess needed. The baby was happy for now, but induced deliveries could often take longer, as well as being more painful, than usual. It had clearly been a long couple of days for Krissy already.

'I don't think I can keep doing this.' Krissy wasn't saying anything that Jess hadn't heard hundreds of times before, but she really did look like she was struggling.

'Is it the pain or the tiredness, or is there something else?' Jacinda had mentioned that Krissy's husband had needed to leave the hospital for a few hours because of other commitments. Although Jess was struggling to work out what could be more important than being at his wife's side, especially as they didn't have any other children. It might be the reason why Krissy was starting to believe she couldn't do this.

'It feels like someone's trying to turn me inside out.' Krissy managed a half-smile for the first time.

'In a way, they sort of are.' Jess had been surprised to discover that Krissy hadn't already elected to have an epidural. Lots of patients being induced chose that option because of the likelihood of increased pain. Jess had always been keen not to make the women she cared for feel like they needed to be heroes. 'Did you talk to Jacinda about the possibility of having an epidural?'

'I'm worried about it making things take even longer and the baby getting into distress. If my blood pressure goes low, it can slow down the baby's heartbeat too, can't it?' Krissy had clearly done her research, but Jess was hoping she could allay her fears.

'It can, but it's very unlikely to harm the baby in any way and it might make the labour easier for you to deal with, which can help with your recovery time afterwards. I'm monitoring the baby closely and if there's any change I promise you we'll deal with it. You don't need to worry about any of that, but this has got to be up to you.'

'I wish Alec would hurry up and get back so I can ask him what he thinks.'

'Is that your partner?'

'My husband.' Krissy nodded as she spoke and Jess's scalp prickled. If a woman in labour needed pain relief, the last thing she should be doing was waiting for her husband's permission. Jess might be small, but she'd never been shy about speaking out when she needed to.

'Only you know how much pain you're in. So, if you think an epidural will help, you don't need to ask anyone's permission.'

'Oh no, it's not that.' Krissy winced again as she shifted position. 'I just need him to reassure me that I won't be failing if I have the epidural. I know you've already said it won't hurt the baby, but I wanted to do this all as naturally as possible. Alec has been telling me all the way through that it doesn't matter as long as me and the baby are both okay at the end of it, but I could do with hearing that again now.'

'Would it help if we called him?' Jess might have misjudged Alec, but she still couldn't believe there was somewhere more important he needed to be right now than by his wife's side.

'He should be back soon. He wasn't going to go, but I didn't want us both to miss Amelia's big day.'

'Amelia?' Jess suddenly wondered if she'd misread the notes and Krissy did have another child after all.

'We're foster carers and Amelia was one of the babies we had placed with us. Today her adoption is being finalised and they're having a ceremony to celebrate. We were both invited and I was originally hoping I'd be taking the new baby to meet them, but obviously this little one had other plans.' Krissy smiled and Jess was relieved to hear that she'd got Alec all wrong. 'The contractions are agony now but they're still a long way apart, so I figured the baby's unlikely to put in an appearance any time soon and fostering's really important to us.'

'I was a foster carer for a little while, but I found it too hard to let go.' Jess still had to blink back tears whenever she thought of Teddy. She'd fallen in love with the little boy the moment she'd discovered him on her doorstep. Somehow, even after all this time, her arms still ached with emptiness when she pictured his face.

'I was like that with a little boy we looked after for almost two years until just after he turned six, but what made it worse was that we gave notice on the placement, so I felt massively guilty as well. We just found it overwhelming never getting a break from the challenging behaviours he had, but... oh my God!' Krissy screwed up her face as the pain took over her body again.

'Like I said before, the gas and air might help, but if you really want to avoid using it, just use your breathing instead. Breathe in through your nose and, when you breathe out again, some women find it helpful to sigh. Don't feel like you have to keep fighting against the pain, though. It really is okay to ask for some help.'

Krissy shook her head, breathing in deeply and then sighing, just as Jess had instructed, three times. Her whole face changed as the contraction finally passed and it was suddenly as though she was just casually passing the time with small talk. When Jess had first started training, she'd been surprised at how, in the earlier stages of labour, some women could be in absolute agony one minute and back to talking normally the next. Sometimes, when the patient had an epidural in, you'd never even guess they were in labour. 'The contractions feel like they're getting stronger. I hope Alec gets back soon.'

'It's okay for you to put yourself first. If you need him, call him.'

'I don't want to let Amelia down. Our social worker suggested we try parent and child placements, after we gave notice on Ajay. They're short-term placements and there's a chance for a break in between. We knew Amelia wouldn't be staying forever, but she was with us for nearly six months, after her birth mum left, and it's impossible not to get attached after having a baby for that long, isn't it?'

'Absolutely.' Jess swallowed hard. Sometimes, just lately, she struggled with that. Holding a newborn for just a matter of minutes was enough to make her feel like she never wanted to let go. She could try rationalising the longing as a biological urge, but that didn't make the feelings any easier to deal with.

'That's why I insisted Alec had to go to the ceremony; we felt like we'd failed when Ajay moved on, so Amelia's family day feels like a huge milestone. When Jacinda said how long the labour was likely to take to get going, I almost shoved Alec out of the door. The ceremony is only down the road and he should be back soon. I just need to hold on for a tiny bit longer and then I can—' Krissy screwed up her face as another contraction took the words out of her mouth.

'Okay, keep breathing like before, that's great.' Jess encouraged Krissy until the contraction passed, watching to see how the other woman was managing the pain.

'How are you doing?' Jess's tone was gentle as Krissy's contraction finally faded away.

'It feels like it's getting harder with every pain.'

'The gap in between is getting shorter too. Are you sure you don't want us to call Alec?'

'I'll call if he's not here by the time I've had three more contractions.' Krissy managed a half-smile. 'I know it sounds weird, but I don't want him to panic either. He probably thinks I'm still waiting for the hormones to kick everything off.'

'And what about the pain relief? I know you said you want to talk to Alec, but if you're even thinking you might want an epidural, I can contact the anaesthetist to come up and talk to you. It could take a while for someone to be free, especially if there are any C-sections in progress. It would be better to arrange it and decide against it later, rather than not be able to get one in time.'

'Are my contractions close enough together for that?'

'Like I said before, things are clearly speeding up. But if you're okay with it, I can examine you again to see if things have moved on since Jacinda last checked? You were three centimetres dilated when you were last examined.'

'Okay, if we can do it before I get another contraction.' Krissy let go of a long breath. 'I just don't want to be disappointed and find out I'm still at three centimetres, when I'm hoping to be at seven!'

'I don't think I can promise seven.' Jess smiled. 'But let's just hope there's an advance on three. That's it, try and relax; I know it's easier said than done.'

Two minutes later, Jess had started the examination and Krissy was obviously desperate to know the outcome. 'What's the verdict?'

'You're at six centimetres. So that's great progress in just over twenty minutes. I think it's definitely time to call the anaesthetist and Alec.'

'I think maybe you're right, but I'm going to tell him that things are only just starting to happen.' Krissy reached for her phone. 'I don't want him to panic and think there's any possibility of missing this. It's taken a long time for us to decide to have a baby of our own, and I just want it to be perfect. That's why I was so determined not to have pain relief, but now I know what the pain is really like, I'm not so sure I want to be a martyr!'

'I'm not sure there are many people who would describe this bit as perfect, but it will be when you've got the baby in your arms. I promise.' Jess moved towards the door. 'I'll go and sort out the anaesthetist and hopefully the baby will decide not to keep you waiting too much longer.'

As Jess opened the door, she tried not to picture the image that seemed to pop into her head at moments like this all the time just lately – of her and Dexter, cradling a newborn baby of their own, with Riley looking on like that proud big brother he was so desperate to be. But no matter how many times she blinked, she couldn't make the image disappear.

* * *

Alec arrived within twenty minutes of Jess suggesting that Krissy call him. When he came through the door of the delivery room, it looked as though he'd run all the way.

'I haven't missed it, have I?' Alec's eyes were wide and it was impossible to tell if it was down to fear or excitement. In Jess's experience, it was likely to be a mixture of both.

'Can you see a baby?' There was a teasing tone to Krissy's voice and she seemed more relaxed now she'd decided to have an epidural. The contractions had shifted to five minutes apart, lasting at least a minute, so she wasn't getting a lot of respite in between any more.

'Sorry, sorry, I just panicked.' Alec kissed the top of his wife's head.

'I forgive you; I was getting a bit panicky myself before Jess arrived.' Krissy gestured towards her. 'But she said the same as you. I don't have to suffer to do this *properly* – whatever that means!'

'Nice to meet you, Jess, and you sound like a very wise woman.' Alec smiled and then turned back towards his wife. 'I still can't believe this moment is finally here. When Bubs decided not to put in an appearance on the due date, and then the days kept ticking past, I started to think it might never happen.'

'No doubts?' Krissy raised her eyebrow. 'Because if you have, it's definitely too late.'

'No doubts.' Alec took hold of his wife's hand and Jess wondered if she should excuse herself, but she had a feeling that might have made things more awkward. 'You know I've never questioned for a moment how brilliant you're going to be at all of this, don't you? I just sometimes wish I didn't know so much about what it's like to care for a small baby. It scares the life out of me that I'm the one who might not be up to the job.'

'I keep telling you it's not going to be as hard with one of our own.' Krissy suddenly caught Jess's eye. 'Caring for the babies we've looked after once their birth parents have left the placement is what's put Alec off trying for so long. But the babies we've cared for have sometimes been withdrawing from drugs and alcohol, and it's not unusual for them to scream for hours on end, night and day.'

'I'd just like to skip the first twelve months.' Alec shrugged. 'You know what, schools should forget all about giving kids those dolls that cry, to cut down on teenage pregnancies, and let them come and see first-hand what can happen when a baby isn't made the priority from day one. I wanted to be 100 per cent ready to do that, because Krissy was born ready.'

'Well, I've never once seen Alec lose his patience or try to dodge taking his turn with any of the babies we've cared for, so I'd say we've got a head start. Oooh—' Krissy dropped her head forward. 'I've got another contraction coming.'

Jess checked the monitor. 'You're doing brilliantly, Krissy. It's only four minutes since the last one, so when you're through this contraction, I'll see if I can find out what's happening with the anaesthetist.'

'Thank God, because I don't think I can stand watching her in this much pain.' Alec shook his head. 'I know, I know, it's not about me.'

'Too bloody right it's not.' Krissy was almost growling.

Krissy's contraction was just easing off as the anaesthetist put her head around the door. 'Anyone here order an epidural?'

'That'll be me and I don't care how big the needle is, after that last contraction I'm ready. Numb me up!'

'We'd better get going then.' The anaesthetist dropped a wink in Jess's direction and within ten minutes the epidural was in place. Sometimes having an epidural could slow labour down, but that didn't happen in Krissy's case and just over an hour later, she was finally ready to push.

'Is everything okay?' Alec looked at Jess as she checked the baby monitor, after Krissy had been pushing for almost thirty minutes. The baby was crowning, but its heartrate was dropping and Krissy was starting to look exhausted too.

'I think we might need to see if we can help the baby out; Krissy is getting worn out and the baby is obviously getting tired too.' Jess gave Alec what she hoped was a comforting smile. 'It's very common to need to do this, so it's nothing to worry about, is it Nancy?'

'Absolutely not.' Nancy, another midwife, had come in to support Jess once it looked like Krissy was getting close to delivery and it was always good to have back-up, especially when things got tricky. 'Are we going to try an episiotomy?'

'I think so.' Jess looked at Krissy. 'If it's okay with you, we're going to need make a cut to help the baby out. You won't feel anything with the epidural in.'

'Will I need stiches?' Krissy looked as though she was struggling to keep her eyes open.

'Yes, but I promise you won't feel any of it and it's the best way to make sure you and the baby are both okay.' Jess turned back to Nancy. 'Do you know if the obstetricians are available? I think we might need to get them up here, in case we need an assisted delivery.'

'I'll find out.' Nancy was out of the room before Jess could respond. One of the benefits of a hospital delivery was having the support of an obstetrician on site.

'Is she going to need a C-section?' Alec was holding on tight to his wife's hand, his eyes wide with concern.

'Sometimes an episiotomy isn't enough to help baby out and given how tired Krissy's getting, I think the doctor might decide to try forceps or a ventouse.' Jess made it sound like the easiest thing in the world. Assisted deliveries were fairly common, but that didn't make it any less nerve-wracking for the woman involved, or her partner. If the doctor made the cut with the forceps already in place, and the perineum at full stretch, it would have the best chance of working and reduce the likelihood of Krissy needing a C-section. But Jess wanted to keep her explanation as simple and as reassuring as possible. 'Having the obstetrician here is always good, because we've got other options if baby still doesn't put in an appearance. Krissy can have a C-section if she needs it, but if we can get over the finish line with the forceps, it'll be the quickest solution.'

'Do whatever it takes to make sure the baby's okay. I don't care any more.' Krissy grimaced. 'But I feel like I need to push again.'

'It's okay, just go with it and as soon as Nancy gets back we'll make a decision about the episiotomy.' If there was no obstetrician available, Jess would do the episiotomy herself and hope it would be enough to get the baby out.

'Okay let's get you up to theatre.' Nancy swept back through the door, almost as quickly as she'd left. 'The doctor's going to meet us there.'

'The theatre? Does that mean a C-section?' The fear in Krissy's eyes was obvious and Jess shook her head.

'No, it's still a back-up plan, but using the forceps in the theatre means we'll be in the right place if baby decides it's too comfy in there to come out. You're in the best possible hands.'

'Are you ready to meet our baby?' Alec kissed his wife, who nodded.

'Let's do this.'

Within minutes, Krissy had been wheeled into the theatre. Jess and Nancy helped her get into position, with her legs up in the stirrups. A catheter had been put in when the anaesthetist had administered the epidural and by the time the obstetrician, Dr Gamble, arrived, they were all ready to go. After that, things happened really quickly.

'I just want you to push the way you've been doing, when you get the next contraction.' Dr Gamble looked far too young to being doing his job and, with the shape of his glasses, there was more than a touch of Harry Potter about him. 'You might feel a bit of tugging from the forceps, but it's nothing to worry about.'

'It won't hurt the baby, will it?' Krissy looked at Jess, who shook her head.

'There might be a little mark from the forceps, but the bones in babies' skulls are much softer at this point and they're designed to pass through the birth canal.'

'I can feel another contraction coming. Can you take my other hand?' Krissy thrust a hand towards Jess and a moment later,

Krissy was squeezing so tightly that the tips of Jess's fingers went purple.

'You're doing brilliantly.' Jess gave the encouragement, ignoring her own minor discomfort in the wake of what Krissy was doing. Watching women give birth was never less than extraordinary, and the day it became routine was the day Jess would know she was finished with midwifery.

'I love you so much, angel; just a little bit longer and we'll finally have our baby.' Alec already had tears in his eyes and Jess couldn't stop the lump from forming in her throat. She so wanted to give that to Dexter and the truth was, she desperately wanted it for herself too. Watching other people give birth was exquisite torture. Witnessing life coming into the world and seeing the start of new families was a privilege like no other, but part of Jess always felt like an outsider. She was there, with her face pressed up against the glass, watching every magical moment, but knowing she'd never have that for herself. And sometimes it felt like every nerve ending in her body was exposed.

'Oh please come on baby, please.' Krissy stretched the last word out, dropping her head down and squeezing even harder. She was clearly giving it every last bit of effort she had and Jess hadn't even realised she was holding her own breath, until Dr Gamble spoke.

'That's it, the head's out. It should be plain sailing now.' Dr Gamble clearly had no concept of what Krissy was going through, but thankfully, when the next contraction came, the rest of the baby came with it.

'Do you want to see what you've got?' Jess interjected to make sure Krissy and Alec had the chance to see for themselves, before they were told. As the baby was placed on Krissy's chest, the tears in Alec's eyes started streaming down his face.

'We've got a little boy.' He couldn't have sounded more surprised if the baby had arrived with a full set of teeth.

'That's the first boy on both sides for nearly thirty years.' Krissy was shaking her head too. 'We've got seven nieces between us, and we were convinced we'd have a girl too.'

'It sounds like he's going to be getting a lot of attention then. Congratulations!' Jess smiled. Dr Gamble might look young, but he'd done a brilliant job and there wasn't a mark on the baby. In a few moments, Jess would have to take him away from his mother for a little while, to check him over properly, but she didn't want to break the spell just yet. The desire to have a baby of her own was becoming more and more overwhelming, but she was starting to wonder if it was because she spent her days witnessing magic and miracles. Maybe it was time to consider taking a leaf out of Alec and Krissy's book and think about fostering again. If she spent enough sleepless nights caring for babies who needed foster care, there was a possibility she might finally get over her longing for a baby of her own. And that would be a tiny miracle all by itself.

5

Meg had been telling herself for weeks that the crippling tiredness, which meant she didn't want to do much more than curl up on the sofa after she got home in the evenings, was the result of working two jobs. But the first of the hot flushes that swept over her left her in no doubt: this was definitely the menopause and her earlier symptoms had ramped up to a whole new level.

'Hello gorgeous.' Johnnie smiled as she opened the door to him. They were supposed to be going bowling in Port Tremellien and then out for a late dinner, but all she wanted to do was order a takeaway and decide whether watching Prime or Netflix was more likely to stop her from dropping off to sleep before 9 p.m. Although if she admitted that to Johnnie, he was going to get a big, fat reminder of the fact he was going out with someone whose energy levels were in serious decline.

'Hey you.' Meg stood back as he came into the hallway. If anything could give her a boost of enthusiasm, it was Johnnie. He was well over six-feet tall with hazel eyes that sometimes looked brown and sometimes looked green, depending on the light. He laughed easily and he made Meg laugh too, more often than she could remember doing in years, maybe even before the accident. But she wasn't going to think about that. Comparing Johnnie to Darren, and the guilt that came with that, had almost killed off their relationship before it had even really started. She'd had to push those feelings down and she'd figured out the perfect way to distract herself fairly early on. Going up onto her tiptoes, she kissed him and when he kissed her back, her body responded in the way it always did, drowning out all other thoughts.

'That's a nice welcome.' Johnnie grinned as he pulled away from her. 'I take it Tilly decided not to come over in the end?'

'She and Ed have gone to visit his parents. It was all a bit last minute.' Meg still hadn't broken the news about Tilly's pregnancy to Johnnie yet. She'd been telling herself that it was because of Tilly wanting to keep it quiet until she got to twelve weeks. But Tilly and Ed were telling his parents over dinner at their house and she'd already said she was happy for Johnnie to know. So Meg had been forced to admit that part of her was truly worried that Johnnie might be bothered about the idea of dating a grandma. There was a chance he'd finally realise she'd been right all along and that one day the age gap was going to catch up with them. As much as she'd reminded herself over and over again that this rela-tionship probably wouldn't last, she couldn't bear the thought of losing him and she didn't want to face it. Not until she had to.

'Are you okay? You look exhausted.' As Johnnie looked at her, she tried to blink back the tears that were suddenly stinging her eyes. 'Oh Meg, what's up? Don't cry. Is it about the boys?'

'N-n-no.' She was stumbling to get the words out and trying not to give in to the tears that were already winning the battle. Johnnie was so sweet, and he'd seen her cry far too often already. She'd always referred to Darren and Seth as 'the boys', and it was no surprise that Johnnie would assume her tears were for them, which made her feel even guiltier. She'd worried about never being able

to laugh again when she'd lost them, but what she hadn't anticipated was the shame that now accompanied so many other
emotions. It seemed so wrong to feel irritated or upset about something minor, when the worst thing in the world had already
happened, but the weird thing was, those emotions didn't just go
away.

'Whatever it is that's wrong, I'm here for you.' Johnnie put his
hands on her shoulders and looked directly at her. 'And I'll do
whatever I can to help.'

'I'm just being stupid; it doesn't matter.'

'It obviously does.' Johnnie let go of her shoulders, taking hold
of her hand instead. 'Let's go and sit down, and you can tell me as
much or as little as you want about what's bothering you.'

'Okay.' Meg was being ridiculous, letting her emotions get so
out of hand over something so silly. If Johnnie didn't want to be
with her because she was a grandma, then it wasn't worth worrying
about anyway, but she couldn't help it. That was probably down to
the bloody menopause, too. Her emotions hadn't been all over the
place like this for years.

Johnnie kept hold of her hand as he sat next to her on the sofa
and she took a deep breath.

'Tilly's pregnant.'

'Wow, really?' Johnnie widened his eyes. 'Are they pleased?'

'They haven't got any money, or a house and it's just... not the
right time.'

'Is there ever really a right time?' Johnnie shrugged. 'Tilly and
Ed seem really solid, and I'm sure she'll be a great mum. She's
learned from the best after all.'

'I'm not ready to be a grandma.' In the end the words had come
tumbling out before she could stop them, but Johnnie just laughed
and she knew she probably sounded crazy. Perimenopause was
sending her hormones into a tailspin, and not even being

completely aware of how ridiculous she was could stop her. How could she cry over the fact that she was now officially old, when neither Seth nor Darren had been given that chance? No wonder Johnnie was finding her behaviour so funny.

'That's not what you're worried about, is it?'

'I know it's stupid, but I already feel worn out and way past my best, and now I'm going to have a label that proves it's true. If I'm going to become a grandma in my mid-forties, I'd at least like to be one of those young, energetic grandmothers.' Meg sighed. 'But the truth is, the thought of going bowling tonight suddenly feels like you're asking me to go mountain climbing and I'm tired just thinking about it.'

'We don't need to go out. I'd be just as happy staying in, as long as I get to spend time with you.' Johnnie was holding her gaze and he looked like he meant every word, but she still couldn't believe it. Why would someone like him choose someone like her, especially now?

'Aren't you worried that the gap between us is just going to keep getting bigger?'

'Not remotely. In fact, I'm hoping that with us changing our plans and staying in, that the gap between us might be about to get a lot smaller.' Johnnie grinned again and she suddenly felt a lot less tired, but then the doubts came crashing back in. The physical side of their relationship had always been the easy bit, but, with menopause clearly rearing its ugly head, there was no telling how long that part would last.

'If you ever change your mind about us, promise you'll just say and not think you've got to stick around for my sake?' It was Meg's turn to search his face and she held up her hand as he started to protest. She couldn't think about a future without Johnnie in it; if she tried it was like a dark cloud closing in on her. It was because of him that Meg had learned to really live again, not just act the part for Tilly's sake. But the idea that he might stay with her out of pity for all she'd been through was even worse than the fear of losing him. So she had to know for sure. 'Just promise.'

'Okay, it's not going to happen, but I promise to tell you if it does.' Johnnie pulled her into his arms again and she made a decision. Living in the moment had served her well since losing Darren and Seth, and especially since she'd met Johnnie, and she wanted to keep doing that for as long as possible. She had no excuse not to see her GP about her menopause symptoms and she was going to make an appointment as soon as she got the chance. Johnnie might not be in her life forever, but, for now, having him in it made things so much better. And she knew, with far more certainty than she wanted to, that *for now* was the only guarantee anyone really had.

* * *

If anyone asked Meg which of the GPs at the surgery was her favourite, she gave the stock answer that they were all great to work with. In reality, there were a couple of them who were harder to like than others, but there was one who was a complete joy to work with. Hamish was also the sort of person who noticed when his colleagues weren't their normal selves, so it shouldn't have been a surprise when he stopped in front of the reception desk at lunchtime on Monday and gave Meg a level look.

'Have you got a minute, Meg?'

'Yes, what's up?'

'I was about to ask you the same thing.' There was no one else in reception and the kindness in Hamish's voice made yet another crop of unwanted tears spring into her eyes. This was getting ridiculous now; she couldn't even have a normal conversation without crying. Maybe she should just ask Hamish to prescribe the maximum strength HRT patch she could have and be done with it.

She wasn't sleeping, the hot flushes were coming all too frequently and she felt old enough to be a great nana, never mind a grandmother. It had taken years to feel even vaguely normal again after losing Darren and Seth, and she was terrified that with all the changes going on in her body the suffocating depression would overtake her again too. If HRT could help keep that at bay, she was willing to give it a go. But despite the promise she'd made herself, she'd done nothing about making an appointment to get checked over.

'I'm fine, I just—'

'No you're not.' Hamish shook his head. 'I've known you for a long time now, Meg, but I haven't seen you look this worried before.'

'I haven't felt like this for a long time.' She might as well tell him. Although there was a good chance he already knew, seeing as her daughter was one of his patients. 'I'm not sure if the hospital contacted you, but Tilly's pregnant.'

'And is she happy about it?'

'Ecstatic.'

'What about you?'

'I'm scared.' There was no point lying to Hamish. She'd first met him when she'd been so deep in the blackness of depression, that she hadn't known which way to turn. Her previous GP had prescribed stronger and stronger medication, but she'd been terrified that Tilly would end up losing her too if she went down that route. She'd ended up moving surgeries altogether, in an attempt to find someone or something that might help her get through the day. Somehow, despite her fears, she'd held it together for Tilly for almost a year by the time Hamish became her GP. By then, on her good days she was emotionless and zombie-like, as a result of the prescription medication. But on the bad days she just wanted to close her eyes and not wake up. She'd have done it, too, if it hadn't been for Tilly.

From the very first consultation with Hamish she'd known he was different. Eventually she'd discovered that he'd lost his wife to brain cancer and been left to raise their two daughters alone. Maybe that's what gave him the empathy and understanding he'd displayed from the moment they'd met. He didn't just write another prescription to drug her into oblivion, so that she could bear the passing of time. Hamish wanted her to move forward eventually, understanding that it would take time and a lot of patience. Finally, bit by bit, she'd begun to do just that.

Hamish had put her in touch with a brilliant counsellor called Heather. He'd also encouraged Meg to attend support groups and given her books that he'd found useful in the aftermath of his wife's death. Although the biggest thing he'd done was to offer Meg a job. She'd tried to refuse it at first, but he'd all but begged her just to try it for a few weeks, telling her that he was desperate and that he had no one to cover if she didn't temporarily take on the job. Of course, none of that had been true, but Hamish had realised she needed a reason not to crawl straight back into bed the moment Tilly went to school. Slowly, without even realising it, she'd begun to create the semblance of a new life for herself. It could never be the life she would have chosen, not without her husband and son in it, but miraculously it somehow became a life she still wanted to live.

'What are you scared of?' Hamish searched her face, but she wasn't even sure what the answer was any more.

'At first, I thought I was just worried about Tilly and I'm still absolutely terrified of something happening to her or the baby. I tried to tell myself that I was just anxious because it was the wrong time for her, but that's stupid because I know the baby will be surrounded by love and that's all they really need, isn't it?' Meg didn't even wait for Hamish to answer. 'Then I started to get scared that something might happen to me and that I wouldn't be around for Tilly and there'd be no family on her side to support her with the baby. I've felt so awful lately and I've been trying to tell myself it's the menopause. But what if it isn't? Then I started thinking about how I'll feel when the baby gets here, and the empty space where Seth and Darren should be becomes even more obvious because the baby's grandfather and uncle aren't a part of its life. I even started to worry that once Tilly has her own family, there won't be room for me in her life the way there always has been. I can't bear the thought of having to let her go, even a little bit. I'm a mess, and I can't tell Tilly any of this because she's got enough to worry about and because I'm just being stupid. I should be crying with happiness, but I've got a feeling of dread that I just can't seem to shake.'

'Oh Meg, you're not stupid or a mess. Every time there's a milestone in my children's lives I feel a maelstrom of emotions because my wife isn't around to see it, and none of those things have even been close to being as big as one of them having a baby. That's a life-changing moment for any parent, even one who hasn't been through as much as you have. It's no wonder you're feeling so many emotions. But if you haven't been feeling well, we need to get that checked out. I know you're going to want to look after Tilly more than ever now, but you can't do that unless you start looking after yourself too.'

'I'll make an appointment.'

'No, you won't.' Hamish gave her another one of his looks. He really did know her far too well. 'Let's do it now. You can talk me through your symptoms, I can take some blood and we can run a few tests.'

'You're not going to give me any choice are you?'

'Absolutely not.' Hamish smiled and Meg felt some of the

weight lift from her shoulders. He was right, she needed to do whatever it took to be around for Tilly and the baby. Even if things didn't work out with Ed, they'd get through it together. They'd got through everything else and, despite her worries, deep down Meg was certain there was nothing on earth that could drive a wedge between her and her daughter.

Happy Ever After: Kate and Coco's Midwi...

6

Jess has just seen her last patient of the day. Glancing at her watch, she sighed. She'd been hoping to have the time to FaceTime Dexter and Riley before the start of the infertility support group meeting, but it wasn't going to happen. The group had been running for over four years, ever since Anna had set it up and then fallen pregnant almost immediately afterwards. It seemed crazy to think that, like Anna, the other early graduates of the group now had children about to go to school. Anna and Brae's twins, Kit and Merryn, would be starting at Port Agnes primary school in the next intake.

Jess was the only original member of the group who was still there. It would have been depressing, perhaps even unbearable, to have been the last one standing if Riley hadn't come into her life and made her a mother in a way she'd never expected. Another thing that had eased the pain of the IVF not working, was focusing on all the women the group had managed to help. A good number of them had gone on to become mothers through IVF and other infertility treatments, including surrogacy. Others had come to terms with the fact that they'd never be biological mothers. Some had gone on to pursue adoption and fostering, but there were also those who'd decided that the journey was over for them and had found a way to not just accept childlessness, but to embrace it. Jess couldn't have admired those women any more than she did. But she'd always known, after Teddy came into her life, that, for her, the journey would never end until she was a mother, in one way or another. Or she'd die trying.

For a while after she and Dexter had got together, she'd hoped that would be the end of her journey to motherhood and she'd counted her blessings every day since the first time Riley had called her Mum. Making that official and adopting him, had truly been the most amazing day of her life. She couldn't imagine anything topping that, even if by some miracle the IVF treatments had worked. But there'd been four rounds now and still no baby. After two, she'd considered giving up, but Riley had started asking when he was going to get a brother or sister and it had become an almost relentless request. Two more rounds of treatment had followed, the last one ending in failure six months ago, and now she was in limbo.

Dexter was amazing and he'd said he was happy to do whatever she wanted. They'd been out of NHS funding after one round of IVF and the other cycles had been funded from their savings, and money that Dexter's parents and Jess's dad had given them. Dexter had since inherited some money from his grandmother, which could potentially fund another two rounds of IVF. It could also replace their decimated savings or pay for the conservatory they wanted to be built, and a trip to Disneyland Paris for Riley. Maybe that would be enough for him; the promise of a meet up with Mickey and Minnie had to be a bit of a consolation prize for not getting to be a big brother. She'd considered fostering again and maybe even adoption, but there was so much uncertainty in the process and she wasn't sure she could go through that again. Not after Teddy.

Thank God she had Riley, because Jess had no idea how she'd have got over losing Teddy without him. She hated not getting the chance to say goodnight to him when she was going to be working late, but she knew Riley wouldn't accept a five-minute chat if she made a video call. He'd want to tell her all about his day and she'd never cut that short. The time would come, probably all too soon, when she'd ask him what he'd done at school and he'd say 'nothing'. For now, he still wanted to share everything with her and she was going to treasure every moment. Instead, she fired off a quick text to Dexter, explaining that her clinic had run late and she was going to have to go straight to the support group. Finishing by telling him that she loved them both, she dropped her phone into her bag. Looking up, she almost jumped out of her skin. Emily was standing right in front of her.

'Oh my God, are you trying to kill me?' Jess clutched her chest and then laughed. 'You'd make a good assassin, being able to sneak up on people like that.'

'Sorry, I thought it might make you jump if I shouted out, but this was probably worse.' Emily was usually the loudest and liveliest person in any room, unless she was competing with Gwen, but she seemed strangely subdued. Jess had taken over as deputy manager of the unit, when Ella had left to become a health visitor, but even if it hadn't been part of her job to keep an eye on the well-being of her staff, she'd have been worried about her friend. The only time she'd seen Emily this nervous before was when she'd been interviewed for a full-time midwifery role, after she'd completed her degree. Jess just hoped nothing had happened with one of the patients.

Midwifery was an amazing job, and it was such a privilege to help women through moments in their lives they'd never forget.

But all of that came with huge responsibility and sometimes even tragedy, which the midwives had to help their patients through too. At some point, Emily would encounter something like that; it was inevitable. And if that moment had come today, Jess was going to be there for her.

'Is everything okay?' She waited for Emily to respond and the younger woman bit her lip. 'Whatever it is, you can tell me.'

'I wanted to ask if I could come to the infertility support group meeting.' Emily shifted from foot to foot. 'Keira and I are thinking of trying for a baby. Well, not thinking; we definitely want to.'

'That's really exciting.' Jess hugged her friend. Emily had been dating one of the nurses from the hospital in Truro for a little over two years, and Jess had been thrilled to see her friend so happy. Before meeting Keira, Emily had never dated a woman and every other relationship she'd had since joining the midwifery unit had ended up as a big, fat disappointment. Then she'd met Keira at a speed dating event. They'd bought a house together eighteen months later, but the news that they were planning to start a family together was a whole different level of commitment.

'It is, but it's a bit scary too.' Emily was still biting her lip as she pulled away from Jess.

'Are you sure this is what you want? Everything with Keira has happened quite quickly, but no one should feel pressured into trying for a baby.'

'Well she's getting on a bit.' Emily smiled for the first time, because she knew Jess was about the same age as Keira. 'And sometimes her biological clock is ticking so loudly it stops both of us sleeping. Well, it does when she nudges me in the side with her elbow to tell me she can't sleep, because she can't stop thinking about trying for a baby. It's not having the baby that scares me. It's just not as easy for us, because there's no way I'm doing this with some weirdo off the internet who wants to donate some of his sperm, but only in what he calls the "traditional" way!'

'Oh God, really?' Jess could tell by the look on Emily's face that she wasn't joking.

'That's just the tame stuff. But it means we've got to go to a clinic, and what happens if the treatment doesn't work? I'm worried about what that might do to our relationship. I know how much of strain it's been for you at times, and Keira seems to think it's going to be so straightforward. She's got a five-year plan all set out. She's going to have a baby in the next year and in about three years' time we'll go for number two and I'll carry the baby. She wants to use the same donor for both, but I've got no idea if any of that's doable. Never mind how she might feel if one of us can't have a baby as easily as she thinks we will. I just want to speak to people who know what it's really like to go through treatment, and I think Keira should too. All those years I spent desperately trying not to get pregnant and now the thing I'm most afraid of is not being able to have a baby.'

'It might not be completely straightforward, but the chances are it'll be okay, especially at your age. There's a bonus with having two women in the relationship too; I could certainly have bene-fitted from a second pair of fallopian tubes being in the mix.' Jess laughed, trying to ignore the twinge that never failed to twist some-where deep inside when she had to face up to her own infertility. 'But you're right, it's good to know your options and there are people in the group who are going through IVF, ICSI and IUI. Have you talked about any of that?'

'Keira thinks we should do IVF to give us the best shot of it working quickly, but there's the cost and the drugs they pump you with.' Emily caught Jess's eye, suddenly looking worried again. 'Oh God, I'm sorry. I know you haven't had any choice about that.'

'There's always a choice, but for me the only alternative to IVF was not to try for a baby of my own at all. You and Keira will have other options.' Jess did her best not to resent people who had more choice. It was relatively easy to avoid being envious of others in the infertility group, because everyone was facing their challenges – even if some people's challenges were much easier to overcome than others. What was sometimes difficult was when she came across cases in her job where women completely took their fertility for granted. The unwanted pregnancies could be difficult too, especially when Jess would have traded everything she owned for the positive test that was someone else's worst nightmare. For a while after the fourth IVF failed, Jess had wondered if she could carry on doing the job she loved, with its daily reminders of everything she might never have. But giving up midwifery would just have broken her heart even more.

'I know we're lucky, but I also know Keira. She takes things hard. When we lost the first house we were trying to buy, after the chain collapsed, she was devastated. In her mind, she'd already moved in and arranged where the furniture would be. She even had our first Christmas there planned!' The smile slid off Emily's face. 'I can see the same thing happening now. Except it won't be so easy to convince her that things happen for a reason, if she doesn't get pregnant. I just want her to go into this with her eyes open, and I think she might be willing to listen to the reality from other people. But if you think it would be wrong for us to be there, when we're not technically infertile as far as we know, I completely understand.'

'Of course it wouldn't be wrong.' Jess put a hand on Emily's arm.

'Thank you so much. I didn't know who else to talk to about this. My mum and my sister...' Emily sighed. 'They still find it hard to get their heads around the fact that I'm with Keira now. It's not that they haven't accepted her, but Mum keeps reminding me that this would all be easier if I was in a relationship with a man. I know it's because she loves me and she doesn't want anything in my life to be difficult, but one thing I don't have any doubt about is that Keira is the one for me. I didn't care where we lived, I just wanted it to be with her. And, for me, if we don't get a baby that's okay, as long as I've got her. But what do I do if she doesn't feel the same and things don't work out?'

'Every time I've seen the two of you together, the way she looks at you... I don't think there's any doubt that you're the most important thing to her too, but you need to talk to her about all of this. It's even more important than hearing the reality from other people in the group.'

'I'm hoping that once we've been to the first session, it'll give us a chance to really talk. About everything.'

'Can Keira get to the group tonight?'

'I've already asked her to meet me there.' Emily's smile was back in situ. 'I was banking on you saying it was okay.'

'Was there ever any doubt?' Jess gave her friend a hug and let go of a long breath. What Emily had confided was a reminder that no one's life was as easy or as straightforward as it might look from the outside. Jess had some tough decisions of her own to make, but helping other people had always been the best therapy and she was so grateful she got the chance to do that every single day.

* * *

The infertility support group meetings were held in the same room the antenatal classes and postnatal parenting groups took place on other days. The infertility group always met in the evenings and used the rear entrance to the building, so that there'd be no chance of any of the members bumping into women attending the clinics or mothers-to-be on their way in to give birth. There was only so much someone going through the trauma of infertility could be expected to take. But they made an exception for pregnant women in the group; no one graduated until they were holding a baby in their arms. Sadly, there was too much that could go wrong up until that moment, and it was even more of a tragedy that some of the group members had experienced that kind of pain first-hand. Even after reaching the holy grail of a successful pregnancy, some of the women made a return to the group, when they were going through further treatment in the hope of having another baby. Nicole was one of those women.

'I still can't quite believe I'm about to go through this again.' Nicole rolled her eyes. 'Here I am, trying to surreptitiously wipe splatters of sweet potato off my top before anyone notices them and I want to add to the chaos. Henry must be the world's messiest eater, but James is convinced we've got a future world champion on our hands, given how far he can fling his dinner. There must be a part of me that wants to make sure I'm covered in regurgitated food for at least the next five years, given how desperate I am to try again.'

'Well who wouldn't want to sign up for invasive and emotionally draining treatment when that's the prize on offer?' Jess gave Nicole a wry smile. The meetings were largely informal, but there was always a catch up at the beginning, where the members would give an update on where they were with their treatments and make introductions to anyone new. Emily and Keira had been warmly welcomed at the start and they were now chatting to Jennie, who was part way through her second round of IVF.

'You're right, we must be crazy to want to board the IVF train again.' Nicole turned to look at Jess. 'How about you? Have you decided whether you're going to have another round of treatment?'

'No.' Jess poured herself a coffee. Every time she'd tried IVF, she'd followed the rules, including cutting out caffeine prior to starting the treatment, but a fat lot of good that had done her.

'It's such a hard choice. I've only been through it twice and I know how lucky I am to have Henry.' The way Nicole was talking, anyone would think it had been a walk in the park for her, but Jess knew exactly how much Nicole had been through and it was a hundred times harder than what she had faced. Nicole might have been successful with both the rounds of IVF she'd had, but her baby girl, Gracie, had been stillborn in her third trimester. As much as the failed rounds of treatment had been devasting for Jess, she'd never known a loss like that.

All Jess had to show for four rounds of treatment were two pictures of a single implanted embryo, and a third with two embryos which had all failed to stick. Her second round of treatment had gone wrong before it had even begun, when the frozen embryo hadn't made it through the process of de-frosting and there'd been nothing to transfer. There hadn't been much chance for hope to grow on any of those occasions and Jess wasn't sure any more that there was even a seed of hope left. Unless she could find one, there was no point even thinking about starting another round of treatment.

'Henry's brilliant, that's undeniable.' Jess managed a genuine smile when she thought about the little boy. 'But that doesn't make this any easier. In some ways it's probably harder, because you want this for Henry as well as for yourselves. But we're here for you, whatever happens. You know that don't you?'

'I wouldn't be able to go through it without you guys.' Nicole squeezed Jess's waist and she didn't need to say anything else. Whatever Jess eventually decided, she knew the friends she'd made in the infertility group would be by her side every step of the way. All of a sudden, she was certain that she was ready for the next step, she just still wasn't sure what that was.

7

Meg had gone through all her symptoms with Hamish and he'd agreed that the most likely explanation was perimenopause, but he'd suggested that he run a range of tests just to be certain. She was seeing him first thing Monday morning, before surgery started, so he could go through the results from the previous week. Hopefully, he'd be able to prescribe something that stopped her veering between a wannabe axe murderer and the Tiny Tears doll she'd had as a child, whose only ability had been to cry.

Talking to Jess and Hamish about Tilly's news had helped too. It probably scared every mother when their child became a parent. After all, being a mother and worrying seemed to go hand in hand every step of the way. When Tilly and Seth were little, Meg had thought that their early years would be the tough part. But the older they got, the more difficult it had become to solve their problems for them, the way she could when they were small. Now Tilly was going to be mother and there would be a whole new generation to worry about. It didn't matter how much stress it would have caused Meg, she'd still have given the world to be able to worry about Seth as an adult. She could just imagine what he'd be up to now, scaring her half to death by threatening to head off back-packing across the Andes, or parachuting out of a plane. Seth would have caused her untold sleepless nights and given the chance, she'd have cherished every single one of them.

The thing that had helped to ease her concerns about Tilly the most were the conversations she'd had with Johnnie. He'd encouraged her to put herself in Tilly's shoes. She remembered breaking the news to her own parents that she was pregnant with Seth and she'd seen the look of disappointment on their faces, even before her father had said they were far too young and financially unstable to be starting a family. It had taken the shine off everything for a long time. She wanted Tilly to feel like it was the best news Meg had ever heard and she was starting to believe that it really might be. She just had to accept that she was never going to stop worrying about Tilly. Even if those worries hadn't been about the baby, there'd have been something else. The truth was, ever since the endometriosis had been diagnosed, she'd thought about how devastated Tilly would be if she couldn't have a child of her own, on top of the pain of the condition itself. She also knew the symptoms of endometriosis could lessen as a result of pregnancy. But the real source of joy would be that there'd be a baby at the end of all of this. A tiny version of Tilly, or maybe even Seth. Darren would be in there too, for sure. He'd had strong genes and Seth had been the double of him, when he'd been in his teens.

Being happy about the baby wasn't just an act for Tilly's sake, Meg was genuinely starting to feel excited. It was why she'd decided to invite Tilly and Ed out to lunch to celebrate their news, but she needed Johnnie there for moral support, too. She only had to look at him to know if she was going down the wrong path and saying something that might inadvertently upset her daughter. He'd give the slightest shake of his head and she'd know she needed to change tack. Johnnie might be over ten years younger than she was, but sometimes he still had to be the grown up.

Johnnie's involvement with the baby was something else that had been on Meg's mind. The chances of him being around in ten years' time, or even five, were slim. She tried not to think about that too often, but she had to remind herself of it, every now and then, when it felt as if they might be getting too close. She couldn't let herself love him too much, because she couldn't face the kind of loss that was bound to come in the end if she completely gave in to her feelings. She had to keep him at arms' length, or at least try. Tilly having a baby complicated things. If the baby formed a relationship with Johnnie, Meg would feel responsible for the loss of that when Johnnie was no longer around. But that was a worry for another day. Darren had often teased her about how much she worried and had constantly reminded her not to borrow tomorrow's sorrows. She was doing her best to follow his advice and today was all about celebration.

'This is so lovely.' Tilly closed her eyes and breathed out. By the View had only recently opened, but it already had the reputation of being one of the best restaurants in Port Agnes. It would usually have been well out of Meg's price range, but this was a special occasion.

'I wanted us to do this somewhere really nice, because it's not every day you get to celebrate the news that your first grandchild is on the way.' Meg reached across the table and squeezed her daughter's hand.

'I wasn't sure how you felt about it when you first found out. I know this is hard. Especially without Dad and Seth.' Tilly fixed her big, brown eyes on her mother, but Meg was still aware of Johnnie and Ed watching them. Neither of them had ever met Darren or Seth, but they were used to them being spoken about as part of the family and nothing was ever going to change that.

'I'm sorry if I didn't show how excited I am. Your dad and Seth would have been thrilled and so am I.' Meg smiled. 'You know me, though, I could make worrying an Olympic sport. But now that you've seen the baby's heartbeat on the scan and you're both okay, it's definitely time to celebrate.'

'Your champagne.' The waiter brought a bottle and four glasses to the table, setting them down. 'Would you like me to pour?'

'No, thank you, I'll do it.' Meg took hold of the bottle herself.

'I can't have any, Mum.'

'I know, sweetheart. That's why I've ordered you this.' She gestured towards another waiter who was walking across to their table with a single drink on a tray.

'Oh my God, really?' Tilly's smile lit up her face.

Meg nodded. 'Do you remember how you used to beg Dad for a grown-up drink every night when we were on that holiday in Spain? He got the barman to make you a non-alcoholic cocktail on the last night and after that, it was all you ever wanted when we went out. I'll never forget the look on that waitress's face, when you asked for a virgin pina colada in Pizza Hut.'

'That was so funny.' Tilly was laughing, but Meg didn't miss the fact that she'd had to wipe tears from her eyes too. Ten years had passed since the accident and yet the memories were still bitter-sweet, even after all this time. 'I wish they were still here to see this.'

'Me too, sweetheart.' Meg squeezed her daughter's hand, suddenly more aware than ever that Johnnie was watching her. 'But every time you talk about them, they're here and, who knows, maybe one day that little jumping bean you're busy growing might start begging you for a special grown-up drink and you'll be able to get one like their grandad got you. He can still be a part of your baby's life and so can Seth.'

'Thanks, Mum. How did you know just the right thing to say?'

Tilly was smiling through her tears and Meg glanced towards Johnnie as she answered.

'Let's just say I had a little help.'

'How are you feeling about being a grandpa, Johnnie?' Ed grinned. There wasn't more than a decade between them.

'I'm not sure I deserve the title, but it's the best news I've heard in a very long time.' If the idea of anyone thinking Johnnie was a grandpa bothered him, he certainly wasn't showing it. 'The big question is how you guys are feeling about impending parenthood.'

'Over the bloody moon.' Ed had red hair and the sort of boyish looks that meant he could probably have passed for someone even younger than his years. Every time Meg felt a jolt at just how young the new parents were, she had to remind herself that she and Darren had been the same age when Tilly was born and even younger with Seth. 'We prepared ourselves for the idea that we might be trying for ages, especially as we decided not to go all out. But then, bam, it happened almost straight away. Sorry, Meg, that's probably too much info for my soon-to-be mother-in-law to hear!'

'You're getting married?' It was the first Meg had heard of it and she took a slug of cold champagne, almost choking as the bubbles hit the back of her throat. It wasn't just the temperature catching her breath. One of the thousand or so things she'd cried about, after Seth and Darren had died, was the thought that Tilly would never get to have her father walk her down the aisle. So much was happening without them.

'We're in no major rush, but we're in this for the long haul.' Ed looked suddenly serious. 'I promise I won't let Tilly or the baby down. I'm working towards a promotion at my firm now that I'm fully qualified and, if all goes according to plan, I'll have a deposit for a house by the time the baby turns two. Living in a one-bed flat in the meantime might not be ideal, but it's not forever and me and

'Tils are going to do everything we can to give the baby everything it needs.'

'I know you will.' Meg allowed her shoulders to relax, as she exchanged a look with Johnnie. He'd been reassuring her, ever since he'd met Ed, that her daughter's boyfriend was a good guy and she trusted Johnnie's judgement more than she trusted anyone else's. She raised her glass, giving Ed her broadest smile. 'Here's to the best possible news and to two people who are going to be fantastic parents.'

'Cheers!' They clinked glasses and Johnnie rested his hand on Meg's leg, giving it a gentle squeeze. In the first few months of their relationship, she'd panicked every time he touched her, worried that he might be thinking how fat her thighs were compared to his thirty-year-old ex-fiancé. But it was just one more thing Johnnie had helped her get past. Now, when he touched her, all she thought about was how good it felt. Part of her wanted to ask Johnnie if he was in it for the long haul too, but she'd promised herself that she was going to take things one day at a time. She just hadn't banked on it turning out to be this hard.

* * *

Johnnie had only had a sip of champagne when they'd toasted the new parents, before insisting on switching to soft drinks so that he could drive Meg home. As a result, she'd drunk a lot more of the champagne than she'd planned to, but if anything, it seemed to be helping her think more clearly.

'I'm going to give Tilly and Ed the house.' Meg made the announcement as they headed along the coastal road towards the hamlet of Trelreath, where her house was situated. It was only a few miles outside of Port Agnes, but it had a much more rural feel.

'You're giving them your house?' There was a definite note of surprise in Johnnie's voice, but he didn't take his eyes off the road in front of him.

'Well, not giving them exactly. Not yet. Ed's still got to prove he can keep the promises he's making, but I want them to be able to live there when the baby's born.' It was suddenly so clear to Meg that she couldn't believe she hadn't suggested it sooner. 'I can move into the flat they're renting. It's right by the harbour and I've always wanted to live closer to the sea. A one-bedroom place will be fine for me. If Ed lives up to his promise, by the time they've saved a deposit, they can re-mortgage the house in their names and I'll take just enough out of the equity to get a little place of my own. Or if they don't want to live in Trelreath long term, we can sell the house and they can put the bulk of the equity down on somewhere new and I'll find myself somewhere smaller.'

'I thought you couldn't bear the thought of selling the house.' Johnnie was still looking at the road as he spoke. He was the only person she'd confided in about not wanting to let go of the home she shared with Darren and Seth, in case they didn't know where to find her. It had sounded crazy, even to her, when she'd finally said the words out loud, but he hadn't laughed or even given her a funny look. He'd taken her hand in his and leant forward to kiss her, which had made her feel able to share all her fears with him. What he saw in someone with her level of neurosis she'd never know.

When Meg had first met Johnnie, he'd only recently split from his long-term girlfriend. Meg had taken a job as a part-time temp at the veterinary practice, where he was a partner, on the days she didn't work at the GP surgery, before she'd joined the maternity unit. During her first week, she'd heard two of the nurses discussing Johnnie, and one egging the other on to 'just ask him out already'. She'd witnessed plenty of the clients flirting with Johnnie too, but he never seemed to notice, and she'd assumed he was busy getting over a broken heart. So, when Johnnie had asked Meg out, she'd figured he'd done it because dating someone of her age was a safe bet for him; no one would expect him to make any long-term plans with her – a middle-aged widow, with a daughter already in her twenties. It was just a rebound thing and they never lasted.

When she'd finally agreed to the date, she'd found out more about Johnnie's last relationship. He told her he'd met his ex, Natasha, who was also a vet, when they'd been working at a wildlife sanctuary in India. It had been Natasha who'd wanted to come back to the UK, but less than two years later she'd decided she was bored of Port Agnes and had started to pressure Johnnie into applying for jobs overseas. When he'd told her he was happy being back in Cornwall and was settled at the practice, Natasha had given him an ultimatum: Port Agnes or her. After they'd split, Natasha had left for a job in Botswana and Johnnie had accepted a partnership in the practice.

Meg had been determined not to let her feelings for Johnnie get too deep, even though she loved spending time with him, because she was convinced all she'd ever be to him was a stepping-stone to his next proper relationship. Yet, here they were, over two years later, still going strong. Whatever happened between them, meeting him had changed her life and she was finally ready to make another big change.

'Darren and Seth aren't in the house and leaving it won't mean we're leaving them. Tilly's reaction when I ordered the virgin pina colada brought it home to me. Seth and Darren will be wherever Tilly and I go. The house is just bricks and mortar.'

'You're right. I know Dad felt that way for a long time about selling the house when Mum died, but in the end he—' Johnnie suddenly slammed on the brakes, as a man stepped into the road just ahead of them. 'Jesus Christ!'

'You don't think he's trying to get himself run over, do you? He looks desperate.' Meg's skin prickled. It suddenly felt like they were in the middle of nowhere and if the man turned out to be as unpredictable as he looked, there was a good chance that no one would pass by for a long time. Ever since the accident, her mind always seemed to go straight to the worst-case scenario.

'He's asking for help.' Johnnie gestured to let the man know he was going to pull over to the side of the road. When he turned off the engine, Meg quickly realised he'd been right about why the man had stopped them.

'Quick, please. My wife needs help, now!' The man was heading towards their car, shouting, but Meg still wasn't sure whether or not he was putting on an act. It would be a good way to get them to abandon their car.

'Are you sure about this?' She hadn't even finished speaking before Johnnie was out of the car, and she wasn't going to sit and wait on her own.

'What's the problem?' Johnnie's voice was calm, but the other man's eyes were still wide and his arms were flailing around as he started to shout again.

'My wife's up the road in our car and the baby's coming; I mean *really* coming. I couldn't get any reception on either of our phones and I need to call an ambulance.' The man took hold of Johnnie's arms. 'Have you got a signal?'

'Let me check.' Johnnie pulled his phone out of his pocket. 'Yes, it's only two bars but it should be okay. I always knew I'd prove one day that sticking to an Android phone was the right decision. Here you go.'

The man grabbed Johnnie's phone, the way a drowning person would grab a life raft, and immediately started stabbing in numbers.

'Do you think your wife would like me to talk to her? I'm no expert, but I've had two children.' Meg spoke as the man waited for the call to connect.

'Yes please. She's freaking out, almost as much as me.' He held up a hand as the call connected. 'Ambulance, please.'

Meg briefly touched Johnnie's hand, before turning and jogging up the road, as fast as her heels would carry her, to where the other car was parked.

'Hi, how are you doing?' Meg spoke gently as she reached the open door on the passenger side of the car. 'I'm Meg; your husband flagged us down and the good news is he's managed to put a call through to the ambulance, so it shouldn't be long now.'

'I don't feel like I've got any time. I'm trying not to push but my body seems to be doing it anyway. Oh Jesus!' The woman gritted her teeth, grasping the gear stick so tightly with one hand that her knuckles went completely white.

'It's okay, your body knows what to do.' Meg wished she did too, but she couldn't control the panic rising in her chest any more than the other woman could stop labour. She'd done a first-aid course when she'd first joined the GP surgery, although it definitely hadn't equipped her for this, but there were some basics she could apply in any scenario and that was what she was going to do. 'Keep breathing, that's it; everything's going to be okay.'

'I wanted an epidural, not this!' The woman shook her head as the contraction eased off. 'I had it all in my birth plan. I'm not one of those women who planned to do it all drug free; I knew my pain threshold was rubbish and I was right.'

'From what I can see, you're doing brilliantly.' Meg kicked off her shoes and crouched down, so she was level with the woman. 'What's your name?'

'Maria.'

'And what about your husband?'

'I've called him every name under the sun in the last twenty minutes.' Maria managed a smile. 'But most people call him Chappers, because our surname is Chapman.'

'He clearly thinks the world of you. He was very worried when he flagged us down.'

'You'd think, being a fireman, he'd have been calmer in a crisis, but I guess all of that goes out of the window when it's someone you—' Maria gritted her teeth again, emitting a low growl as she bore down. 'Oh God, it really feels like the head is coming.'

'Do you want me to take a look?' Meg was half hoping that Maria would turn down her offer, but, when the other woman nodded, she took a deep breath. It was time to woman-up and do whatever had to be done, even if the prospect was terrifying. 'Okay, do you think you can get out of the car and into the backseat before the next contraction comes?'

'I'm scared that if I move at all the baby's head might just drop down.' Maria had the same wild-eyed expression her husband had been wearing moments earlier. 'Can I just push the seat back and stay here?'

'If that's what you want to do.' Meg sat on the edge of the car's doorframe, as Maria pushed the seat back. 'Do you need me to help you take your underwear off?'

'If you don't mind. Oh God, I'm so sorry. There you were, just out for the afternoon and now you've got to look at a stranger's noo-noo. I'm sure that wasn't what you were expecting.'

'Well, it's not boring, that's for sure.' Meg smiled, silently praying that this would end up being a hilarious story she'd be able to tell her colleagues, and not something she'd never be able to forget for all the wrong reasons. 'Okay that's it, the knickers are off now.'

'I suppose I should be embarrassed, but I'm just taking heart from the fact that you probably won't recognise me by my face if we ever meet again.' Maria started to laugh and then broke off as another wave of pain threatened to overwhelm her.

'The call handler wants to speak to you.' Chappers skidded to a halt in front of Meg, holding out the phone. Johnnie was behind him, but at enough of a distance to preserve whatever dignity Maria might have left.

'They want to talk to me?' Meg had a feeling that the wild-eyed stare had spread to her, as Chappers nodded.

'Please. They want to talk us through things in case...' He didn't need to finish the sentence; the implications were obvious. 'I can't do it, I just can't.'

'Okay.' Meg took the phone. 'Hello?'

'Hi Meg, my name's Alison. I'm from the ambulance call handling team and I'm trained to talk people through delivering a baby, if the paramedics can't get there in time. I spoke to Chappers and he tells me you're with his wife, Maria, and that she's in advanced labour. Is that right?'

'I think so. I was just about to have a look; Maria thinks she can feel the head.'

'That's great, Meg; if you can take a look and tell me what you can see, it'll really help us work out exactly how close she is to giving birth.'

'Right.' Meg took a deep breath for the second time. She'd have given anything for Jess or one of the other midwives to be there. Pushing Maria's dress further up her thighs, Meg did as she'd been instructed. 'I can see the top of the head.'

'The ambulance is en route, but it's almost half an hour away, so there's a chance it might not get there before the baby does. I'm going to stay on the line until the paramedics arrive and I can talk you through it if things start to progress.'

'I really need to push; it feels like there's a boulder trying to get out.' Maria was gritting her teeth again and, as another contraction took hold, Meg could immediately see more of the baby's head.

'It's definitely coming; she's having another contraction and I can see more of the top of the baby's head as she's pushing.'

'Okay, keep encouraging her to breathe, in through her nose and out through her mouth. She just needs to bear down with the contractions, but tell her to try not to push in between. Listening to her body is the most important thing she can do.'

'I'm going to put you on speaker so I can keep my hands free.' Meg set the phone down in the console between the two front seats. 'You're doing brilliantly Maria. All you've got to do is keep breathing, that's right, in through your nose and out through your mouth, and just bear down as hard as you can when the contractions come. But make sure you stop pushing when the contraction eases off. Your body's helping you do this; you just need to listen to it.'

'It's starting to burn.' Tears were streaming out from the corners of Maria's eyes, even after she closed them.

'It won't last forever, I promise.' Meg squeezed Maria's leg and leant across to the mobile phone. 'She says it's burning; is there anything I can do to help?'

'What you're telling her is right; it's not going to last and the burning sensation is a sign that the baby is crowning. You both just need to keep doing what you're doing.'

'I've got another one.' Maria's eyes flew open again. 'Chappers, where the bloody hell are you?'

'I'm here darling, you're amazing. I can't believe you're doing this all by yourself.' Maria's husband took hold of her hand. Meg was kneeling in the footwell now and there was no avoiding facing the situation head on.

'That's it, Maria, you're doing so well. The baby's head is out.' Meg could barely catch her breath and she wasn't even sure whether Maria had heard what she'd said, because the next contraction was already coming. 'The baby's coming really quickly; I can see the top of the shoulders – oh wow, that's it, the baby's out.'

'Here, take this.' Johnnie passed her a towel, still managing to look away from the car as he did. 'It's all right, it's clean. It was in my gym bag, but everything in there is washed and ready for the next time I go.'

'Thank you.'

'Is everything okay?' Alison's disembodied voice called out from the mobile, as Meg wrapped the baby in the blanket, being careful not to damage the umbilical cord, which was still attached.

'The baby's here.'

'Brilliant, well done. If everything looks okay you can place the baby on Maria's chest, but the important thing is to make sure they're both kept warm.'

Meg did as Alison had instructed, but the baby still hadn't made a sound and she grabbed the phone, taking it off speaker mode. Lowering her voice, she stood upright and moved slightly away from the car, confident she wouldn't be heard over the sound of Chappers' and Maria's excitement at the delivery of their child. No one could miss the wonder in Maria's voice when she discovered she'd got a daughter. Meg really wished the baby would cry; she just hoped Alison could convince her the silence was normal. 'Should the baby be crying by now?'

'Because the baby's still attached to the placenta, which is supplying its oxygen, it's not unusual that it hasn't cried straight away.' Alison made it sound so routine, but this definitely wasn't the sort of thing that happened to Meg every day.

'She looks a bit floppy.'

'Was the cord free of the baby's neck during delivery?' Suddenly there was an increased urgency in Alison's voice.

'Yes.'

'And can you see if the baby is breathing now?'

'She is.' Meg could see the baby's chest expand and contract, as she lay on Maria, part of her rib cage just visible above where the towel was draped.

'That's good. She might need some stimulation. The delivery sounds like it was very quick and sometimes the baby can go into a bit of shock.'

'How do I do that?' Meg had never been able to bear the sound of either of her babies crying – she'd had to comfort them straight away – but there'd have been no sweeter sound than the piercing cry of a baby at that moment.

'You can try patting the baby's feet, but rubbing her back and chest might work best. If you've got something you can use to rub her dry that might help.'

'Right okay.' Meg painted on a smile and turned back towards Maria and Chappers, slipping the phone into her pocket. The baby looked like a doll lying on her mother's chest and she still wasn't moving. 'The call handler says we need to dry the baby to help keep her warm.'

'It might be easier for you to take her. There's not much room in here.' Maria didn't seem to have noticed how still her baby was, but there was a good chance she was in shock too. Everything had happened so fast.

'Come here sweetheart.' Meg carefully lifted the baby, trying not to panic about the fact that the umbilical cord was still attached. 'Johnnie, if I hold her, can you rub her with the towel. I'm worried about her slipping otherwise.'

'Should I just pat her dry?' He looked almost as uncertain as Meg felt, but she shook her head.

'You need to give her a rub, like she's just come out of the shower. But the cord needs to be kept out of the way so we don't damage it.' Meg remembered enough from her antenatal classes to know that could be dangerous, although she had no idea if they were doing the rest of it right. But if the baby needed stimulating, she could only assume it needed to be fairly rigorous. She couldn't help wishing that Jess or one of the other midwives had been on the road instead of her, only life didn't often work out like that.

'I don't want to hurt her.' Johnnie looked terrified now, but he started rubbing the towel up and down her chest and back, and over Meg's hands, as she kept a firm grip on the baby's body.

'Keep going.' Meg kept her eyes fixed on Johnnie's face. She'd trust him with her own life and she was silently praying that she could trust him with this baby's life too. And, just when she was starting to think it was never going to happen, the baby let out a wail. If Meg hadn't been holding on to her like the universe depended on it, she'd have kissed Johnnie there and then. Any attempt she'd been making to sound calm had gone out of the window too. 'Oh thank God, she's crying.'

'I hadn't even realised she was so quiet.' Maria's eyes widened, but as Meg laid the baby back on her mother's chest, the little girl continued to complain very loudly about her rude awakening.

'She's going to be fine; you can see how strong she is. It was probably just a bit of a shock arriving into the world so quickly.' Meg could hardly believe it was her talking. She actually sounded like she knew what she was doing, even if it still didn't feel like it. 'I'd better let the call handler know what's going on.'

Taking the phone out of her pocket, Meg put the handset to her ear. 'Did you hear all of that?'

'I heard the crying!' Alison sounded as relieved as Meg felt. 'How's mum doing? Any sign of the placenta yet?'

'Not yet. I keep wondering if I should call one of the community midwives I work with, to see if they can get here before the ambulance. I'm a receptionist at the Port Agnes Midwifery Unit.'

'It's probably not worth it, unless they're very local to you. I've just had an update from the paramedics and they should be there really soon.'

'I'm worried about the placenta, in case it doesn't come out on its own.' Meg had suffered a retained placenta after Seth's birth and had needed a manual removal. The midwife who'd delivered him had warned her what might happen if the placenta wasn't delivered quite quickly after the birth, so she knew it could lead to a life-threatening bleed.

'Is there any reason to think it might not? Is the cord still intact?'

'Yes it seems to be.' Meg looked over at Maria, trying to work out if the other woman was just exhausted, of if her pallor was something to worry about. It was no good; she couldn't just sit and wait for the ambulance to come. She turned to Johnnie.

'I'm just going to go and grab my phone from the car. I need to get hold of Jess and see if she or one of the other midwives can get here.'

'Can you hear that?' Johnnie looked up the road as he spoke. 'I think it's a siren.'

'Are you sure?' Meg wanted him to be right more than anything, but for a moment she couldn't hear it. Then, there it was, the unmistakeable wail of a siren as the ambulance headed towards them along the country lane.

'The ambulance is coming, Maria.' Meg rushed back to the side of the car, relief flooding her body and making her giddy.

'I can see them.' Chappers seemed determined to jump out and stop the vehicle, even though the ambulance was already headed straight for them. He stepped into the middle of the road, waving his arms again like he had when he'd flagged down Meg and Johnnie's car.

The ambulance pulled in about twenty feet in front of the car and Chappers rushed towards it, before the paramedics even had a chance to get out.

'How are you doing? The experts are here now.' Meg leant into the car. Maria was cradling the baby against her chest and the little girl already seemed to be rooting around for a feed.

'I don't know if she's hungry.' Maria looked worried and Meg recognised her expression. When Seth was first born, she'd been scared he would starve to death during the first night, when he wouldn't latch on properly and her milk didn't seem to be coming in. It seemed crazy thinking about it now, but she'd been convinced if he didn't feed regularly within the first few hours, he wouldn't make it.

'Why don't you try feeding her? Even if you're not planning to breastfeed, the midwife told me when I had my son that it can help deliver the placenta.'

'I don't suppose my placenta suddenly dropping into the footwell of the car could make things any more embarrassing than they already are.' Maria pulled a face. Chappers had used a jacket that was on the back seat, as a makeshift blanket for his wife, so at least a tiny bit of her dignity was protected.

'You've got nothing to be embarrassed about. Look what you've just done, you've made a whole new person.' Meg couldn't help thinking about Tilly as she watched Maria with her new baby. Her daughter was going to do something just as amazing, and Meg suddenly felt certain that nothing was going to stop her loving the baby with everything she had. Just because Seth and Darren couldn't be there, it wouldn't diminish how special the moment Meg first saw her baby with a baby of her own would be. And she couldn't wait. 'Look at that little sweetheart, she's latching on like a total pro.'

'She really is.' Maria's whole face relaxed and it was like a sense of calm had descended by the time the paramedics reached the car.

Within minutes, they had everything under control and had carefully transferred Maria and the baby to a stretcher to get them into the ambulance. Chappers couldn't stop smiling, but his wife suddenly grabbed his arm, as if she'd been hit by another contraction, and all Meg's worries about her came flooding back.

'Make sure you get Meg and Johnnie's numbers before we get into the ambulance. We owe them the world and we can never repay that, but we can at least sort out a slap-up dinner once things are back to normal a bit.'

'You don't owe us anything.' Tears filled Meg's eyes. 'It was an absolute privilege to see your little girl arrive into the world and I'm never going to forget it.'

'Meg's right. You don't owe us anything. Maybe just name her after me?' Johnnie winked. 'I mean, maybe not Jonathan, but Joanna-than has quite a ring to it!'

'We'll think about it.' Chappers laughed. 'But I know my wife, and if I don't get your number she'll refuse to go to the hospital until I do.'

Johnnie reeled off his number and Chappers put it into his phone, before following his wife into the ambulance. With one more wave from Maria before the doors were closed behind her, Meg felt suddenly bereft. She'd known Maria and Chappers for less than forty minutes, but somehow she missed their new little family already and she didn't even know the baby's name.

'Are you okay? You were completely amazing.' When Johnnie looked at Meg, his eyes were shining. There was no doubt the emotion was getting to him too, and she couldn't stop herself from asking a question she wasn't even sure she wanted the answer to.

'Don't you want that?'

'What, a medical emergency in a layby?' Johnnie was trying to joke his way out of it, but he wasn't getting away with it that easily.

'No, a baby. I saw the look on your face when you were

watching Chappers with his daughter and I know you'd be a great dad. I can't believe you don't want that.' Having children had been the best thing to ever happen to Meg and even losing Seth hadn't made her regret it for a second. Johnnie deserved the chance to have that too.

'Not if it means losing you.' He put his hands around her waist. 'Meg, I need you to look at me when I say this.'

'I am looking at you.'

'No, you're not. I don't mean look at my shoes; I want you to look at my face.' Johnnie waited while she dragged her eyes upwards until they finally met his. 'What I want is you. And it doesn't matter how many times you question it, or how often you tell me that what we've got will be nice while it lasts. Because, unless you get fed up with me and kick me out of your life, I'm not going anywhere. When Tilly's baby arrives, we can have fun helping out and getting our fix of baby time whenever we want it. But we can also give the baby back and go out to dinner at By the View. We can sip cocktails at the weekend without feeling a shred of guilt that we should be at a soft play centre instead. I want you Meg Sawyer, and the only thing you could do to make me even happier than you already have is to accept it's true.'

'How can I prove I've accepted it?' He'd never given her a moment's reason to doubt him and if he said all he needed was her, she owed it to him to show she believed it.

'Move in with me.' Johnnie's eyes never left her face, even when she took a step back in shock. 'It makes sense. You want Tilly and Ed to move into your place, to help them out. And, this way, they'd have no reason to feel guilty about doing it.'

'I-I...' Meg couldn't find the words to finish the sentence.

'Unless you don't want to. The last thing I want to do is to put any pressure on you.'

'Of course I want to.' Suddenly the words were out there, before she had a chance to weigh up all the pros and cons, or to worry about what other people might think. Johnnie wanted to be with her and there was no doubt in her mind that she wanted to be with him too. No one had the guarantee of forever anyway, she knew that better than anyone. Right now, she had a second chance to grab happiness with both hands and she wasn't going to let it pass her by.

8

By Sunday evening, Chappers had already sent a text to Johnnie, letting him know that they'd decided to call the baby Daisy, after the road she'd been born in. The little girl was lucky that her surprise arrival had been in Daisy Fields Lane and not Duck's Bottom Loop, which was only about half a mile away from where she'd been born. But it was lovely that she'd know all about her unusual entrance into the world and that she'd have a memento of it forever. Even better news was that both Maria and Daisy had been given a clean bill of health and they were already back at home, ready to start their new lives as a family of three.

Meg had arranged to meet Hamish before surgery started, to go through the results of her tests, but the worries she'd felt about him confirming she was menopausal had disappeared. Johnnie knew what he was getting into and he didn't care. Everyone who'd heard that Tilly was expecting had told her no one was going to believe she was a grandma and she'd decided to focus on the positives. It was going to be great hitting these milestones before she'd expected to. It was easy to see the positives of being a fun nana, who could keep up with a toddler and do all the fun stuff that kids liked to do. It might be a bit harder to see the upside of an early menopause, but she'd be getting that out of the way too. By the time she hit her fifties, it would all be behind her.

'Morning.' Meg smiled as she walked into Hamish's consulting room and he looked up at her, returning the smile. But there was something in his eyes that made the nerves she'd thought had completely vanished flutter in her stomach like leaves in the wind. There were worse things than an early menopause. Far worse.

'Grab a seat and I'll go through the results with you.'

'Just tell me. Is it bad news?' Meg wasn't sure she could face this, not without Johnnie. If this was the thing she feared the most – having the sort of illness that meant she might leave Tilly too – the only person she wanted with her would be Johnnie.

'That depends...' Hamish held her gaze and it felt like time had stopped, until he finally spoke again. 'On how you feel about having a baby.'

'What?' For a moment Meg was confused, but then she shook her head, realising what he meant. 'It's okay, I know what you're going to say. That that ship has sailed. So I'm officially menopausal?'

'No, you're officially pregnant.' Hamish smiled again, but any minute now he was going to burst out laughing, because this had to be a joke.

'I can't be. I haven't been having proper periods for almost a year and, well... I just can't be.'

'There's a good chance, given how long your symptoms have been going on for, that you have entered perimenopause, but that doesn't mean you can't still become pregnant. Your periods can become irregular due to fluctuating hormones, but if you're still ovulating – even if it's not every month – then you can become pregnant.' Hamish's tone was gentle. 'I assume from your reaction that you weren't trying to get pregnant?'

'I didn't think I could, but we always used condoms just in case.' Meg might have been embarrassed about the conversation, if she hadn't been so shocked she could barely remember her own name.

'Is it something you think you might want?'

'Are you sure the test is right?' She couldn't even think about the answer to Hamish's question, because she couldn't picture a universe in which she could possibly be having another baby. Not at forty-six. And what was Tilly going to say? 'Oh God, I feel sick.'

'It's going to be okay.' Hamish had come around from his side of the desk. 'Do you really think you might be sick?'

'My stomach's churning. I can't be pregnant. I can't.' If she kept saying the words over and over again, maybe that would make them true.

'You're definitely pregnant, Meg, and the other tests have shown there's nothing wrong with you. Whatever you decide about the baby, there are options. But this could be good news, once it's sunk in. Either way, a clean bill of health is something to celebrate.'

'*Pregnant.*' Meg shook her head again and looked at Hamish, without really seeing him. Coming to terms with Tilly having a baby had taken her long enough, but this was a whole other level, and for the first time in a long time, it wasn't Johnnie she wanted to turn to first. Meg had to work out how she felt before she talked to him and she had no idea where to start.

* * *

Jess had heard all about Meg's stint as a stand-in midwife and she'd suggested to the rest of the team at the midwifery unit that they throw a little celebration for her, next time she was working. It was nothing big, just some cakes and a few balloons, but by all accounts, Meg had been absolutely amazing at Daisy's delivery and that deserved to be celebrated.

Izzy ran into the staffroom. 'Her car has just pulled into the car park.'

'Do you think the party poppers are too much?' Jess was suddenly worried that Meg wouldn't want any of this. After all, she hadn't told Jess or the others about delivering the baby.

'It's just a bit of fun.' Anna smiled. 'But the cake looks amazing.'

'Jago did a great rush job on it. I only phoned him lunch time yesterday and he let me pick it up first thing.' The cake was in the shape of a car, with a baby sitting on the bonnet made from fondant. It was brilliant and it was no wonder Jago Mehenick's bakery was famous for miles around.

'I think I can hear her coming.' Toni shushed everyone and for a moment the sound of footsteps coming down the corridor was all Jess could hear. Then, when the door opened, a chorus of 'surprise' went up around the room.

'Oh my God!' Meg dropped the bag she was holding and for a moment Jess was worried her friend was going to pass out. Maybe Meg had had enough of surprises. Finding a woman giving birth by the side of the road would have been nerve-wracking even for a trained midwife, so it must have been a real shock for Meg.

'Sorry, this was supposed to be a nice surprise, not scare you to death.' As Jess put an arm around Meg's waist, she realised her friend was shaking. 'Hey, it's okay, we just wanted to celebrate the news about the baby.'

'You know about the baby?' Meg's voice was so high it made Jess wince, but she needed to hear how amazing they all thought she was.

'Of course we do, everyone does. It'll be the talk of Port Agnes soon. It's fantastic and, from what I've heard, the *Three Ports News* want to make it their front page story. We're all so proud of you, aren't we?'

'Why the hell would the Three Ports News be interested in a story about my—' Meg suddenly stopped and shook her head again, some of the colour coming back into her face. 'Oh, you mean the baby at Daisy Fields Lane.'

'What other baby did you think we meant?' Gwen tilted her head and looked at Meg.

'I just, it's...' Meg stopped and Gwen narrowed her eyes.

'You're not—' In that instant, Jess knew she had to cut Gwen off before she had the chance to blurt something out that she might regret.

'Gwen!' The word came out more sharply than expected. 'Sorry. I've just realised I left the balloons in the car and what's a party without balloons?'

Jess turned to Meg. 'Do you mind popping down to the car with me and giving me a hand?'

'I can do it; we don't want Meg missing her own party.' Gwen was still looking at Meg quizzically. Jess had no idea how she was going to explain it when she walked back in without the fictional balloons, but all that mattered for now was getting Gwen and Meg out of the room. And she clearly wasn't the only one who thought so.

'We can all go.' Meg took hold of Gwen's elbow without even giving her the chance to answer, and pulled her out into the corridor, with Jess behind them. The rest of the team were left standing open-mouthed in the staffroom, on the other side of a firmly closed door, probably wondering what the hell was going on.

'Are you okay, Meg?' Jess didn't really need to ask; she could tell by the look on her friend's face that she was far from okay.

'Yes, it was just a bit of a shock, seeing you all standing there.'

Jess could see the heat rising up Meg's neck and flushing her cheeks, and Gwen was nobody's fool.

'It's not just the shock, is it? You're pregnant, aren't you? When you stepped back after we shouted surprise, you put your hands over your belly. You probably didn't even realise you'd done it, but it's instinctive.' Gwen had been a midwife for over forty years and she didn't miss the subtlest of signs.

'I don't know what to do.' Meg seemed to be finding it hard just to breathe in and out. 'How am I supposed to go in there and try to pretend everything is okay, when I'm completely freaking out?'

'I can just go back in and tell them you felt a bit strange when we got to the car and needed to go home. You don't have to tell anyone about this until you're ready. If you ever are.' Jess put an arm around Meg's shoulders.

'They're not going to believe that.' Meg was shaking her head and she was right. Jess was terrible at lying and the balloon story wouldn't have fooled anyone, especially when they came back empty handed.

'I'll tell them I opened the door to Jess's car, got distracted by that good looking traffic warden who always seems to be patrolling the road outside the unit and accidentally let all the balloons float away. They'll believe anything of me! But Jess is right, you don't owe anyone an explanation if you don't want to give it to them.' Gwen could sometimes be as subtle as a brick, but there was such kindness in her eyes when she looked at Meg.

'Thank you, but it's okay. I think I need to tell them the truth. Maybe my subconscious knew I needed to tell someone before I did, and where better to start than a room full of midwives?'

Before Jess or Gwen could say another word, Meg pushed open the door to the staffroom and everyone fell silent.

'Everything okay?' Anna's face was filled with concern.

'I've got something to tell you.' Meg seemed to freeze for a moment and then she took a deep breath. 'I'm pregnant.'

'Oh my goodness, that's fantastic news!' Anna clapped her hands together.

There was an instant flurry of congratulations from around the room, echoing Anna's words, and Meg looked as if she was trying to smile, but then something very weird started happening to her face, and it crumpled as she started to sob.

'Oh sweetheart, it's okay. It's going to be okay.' Jess knew Meg was freaking out about being pregnant but she still had no idea why. Having a baby at forty-six was high risk, but there were any number of reasons why her friend might be upset that had nothing to do with her age. But for now, one thing was certain: Meg needed a hug.

* * *

'Are you feeling any better now?' Jess sat down next to Meg, who was nursing a cup of tea and still looking completely shell-shocked. They were in one of the consulting rooms and it had been clear that despite wanting to tell them all, the last thing Meg needed was an interrogation from the whole team once the news was out there.

'I don't know. I've been numb since yesterday morning, when Hamish told me. I think I've spent the whole time since then trying to convince myself it was a mistake. I haven't even told Johnnie, and then I thought you guys somehow knew about the baby. I still can't process it.'

'Maybe talking to Johnnie would help.' Jess had met Johnnie several times and he seemed like a nice guy, but maybe there was a reason Meg wasn't ready to talk to him yet. 'Do you know what *you* want to do?'

'I can't have a baby.' Meg was still staring straight ahead. 'I'm twice the age I was when I had Tilly and Seth would have been almost twenty-five by now. I'm going to be a grandma in six months' time.'

'If it's just age worrying you, then don't let it.' Jess had supported pregnant women across a wide age range, and there was a member of the infertility support group currently going through IVF by egg donation, who was coming up to her fiftieth birthday. Meg might find she had less energy than the first time around, but it was obvious she'd been a great parent to Tilly and Seth, so she definitely had what it took.

'It's not that. I don't even know whether Johnnie wants children. He keeps saying he's not worried about having them, although I'm not sure if that's just because neither of us thought it was a possibility for me.'

'You know the best way of finding that out, don't you?' Jess gave her a gentle smile. 'But maybe you need to go into that conversation knowing what *you* want, because as involved as Johnnie will be, ultimately, it's down to you.'

'That's the thing; I've got no idea.' Meg bit her lip. 'I can't even imagine having another baby and, when I try, I have so many different emotions battling each other. I'm scared, guilty and sad, but there's something else too, and in a way that frightens me even more.'

'Do you want to talk about it?' Jess didn't want to force Meg to open up, but talking about it might help her to process things.

'It makes no sense, because it's the tiny spark of excitement that frightens me the most.' Meg looked at Jess properly for the first time. 'What if I let myself want this and then it all goes wrong? At my age, the likelihood of this working out and going full term is much smaller than it would be at your age.'

'Age doesn't guarantee anything.' Jess was living proof of that, but this wasn't about her and she tried to ignore the all-too-familiar ache in her chest.

'Oh God, Jess, I'm so sorry.' Meg's face fell. 'I can't believe I'm whingeing to you about being pregnant. I'm so bloody selfish.'

'Of course you're not and you don't have to want the baby, just because some people can't have them.' Jess swallowed hard. 'This is about your life. You've been through so much and you deserve the right to choose where life takes you next. I know you might not know the answer to this yet, but I think you need to be really clear about one thing before you talk to Johnnie. Do you want this baby?'

Meg was silent for a moment and the myriad of emotions she'd described earlier looked as though they were passing across her face. Finally she looked at Jess again. 'I do. I want this baby.'

'Well, that's a start then.' Jess gave her friend the hug she'd known she so badly needed. Meg might not know exactly where the path ahead of her was going to lead, but at least she knew which direction she wanted to go. And maybe it was time for Jess to work out the same thing.

9

Jess was working another shift at the hospital, but her mind was miles away, back in Port Agnes. She hadn't told anyone yet, not even Dexter, but Ella had put her forward for a senior role with the maternity team at the new hospital. It would mean a big increase in salary and a permanent management position as deputy matron, but it would also take her out of community midwifery and away from the colleagues she thought of as family. There'd be more shift work, too, and that would make going back to work, if she ever managed to have a baby, even more of a wrench. The flipside was that it would give her a greater breadth of experience and further her career, something she had a feeling she'd want if her dreams of giving Riley a sibling came to nothing.

There was always the option of adopting, but the chances of being matched with a newborn were almost nil. The role at the hospital wouldn't be a good fit for fostering either, but things would have to change drastically either way if she and Dexter did decide to foster a child who they hoped could become a permanent member of the family. First time around, Jess had only committed to respite fostering, so she could fit it around her work.

But then Teddy had come into her life and changed it forever. Sometimes, when she closed her eyes, she could still remember what it felt like to stroke the velvety soft skin of his cheeks. She wanted that again, more than she wanted to go after any job, no matter how much of a pay increase it would mean. Except the job was within her grasp and having a baby just seemed to be getting further away.

After her fourth round of failed IVF, she was due to go back to the clinic for a follow up appointment. Jess would be having some tests to check her ovarian reserves and hormone levels, before she could even consider the next round of treatment. She'd been trying to decide whether or not to cancel the appointment altogether, and sometimes she changed her mind as often as three times a day.

'Morning! It's good to have you on shift again.' Jacinda smiled as Jess walked along the corridor towards her.

'Morning, it's nice to see you again too.' Jess breathed out, and it already felt as if some of the burden of constantly thinking about making a decision had lifted. That was the thing about her job, it stopped her having the time to overthink everything. 'I don't want to mention the Q word, but it looks fairly calm today.'

There was a tradition at the midwifery unit in Port Agnes never to comment when things were quiet, because it always seemed to result in the flood gates opening and three women in labour all turning up at the same time, with a home delivery thrown in for good measure. But looking at the board, it was an unusually quiet morning in the hospital so far. There was only one woman in active labour and another having an oxytocin drip to induce labour. It had never been anywhere near as quiet on any other shift that Jess had worked there.

'Definitely don't mention the Q word.' Jacinda put a finger to her lips. 'If we're lucky, we might even have time for some cuddles.'

'I really like you, Jacinda, but I'm not sure we're quite at that level yet.' Jess laughed and Jacinda shook her head, joining in.

'Luckily for you then, the cuddles will be with Krissy and Alec's baby.'

'Really? That sounds great, but surely she's not still here?' Jess had delivered the couple's baby on her last shift at the hospital. But even with a forceps delivery, it would have been usual for the new family to head home within twenty-four hours. It had been almost two weeks.

'They went home, but Krissy had a breast abscess and it didn't respond to the antibiotics, so she had to have it surgically aspirated and she's been back in hospital. I literally bumped into Alec in the corridor; bless him, he looked totally washed out. He said that Krissy's being sent home today and that they'll pop up and see us with Caleb before they leave.'

'Poor Krissy.' Jess involuntarily folded her arms across her chest at the mere thought of a breast abscess. 'At least they've managed to agree on a name. When I last saw Krissy they still weren't sure. Alec wanted to call him Leonard, but I think Krissy's words were something along the line of *over my dead body.*'

'I'm not sure I could ever look at a baby and come up with the name Leonard.' Jacinda pulled a face. 'But I know how hard it can be to come up with names you both agree on, especially by the time we got to our third! We've never bickered so much about anything.'

'I've got no idea how you manage shifts with all you've got going on.' Jess didn't know exactly how old Jacinda's children were, but she'd mentioned having one in pre-school and another who was with a childminder, because he was too young for the same nursery her daughter went to. She'd talked about how rounding up her kids after work from their various pick-ups was like a military operation, and Jess could well believe it. But none of that stopped her feeling envious. If she wanted to pick out a name, at this rate she'd have to buy a dog; maybe Leonard might work for a Labrador. Jess's beloved cat, Luna, had died a year ago and she'd been wanting to get a dog for Riley almost as much as the little boy wanted it for himself, but it had never seemed like the right time.

'Sometimes it's tough and it's about to get tougher.' Jacinda put a hand on her abdomen. 'We've got nearly six months of bickering ahead of us before we have to decide on a name for this one, though.'

'Oh, congratulations!' Jess hated herself for the way her skin was prickling. This wasn't just envy, it was full blown jealousy, especially when she heard what Jacinda had to say next.

'We were being really careful, at least I thought we were. Dev even had the snip the month before we found out, but they told us to keep using contraception for at least eight weeks. And we did, except for one night when... Well, let's just say there might have been a few too many G&Ts at a family wedding we went to. And oopsie, here I am, having number four. But this is definitely it; I'm not letting Dev near me again after this one until we know for certain. I'm going to have my tubes tied too. Belt and braces is what my friend in gynae calls it!'

'Four's a nice round number.' It was a number Jess desperately wanted to be a feature of her life. Not four children, she wasn't asking for the moon. Just a family of four – Jess, Dexter, Riley and one more. A Labrador, no matter how cute, could never fill that gap. Not for her. It was hard to describe the feeling of an empty space that had never been occupied, but it made her feel restless, like she was constantly searching for the final piece that would complete the jigsaw. The last thing she wanted was to become bitter, but seeing how easily other people created their families made her chest ache. She wondered, not for the first time, if she could really stay in a job which forced her to confront that every single day.

* * *

Jess had been asked to assist with delivering the baby of the lady who'd been in labour when she'd arrived on shift.

Abigail was in the delivery suite with her twin sister, Phoebe, and according to Geraldine, the lead midwife, she'd been in labour for sixteen hours.

'Hi Jess, thanks for coming down.' Geraldine looked up as Jess came into the room. 'We can already see baby's head, so it won't be long. But Abigail's been in labour since six o'clock last night, so she's more than ready and another contraction should be along any time.'

'Are you sure it won't be long? I don't think I can handle much more of this.' Abigail's twin sister looked as though she meant every word. 'Seeing Abs in this much pain is killing me!'

'You're just lucky twins don't really feel each other's pain, because I'm sure this kid is coming out sideways. No one ever said it was this bad!' On cue, Abigail's face twisted until it was almost unrecognisable as another contraction took hold. The good news was that the baby wasn't coming out sideways, but head first and face down, exactly as it should be. It still took another twenty minutes before Abigail's baby girl made her appearance into the world, though.

'I'm so proud of you.' Abigail's sister leant over and dropped a kiss on the top of her head, as her newborn niece lay on her mother's chest.

'Me too.' Abigail laughed. 'I couldn't have done it without you, Phebes.'

'Watching you giving birth, I half wished it was me having the

baby for you, instead of having to see you in that much pain.'
Phoebe wrinkled her brow as if it was a genuine dilemma. 'Either
way, it would all be worth it for this little one.'

'She's amazing, isn't she?' Abigail exchanged a look with her
sister that said so much, without a single word being spoken.

'I'm really sorry but I need to borrow the baby for a few
minutes.' Jess always felt guilty about this bit, but now that Abigail
had had some time to bond with her little girl, she needed to check
the baby over while Geraldine oversaw the delivery of the placenta.

'That's fine, I've got the rest of my life with her. Just the two
of us.'

'Not just the two of you, because you've got me as well. Both of
you have. Forever.' Phoebe's tone was serious for a moment and
then she laughed again. 'Because I might never have a baby of my
own after watching that.'

'You'd better tell Ricky I've ruined all your plans then.' Abigail's
face suddenly crumpled. 'Do you think she'll hate me later for not
giving her a dad?'

'She's not going to hate you; she's going to love you for being
the best mum ever and, if you like, I can remind you of all the
reasons why I know that's true, while Jess is checking the baby
over.'

'Right, come on then little one, let's get you sorted.' Jess picked
the baby up and left the sisters deep in conversation. She'd never
had a sibling and she knew plenty of people who were far closer to
friends than they were to their siblings, but she still wanted to give
Riley the chance of having a bond that could last a lifetime. It
sounded as if Abigail had taken the decision to have her baby in a
slightly unconventional way, but if Jess wanted a baby, she'd have
no choice about taking an unconventional route. There were
plenty of options for becoming a parent and the members of the
infertility support group had tried almost everything, including

two of the group who'd used surrogates. It wasn't something Jess had ever really considered, but maybe it was time to do a bit more research and to find out how Dexter felt about it. Carrying her own baby might have been part of the original dream, but it wasn't the important bit. She was more certain of that than ever.

* * *

Krissy and Alec came up to the maternity ward as promised, and Alec was carrying a big cardboard box filled with packets of sweet and savoury biscuits, chocolates and cakes.

'Krissy sent me to the supermarket to get some stuff as a thank you, but I was thinking about all the things I like to eat!' Alec grinned.

'Listen, those sorts of empty calories always go down a treat when we're on a long shift.' Jacinda took the box off him, but Jess's fingers were already itching to reach out and take baby Caleb. Her job meant she got the privilege of holding other people's babies in her arms more than most, but it was usually fairly fleeting, so the prospect of getting to give the baby a proper cuddle was very welcome.

'How are you feeling now?' Jess turned to Krissy, keeping her arms clamped down by her sides in an attempt to make her desperation to hold him less obvious.

'Just about human again, at last.' Krissy was pushing Caleb in a pram, but she looked as if she was ready to have a lie down herself and her next words confirmed it. 'I think this giving birth lark might be a one and done for me.'

'It's early days; I wouldn't rush into a decision just yet.' Jess didn't seem to be able to stop her fingers from twitching as she looked at Caleb.

'I know, but I don't think Alec wants to do it again either. I was on the ceiling with pain from the abscess, and we've got the foster-ing. So if I ever miss the newborn stage, I can easily get my fix.'

'I've been thinking about that lately too.' The truth was, Jess had barely stopped thinking about Krissy and Alec since she'd met them. She'd considered every possible way to have a second child, but some options were starting to feel like a better fit for them. If she and Dexter decided to try and adopt a second child, she knew she'd never experience the newborn stage. If they started fostering again, they could apply for parent and child placements. One or both of the baby's parents would move in too and be shown how to care for their child, with the foster carer assessing their progress. Sometimes this would mean the families staying together and sometimes the parents left the placement, with the foster carers looking after the babies until the court process was finalised and they could be adopted or returned to birth family members. Maybe that was all Jess needed, to have the experience of caring for a newborn for longer than she'd had Teddy, and to get to do it with Dexter by her side. If that was something she could get out of her system, so that she could move on to adoption without feeling even a tiny twinge of regret about what might have been, it had to be a good thing. Any child who was adopted deserved to feel like they were everything their adoptive parents had ever wanted and to be seen as every bit as precious as they were. And until Jess got to that point, she knew she wouldn't be ready to adopt again.

10

Meg had thought of twenty different ways to tell Johnnie she was pregnant. She could picture herself breaking the news every time, whether it was blurting it out, handing him a positive pregnancy test, giving him some baby booties, or even getting Jago to ice it on a cake. But what she couldn't picture, in any of the scenarios, was what Johnnie's reaction was going to be. 'I just want you.' His words from the last conversation they'd had about having a baby kept coming back to her. When he'd said them, she'd been terrified that he might not mean them. Now she was terrified that he did.

'Are you okay? You look worn out.' Johnnie's face was full of concern when she opened the door to him. They were standing in the hallway, which was still lined with pictures of Darren and Seth. She couldn't just blurt it out, not in front of them.

'I haven't been sleeping well, that's all.' She turned back down the hallway. 'Come on in.'

'Why aren't you sleeping? Are you still worried about Tilly and the baby?' Johnnie followed her through to the kitchen, the smell of the food she was cooking hitting her as she went in, making her stomach turn. If she couldn't even keep down a simple pasta bake, it was going to give the game away whether she was ready or not.

'The baby has been on my mind.' Meg had never liked lying, but this way she was just stretching the truth.

'Have you spoken to Tilly about my offer for you to move in with me?'

'Not yet.' Meg took some pasta bowls out of the cupboard. 'Sit down and I'll get us a drink.'

'Not until you tell me what's really the matter.' Johnnie gently took hold of her arms, forcing her to stop laying the table and look at him. 'Did the doctor say something?'

Johnnie looked really worried now, and she wished she'd never told him she was going to see Hamish, but it wasn't fair to leave him wondering and suspecting the worst. Whatever his reaction, the news wasn't the worst thing she could say. And, if he didn't want anything to do with the baby, that was his choice.

'Something showed up on one of the tests.'

'Oh God, Meg, whatever it is, we'll get through it together.' Johnnie took hold of her hand and she blinked back tears. It was early days in the pregnancy and there was a possibility it could be over soon anyway. She hadn't even had a scan yet. Meg had thought about trying to keep it to herself until she knew whether it was likely to go any further, but the truth was she didn't want to face that alone either. She and Johnnie were in this together, and he had a right to know.

'I hope so, because I'm pregnant.' It was just two words, but they changed everything. She wasn't even sure Johnnie had heard them, because he was staring at her open-mouthed. Nothing in his expression gave away what he was thinking; his face was completely blank. 'Did you hear what I said?'

'We're having a baby?' Johnnie still looked stunned, but his words said everything. There were so many ways he could have worded it, but he hadn't said 'You're pregnant?' or 'You're having a baby?', he'd said 'we' – 'we're having a baby'. She was certain then, whatever happened, they really were in this together.

'Well, yes, if it sticks. But at my age...'

'Of course it's going to stick. Oh my God, Meg, Meg.' Johnnie kissed her gently and then pulled away to look at her again. 'I can't believe this is happening.'

'But is it what you want?' Meg was almost certain she knew the answer, but she needed to hear it from Johnnie.

'I want you, but a baby...' Johnnie shook his head and for a moment Meg's heart sank. 'That wasn't something I ever let myself think about, because until I met you there was never anyone I wanted to do that with. But when I met you, it was different. Almost from the start I knew you were the person I wanted to be with, for the rest of my life. I needed that feeling to commit to having a baby, but I didn't think it could happen for us. I knew I could be happy if it was always just the two of us, so it was easy to accept that's how it would always be. Now you're saying we can have that too. Oh Meg, darling, it's honestly the best news I could ever have had.'

'I didn't know what you'd think and I had no idea if this was something you'd want...' Meg's voice trailed off, sounding small, even to her own ears. Her hands were trembling, from a mix of adrenaline at building up to the news and relief at how he'd taken it. She wished she could share his joy with him, but something was blocking her. And Johnnie could see it too.

'What worries me, is what *you* think. I know this must be really hard for you after losing Darren and Seth.' His hand was warm as he put it over hers and it made her feel safe enough to tell him the truth.

'You're right, it is hard. I feel guilty that I'm moving on and starting a life that neither of them can be a part of, but that started the moment I met you.' She looked up at him, her eyes filling with tears again. 'I'm absolutely terrified too, of letting myself get attached to someone else I might lose. But that's another risk you've already forced me to take. So it's a bit late to try and put the brakes on it now, isn't it?'

'I think it probably is.' Johnnie squeezed her hand again. 'I know this isn't going to be easy for you, but I want you to be able to tell me what you're thinking. I'm not going to get jealous or be funny about things, if this rakes up difficult memories. I want you to be able to tell me about all of that.'

'I want to, but I don't even know how Tilly is going to take it.'

'You haven't told her yet?' Johnnie looked almost as shocked as he had when she'd first told him the news. He knew Meg and Tilly usually shared everything, and she'd picked up the phone to ring her daughter at least six times since the consultation with Hamish. But she still hadn't been able to go ahead and make the call. She'd have to do it soon, now that the other midwives knew, but, until she had a scan, there was still a chance there might not be a lot to tell.

'I've got my first scan tomorrow to work out exactly how far along I am. I don't want Tilly to have to deal with all the feelings that this is bound to rake up for her, until I know if the pregnancy is viable. The truth is, I was planning to save you from all of that too, but I just couldn't face the thought of going to the appointment on my own.' Meg looked at him again, knowing the answer to her next question before she even asked it. 'Will you come with me?'

'Just try stopping me. I love you and nothing's going to change that.' Johnnie smiled again, but another waft of the garlicky pasta sauce cooking on the stove made Meg's stomach lurch.

'I think I'm going to throw up.'

'Not quite the response I was hoping for.' Johnnie laughed,

grabbing the washing up bowl from the sink. 'You go and lie down and take this just in case. I'll turn this lot off and whip down to the shop and get you some ginger biscuits; they used to work wonders when my sister was pregnant with her boys.'

'What about dinner? I promised to cook for you tonight.'

'I'll sort something for us later if you fancy it and, if not, I'm more than capable of looking after myself. It's time you let someone else take care of you for a change, Meg, and that's the only thing I'm going to insist on.'

'Thank you.' There was so much more Meg wanted to say, but nausea was bubbling in her stomach again and if she didn't get out soon, Johnnie was going to see a side of her she wasn't quite ready for him to witness yet. She'd have to get past all of that soon, though, because there was nothing in the world as intimate as sharing the experience of having a baby – the good, the bad and the ugly bits. And there was no one else on earth she'd rather share that with than Johnnie.

* * *

If Meg was going where there might be a lot of people whose elbows had the potential to come within a six-foot radius of her chest area, she was going to do it wearing a puffer jacket. Even if the weather on the Cornish Atlantic Coast in early June was promising a long, hot summer ahead, Meg would rather look ridiculous in a quilted jacket, than risk anyone accidentally brushing against her chest, let alone banging into her. She'd forgotten the incredibly painful, burning sensation that had made the early stages of her other two pregnancies almost unbearable. Even the thought of putting a bra on made her wince.

While she didn't enjoy the discomfort, it meant Meg was confident the sonographer was going to find a baby when they scanned her. Ever since Hamish had told her she was pregnant, she'd been trying to work out when she might have conceived, but there was no real way of knowing. Meg hadn't had a proper period in over a year, but that couldn't be any indication of when she'd fallen pregnant – otherwise she'd be going into the *Guinness World Records* for the world's longest gestation. It wasn't even as if she could tell just by looking; her stomach hadn't been flat since she'd had Tilly by C-section, after she'd flipped into the breech position two weeks before her due date. The surgeon seemed to have somehow crimped the edges of the scar together and her belly had been left looking like a giant Cornish pasty. When she and Johnnie had started sleeping together, she'd frozen every time he touched her abdomen. Leaving the lights on hadn't even been an option. But if Johnnie had noticed, he'd hadn't given the slightest indication. Instead he'd told her how beautiful she was so often that she'd finally started to relax. She might never believe she was beautiful, but she did believe that he thought she was and somehow that was enough.

'It's going to be okay.' Johnnie held her hand and she silently prayed he was right. Going back to the nappies and sleepless nights phase didn't even feature on her things-to-worry-about list. At the top of it right now was seeing a viable embryo. After that, it would be telling Tilly and Ed, and then the tests that would inevitably be suggested for a mother-to-be of her age. But one thing she'd learned from the counselling she'd had after losing Darren and Seth was to go hour by hour when life was at its most overwhelming. She just needed to get through the scan, then the next step, and the one after that until she reached the end of what-ever this turned out to be. She couldn't do anything to control whether or not she ended up with a baby in her arms, but she wasn't going to risk thinking that far ahead either and falling in love with a person who might never exist.

'I really need a wee.' Meg had been told to drink water in the hour prior to her scan, but they were running about twenty minutes late and she wasn't sure she was going to be able to hold on.

'Megan Sawyer?' A woman in a light blue uniform came out of a room and called Meg's name, making it feel like her heartbeat had suddenly doubled its pace.

'Promise you won't let go of my hand.' She turned to Johnnie, who nodded.

'I promise.' True to his word, he kept hold of her hand as they followed the sonographer into the room, only letting go long enough for Meg to lie on the bed and undo her trousers, before he grasped her hand again.

'Can I check your date of birth?' The sonographer peered at the screen in front of her and Meg dutifully announced that, yes, she really had been born forty-six years ago. The sonographer gave a little nod and turned to face them. 'And your notes say you're unsure how far along you are; is that correct?'

'Uh-huh.' Meg felt her face colour. The sonographer looked around the same age as Tilly and she suddenly felt uncomfortable admitting that she had no idea when she'd conceived. People that age probably thought that middle-aged women like Meg had sex once in a blue moon, if at all, so it should be easy to pinpoint when she'd fallen pregnant. But neither of those things was true in her case.

'And you can't be certain whether you're before or after the eight-week point either, is that right?'

'I'm afraid not.' There were two spots of heat burning on Meg's cheeks now, but it would all be over soon.

'In that case, I'll start with an abdominal scan, but there's a chance I might have to perform a transvaginal scan if you're still quite early on.' The sonographer gave her a level look. 'That's an internal scan using a probe; will you be okay with that?'

'I can't say it was at the top of my bucket list, but I'm sure I'll cope.' Meg smiled and the sonographer laughed, immediately lifting some of the tension in the room.

'I don't think it's many people's idea of fun.' The young woman took the bottle of gel from the stand at the side of the examination table. 'I'm going to squirt some of this on to your abdomen and I'm sorry if it's a bit cold. Don't worry if I go a bit quiet when I first start the scan; it can take a bit of time to work out where things are.'

'Okay, thank you.' Meg hadn't even been sure she'd be able to look at the monitor when the scan started. If she watched Johnnie's face instead, it would tell her all she needed to know. But in the end her eyes were drawn to the screen as if by some invisible force.

'Right, well I didn't need to spend much time looking for that.' The sonographer smiled and indicated towards the screen. 'I'm sure you can see what I can, right here, looking very settled and, at a guess, I'd say you were around sixteen weeks pregnant.'

'As much as that? Are you sure?' Meg's mouth had dropped open, but there was no denying that this wasn't just a tiny bean, with a flickering heartbeat and not much else discernible on the screen. The image was quite obviously of a baby, with distinct limbs and a tiny little hand raised above the rest of its body, waving at its stunned parents. Her overwhelming emotion might have been shock, but there were so many feelings bubbling just below the surface. This baby on the screen was a part of her and a part of Johnnie, and the desire she felt to protect it had taken her breath away from the moment she saw it.

'I'll do the measurements in a moment, but, yes, I'd say you're well into the second trimester and only a few weeks off the halfway point.'

'But I haven't been doing any of the right stuff.' Meg couldn't take her eyes off the image on the screen, guilt fighting its way to the top of the pile of emotions and making the skin on the back of her neck prickle. She was terrified that if she looked away from the screen for even a second, the baby might suddenly disappear. It was bad enough that she was as old as time, but she hadn't taken any pre-natal vitamins and she'd eaten and drunk far too many of the wrong things. 'I didn't even have any symptoms until my GP told me I was pregnant. How can I have missed all of that for sixteen weeks?'

'Symptoms can be written off as other things and, if you're busy and the signs are mild, it's sometimes possible to ignore them altogether.'

'I put most of it down to the menopause. But I've only started getting morning sickness this week.' There was no way Meg could have ignored the nausea she'd been experiencing for the last two days.

'It's possible for mild nausea to get much worse in the second trimester, but it's quite rare and there's always a chance it could be something else that isn't related to your pregnancy. The best thing you can do is to speak to your midwife about all of that as soon as possible. You'll be given another scan at twenty weeks to look in a lot more detail at the physical development of your baby, but, for now, try not to worry too much. I'll do the measurements and see if there's anything else to report, but the baby has a very strong heartbeat.'

'I still can't believe that's our baby.' Johnnie took the words right out of her mouth and when she turned to look at him, there were tears streaming down his face. 'It's our baby, Meg. Ours.'

'It is and I really love you.' She'd been saying those words to him for a whole year, despite the plans she'd had at the start not to fall in love with Johnnie. They'd been hard to say at first, because Darren had been the only other man she'd ever said those words to. But she'd been absolutely certain, by the time she finally said them, that she meant them and never more so than now. She loved Johnnie and she already loved this baby, more than she'd ever thought possible, even half an hour ago. She just had to pray her body wouldn't let any of them down, because now they'd been given the chance of a baby of their own, she had no idea what they'd do if that was taken away.

11

Jess hated asking Dexter to miss work. His wasn't the sort of job you could easily take a day away from and, as a social worker, there always seemed to be more to do than there were hours in the day. But she couldn't face going to get the results of her tests at the fertility clinic alone.

'What if the results suggest we should start treatment sooner rather than later?' Jess shivered; just the idea of starting up treatment again made her stomach churn. She'd spent a good chunk of the last three years feeling sick with nerves. It was no surprise that they called IVF a rollercoaster, because you spent the whole time not knowing whether what was around the corner would be a massive high, or a devastating low.

'It doesn't matter what the tests say. It's what we want that's important.' Dexter turned her to face him, as they reached the entrance to the clinic. 'Do you know what you want?'

'Not to waste any more time.' Jess looked up at her husband, wondering if she was about to rob him of one of his dreams, but suddenly she was more certain of what she wanted than she'd been at any point since the last cycle had failed.

'On having treatment?' Dexter's eyes never left hers, even as she nodded.

'I don't want to miss out on any more of our lives together – you, me and Riley. When we're going through the treatment, we're always working towards the next stage. First of all, it's whether or not the drugs are working, then we have to worry about whether we're going to get any eggs. Even if we do, they might not mature and if we're lucky enough to get some embryos, there's the hell of waiting to find out whether or not they've implanted. We've had four rounds of treatment and got all the way to the two-week wait hell three times, but we still don't have a baby. Instead, we've wasted months where we couldn't book a holiday in case we missed an optimum window for treatment, and we couldn't eat or drink what we really wanted to, in case it made half a per cent's difference to the chances of me falling pregnant. I don't want Riley to look back on his childhood and feel like we were always wishing for something more, instead of making the most of what we've already got.' She was terrified that she might be about to break Dexter's heart, but she didn't want to live like this any more, no matter how much she wanted another child. Tears were choking in her throat at the thought of hurting him and for all the failed attempts that hadn't got them any closer to having the baby they so desperately wanted, but she couldn't cry, she was too exhausted.

'Are you saying you don't want any more treatment?' Dexter's tone wasn't giving anything away, but there was no backing out now. She had to be honest.

'I think I am.' Jess wasn't sure how she'd expected to feel when she finally said the words out loud, but her overriding emotion now was relief. She just needed to know what Dexter was thinking.

'Would the results from your test make any difference to how you're feeling?'

'Not to me, but if you want us to try again—'

'No.' Dexter didn't even give her the chance to finish. 'I'd have supported you with whatever you wanted, you know that. But the thought of you going through all of that again... I've always known that you and Riley would be enough for me. I don't want to waste any more time either.'

'Shall we go up and cancel the appointment?'

'No, let's ring them from the car. We can go out to lunch, eat and drink whatever we want, and talk about where we're going to take Riley on holiday this year.'

'Are you sure you haven't got any doubts?'

'Not a single one.' Dexter took her hand in his as they turned away from the entrance to the clinic, and it was all she could do not to break into a run.

* * *

Jess packed the muffins into the picnic basket, ready for the trip to the beach that Riley had been asking for all week. They were heading down to Ocean Cove and they had to time it right to make the most of it, before the cove had to be cleared at high tide. Riley had been checking whether it was time to go yet, almost from the moment he'd got up.

'Are you ready?' Jess looked up and smiled as Dexter came into the room. He had a huge bag, filled with buckets and spades, a football, towels and she could even see the top of a cricket set poking out.

'I think I've got everything we could possibly need for a few hours on the beach, or maybe even a fortnight's holiday.' Dexter grinned. 'Do you need a hand with anything?'

'No, I think I'm all set.' Jess called down the hallway, 'Riley, it's time, sweetheart.'

'At last!' Riley skidded to a halt on the wooden floor outside the doorway. 'Come on then, Mum. Are we going, or not?'

'I hope you've got your trainers on.' Dexter laughed. 'Because I think our son is going to want to run all the way to the beach.'

'I think he is.' Jess picked up the picnic basket and followed her husband and son out into the sunlight. It was going to be a beautiful day.

* * *

The best thing about Ocean Cove was that only locals really knew it was there. Port Agnes owed a lot to the tourists who brought income to the town and created lots of extra jobs, especially during the summer, but there was something special about the little stretch of sandy beach that was hidden away from the main bay, and hardly ever had more than a handful of people on it – even in the height of summer.

'Dad, I'm going to dig a really big hole so that I can bury you in it.' Riley picked out the longest spade from the collection that Dexter had brought and started digging with a look of real determination on his face.

'Rather you than me.' Jess couldn't help laughing at the expression on Dexter's face.

'Yeah, how come he collects pretty shells for you and digs a massive hole to bury me in?'

'I should probably worry that he's pigeon-holing us on the basis of gender, but if it means I get to keep the sand out of my pants, then I think I can live with it!'

'Who knew it was so easy for you to throw your principles out of the window?' Dexter put an arm around her and pulled her towards him. 'Have you got any idea how much I love you?'

'Some, but I don't mind you showing me every now and again.'

'It won't be long before Riley is horrified at the idea of his mum and dad having a cuddle. He'll refuse to be seen with us then.' Dexter smiled, but as Jess looked across at the boy she couldn't have loved any more if she'd given birth to him, she wished she could slow down time. She hadn't had the baby stage with him, but now even the primary school years seemed to be hurtling by. From what friends had told her, Dexter was right, and Riley would want far less to do with them once he started secondary school. She wasn't ready to say goodbye to everything that came with parenting a younger child, and she needed to talk to Dexter about what came next, now that they'd decided against any further fertility treatment.

'Anna keeps reminding me that I need to put in an application for the deputy matron's role, if I want to be considered for when the new hospital opens. They're trying to get staff in place well in advance, so that the new teams can have some input into how things are set up.'

'That's a bit of a change of subject, but I won't take it personally.' Dexter gave her a long look. 'Do you think you'll want to apply? I know you were a bit undecided before.'

Jess sighed. 'If I'd been planning on having more treatment, I wouldn't have even considered it. The extra stress definitely wouldn't have helped, not to mention having to go straight on maternity leave, if by some miracle the IVF had worked this time.'

It was still hard to say that, despite the fact that she hadn't had any doubts since making the decision. She felt so much freer now she was no longer a prisoner of hope. But the finality had the power to catch her unawares, nonetheless. Dexter must have seen it on her face. 'Something came in the post yesterday and I've been debating whether or not to give it you.'

'What is it?' Jess had a feeling she knew, just from the way

Dexter was looking at her. When he handed her a crumpled envelope, she was certain she was right.

'It's your test results. But I can get rid of them if you don't want to read them.'

'You might have to set fire to them to stop me from searching the house for them, if I don't open them now.'

'I thought screwing them up and chucking them in one of the dog poo bins might do the trick.' Dexter laughed and she pulled a face.

'Maybe we should just open them. It won't change my decision, but I think part of me will always want to know.'

'Let's do it then.' Dexter ripped open the envelope and passed her the letter inside.

'The AMH test result is 0.16.'

'What does that mean?'

'It means that my ovarian reserves are ultra-low and that the chances of me conceiving, even with IVF, are incredibly low too.' Jess had learned more about fertility tests than she'd ever wanted to know over the past few years. For a couple of moments, she stared at the letter, not sure how to feel, but then it came: another wave of relief. She really had made the right decision.

'Are you okay, darling?' Dexter put his arm around her again and she nodded.

'I really am. I can move forward now without the worry that I'll suddenly change my mind and want to try again.'

'Does that make the decision about the job easier too?'

'Not really.' Jess looked at her husband. She knew him better than anyone else, but she still wasn't sure how he was going to react when she told him what it was she wanted to do.

'I know leaving all your friends at the unit must feel like a tough decision, but things are going to be very different anyway, once the hospital opens.'

'It would be really hard not to be able to work with them any more, but it's not just that.' Jess took a deep breath. 'I think I want to foster again and I want to focus on parent and child placements.'

'Are you sure? After everything that happened with Teddy...?' He'd witnessed her pain first-hand and had seen how close to the edge losing Teddy had taken her, but a lot had changed since then.

'I know you probably thought I was going to suggest adopting again and one day I might be ready to do that, but for now I just need to get this out of my system. I'm never going to have a baby of my own, and there's a better chance of us winning the lottery than adopting a newborn, but I want to have the baby stuff for longer than I did with Teddy. I know the parent who's placed with us is supposed to take the lead, with our support, but having a baby in the house is just something I need to experience. And if I know from day one that I've got to let the baby go, it will make saying goodbye so much easier than it was with Teddy.'

'It might be harder than you think, even if you know they're not going to stay.'

'I'm tougher than I look.' Jess's eyes met Dexter's.

'I know you are; I just wish you didn't have to be.' He kissed her gently and then pulled away to look at her again. 'I can tell this is something you really need to do, and I'm with you all the way. If it was anyone else, I'd question whether you really understand what you'll be putting yourself through, but there's no one else like you, Jess.'

'So, we can apply to foster again?'

'Absolutely. Now, what do you want me to do with this letter?' Dexter held up the piece of paper, no doubt expecting her to tell him to get rid of it, but she had other plans.

'Let's keep it and, one day, if we decide to adopt again, we can tell our son or daughter how it all started, why we chose them, and why that makes them so very special.'

'I'll put it somewhere safe.' Dexter pulled her towards him again and Jess looked across to where Riley was still busy digging his hole. He was chatting to a little boy of about four, who'd wandered over with his mum to take a look at what Riley was doing. He was going to make a fantastic big brother one day, but for now, fostering would bring something new to all of their lives and she couldn't wait to start.

12

Jess had been out on home visits for the morning, before heading back to the unit to run an antenatal clinic. Her last appointment of the day was a booking-in for a newly pregnant lady called Charmaine Jenkins. Jess enjoyed clinics and home visits even more than delivering babies. In a small community, there was a chance of her getting to know the expectant mother quite well, especially if they were coming back for a second or third time. Charmaine's notes said she was a second-time mother, but she hadn't been cared for at the unit the first time around, so Jess had no idea what to expect. Booking-in appointments were usually an exciting time for the mother-to-be, but they were often filled with anxiety too, especially if the woman involved had experienced a previous loss, or a traumatic labour.

'Hi Charmaine, come on in. I'm Jess.'

'Is it okay if my auntie Jayne comes in with me?' Charmaine hovered at the entrance to the door for a moment, until Jess nodded.

'Of course. Nice to meet you both. Come and take a seat.'

'Good to meet you too.' Jayne smiled as she followed Charmaine into the room, the two of them sitting opposite Jess.

'Congratulations first of all. The notes from the GP surgery say you think you're eight weeks pregnant, is that right?'

'Yes.' Charmaine shifted in her chair. 'Based on my last period, I'll be nine weeks on Tuesday, but I didn't want to jinx things by coming in too early.'

'Is there anything in particular that's concerning you?' Jess's tone was gentle, but Charmaine shook her head.

'I lost my second pregnancy at six weeks, but I never even got to the booking-in stage, so it won't be on my records.'

'I'm sorry to hear that and I can completely understand why that would make you more anxious.' That was the one thing that Jess had been grateful for during IVF. Getting a positive pregnancy test and then having a miscarriage would have felt crueller still – like someone handing her hope and then snatching it away again. When she'd talked about that at the infertility group, not everyone had understood. Alesha, who was also going through IVF, had said that a positive pregnancy test would at least prove she *could* fall pregnant, even if she lost the baby. But, for Jess, it was somehow easier to know for certain that it wouldn't happen.

'I just want things to be normal this time.' Charmaine exchanged a look with her aunt. 'With my little boy, I got postnatal depression afterwards and we ended up moving in with Auntie Jayne and Uncle Paul. They more or less raised Carter for the first year.'

'We just did what any family would do.'

'Hardly.' Charmaine shook her head and turned to Jess. 'Jayne underplays everything. She looked after me for over a year when I was a baby too, after my parents split up and Mum couldn't cope. I don't know where I'd be without her.'

'It was my honour to do it.' Jayne smiled. 'Paul and I never had kids of our own, but I don't feel like I missed out, because I've got such a good relationship with Char, and my brother's two boys. I looked after them from when they were tiny, while my brother and his wife were at work.'

'That's why we all come to Auntie Jayne when we need support with anything.' Charmaine nudged her aunt's arm. 'And it was why I knew exactly who I wanted to come with me today, when my partner, Brandon, couldn't get the time off work.'

'It sounds like you've got a lovely relationship.' The support that Jayne had offered her niece might be a bit different to what Jess could offer someone in a parent and child placement, but there were some parallels. She'd thought about what might happen if the parent in the placement decided not to stay, and she and Dexter were left with the baby. But until now she hadn't thought about what might happen if the placement worked out really well. That was always the aim, of course, but a lot of the forums Jess had been reading had focused on fostering a baby through to adoption, after the parent had left. There was a chance, though, that one day she might be someone's 'auntie Jayne'. The person who was there for them and their baby when they needed support the most. She wished she could ask Jayne whether it had been hard to let Charmaine go, once her sister had got herself together again, but it wasn't the time or the place.

'I'm so lucky to have the support that I do and Brandon's great with our eldest too, although I'm already worried that Carter is going to have his nose put out of joint when the baby comes.'

'He might be a little bit possessive of you at first, but kids are remarkably adaptable.' Jess didn't need to worry about that with Riley; he asked when he'd be getting a sibling at least once a month. She and Dexter had told him that not all parents could have their own baby. Jess had wanted to tell him really early on, when he was only about six, that it was her tummy that was broken and she'd even found a book that explained things, in a language he'd understand. But Dexter had been adamant that, if they gave him any details, it should be that the two of them couldn't have a baby, not just Jess. Now that he was older, he understood that the doctors had been trying to help them have a baby, and she'd been dreading telling him that they weren't going to ask the doctors to help them any more. It didn't seem to faze him at all, though. He'd just shrugged and reminded them – as if they needed it – that he was adopted, so not being able to have a baby shouldn't stop them giving him a brother or sister. He seemed to think it was as easy as he made it sound, and Jess wished with all her heart that it was.

'You're probably right and Carter will just take it in his stride.' Charmaine frowned. 'But I'm sure you've already worked out that being anxious is like breathing to me. I'm panicking about the postnatal depression coming back too.'

'That's understandable, but there's plenty we can do to reduce the likelihood of that and to minimise the impact if it does come back.'

'Like what? I don't want to take any medication while I'm pregnant.'

'The first thing we can do is make a postpartum plan.' Jess had recently completed a part-time master's degree in mental health nursing and she was now the unit's specialist mental health midwife. Being able to help women like Charmaine made all the hours of study worthwhile. 'We can make some additional appointments and talk through your experiences from the first time around, including whether you remember any particular triggers for your depression and what kind of things helped you. You might also want to think about some counselling and if you'd consider taking medication as soon as the baby arrives. But if that's not an option, we can look at things like diet and exercise, and the support groups available locally.'

'Having a plan always helps me feel a bit calmer.' Charmaine let go of a long breath and Jayne patted her arm.

'Me too.' Jess made a note in Charmaine's file. Having a plan about what to do now that the fertility treatment was over had really helped Jess to move on, and she wanted to carry out step one of the plan as soon as possible. Setting up a meeting with the social worker, to discuss re-assessment as a foster carer, was where the next chapter of her life with Dexter and Riley would start.

* * *

Once Jess had finished her appointment with Charmaine, she was desperate to go home and put the call through to the local authority's fostering team, to request a new assessment. But when she got to reception and spotted Meg, she stopped.

'Are you okay? You look really pale.' Jess would have been concerned just as a friend, but Meg had also asked if Jess would be her midwife. They were still waiting to hear back from the hospital about whether they'd let Meg have her antenatal care from the community team, given her age and the complications in her previous pregnancies, or whether she'd need to have consultant-led midwifery care. Jess had a feeling it would all hang on the results of Meg's twenty-week scan, but for now she looked as though she needed Jess's support either way.

'I'm just tired. I've barely slept the last two nights.' Meg was usually a smiley person, which made her a wonderful receptionist, and someone Jess had always looked forward to seeing when on shift. Today she barely looked like the same person.

'Have you had any pain?' It was the one thing Jess dreaded about being a friend's midwife. It was horrendous enough when any patient suffered a loss in pregnancy, but it didn't bear thinking about when it came to one of her friends.

'No, nothing like that.' Meg looked close to tears all the same. 'I need to tell Tilly today, about the baby, and I've got no idea how she's going to react. Most of the time I still can't believe it myself and I keep wondering if I'm crazy at my age... but it's too late now.'

'You want the baby though, don't you?' When Meg had first blurted out the news in a flurry of tears, that was the one thing that had been clear – she definitely wanted this baby.

'I do, but I want to be ten years younger, except then Darren and Seth would still be here and I'd never have met Johnnie, so there'd never have been another baby. Darren always said two was enough; we got lucky and had our perfect little family by the time I was twenty-three and he was twenty-six. We had a scare once that we might be having a third, but deep down I think we were both relieved when it turned out to be a false alarm. He always talked about what we'd be doing when we got to our forties and the kids had left home. Darren used to joke about us partying in Ibiza or Ayia Napa, like a lot of our mates did back when we were in our twenties and were at home, knee deep in nappies. I never wanted it any other way, though. We might not have had a lot of money in the early days, but we had bags of energy and we had so much fun with the kids. What if I can't do that for this little one? What are people going to say about someone my age having another baby?' Meg's hands shifted down to her bump. 'Darren would have been horrified about me having a baby at forty-six.'

'This is not Darren's baby, or Tilly's, or anyone else's. It's yours and Johnnie's.' Jess spoke as gently as she could. There was so much trauma in Meg's past, and she could understand why her friend was finding it so hard to separate her old life from this new one, but she had to, at least a little bit. 'All that matters is what the two of you think. There are always some people who have plenty to say on any subject. I've had lots of patients who've been told that they're too young to have a baby, and others that they're too old, or too thin, or too fat. Whatever your circumstances, some people will decide to judge you and there's nothing you can do about it. You know that saying, that other people's opinions of you are none of your business? Well, it's true and there's almost nothing you can do to change those opinions, because they're influenced by so much more than whatever it is you're doing. And they're not worth a moment of your worry as a result. As for Tilly, of course what she thinks is going to matter to you, and at first she might not react the way you want. The two of you have been through so much and that complicates things, especially as she's pregnant too. But Gwen always says that babies bring their own love and it's so true. Once your little one is here, Tilly's going to love being a big sister and hopefully the baby will be a playmate for her baby too.'

'Thanks Jess, you always seem to know what to say.' Meg managed a smile for the first time. 'Is there any chance of one of your famous hugs?'

'Always.' Jess walked around to the other side of the reception desk, as Meg stood up, and, when they embraced, her friend's growing baby bump was clearly evident. It was time for Meg to tell Tilly, however difficult a conversation that might be. Because, if she didn't, Tilly would find out for herself first and there was no way that would end well.

13

Meg felt a huge wave of nausea as the smell of the curry Johnnie was cooking wafted in the air, but this wasn't morning sickness. After the sonographer had told her it was unusual for the nausea to suddenly get worse during the second trimester, she'd spoken to Jess about it and it had quickly become apparent that it was anxiety causing it. Which made complete sense given how sick she was feeling right now. At any minute, Tilly and Ed would be arriving for dinner, and Meg would sit across the table from them, knowing that once they'd finished their food she'd have to tell them about the baby. Just before she'd called Tilly to invite her over, Meg had felt the first fluttering of movement and it was as if the baby didn't want her to forget for a second why she was calling her daughter. It was a reminder that there was a brand new person growing inside her, who'd one day have their own opinions about being brought into a family like this, where two of its members cast long shadows over a group they were no longer even physically a part of.

Seth and Darren still had their own chairs at the dinner table. It was a big piece of furniture, that Darren had made himself, and there was enough seating for eight. But now there were only six available spaces, because the empty chairs would always stay empty – reserved solely for Darren and Seth. The ever-present shadow of Tilly's father and brother was the reason her relationship with Johnnie had got off to such a rocky start when they'd first met, over one of Meg's Sunday roasts. Every other time he'd been over to eat before then, it had just been him and Meg, and they'd always sat next to one another on the side of the table closest to the cooker. But with Ed and Tilly joining them, Johnnie had naturally left space between him and Meg, and had sat down at the top of the table, in what he'd had no idea was Darren's seat.

Tilly had burst into noisy, almost hysterical, tears and it had taken everything Meg and Ed had to calm her down. She'd apologised to Johnnie afterwards, explaining how difficult it was to see someone else sitting in her father's seat, even after all this time. And Johnnie, for his part, took it like the amazing person he was, telling Tilly that he understood completely and that it was him who should be sorry for not checking first. The truth was, it had all been Meg's fault. She was the one who should have told Johnnie a long time before about why they never sat at the other end of the table, and just how attached Tilly had become to these ways of coping with their loss over the years. Meg had needed them just as much in the early days, but she would probably have let them go if Tilly had been ready. Now she had a horrible feeling that she'd left it too late to encourage her daughter to stop using those coping mechanisms and she was scared Tilly might never feel ready. Which was why she was so worried about how she was going to react to the news about the baby. Meg was definitely going to be sick.

'Something smells great. Please tell me that's your chicken korma, Johnnie, because it's my favourite.' Tilly came into the kitchen, with Ed following on behind. She still had her own key and could come and go as she wanted, which she often did without warning. It was something else that Johnnie had never complained about, and just one more reason why Meg loved him.

'I know, that's why I made it for you.' Johnnie smiled and Tilly reached up to give him a peck on the cheek. Their relationship had come a long way, but Meg couldn't help thinking it was because Johnnie was always so careful to make sure he never overstepped the mark again after that first dinner. It was typical of him to be like that, but he shouldn't have to spend his life treading on eggshells around her daughter.

'You could be worse, you know.' She grinned and tiny bit of the tension left Meg's body. The fondness that had developed between Tilly and Johnnie was bound to help with the news about the baby. Surely.

'How are you feeling sweetheart?' Meg stood up to give her daughter a hug, hoping she wouldn't notice how weirdly she'd angled her body to make sure there was no chance of Tilly realising there was a baby bump hiding under all the layers she had on. Or how weird her choice of clothing was, given that they were in the midst of a Cornish summer. If Tilly had noticed that the shirt, jumper and cardigan combo she was wearing was very odd, she hadn't said anything. But then Tilly had her own problems to think about.

'I feel sick until about 11 a.m. every day. I think I'd feel better if I actually was sick, but it's just constant nausea.' Tilly rolled her eyes. 'But then I'm ravenous for the rest of the day. At this rate, I'm going to be the size of a house by the time this baby arrives.'

'No you won't.' Ed slipped an arm around her waist. 'And even if you are, I'll love you anyway.'

'This is another side effect I did not see coming.' Tilly laughed. 'It's made Ed completely soppy. He cries more than I do!'

'Nothing wrong with that.' Johnnie exchanged a knowing

look with Meg. There was no question that he'd been more emotional since they'd found out about the baby. He and Ed would have a lot to talk about once they broke the news; that was if Tilly didn't walk straight out. 'Right, who's ready for some food?'

'More than ready.' Tilly sat in her old space, the way she had from the moment her highchair had first occupied the spot. True to her word, she ate as though it had been a month since her last meal, so there was no chance of her noticing how little Meg was eating, as she pushed the food around her plate.

'What's new with you, Ed? How's work?' Johnnie looked across at the younger man, waiting as he finished the mouthful he was eating.

'Yeah, it's good. I've been doing extra hours to put some money aside for the deposit and to top up the bills while Tilly is on maternity leave.'

'I wanted to talk to you about that.' Meg had barely got the words out before Tilly cut in.

'We're not taking your money, Mum. I've told you that.'

'I'm not offering you money.' That had got her nowhere before and she knew her daughter well enough to accept that Tilly wouldn't change her mind. 'I want you to have the house.'

'This house?' Tilly shook her head. 'You can't give us this house.'

'I'm not giving it to you, at least not yet. But it makes total sense for you to have this place, instead of paying out rent, and for me to move—' She'd been about to say 'somewhere smaller', but that was no longer the plan, so she paused for a few seconds before she went on. 'For me to move in with Johnnie.'

'I didn't realise things were that serious.' There was a defensive tone to Tilly's voice already and this was only the start.

'They've been going out for over two years, Tils. What did you expect to happen, for them just to date forever?' Ed's tone was reasonable, but that didn't stop Tilly from bristling in response.

'Well, I didn't expect *this*. Not out of nowhere.' Tilly narrowed her eyes. 'Are you getting engaged too?'

'I'd marry your mother tomorrow, but there are no plans for that just yet. She'd have to say yes first.' Johnnie reached under the table and squeezed Meg's hand. She wondered if he could feel her shaking.

'What if you move in together and you realise it's not that sort of relationship? Let's face it, you're at different stages in life.' Tilly didn't even wait for them to answer. 'I suppose Mum could just move back in here with us; there's plenty of room and it would be great to have help with the baby.'

'I won't be moving back in.' Meg finally found her voice, but Tilly was already shaking her head.

'You can't know that for sure. When Ed and I first started living together, it was touch and go for a bit and I nearly came home several times and that's without a massive age gap.'

'I won't be moving back, because Johnnie and I will find a way to make it work, even if things are a bit difficult at first. We've got to.' Meg could feel her breathing speeding up. Part of her just wanted to blurt it out and leave the room as quickly as possible, before Tilly reacted. But Johnnie was still holding her hand, his thumb gently circling her palm. Just knowing he was there and completely on her side made more difference than he would ever realise.

'What do you mean you've *got* to make it work?' Tilly was leaning forward in her chair now, and Meg was going to have to say the words she'd rehearsed so many times.

'Because we're having a baby.'

'You're *what*?' Tilly was up on her feet in an instant. 'Surely that's not even possible at your age?'

'We've got the scan pictures to prove it.' Johnnie couldn't seem to help smiling every time he talked about the baby, and he looked ready to whip the pictures out of his wallet at any moment.

'How far along are you, if you've had a scan? I can't believe you've been keeping this to yourself all this time!' Tilly's voice had gone high and reedy, and even when Ed put a steadying hand on her arm she didn't move to sit down.

'We had no idea until a blood test I had at the doctor's, for something else, showed it up. Hamish sent me for a scan and they said I was sixteen weeks pregnant.' Meg knew she sounded as if she was apologising and the truth was she did feel guilty for dropping this surprise on Tilly, now of all times. 'That was last Wednesday.'

'And you're only telling me now? What else are you keeping from me? That it's twins or something?'

'There's only the one in there but seeing as it's more than I could ever have hoped for, you won't hear any complaints out of me.' Johnnie was still smiling, despite the icy atmosphere.

'So you're what, almost two months ahead of me?' Tilly suddenly sat back down with a thud and Meg shook her head. 'At least my baby won't have an aunt or uncle who's younger than them. That's something.'

Meg hadn't expected Tilly to do cartwheels with joy at the news that her mother was pregnant; in fact, she'd half anticipated one of her daughter's meltdowns. She'd got used to them over the years, when things didn't quite go Tilly's way, and she'd made excuses for them both to herself and other people. Tilly had lost her father and brother; she was bound to be difficult to be around sometimes. But the implication that Meg's pregnancy was little more than an embarrassment to her daughter was somehow harder to take than an all-out meltdown. Meg had got used to hiding her disappointment over the years, when Tilly found it hard to see the good in things or the effort Meg put in to try and make her happy, but it still hurt.

'Why would it matter if our baby was older?' Ed looked genuinely nonplussed and Meg's opinion of her daughter's boyfriend was increasing with every passing moment.

'It's just so... you know.' Tilly's shudder gave away what she was thinking, even if her words were vague. Meg was with Ed; if babies were loved and wanted, nothing else really mattered. But the truth was, she hadn't been so very different from Tilly when she'd first found out that her daughter was expecting. She was worried about her and Ed managing financially, and putting their career plans on hold, so she couldn't really blame Tilly for expressing her worries about Meg and Johnnie having a baby. Even if the reasons behind those worries were very different.

'It will be nice for the babies to be so close in age.' Johnnie was determined to see the bright side of everything, but Tilly still looked as if she was having trouble processing any of it and Meg could hardly blame her for that either.

'At your age... I wouldn't have even thought it was possible.' Tilly shook her head, repeating what she'd said earlier. 'Were you trying?'

'No, it was an—' Meg had been about to say accident, but Johnnie had already suggested they should reframe it. No one could want this baby more than he did, so calling it an accident felt wrong. 'It was a surprise. I never thought it would happen at my age either. It didn't even enter my head.'

'I think it's brilliant news! Congratulations, both of you.' Ed raised his glass and clinked it against Johnnie's, but Tilly still looked frozen to the spot, so Meg didn't move either. Then Tilly turned towards her mother and blinked three times, before she finally spoke.

'Yes, congratulations. I can't say it isn't a huge shock, but baby news is always happy news, right?' Tilly was clearly trying her best to smile, but her eyes had filled with tears. 'I just hope you'll still have time to be a doting grandma, because I'm going to need you too.'

'Just try stopping me.' Meg reached out and handed Tilly a napkin to dry her eyes. She'd expected to feel relief once she'd told her daughter the news, especially since Tilly seemed to have accepted it without too much drama, but there was still a nagging feeling in her gut and a lump in her throat that made it difficult to swallow. But she knew exactly why; there was still someone very important she hadn't told.

* * *

Gwen's seventieth birthday party was always going to be a grand affair. There was hardly a person in the Three Ports area who didn't have a connection to her in some way or the other. Meg had known who she was even before she'd been her midwife when she'd been pregnant with Tilly. Back then, Gwen had worked in the hospital in Truro and she'd been present when Tilly was delivered by caesarean section.

Darren had almost seemed relieved when Tilly had turned breech, so that the only option was a hospital delivery. Up until that point, Meg had been determined to have a home delivery, despite having had a retained placenta when Seth was born. Darren had thought she was mad wanting to have the baby at home, and had asked – with a very worried look on his face – whether it meant they'd also be expected to have placenta chilli in the days that followed their second child's arrival. Meg could hardly blame him when the only other couple they knew who'd chosen a home birth had done just that.

Despite knowing that their second child would be born in

hospital, Darren had still worried about the birth – right up until the moment he'd held his newborn daughter in his arms. All that wasted worry the two of them had had in the years they'd spent together, mostly about things she couldn't remember any more, and yet she'd never worried about him going to work. It wasn't like he was in the army, or the police, or even one of the local fishermen, who set out to sea in rough weather. He had a small construction firm, taking on modest jobs, and yet somehow that had still ended up killing him and taking Seth from his mother too.

Meg shivered as she looked around the crowded room. Everyone was there to celebrate Gwen's big birthday, but there were two people missing, as there always were. Darren and Seth would definitely have been at the party too, if they'd still been alive. Gwen's husband Barry had been the president of the local cricket club for almost three decades, and both Darren and Seth had played for the club at different times. Gwen's cakes, her contribution to the cricketing teas, were famous, not just with the Port Agnes team, but with their opponents from across the county too. Gwen had attended the matches as often as she could and she'd cheer loudly every time a ball was struck well, whether it was for Port Agnes or the opposing side.

It was strange the things Meg had missed once the boys were gone. Of course, there were all the things she would have expected to miss: cuddling up to Darren in bed and warming her freezing feet on his legs, or the way that Seth would still sidle up for a hug every now and then, despite being fifteen and over six feet tall. But then there were things she'd never have expected to miss, like the hours spent watching cricket, a game she hadn't ever really understood, and trying desperately to get the grass stains out of the cricketing whites before the next match. Meg's and Darren's roles had always been fairly traditional; she'd largely been a stay-at-home mum taking on the bulk of the household chores. She'd been happy with that, but she hadn't expected to miss the mundane chores that no longer existed when Seth and Darren were gone.

'Are you okay? You look miles away.' Hamish put his hand on her arm, jolting her back to the present.

'Just thinking about all the years I've known Gwen.' Meg swallowed hard and painted on a smile that probably looked every bit as fake as it felt. 'And wondering if I'll be able to remember the steps for the dance.'

'You'll be great.' Nadia, who worked at the unit with Meg and was also Hamish's partner, nodded as she spoke. 'I think it's a lovely idea; I caught the end of one of the rehearsals when I was picking Remi up from her tap class.'

'I just don't want to let the side down. I swear I was born with two left feet and I don't think I'd have learned anything in the last eight years, if Nicky wasn't such a great teacher. Let alone learned this routine.' Meg and Tilly had started dance classes with Nicky Kirby, who ran the Port Agnes Quicksteppers – a dance school that catered for pupils aged two to eighty plus – about eighteen months after the accident. It was something Meg's therapist had suggested to get them out and about, doing things together and making memories that didn't come straight back to Darren and Seth. Tilly had taken to the dance classes like a duck to water, whereas Meg had looked more like a duck about to lay an egg.

The social life linked to the dance school had been really good, though, and the classes themselves had probably done more to help them start moving forward than almost anything else. There was a natural high with any form of exercise, but nothing could beat the feeling that came when you finally cracked the choreography and truly felt like part of the group you were dancing with. Gwen had joined the quicksteppers about five years after Meg, but she'd fitted right in. So, when Nicky had suggested choreographing a routine for Gwen's fellow dancers to perform as part of the celebrations for her seventieth birthday, every single member of the group had been willing to do so. Keeping the whole thing a secret from Gwen was probably the hardest part for most of them. But not for Meg; the choreography was undoubtedly the hardest part for her.

'Does anyone want a drink?' Bobby came over to join the group, with Toni just behind him, followed by Anna and her husband, Brae, as well as Jess and Dexter, Nadia's mother, Frankie, and her partner, Guy. It wouldn't be long before the whole unit was there, all ready to watch the dance. None of that did anything to calm Meg's nerves and, if she wasn't almost five months pregnant, she'd have asked Bobby for the biggest G&T he could carry.

'Johnnie's already getting me a drink, but thank you.' Meg looked over towards the bar. 'He's on his way back with the others.'

Johnnie was a bit like Gwen, in the sense that he knew almost everyone in Port Agnes. He'd been born and brought up there, but had spent almost a decade away, before coming home to Cornwall and eventually becoming a partner in the town's veterinary practice.

Now Johnnie was walking towards her, with Ella and Dan, Emily and Keira, and Izzy and Noah, all following in his wake. Meg knew she could have asked anyone in Port Agnes what they thought of Johnnie and they'd all say the same thing: he was a miracle worker. He had a reputation for being able to help animals that other vets had written off. People from miles away often came to him, because he seemed able to treat the untreatable, and save the unsavable. It was why almost everyone in Port Agnes knew and loved him, and Meg still couldn't quite believe he'd chosen her.

'God, this reminds me of how much I miss you lot.' Ella looked around, as Johnnie and the others reached the rest of the group. 'I love the team at the surgery and it's nice doing handovers with you guys when the midwifery ends and the health visiting starts, but I don't think anything will beat my memories of working at the unit.'

'And no one can take your place either.' Anna gave her best friend a hug. Ella had left before Meg joined the unit, after a diagnosis of MS had prompted her to rethink her plans for the future. She'd retrained to become a health visitor, so that she could continue to help new mums and their children, and she was now attached to the GP surgery. As a result, Meg had got to know Ella well, but she'd have heard plenty about her even if she'd only worked at the unit. The other midwives still spoke about her with a lot of affection.

'And what on earth are we going to do when we've lost Gwen as well? It's going to be so quiet.' Toni shook her head and leant into her husband, Bobby.

'I might be taking a bit of a sabbatical too.' Jess could barely make eye contact with the rest of the team, and Anna, who managed the unit, took in an audible breath.

'You're not going full time at the new hospital, are you?'

'No.' Jess took hold of Dexter's hand as she spoke. 'I'll be taking a break from work completely, if it goes ahead. We're getting assessed to foster again, for parent and child placements this time. I just feel like I need to have the opportunity to care for a baby, so I can get the need to do that out of my system. I know we'll be supporting the birth parents, rather than fostering the babies. But, from talking to other foster carers, there's a lot of direct care for the babies involved too. And sometimes they care solely for the baby, until a long-term plan is made, if the mother or father decide not to see the assessment of their parenting skills through to the end and leave the placement., If we get accepted, it'll be my full-time job and I want to do it for at least a year. After that, we'll apply to adopt again and I'll come back to work, until we get matched with a child.'

'That all sounds amazing, but we're going to miss you so much at work.' Frankie touched Jess's arm.

'Although there's the huge bonus of us getting to be grandparents again!' Guy put one arm around Frankie and the other around Jess. Meg knew that Jess's relationship with her father hadn't always been perfect, but ever since he'd come back to Port Agnes and got together with Frankie, he'd been a model grandparent to both Riley, and Nadia's two children, Remi and Mo. The team at the unit called themselves one big family and they really were.

'Is this the bit where Izzy tells us she's pregnant! That's what happened with Toni last time Jess was working reduced hours and Anna was still part-time after her maternity leave.' Emily laughed; she was shaping up to be Gwen's apprentice, asking the questions most people wouldn't and possessing the same uncanny knack of hitting the nail on the head. And, judging by the look on Izzy's face, she'd done it again.

'Did you say something to Emily?' Izzy gave her husband, Noah, a pointed look, but he was already shaking his head.

'Not a word.'

'I'm sorry, Anna, I would have said something, but it's early days and I wanted to wait until after the twelve-week scan.'

'Don't be sorry. It's fabulous news; you and Noah are going to make such great parents.' Anna's tone was warm, but she was looking a bit shell-shocked all the same and Meg didn't blame her. The team were dropping like flies. 'Just promise me that none of the rest of you are going to make an announcement, because if you are, I might need to sit down first.'

'Not me.' Emily shook her head. 'Keira's going to be the one having our first baby and we don't have the problem of getting pregnant unexpectedly after a few too many beers at the weekend.'

'At my age I've shut up shop. I just wouldn't have the energy at forty-one.' Toni suddenly seemed to realise that she was standing next to Meg, who had five years on her. 'But not everyone slows down like I seem to have done since I hit forty. There are plenty of woman who are whirlwinds into their fifties, sixties and beyond. Just look at Gwen.'

'Well if I fall pregnant, the news teams are going to descend on Port Agnes, to report on a medical miracle.' Frankie laughed. 'Although, as Guy said, we haven't given up hope of more grand-children.'

'You'll have to rely on Jess and Hari for those then.' Nadia raised her eyebrows and leant into Hamish. 'We've already got four between us and we've got big plans once Mo heads off to uni in ten years' time. There's a whole lot of world we want to see.'

'I'm just happy that she's willing to plan ten years ahead with me.' Hamish's smile said it all and Meg couldn't help smiling too. Even though she couldn't even begin to imagine life that far ahead. By then, she and Jonnie would have a child almost ready for secondary school, and so would Tilly and Ed, but Meg would only be a few years off her sixtieth birthday. She could still remember thinking that Seth would be forty by the time she hit sixty, but the new baby wouldn't even be the age Seth was when he died. It was all too much for her to get her head around. Johnnie suddenly took hold of her hand, as he often seemed to do when she was starting to overthink everything. It was as if he could read her mind. What-ever the reason for him doing it, she was glad he had, and she immediately felt the panic begin to subside.

'Mum, Nicky's telling us all to come over, so we're ready for the routine.' Tilly appeared at her side out of nowhere.

'How are you feeling, Tilly?' Jess smiled at Meg's daughter.

'Too fat to be dancing.' Tilly pulled a face. 'Although if Mum can do it, I've got no excuse, have I? After all, everyone is a lot more worried about her than they are about me.'

Meg was probably reading too much into it, but there was

something in Tilly's tone that made the worry creep in again. She couldn't help wondering whether her daughter resented having to share her pregnancy with someone who should have been lavishing all the care and attention on her. But there was nothing either of them could do about it.

* * *

In the end, the performance had gone smoothly and Gwen had been completely thrilled with the dance routine that would forever be known as the Gwen Jones Cha-cha. Afterwards, she'd taken straight to the dancefloor herself, and proved that seventy-year-olds could twerk, whether you wanted them to or not. One of her grandsons, Rory, who must have been about eleven, had walked past Meg muttering something about never being able to unsee what he'd just seen.

'You did brilliantly.' Nicky, Meg's dance teacher, had an infectious smile and always looked like she was ready to burst out laughing. Especially when her sister, Laura, who also worked at the dance school, was around. 'You must be worn out, but it didn't show.'

'I felt like the sugarplum fairy!' Meg was just glad it was over. She could enjoy the rest of the evening now, catching up with old friends. And no one here would judge her if she needed to head home by ten o'clock, except perhaps for Gwen.

'Is everything okay with you and Tilly?' Nicky's tone was gentle and Meg knew her well enough to know she wasn't just being nosey. Nicky seemed to genuinely care about all of her dancers like they were part of her family.

'I think so. It's just a bit tough at the moment, what with us both being pregnant.' It was no secret any more. Tilly had announced the news on social media, the moment the hospital had confirmed she was expecting, but it had taken Meg slightly longer to share her pregnancy with anyone but her closest friends and family. But now everyone seemed to know and there'd been plenty of jokes about her family needing their own parking space at the hospital, or getting two for one on nipple pads. Despite the terrible jokes, there was no malice in the comments. The only person who didn't seem to find any of it remotely amusing was Tilly. She'd been sniping at Meg during the dance routine and Meg had had to resort to counting in her head to drown Tilly's remarks out. It was hard enough performing in front of an audience of people she knew, without her daughter's running commentary every time she was even slightly out of step.

It was typical of Tilly, if Meg was honest. The constant pick, pick, picking at her mother, which she wouldn't stop until she got a reaction. It happened when Tilly was looking for an argument. Meg had often wondered if her daughter did it to let off steam, when the anger and sadness at losing Darren and Seth got too much for her. She needed someone to lash out at, and deep down Meg knew she'd allowed herself to become the scapegoat for her daughter's negative emotions. Tilly could be incredibly loving, but she could be nasty too. Meg had never retaliated, because of what her daughter had been through, but there'd been times when Meg had walked into the woods near their home and screamed until her throat burned. Now it just made her sad when Tilly started sniping at her, the way she had today. She wished they could talk like adults about what was bothering her daughter, but the way Tilly was acting had become a habit that neither of them seemed able to break.

'She's always seemed a little bit impatient with you, ever since you joined the dance school, but I just wanted you to know I thought you handled it really well today. You always do, but it must get hard walking on eggshells so much of the time.'

'It's just Tilly, she's sensitive and ever since the accident...' Meg trailed off. For a long time she'd been excusing the way her daughter sometimes behaved, but she wasn't sure if doing that had really helped.

'I can't even imagine what it was like losing your husband and son, or for Tilly to lose her father and brother.' Nicky shook her head. 'This is none of my business and you can tell me to butt out if you like, but it is okay to put yourself first every once in a while. Sometimes you need to allow yourself to lean on the people who want to be there for you, and distance yourself a bit from the people who only ever lean on you. There's this theory I've got that people are either radiators or drains, and you're definitely a radiator. But, right now, you need to be careful not to allow other people to completely drain you.'

'Even when it's my own daughter?'

'I'm not saying that you can't be there for her; no one could stop you if they tried. But it seems to me that your whole life has been all about Tilly for so long, and now it's not. That's going to be hard for her to adjust to, but you needed to do some adjusting too.'

'If I didn't know better, I'd think Johnnie had bribed you.' Meg half wished it was true, but the fact was, Nicky was right. It was time for Meg to start putting herself first every once in a while, but she had a horrible feeling Tilly wasn't going to like it one little bit.

14

The anniversary of Darren's and Seth's deaths was always difficult, but never more so than when good weather meant the summer sun seemed to be at its brightest – just like it had been on the day they'd died. The very least the universe could do was match the weather to the event. When the two police officers had turned up outside Meg's front door, it had already been ajar to let a breeze circulate through the house. She'd seen a glimpse of one of their uniforms as she'd headed down the hallway in response to their knocking.

There must have been fewer than thirty steps between the point when she'd realised there were police officers outside her door, and getting to where they were standing. But somehow she'd still managed to come up with a dozen reasons they could be there that didn't involve bad news. Maybe they were trying to recruit for a new neighbourhood watch scheme, or they were going door to door to see if anyone had spotted suspicious behaviour before a burglary up the road. She refused to believe it could be about anything else, even when they asked her to confirm whether she had a husband called Darren Sawyer, and a son called Seth.

Despite the scream that had filled the air when they'd finally told her that falling masonry had killed her husband and son, she hadn't really taken it in. The reality was it had taken months to finally accept they were never coming home and grief had seemed to start all over again when it finally sank in. She'd hidden it from Tilly, though, never letting her see how devastated her mother really was.

The only time she fully released her emotions was at Seth and Darren's graveside. They'd been cremated and their ashes buried together in the churchyard at St Jude's. Meg still visited as often as she could, even if she was just passing on her way home from work. She and Tilly would be making a special trip to the grave later to mark the anniversary, but she'd wanted to come on her own first, too – so that she could talk to Darren and Seth by herself. It would probably sound mad to anyone else, but this conversation was just between her and them, even if they could no longer hear a word she said.

'Hey you two.' Meg rested a hand on the stone that marked the place where their ashes were buried. The sun was so strong that even the stone was warm to the touch. Blinking twice, she forced the images out of her head of the last time she'd seen Darren and Seth, at the undertaker's. The feel of their skin beneath her hand had been cold, but it wasn't really them lying there; they'd gone already.

'It's a lovely day today.' She was making small talk, even though she was there to tell them something huge. 'I miss you both so much. I love you.'

If she closed her eyes and tried really hard, she could picture them telling her they loved her too. Darren had said it all the time, but it had dwindled with Seth over the years. At fifteen, he'd said it maybe once every couple of months, if she was lucky, but somehow that had given the words even more meaning. It wasn't the same phrase he'd repeated parrot-fashion as a three-year-old; when he said the words as a teenager he'd really meant them.

'If you're wondering why I came here without Tils, don't worry, we're both coming back later, but there's something I wanted to talk to you about first.' Meg paused as a seagull flew overhead. Its cacophonous squawking seeming to fill the air around her until it had disappeared out of sight.

'You remember I told you about Johnnie?' It was something Meg had done about six months after they'd started dating, when she'd been sure that the relationship wasn't just going to fizzle out. It had almost felt like admitting an affair, but she'd needed to say the words out loud, even if all they'd done was drifted into the ether.

'Well, something has happened.' The same guilt she'd felt telling them about dating Johnnie was washing over her again. 'We're having a baby. Me and Johnnie.'

Meg wasn't sure what she'd expected to happen – a bolt of lightning coming from the sky? – but the response was a resounding silence.

'It doesn't mean I'm replacing you, because I'd give anything to have you both back.' She couldn't bear to think about what would happen if she was actually faced with that choice, because she never would be. She wasn't sure she could give Johnnie up, if Darren suddenly walked through the door, but then she wouldn't have been able to give Darren up either. Before Johnnie, Meg had never really believed it when someone said they could love two people equally – as far as she was concerned that was just having your cake and eating it – but now she completely understood.

'I hope you're not upset with me, because I really do love you both as much as ever.' For a moment, the silence continued to still the air and then a shaft of light moved from behind the trees and across the ground where Meg was standing. Deep down, she knew it was just a coincidence, but she was going to take it as a sign anyway. Telling Darren and Seth about the baby had been weighing on her mind, but now they knew. She just needed to sort things out with Tilly and then she might finally be able to start looking forward to the baby arriving.

* * *

'This doesn't feel like a celebration for Dad and Seth, not with Johnnie cooking.' Tilly was sitting on the loveseat her father had made for his and Meg's tenth anniversary. It was in Meg's favourite spot in the garden, under the apple tree. In the days after the accident, she'd spent hours looking up the track across the field behind the house, which she could see from the loveseat, waiting and praying for Darren and Seth to suddenly appear, with Darren's Jack Russell, Dotty, following on behind. Dotty had taken Darren's place in the bed, next to Meg, for two years after his death. Cuddling up to that warm, little body had probably saved her life. When Dotty had died at the age of thirteen, it had broken Meg's heart all over again. She'd never see the three of them coming down that track again, but she still loved sitting under the apple tree, because it was so easy to picture them when she did. Tilly had always loved that spot too, and every time she came home, she claimed it as her own. Only Ed was ever allowed to sit next to her.

'Johnnie and Ed enjoy the barbequing and I thought you'd fancy a bit of rest; I know I will.' Just mentioning the barbeque was giving Meg indigestion. She'd forgotten how she used to chug Gaviscon like water when she'd been pregnant with Seth and Tilly, but it was all coming back to her now. Meg was trying to do what Nicky had suggested and start putting herself first, which was why she'd asked Johnnie to take over the cooking for Darren and Seth's anniversary. They'd only just got together on the anniversary two years before, and she hadn't invited him over the previous year either. This was the first time he'd been part of it, so she could understand why her daughter was finding it hard. But Meg and Johnnie were having a child now and she couldn't cut them out of the other half of her family.

'Well, I'm not as far along as you, am I?' Tilly was even more snappy than she'd been at Gwen's birthday and Meg had a feeling it was going to take a while for both of them to get used to any new boundaries she tried to put in place.

'The first twelve weeks are really tough, but this isn't a competition, darling. If you're struggling with anything, you know I'm here for you, don't you?'

'You've got your own stuff going on; you haven't got time for my problems.' Tilly looked at her, wide-eyed, tears already threatening to fall.

'Oh sweetheart, don't say that.' Meg was up on her feet in a flash, ignoring the stab of sciatica that always seemed to strike if she moved too quickly these days. Her daughter needed her. Taking hold of Tilly's hands, she crouched as best as she could down by her feet. 'What's going on?'

'I feel sick all the time and every time I get a pain I'm scared something bad is going to happen. I'm worried about money and whether we were stupid to have a baby now, but I couldn't bear the thought of leaving it too late and not being able to have one at all.' Tilly sniffed. 'But most of all I'm sad that Dad's never going to know he's got a grandchild, or that Seth's an uncle. I wanted to tell you about all of this, but how can I when you're starting over? If Johnnie proposes, you'll have a new husband, and if you have a little boy, you'll have a new son. I'm never going to get my Dad back, and your baby will only ever be my half-sibling; it won't replace Seth.'

If someone had plunged their arm into Meg's chest and twisted her heart in their hands, she didn't think it could have hurt any more. But she had to make Tilly understand how wrong she was. 'Nothing will replace your Dad and Seth for me either. I love Johnnie too, though, and I'm going to love this baby as well. Just like I'm going to love your baby so much that it will be enough for me, your dad and Seth put together. We can't get them back, and I decided, about a year after they died, that I owed it to them to start living again. Otherwise I might as well have died too. They both loved life and they'd have been so angry with us if we'd stopped having a life worth living, when they'd have given anything to be here. It's why I dragged you to all those activities, when it would have been easier to just curl up and cry. And it's why I eventually allowed myself to be open to meeting someone again.'

'I don't want Johnnie coming when we visit the grave. Please.' Tilly hadn't acknowledged anything else her mother had said, but the tears were rolling down her face now.

'Okay.' Meg knew, without even having to ask Johnnie, that he'd happily respect Tilly's wishes. He'd been brilliant at never over-stepping the mark and he'd probably take his dogs, Cagney and Lacey, out for a walk when they went down to the church. But she'd miss him and, if it was up to her, she'd probably have asked him to come along. But this was one thing she couldn't be upset with Tilly about. Her daughter needed the space to grieve for father and brother, and the fact that Johnnie understood that demonstrated once again what a wonderful person he was.

Meg and Johnnie were virtually living together now, but they'd never slept in the room she'd shared with Darren. It was another reason why it was time to let the house go. It hadn't felt right for them to use Seth's or Tilly's old rooms either, but sleeping on a sofa bed, at almost five months pregnant, was crazy. Especially when there was a solution that could work for them all.

'As for the other things you're worried about, maybe I can help with them too. There's no reason for you and Ed to put off moving in here; I'm spending half my time at Johnnie's anyway. As soon as you can get out of your rental agreement, why don't you move in? That should alleviate some of the financial burden and help you save a little bit for when you're on maternity leave. I know you said you don't want any money, but I can help out with some of the other bills, if you need it. Dad would have been happy for me to use some of the insurance money that's left for your baby. That way he'll still be doing his bit for his grandchild. He'd love that.'

'He would have been such a brilliant grandad.' Tilly blinked and a fresh crop of tears filled her eyes. There was nothing Meg could do about Darren not being around any more. And it was just as well she didn't expect any thanks from Tilly for offering to help, because she clearly wasn't going to get it. But she'd learned a long time ago that that wasn't what motherhood was all about.

'And as for feeling sick, and worrying that something bad is going to happen...' Meg breathed out. 'Pregnancy isn't easy, but your midwife will probably be able to suggest something that can alleviate the symptoms. I always found ginger biscuits and water crackers helped a bit, but I know some of the patients at the unit use travel sickness bands and find that works for them. It's the hormones that will be making you feel sick and maybe you can take that as a good sign. It means you've got plenty of pregnancy hormones swirling around your body.'

'Oh Mum, don't say swirling.' Tilly blew out her cheeks.

'Sorry, sweetheart. And the worrying bit? Well, I'm afraid you're in that for life now, Tils, because I've never stopped worrying about you and I never will.'

'Deep down I know this is all normal, but it's just so hard.' For the first time Tilly returned the squeeze of her hand. 'I'll talk to Ed about moving in here as soon as we can. And you're okay to ask Johnnie not to come to St Jude's?'

'I'll go over and talk to him now.' Meg struggled to her feet. She wasn't doing very well at following Nicky's advice, but that was just one more thing she was going to have to take day by day. Tilly still needed her and she was never going to let one of her children down again.

* * *

'Are you sure you don't mind?' Meg stroked the hair at the nape of Johnnie's neck, as she stood next to him. Ed had gone over to get Tilly a drink and they were now deep in conversation, no doubt about moving into the house.

'It's not my place to come to St Jude's, I get it, and I understand how Tilly feels about that.' There was something about the way Johnnie emphasised the last two words that made the nerves bubble in Meg's stomach.

'Don't be cross with her.' Meg dropped her hand away from Johnnie's neck and touched his arm instead. 'Days like this are hard for her.'

'I know how hard they are for *both* of you.' He turned towards her. 'I'm just worried she's never really going to get used to us being together and with the new baby coming...'

'I've spoken to her about that and told her it's time for her to move in here, so that you and I can be together properly. She's got pregnancy hormones to contend with, as well as all the emotions days like today bring. It's just going to take her a bit of time, I think.'

'It's okay, I really do get it and it's fine. Even if it wasn't Seth and Darren's anniversary, I'm big enough and ugly enough to understand when Tilly wants some one-on-one time with her mum. But what I don't want to happen is for our baby to ever feel like they aren't welcome with Tilly. That's all.'

'She wouldn't do that and, even if she tried, I wouldn't let it happen. I know better than anyone how important family is, and that it should never be taken for granted.' Meg felt a wave of nausea that had nothing to do with the hormones taking over her body. She was nowhere near as confident as she was pretending to be that Tilly wanted the baby to be a part of her family. Meg couldn't bear the thought that the baby might grow up in an atmosphere of Tilly's creation, where there was always an undercurrent of tension. She'd spent the last ten years accommodating her daughter's moods and adjusting life to fit around her, and she had no idea how Tilly would react when that stopped. But she knew it had to.

'Meg, you're a beautiful person, inside and out. You know that, don't you?' Johnnie kissed her gently and she tried not to worry that Tilly might be watching them; Meg had to find some balance in this new life of hers, that made room for Tilly, Johnnie and the baby. She just needed to get the anniversary out of the way first and then they could all make a start on finding their way forward.

15

Jess could still remember getting ready, when Dexter was coming over to start her fostering assessment. She'd worried about whether the biscuits she'd bought would be ones he liked, and whether her apartment at Puffin's Rest would be deemed suitable or clean enough. Before she'd met him, she'd expected Dexter to be a stereotype of all the social workers she'd seen depicted in the media, but he'd been absolutely nothing like that. What she hadn't expected, in her wildest dreams, was to make the kind of connection with him that she had, much less to fall in love with him. She'd sworn off men completely after her first marriage had failed in spectacular style, with Jess's ex blaming her infertility for him being unfaithful. It had taken her a long time to let her guard down with Dexter, despite the fact that the assessment meant she'd had to begin telling him her life story from day one.

Now the two of them were going to have to share their life stories again, as well as the details of their relationship, with another stranger. Dexter knew her so well, and he could obviously tell how nervous she was in the hours leading up to their first appointment with the social worker.

'Do I need to be worried?' If Dexter's mouth hadn't been lifting in the corners, Jess might have started to panic more than she already was. But he looked as if he was trying not to laugh.

'Worried about what?'

'You falling in love with our social worker; you know you've got form.' He gave in to the laughter that had clearly been bubbling just below the surface, as she nudged him.

'Carry on like that and you might have to watch out.' She let him catch hold of her and pull her into his arms.

'There's no way I'm ever letting you go and this will all be okay, I promise.'

'What if they turn us down?' Jess could feel her heartbeat pulsing in her ears. There was so much riding on this.

'Why would they do that? You've already proven how brilliant you are with Riley, and when you were caring for Teddy.'

'I'm worried they'll think I just want to foster to make up for the fact I can't have a baby. But I already know it's not going to fill that gap. I just want to have had the experience of caring for babies, and hopefully help to give them the best possible start in life. I need to do that before I can feel ready to adopt an older child.'

'I understand exactly what you mean, you know that.' Dexter caressed the back of her hand with his thumb. 'I just think we need to be careful about how we word things with the social worker, because they might not understand.'

'So what am I supposed to say?'

'Just tell the truth about the fact that we've worked through our feelings about IVF and we've got no intention of trying for a baby of our own again. Then just say what you've said to me, that you want to offer parent and child placements to help give those babies the best possible start in life.'

'Will you kick me under the table if I say the wrong thing?' The pulsing sensation was back in Jess's ears, but Dexter shook his head.

'You won't say the wrong thing and, if they can't see how amazing you are, then there's something wrong with them, not you.'

'See. *This* is why I fell in love with you.' She was about to kiss him when the sound of the doorbell ringing suddenly echoed down the hallway. This was it. The moment of truth.

* * *

Kelly Roberts peered at Jess over the top of her glasses. She'd already asked them what felt like a thousand questions, and Jess was finding it really difficult to assess how it was going. Kelly's face gave nothing away and she hadn't even touched the biscuits Jess had put out.

'How would the two of you feel about being fast-tracked?' Kelly raised her eyebrows and Jess looked at Dexter.

'I think we'd like that, wouldn't we?' He turned towards her as he spoke, but Jess still wasn't sure she'd understood Kelly's question.

'Do you mean fast-tracked through the assessment, or fast-tracked to a *thanks-but-no-thanks* decision?' If the question made Jess sound stupid, she didn't care. She couldn't risk getting her hopes up until she knew for sure.

'Ha!' Kelly laughed for the first time, her whole face completely changing when she did. 'Of course I mean fast-tracking you through the assessment. We're desperate for carers with your kinds of skills, and what better credentials could there be for parent and child carers, than a midwife and a social worker? Especially when you've already got experience of fostering and adoption. I mean, come on, I felt like I'd won the lottery when I read the notes about you. Maybe not the proper multi-million-pound-winning lottery, but at least one of those charity ones where you can win cash enough for a holiday. Because, trust me, your assessment is going to feel like a holiday compared to most!'

Jess was still processing the fact that Kelly had a sense of humour and was now cracking jokes, instead of staring at her intently as she had for the last hour. So it was down to Dexter to respond. 'That's really kind of you to say, and we'll do our best to make this as easy as possible for you, I promise. We're pretty open people and we've been through the process before. Am I right in thinking a fast-tracked assessment should only take about two months?'

'Yes, we'll run the statutory checks alongside the assessment, instead of doing them separately, which means stage one and two of the process will be running at the same time. I'll be doing the same number of interviews with you, but they'll be a lot closer together than they usually are. We'll get a panel date provisionally booked in and, as long as none of the checks or references are held up, we should be good.'

'Two months.' Jess's pulse was suddenly racing again. It didn't give them very long to get everything organised, but sometimes you just had to take the leap.

* * *

When Meg had been a year into her relationship with Johnnie, her parents had finally fulfilled their dream of retiring to the South of France. Meg was glad they were living their own lives again, after putting their plans on hold for her and Tilly for so long, and they'd managed to maintain a close relationship despite the physical distance. Her parents had been excited about the news of a new grandchild and Meg got a text every couple of days asking when they were planning to visit again. She loved spending time at her parents' place and, when she'd gone out to spend their first Christmas in France with them, it had felt as though she was suddenly a child again, sneaking around and looking for her presents, the way she always had as a kid. That was her all over, though. Waiting for a secret to be revealed had never been her strong point. So, despite the first available appointment for a private gender scan only being ten days before she was due to have her twenty-week scan at the hospital, she hadn't been able to resist booking it.

Johnnie had come to pick her up for the scan. The moment he'd begun talking, the baby had started to move. It recognised its father already and it made Meg want to cry tears of happiness and sadness, all at the same time.

'Are you okay? You've gone a bit of a funny colour.' Johnnie was instantly at her side and she nodded.

'I can feel the baby moving, that's all.'

'I wish I could.' Johnnie had a wistful look on his face.

'It won't be long before you'll be able to as well. And, if it's any consolation, the baby always moves more when you're around. I think it's the sound of your voice.'

'Really?' Johnnie's face lit up and Meg felt a warm glow from knowing just how much he was looking forward to becoming a father. The fact he'd been willing to give up something he must have always wanted deep down, just for her, was amazing too.

'Our baby knows you already.' Meg breathed out as Johnnie folded her into his arms. She was desperately hoping that, by the end of the day, she'd be able to say *she knows you already*. But Meg hadn't admitted to anyone, even Johnnie, how much she wanted the scan to show they were having a daughter. She was terrified of how she'd feel about another little boy coming into her life, or of people thinking it would suddenly cancel out her loss if she had a second son. It didn't work like that, because Seth was truly irreplaceable.

'As nice as this is, I suppose we'd better get going.' Johnnie pulled back and gently stroked the hair away from her face.

'Uh-huh.' Suddenly she wished she'd been able to wait for her NHS scan. That way there'd be another ten days of ignorance. So, when her phone pinged with a text, she couldn't help hoping it would be the clinic cancelling the appointment. 'I'd better just check that.'

✉ Message from Tilly

Sorry for the things I said on Dad and Seth's anniversary. Ed and I had a chat, and he gave me a few home truths. I know you'll be a really good grandma, even while you're busy being a new mum. If you can forgive me, we'd really like you to come to the twelve-week scan. I always pictured having you by my side when I went through all of this and I don't want that to change xxxx

God bless Ed. Meg had no idea what it was he'd said to Tilly, but he already seemed to have developed the knack of knowing how best to handle things. Ed clearly wanted the best for her daughter and he was a peacemaker, which would help balance things out when Tilly lashed out the way she sometimes did.

'Is it anything you need to deal with, or shall we go and find out whether our little miracle is a boy or a girl?' Johnnie searched her face. 'You're not as excited as I thought you might be and if you've changed your mind, I'm more than happy to wait.'

'Are you sure you don't mind? We'll lose the money.' It wasn't just the fear of finding out she might be having a boy that was stopping Meg. Finding out the gender of the baby could wait, because even if they knew, she wouldn't be able to tell anyone else. She wanted to concentrate on Tilly's scan and make sharing that moment with her as special as it could possibly be. Tilly's baby needed to be the focus of the next couple of weeks, because the truth was, once Meg's baby arrived, she wouldn't be able make grandparenthood her top priority. And she really needed to make the moments where she could share in her daughter's pregnancy count.

16

Meg's bump was now getting impossible to hide and every outfit she'd put on when she'd been getting ready for Gwen's retirement do was either too small or left her looking and feeling like she was wearing a muumuu. She really did need to buy some maternity outfits, but she'd set an arbitrary goal in her head of getting past the twenty-week scan first, so that she didn't tempt fate. In the end, she'd settled for a black woollen dress, that wouldn't have been the best thing for a summer's evening, even if she hadn't been carrying a built-in hot water bottle.

Unlike Gwen's big birthday bash, the retirement party was just for her colleagues and ex-colleagues from the maternity unit. Anna had booked a table at Casa Cantare and then they'd be following the tradition of most of the unit's nights out and indulging in some bad karaoke.

'Do you think you're going to be able to handle all of this without alcohol?' Izzy smiled as she joined Meg at the bar. The sound of raucous laughter was already coming from behind them and the rest of the team appeared to have made up for Izzy's and

Meg's abstinence by drinking their share already. It was going to be one of those nights, if early indications were anything to go by.

'I'm not sure about the karaoke part; I usually only get the courage to sing when I've had a couple of glasses of something, but it's entertaining watching the others. I always think Bobby should have been a singer. I couldn't believe how good he was the first time I heard him.'

'He's amazing, isn't he?' Izzy smoothed her top down, and if Meg hadn't known she was pregnant too, she'd never have guessed. 'I was a bit worried he wasn't coming when I first got here, but Toni said he's dropping the kids off at his parents and then walking over, so he should be here soon. No one will nag us for not having a turn on the mic if he's performing. I'm looking forward to seeing what Gwen's got in store for us tonight, too. Apparently she's been planning a special farewell performance.'

'That's bound to be memorable! I can't imagine the unit without her, but I've probably only got two or three months before I go on maternity leave anyway. Everything's a bit more high-risk at my age and I don't want to take any unnecessary chances.' Meg didn't voice the fact that she still wasn't taking anything for granted. She didn't want to talk about the possibility of something being wrong with the baby, especially not when Izzy was pregnant too. Izzy was almost fifteen years younger and the risks for her would be far lower, but that didn't mean she wouldn't have her own fears. 'How are you feeling? I've been hoping that you've managed to avoid the sickness. Tilly has been really struggling with that and I think the first twelve weeks are the hardest, apart from the bit right at the end. This middle bit is quite easy in comparison.'

'I've been really lucky so far; I've hardly had any symptoms and you're looking great. You've got that bloom that everyone talks about and, despite being a midwife, I don't see anywhere near as much of that as you might expect.'

'It was all a shock at first, and I still can't believe I've been this lucky.' Meg wished she could shake off the nagging thought that something might still go wrong. So much was hanging on the twenty-week scan.

'Come on you two; the starters are here,' Frankie called out from the table behind them, and Meg followed Izzy over. There were platters of mixed starters and a big plate of raw oysters right in the centre.

'Who ordered these?' Toni picked up one of the oysters, her face a picture of disgust. 'It looks like something that someone with a terminal lung condition might cough up. How the hell are these supposed to be an aphrodisiac?'

'Don't knock it unless you've tried it! I ordered them so we can all have a great night, even after we get home.' Gwen turned towards Toni. 'The reason they're an aphrodisiac is because they improve the circulation and make sure the blood reaches all parts of the body. If you know what I mean.'

'All I want to do when I get in is to make the most of a childfree night by going to bed and knowing I can have a lie in. Now that really is a turn on.' Toni prodded the oyster with a fork. 'I don't think I could put this in my mouth, even if it promised to make me a size twelve.'

'Come on, try something different.' Gwen fixed her with a look. 'Me and Barry have decided we're going to try as many new things as possible now we're retired.'

'You're already doing the dancing and the magic shows, not to mention volunteering when the new hospital opens. Is there anything left for you to try?' Frankie raised her eyebrows.

'Oh you'd be surprised. We've got the first thing lined up already.' Gwen tapped the side of her nose.

'Dare I ask?' Nadia looked nervous.

'We're going newsraiding.'

'I know I'm going to regret this, but what's newsraiding?' Anna filled Ella's wine glass as she spoke.

'It's where you appear in the background of live broadcasts. It takes some planning, but Barry's been following a load of people who work for ITV West Country on social media, and we've set ourselves a target of appearing in at least two segments in the first month. You've just got to be willing to do whatever it takes to make sure you get seen.'

'Here we go.' Ella widened her eyes. 'Is this the bit where you tell us you'll be doing it naked?'

'No, that's the paddleboarding we're planning to do the month afterwards.' Gwen was completely straight-faced. 'We're going to Norfolk on holiday and we've already booked paddleboards at Holkham Bay. The western side of the bay is a nudist beach and, believe it or not, that's something we've never done either.'

'Gwen, I want to be you when I grow up!' Emily grinned. 'And I for one am going to down this shell of jelly and mucus, because if it works for you then I'm willing to give it a try. I think we should all do it together.'

'Can I do it with my eyes shut?' Jess peered at the oysters and then looked away again. 'Although I might have to hold my nose too.'

'I think Meg and I are going to have to opt out.' Izzy winked at Meg. 'But we'll make do with the bruschetta.'

'Should we wait for Bobby?' Meg didn't want him to feel left out, although he might be glad if he felt the same way about oysters as his wife clearly did.

'No, he won't mind, and I want to get this over and done with as soon as possible.' Toni screwed up her face again.

'Right. All for one and one for all. Here's to our Gwen and the endless antics she's going to get herself involved in now she's retiring.' Anna lifted her oyster into the air and everyone followed suit. 'One, two, three.'

Meg was laughing so much at some of the faces being pulled that she couldn't even take a bite of her bruschetta. But it was Toni who outdid everyone else by chewing on her oyster like it was made of rubber before trying and failing to swallow it, then depositing it as elegantly as she could back into its shell. And suddenly Bobby was at her shoulder.

'Ooh oysters. I love these.' Before his wife could even try and speak, Bobby had pinched the oyster off her plate and eaten it.

'You should probably have asked Toni if it was okay for you to have that.' Jess looked as though she was going to burst out laughing at any moment.

'It's all right, I know she hates shellfish. Don't you, darling?'

'Yep, which is exactly why I just spat it out!' When Toni started laughing, everyone else joined in – even Bobby – and it turned out to be the soundtrack to the whole night. Meg would be sad to leave the unit when the time came. But, like Gwen, she was praying she'd have plenty to look forward to.

* * *

Jess was running late for the infertility support group meeting because she'd had another one-to-one interview with her social worker, Kelly. The pace of the assessment was full-on, but there was no way she was letting the other members of the group down, even though her own infertility treatment had now come to an end.

'Sorry, I got held up.' Jess rushed into the room and dropped her bag on to an empty chair. The group had grown so much over the years and there were still too many women who'd been attending for a very long time. But seeing others, like Nicole, finally get their longed for babies, gave them all hope.

'I got the teas and coffees sorted while we were waiting. Hope you don't mind.' Nicole smiled. She'd been supported through her two previous pregnancies by the team at the unit, and had become so close to everyone that she was almost like one of them. The fact that she and her husband James were still raising funds for the unit in their daughter Gracie's name made Nicole's relationship with the team even more special.

'Of course not, you're a star.' Jess let go of a long breath. Thanks to Nicole, the other members of the group seemed content to be chatting amongst themselves. Nicole had also managed to find some very nice looking chocolate biscuits from somewhere. Although, knowing her, she'd probably made them herself. 'How's everything going?'

'I'm going for a scan tomorrow to see if my womb lining is feeling friendly.' Nicole rolled her eyes. 'Then if one of the frozen embryos I've got defrosts okay, I can go back for the transfer.'

'It's such a rollercoaster isn't it?' As much as Jess would have loved a baby, listening to Nicole made her more certain than ever that she didn't want to go through any of that again. She couldn't.

'It is and... Oh my goodness.' Nicole suddenly stopped mid-sentence and turned towards the door. 'I didn't expect to see you back here.'

Jess swung around, and experienced a sharp intake of breath as she spotted who Nicole was talking too. Jemima was a good friend of Ella's, who'd introduced her to Jess when Jemima had begun to think about trying for a baby with her husband, Leo. An accident had resulted in Leo becoming paralysed from the chest down, which meant that he and Jemima had needed fertility treatment. It had been a smooth journey in terms of the treatment itself, but the emotional impact on Jemima had been very hard. She'd had doubts about coping with caring for both Leo and a newborn baby, and had ended up changing her mind several times before finally going ahead with treatment. Eventually she'd given birth to a son, Dillon. Jess had never expected to see her back in the group, and neither had Nicole by the sounds of it. And they clearly weren't the only ones.

'I never expected to be back here either, if I'm honest.' Jemima shrugged. 'But I really want another baby and so does Leo. We might be mad, but the heart wants what the heart wants, doesn't it?'

'It certainly does.' Jess was certain she'd have felt that familiar twist of the knife in her gut only a couple of weeks before, but this time it didn't come. That didn't stop Jemima slapping her hand over her mouth and looking mortified, though.

'Oh my God, Jess, I'm so sorry. Here I am blabbing on about wanting another baby, when I should just be grateful I've got one.'

'It doesn't work like that, though, does it? And I'm fine anyway, I promise.' Jess gave her a hug. 'I'm really glad that you and Nicole have come back to get support and I don't want you to feel like you've got to pretend life is all rosy because of me. No one wants to go through this treatment, and most people get to choose when to have more children without having to do all of this. I know none of this is easy, and so does everyone else in this room. But I also know it's not for me any more.'

'So, you've made a definite decision?' Nicole's tone was soft. Jess had already told her how uncertain she was about having any more treatment, but no one at the group knew yet that she and Dexter had already started a fast-track assessment for fostering.

'We've applied to foster again, with parent and child approval this time. Then, when we're ready, we're really hoping we'll be able to adopt another child. That needs to be timed around what's best for Riley, though. The likelihood is that we'll be adopting a child who's around the age Riley is now. We think it's important he retains his identity within the family, as the eldest, so it will be a while before we even think about that. Fostering in the meantime will allow us to help more children, and it will also give me the opportunity to care for babies for longer than I looked after Teddy.' Jess felt a genuine sense of excitement explaining her plans to her friends. She really couldn't wait to get started. 'They've already got us on a fast-track assessment.'

'That's amazing, Jess.' Nicole, whose emotions were always close to the surface, was crying as she spoke. 'I'm so happy for you.'

'Me too.' Jemima looked across at Jess. 'But you'll still be around, won't you? I know it's selfish, but I'm not sure I can get through this without you, Jess.'

'I'll still be around, don't worry.' She meant what she said. Life might be about to get very busy, but living in Port Agnes had given her a sense of belonging, community and family that had been missing from her life for so long. And she never wanted to let it go.

17

Meg had never felt as old as she did waiting to go in for her scan at Truro Hospital. It was probably bad timing, but there didn't seem to be another mother-to-be in the room who was out of their twenties, let alone out of their thirties. And there was Meg, closer to fifty than forty. A couple of the expectant mothers had older women with them, who Meg assumed were their mothers. She'd seen one of them giving her several sideways glances, probably wondering if she was as old as she looked. Some of her friends from school were already grandparents and she would be soon too. Tilly had even asked if it was going to bother Meg when people assumed that both babies were her grandchildren. Her words had stung, having their desired effect, but Meg couldn't care less any more. As long as the baby was born healthy, she didn't give a damn if people thought she was its great-grandmother.

'I can't wait to see the baby again.' Johnnie was on high alert, sitting up straight whenever one of the sonographers came out to call someone's name. He was halfway out of the chair every time, but they were twenty minutes late now and still waiting.

'Me neither.' The truth was that Meg couldn't wait for it to be over. Not because she didn't want to see the baby every bit as much as Johnnie did. But there was something she wanted even more – for the baby to be given a clean bill of health. After that, they'd only have one day to wait until Tilly's scan and the fact that all of this was happening might start to feel a bit more real.

'Are we going to find out the gender?' Johnnie took hold of her hand as he spoke. 'You know I don't mind either way.'

'I'm not sure.' The fear she had about being told she was expecting another son was way down the list right now, but if they were lucky enough to be told that everything with the baby looked good, she didn't want anything to take the shine off that. Even a tiny bit. She knew she'd adjust to having another son and learn to manage the feelings that came with that. What she knew she wouldn't be able to deal with was being told that the baby wasn't going to make it. It wasn't just because she knew how much Johnnie wanted the baby; she did too, more than she could ever have imagined possible before discovering she was pregnant. It was like being told you could have the impossible and then having to wait nine months to find out if you really could.

'Megan Sawyer.' The sonographer finally called her name and she kept a firm grip on Johnnie's hand as they followed the woman into the room.

'Right, if you can get yourself comfortable on the examination table, we'll make a start. My name's Liz by the way, and is this dad?'

'That's right.' Meg lay down as instructed, rolling down the top of her leggings and her pants, as Liz tucked a paper towel under the lowered waistband.

'Sorry if the gel is a bit cold.' Liz squirted a dollop of the liquid on to Meg's increasingly generous belly. 'We'll be doing a more detailed scan today than any you've had earlier in your pregnancy.

I'll be looking at the baby's heart, brain, kidneys, spinal cord, bones and abdomen.'

'Okay.' Meg exchanged a look with Johnnie. By the time they'd discovered she was pregnant, it had already been past the optimum date to have the nuchal fold test or the combined ultrasound and blood test, which could detect whether the baby might be born with either Edwards' or Down's Syndrome. She and Johnnie had discussed it and they'd agreed that, unless the twenty-week scan detected a condition that was incompatible with life, they'd be continuing with the pregnancy. The first thing she wanted to see was the baby's heart beating strongly. She'd felt it moving on the drive over, so it should have been a given, but she still needed to know for certain.

'It's going to be okay.' Johnnie mouthed the words to her and she clung to his hand again, as the sonographer began moving the scanner across her abdomen. Meg knew it wasn't possible, but it felt as though she barely took a breath for the next fifteen minutes and, every time she glanced in Johnnie's direction, he was staring wide-eyed at the screen.

'Well I can safely say you've got the most compliant baby I've scanned all week. Usually I have to work really hard to get all the images I need and sometimes I even have to get patients to go for a walk to encourage the baby to change positions, but your little one has been a real star.' Liz smiled as she turned back towards Meg and Johnnie.

'Is everything okay?' Johnnie asked the million-dollar question.

'Everything looks good. Almost textbook in fact.' Liz didn't quite manage to hide her surprise, but then she smiled again, neither the sonographer or Johnnie having noticed that tears were streaming down the side of Meg's face and into her hair. 'The only other thing I wanted to check is whether you'd like to know the baby's gender.'

'Do we want to know?' Johnnie looked straight at Meg, catching his breath as he finally realised she was crying. 'Oh sweetheart, what's wrong?'

'I'm just so happy.' Meg was doing that half-laughing, half-crying thing that made the words come out in breathy bursts.

'You're going to make me cry in a minute.' As Liz spoke, Johnnie leant down and kissed Meg gently, before pulling away again.

'I don't think I've ever been happier, and I don't care about what gender the baby is, but I thought maybe you might need some time to get your head around things if it's a boy.' Johnnie had worked out what was worrying her, without Meg even having to say a word, and she couldn't have loved him any more than she did at that moment.

'I want to know.' Meg squeezed his hand again, suddenly certain, and they turned towards Liz, who smiled back at them.

'Well, like I said, the baby has been *very* cooperative.' Liz paused like a presenter about to announce the winner of a reality show, before she finally went on. 'And *she* gave me every opportunity to check for gender too. Congratulations, you're expecting a daughter.'

'Yes!' Johnnie punched the air and a fresh crop of tears filled Meg's eyes. She couldn't have asked for more and, for the first time in more than ten years, life felt as perfect as it was possible to be.

* * *

'I hope I'm having a boy.' Tilly rested a hand on her non-existent baby bump. It was Meg's second day in a row sitting in the waiting area for an ultrasound. Ed was on the other side of Tilly, and Meg had given them the news about her scan over the phone the night before. She'd considered waiting until after Tilly's scan, to keep the focus entirely on her daughter, but she'd almost certainly have let it slip by accident. At least this way, she couldn't accuse Meg of keeping it from her. Tilly had said all the right things, but her tone had been subdued and it had been hard for Meg not to take it personally.

'Why do you want a boy?' Meg knew she was probably asking for trouble, but she couldn't seem to help herself.

'I just don't want everything we're doing to be the same.' Tilly must have seen the look Ed shot her, because Meg did. 'And I'm also hoping that, maybe, if I have a boy, he'll have a bit of Seth and Dad in him. You're not going to get that, are you? Well definitely not a child that's anything like Dad anyway.'

Meg caught her breath, digging her nails into the palms of her hands in the hope that the physical pain might somehow alleviate the effect that Tilly's words had on her. Just lately, spending time with her daughter was like death by a thousand cuts. What Tilly had said might have been true, but that didn't make it any easier to hear.

'I bet Johnnie's thrilled.' Ed smiled, leaning forward to look past Tilly. 'I'll be really pleased if we're having a girl. Dads and daughters always seem to have such a great relationship, but I don't really care what we're having. And we won't be able to find out today anyway.'

'Don't be so sure.' Tilly shook her head. 'When my friend Sophie went for her twelve-week scan, the sonographer told her what they thought the gender was. They said they could only be 60 or 70 per cent sure it was a girl at that stage, but they were right. If it's a boy, it'll be definite, though, because if there are dangly bits there's no mistaking it.'

'You're going to love that baby like you've never loved anything else in your life, whatever gender it turns out to be. It's unconditional.' Meg squeezed her daughter's hand. Sometimes over the last couple of months the love she had for Tilly had needed to be unconditional, but Meg had never once doubted it.

'Tilly Sawyer?' The sonographer who came out to call her name introduced himself as Tim. He got Tilly settled, explained what he'd be doing and made the same apology about the coldness of the gel. But that was where the similarity between Meg's scan and Tilly's ended.

Meg knew something was wrong almost straight away and the silence in the room was torturous as Tim moved the scanner across Tilly's abdomen. The sonographer clearly hadn't perfected a poker face over the years he'd been in the job and his mouth was dragged down at the corners, as he turned to looked at Tilly and Ed.

'I'm really sorry.' He'd barely got the words out before Tilly started to sob.

'No, no, no, no, no!' She was attempting to get up from the examination table, even as Ed tried to put his arm around her. 'I can't have lost the baby; I haven't had any bleeding. I'm still getting morning sickness too.'

'It's what we call a silent miscarriage.' Tom's voice was soft, but it did nothing to lessen the blow and it was all Meg could do not to scream. She couldn't bear seeing her daughter in so much pain. 'Unfortunately, it looks like your baby stopped developing at about eight weeks and died shortly afterwards. When it's a missed miscarriage like this, there are often no symptoms and sometimes the body still thinks its pregnant, which explains the sickness. I know it must be a horrible shock.'

'Oh baby, I'm so sorry.' Meg got to her feet and moved closer to the bed, but Tilly wasn't ready to be comforted.

'This shouldn't be happening to me.' Tilly's nostrils flared, as she turned towards her mother. 'How can your baby be okay and mine isn't? This should be you, not me.'

Her words were like a physical blow and all Meg could do was stand there. It was Ed who had to intervene. 'Tils, sweetheart, I know you're heartbroken, but you can't lash out at your mum like that.'

'Why not? She never wanted me to have a baby in the first place and she's probably glad she hasn't got to pretend to be interested in our baby, when she'd rather be playing happy families with Johnnie. Well, I don't want to be a part of it. It's not like it'll really be my sister, not when the baby isn't Dad's.'

Meg couldn't answer. A wave of grief had washed over her, like it used to suddenly do in the early days after the accident. And just like back then, the sadness was so overwhelming that words just wouldn't come. Meg's chest felt as though someone was sitting on it and, if she hadn't known better, she'd have been scared she was having a heart attack. But she had to face it now; she hadn't just lost Seth and Darren in the accident, she'd lost the person Tilly had been back then too. Sometimes, the version of her daughter that had been left behind was a person Meg didn't even recognise.

When Meg looked at Tilly again, there was guilt mixed in with the sadness, because her daughter had just lost someone else, and Meg was terrified that the young woman standing in front of her might be about to become even more of a stranger. But she still couldn't find the words she needed to say, and it was Ed who filled the silence.

'Tilly, for God's sake, stop it, please. You don't mean any of this and you're going to regret it so much when—' Ed stopped mid-sentence as Meg turned away. If he said anything else she didn't hear it. She had to get out before she threw up, or her legs gave way, or both. The euphoria she'd felt less than twenty-four hours earlier, just two doors along the corridor, felt a hundred lifetimes away. Tilly had lost her baby, and she hated Meg for still having hers. There were some words that could never be taken back and, even if they were, they could never be forgotten. Meg had no idea where they went from here, all she knew was that she needed to leave.

18

Meg hadn't cried this much in years, not since the first year after the accident, when every event that came around made Darren and Seth's absence even more painful than it already was. But this was different; this was fresh grief, but the anger and sadness that came with it were so mixed up that Meg was struggling to make sense of her feelings. She was crying for the child that Tilly and Ed had lost, and for the pain they were going through as a result. That wasn't the sole reason for her tears, though. She was crying for how fractured her relationship with Tilly had become, and the mistakes she'd clearly made in trying to make life as easy as possible for her daughter, which seemed to have made her lose all empathy for anyone else's pain. Looking back, Meg should have pulled Tilly up on things a long time ago, but it was too late now.

What she'd said about Meg being the one who should have lost her baby was burned into her brain. As desperate as she was to forget them, it was like they were playing on a loop in her ear, and all she could do was stay curled up on the bed in Johnnie's house, her arms wrapped protectively around her bump, waiting for him to come home from work.

Johnnie had given her a key months before he'd ever suggested that she move in with him, but this was the first time she'd ever used the key without telling him first. She couldn't face ringing him when she'd left the hospital, tears streaming down her face so fast that she could barely see to drive. Meg couldn't go back to her place either. Tilly and Ed had already started to move some things in and they'd given notice on their flat. It was their home now and she didn't want to risk them turning up half an hour after she got in. She wasn't sure when she'd be able to face talking to Tilly again and she needed some time to process what had happened before she spoke to Johnnie. That way, she might be able to get to a point where she didn't burst into tears as soon as she started talking. The trouble was, Meg would probably have needed him to stay at work for another three weeks for her to do that, but he turned up about an hour and a half after she got home and he couldn't miss seeing her car parked on the driveway.

'Meg, are you here?' he called out as she heard the front door open and the sound of his dogs racing excitedly down the wooden hallway as they came in with him.

'I'm upstairs.' Catching sight of herself in the mirror on the dressing table, she tried to wipe her eyes, but even a professional makeup artist with half an hour to work their magic would have struggled to disguise her red, swollen eyes. So Meg had no chance.

'This is a lovely surprise.' Johnnie was smiling as he pushed open the door, but then his face changed completely. 'Oh my God, what's wrong? Are you okay? Is it the baby?'

He was at her side in an instant and all she could do was lean into him and sob. Any ideas she'd had about trying to get through the explanation without crying were forgotten, because it was impossible. She managed to say one thing, though.

'The baby's okay.' Saying it made her cry even harder. How

could the baby really be okay, when her older sister already wished she didn't exist? Meg had never had siblings and she'd been desperate to give that gift to her children. There was no guarantee of siblings getting along, or even being close, but Tilly and Seth had been inseparable from day one. Seth would bring his toys over to her cot, when she was sleeping, so he could be near her while he was playing. He was barely two when she was born, but he'd taken to the role of big brother like a duck to water. When all of that had been taken away from Tilly, it had added another layer of heartbreak for Meg. Nothing could ever replace their connection and, with the huge age gap between them, Tilly's relationship with her little sister would never be the same as it had been with Seth. There was still a chance to build something special, in a different sort of way, if Tilly wanted to. Except she'd made it very clear she didn't.

'I'm here when you're ready to tell me what's wrong.' Johnnie stroked her hair, which was wet with tears, away from her face. 'And even if you don't want to tell me, I'm still here. I love you.'

'I love you too.' Meg mumbled the response, but it was still a couple of minutes before she finally got herself together enough to explain things to Johnnie.

'Tilly's lost the baby.' A fresh crop of tears filled her eyes, as she saw the expression on his face. He was such a good man, and he was clearly heartbroken for Tilly and Ed, but he hadn't heard the whole story yet.

'Oh my God, I'm so sorry. They must be devastated, and it's obvious you are too, sweetheart.' Johnnie folded her into his arms again. 'Is there anything I can do to help, even if it's just practical stuff like dropping off some food so they don't have to think about cooking?'

'I don't think Tilly wants any help, especially not mine.' Meg was trying desperately not to picture the look on Tilly's face when she'd shouted at her after the scan, but it was proving just as hard to try and forget as the words were. Meg forced herself to look at Johnnie, the tears still burning at the backs of her eyes. 'When she found out she'd lost the baby... I know she was hurting like hell, but she said some terrible things.'

'About you?' Johnnie's face was already changing and she knew she wouldn't be able to take anything back if she told him the next part, but she couldn't keep the words in. It felt like they were poisoning her from the inside out.

'It was about the baby.' Now she'd started, she just wanted to get it out. 'She said that I should be the one going through a miscarriage and that she doesn't want to be a part of the baby's life, because she won't be her real sister anyway.'

There was a muscle going in Johnnie's cheek. Meg had so rarely seen him angry and he suddenly looked like a different person. She could understand why. When he finally spoke there was a bitterness in his tone that she'd never heard before. 'I wish I could say it's completely out of character and to put it all down to her loss, but it's far easier than it should be to imagine those awful things coming out of her mouth. I know she's hurting because of the miscarriage, but there's no excuse for this, Meg. None.'

'I think even Ed was shocked.' Meg shook her head. 'But it's all my fault.'

'How on earth did you come to that conclusion?' Johnnie was pacing now, looking capable of making a bolt for the door at any minute to go and have it out with Tilly.

'I've made too many excuses for her since Darren and Seth died. It was so hard for her and I tried to protect her from any other hurt or disappointment that came her way. I spent half my life trying to fix problems before they even happened, but I can't do anything about the miscarriage. It's my fault she lashed out the way she did, because I've let her do that to me every time something has gone wrong. I was willing to do anything that might ease her pain. She's right, too; the odds are it should have been me.'

'Please tell me that isn't what you're wishing.' Johnnie stopped and looked at her, his eyes wide. So much hung on what she was about to say, but all she could do was tell him the truth.

'That's the thing, I'm not, even a tiny bit. I want this baby and to start a life with you more than I've wanted anything for a long time and I wouldn't give that up for anyone. Not even Tilly.'

'I think maybe she needs to hear, for once in her life, that she doesn't always come first.' Johnnie moved closer to Meg again, taking hold of both her hands. 'And if she can't accept that and apologise for what she said, I'm not sure where we go from here. This is your call, Meg, but I can't stand around and watch her treating you like this. If things don't change, I can't see me wanting to be around Tilly any more. I'm putting you and our baby first.'

'I know I need to talk to her and I know it's hard for you not to hate her for what she said, but I really want us all to be able to get past this.' Meg had no idea if Tilly would even be willing to talk, let alone to listen to what her mother had to say. But Johnnie was right, it was time for some home truths. It would be painful for them both, and there was a chance she could lose Tilly because of all of this. But it was still a chance she needed to take, even if losing her daughter would mean her worst fear coming true.

* * *

To Meg's surprise and relief, it was Tilly who reached out first. The apology came by text, as they always did when Tilly realised she was in the wrong.

✉ Message from Tilly
Mum, I'm so sorry. I didn't mean what I said. Ed is really angry with me.
I was lashing out because of losing the baby and it's all a blur. Ed told
me I said some terrible things. I was in such a state, I don't remember
what I said, but I am really sorry. I love you. T xxxx

That was the thing with being a mother. There was a capacity
to instantly forgive behaviour from your child that you wouldn't
forgive anyone else in the world for, no matter how hard they tried
to make amends. But Meg knew it wouldn't be enough for Johnnie.
He'd want to know she'd spoken to Tilly face to face and that her
daughter was willing to prove she meant it when she said she was
sorry. They needed to meet in person.

✉ Message to Tilly
I love you too, but what you said really hurt me. I think we need to meet
to talk a bit more. Xx

Meg had contemplated leaving the kisses off altogether, but she
couldn't do it. Tilly might have some ground to make up, but Meg
would always be willing to meet her halfway.

✉ Message from Tilly
I'm back at home. We came straight back here from the hospital
yesterday and Ed is out now moving the rest of our stuff from the flat.
When I'm better, I want to be here so I can help you for a change. I'm
not going anywhere, so just come home when you're ready xxx

✉ Message to Tilly
I'll be there in half an hour xx

Meg didn't know how to feel about the fact that Tilly and Ed were going ahead with their plan to move out of the flat. She'd expected Tilly to hide out there until she'd recovered, at least physically, from the miscarriage. The move felt like a turning point, but Meg still wasn't sure what direction things were going.

'Oh Mum, I'm so glad you're here!' Tilly almost threw herself at Meg the moment she walked through the door of their old family home. Her daughter looked pale, with dark hollows under her eyes, as if she hadn't slept for days, but it had only been twenty-four hours since Meg had last seen her.

'You look exhausted; should you even be back home yet?' Meg had worked in healthcare long enough to know that miscarriages happened all too frequently and that patients were usually sent home straight away, but Tilly did look terribly pale and Meg's own maternal instincts were kicking in. 'Why don't you go and sit down on the sofa and I'll make us a drink.'

'No, I'm okay, but if you want a drink I can do it.' Tilly went through to the lounge and Meg followed her, suddenly feeling like a guest in her own home.

'Did the hospital give you anything?' Meg sat next to her daughter on the sofa and, as they faced one another, she was aware of her growing bump filling the space between them. She had to fight the temptation to grab a pillow to cover it up.

'Painkillers and some medication to try to bring on the bleeding, but if it hasn't started by tomorrow, I need to go in for a D&C.' A single tear rolled down Tilly's face. 'I'm scared of what might happen if they need to do that, because some of the websites say I should wait three months afterwards to start trying. But I don't think I can wait that long.'

'You need to make sure you're ready and there's no rush; you've got age on your side. Allowing yourself time to grieve for what you've lost first is really important.' Meg was desperately trying not to say the wrong thing, but, as she'd said to Johnnie, she couldn't fix this for her daughter and it was unfamiliar territory as a result.

'Will you stay with me? Until after the baby has gone. Please, Mum? I can't go through this without you.' Tilly looked at her with such desperation in her eyes, that all Meg could do was nod. There was no way she could leave her daughter to go through this alone, whatever else had happened. 'They've given me a couple of weeks off work and, once I'm over the op, if I have to have it, I can start looking after you for a bit. I think us being together and me caring for you for a little while, for a change, will really help me bond with my baby sister, before she even arrives.'

'I don't need you to take care of me, I'm—' Tilly cut her off before she could finish.

'Already being looked after by Johnnie?'

'No, because I'm fine.' Meg tried to stop her tone from becoming defensive, but it was difficult after everything that had happened.

'I need to do this for you, Mum, to show you I really am sorry and that I do want to be a part of the baby's life. I've already lost Dad and Seth, and I can't lose you too.' Tilly was still crying and Meg reached across the space between them. She had to let Tilly make amends and she had to be there for her daughter, at least until after she knew if she'd be having the operation, even if Johnnie might not understand.

'You'll never lose me, sweetheart, and I promise I'll stay with you until after the operation.'

'And you'll let me take care of you for a while after that, too?' Tilly widened her eyes.

'Just for a little while, but then you and Ed will be more than ready to get on with your new lives here together. It might be nice to be pampered for a while, though.' Meg smiled, but she was already dreading telling Johnnie. He wanted to be the one to take care of her, if she needed it; he'd shown that time and time again. Sometimes the pull between the family she'd built with Darren and the one she was building with Johnnie, felt like it was tearing her in two. And this was definitely one of those times.

* * *

'If that's what you really want.' Meg couldn't see Johnnie's face as he spoke, but she could tell by the way he was clattering the pans that he wasn't happy.

'She wants to make it up to me and she thinks this is the best way.' Meg went up behind him and slid her arms around his hips, resting her head against his shoulders. 'It'll only be for a few days, a week at the most.'

'I just don't want you ending up looking after her when she's already got Ed. You need to start looking after yourself first.' Johnnie spun round, so that they were face to face. 'I know she needs your support, but I've seen the two of you together. You can't stop yourself from attending to her every need and she can't help taking you for granted. Neither of you will mean for it to happen, but it will anyway.'

'I promise to keep an eye out for us slipping back into old patterns.' Meg reached up and kissed him, before pulling away again. 'And I'll be back by the end of next week at the latest. After that you'll have me and my enormous belly living here full time, for good.'

'Do you promise me that too?'

'I do.'

'I can't wait. You know that, don't you?' Johnnie took her face in his hands and she nodded. In some ways, she'd been incredibly unlucky in life and losing the boys had felt like the cruellest blow fate could possibly deal. But to have been loved this much – not once, but twice – was something she'd never stop being grateful for.

19

When Jess had posted in the Port Agnes Facebook page, asking for recommendations for somewhere that specialised in cutting children's hair, she'd been inundated with suggestions to go to Simeon Tobi's Barber's Shop. Riley had been reluctant about having haircuts since the very first time and had screamed his way through the first couple of appointments Jess had taken him to. It had resulted in a very wonky fringe each time and, when a pair of scissors had nicked Riley's ear on the second occasion, he'd developed a full blown phobia of having his hair cut. After that, Jess had resorted to cutting his hair herself, which had been achieved with the aid of hair clippers. But, at eight years old, he was starting to demand slightly more complex hairstyles than Jess's limited skills could offer him.

'What are you after today then young man?' Simeon, who owned the salon with his brother, Tobi, had immediately put both Riley and Jess at their ease. Riley might be too old for the salon chair that looked like a racing car, but Simeon and his brother obviously knew how to handle clients of all ages. Tobi had already offered Riley a choice of films to watch on the iPad, when his haircut began, and Simeon had let him watch another child having their hair cut, to help gain his trust.

'How long have you been cutting hair?' Riley narrowed his eyes, as he looked at Simeon's reflection in the mirror.

'More than ten years.'

'And have you ever cut someone's ear when you've been doing it?'

'Never.' Simeon feigned a very serious expression, but Jess didn't miss the twinkle in his eye. He was clearly trying very hard not to laugh. 'You can ask my brother if you like.'

'He's telling the truth.' Tobi mirrored his brother's deadpan expression, with only the slight twitch of his lips giving him away.

'Okay, that's good, but how many bad haircuts have you done?' Riley would make a good barrister, the way he was cross examining Simeon.

'Only one, but that was on my brother when we were both about your age.' Simeon winked.

'He did that on purpose, because I've always had the best hair out of the two of us.' Tobi shrugged. 'And I can promise you he hasn't done a bad haircut since he finished his training.'

'Really?' Riley breathed out slowly.

'Really.' Simeon smiled at him in the mirror.

'Well, in that case, I'm willing to give it a go.'

'You sound about forty-three.' Jess couldn't help laughing. 'But you're going to have to let Simeon get on with it, my darling, because I've got to drop you at Grandad Guy's before me and Dad go to our meeting.'

'Grandad Guy has quite cool hair.' Riley looked at the barber's reflection in the mirror again. 'Even though he's really old.'

'Do you want a haircut like your grandad's?' Simeon really did have the patience of a saint.

'Nope, I want a fade, like all my friends at school. Can you show him the picture on the phone, Mum?'

Jess got her phone out as instructed and showed Simeon the picture Riley had chosen when they'd looked online together. 'This is it.'

'Do you think that's something you can do?' It wasn't just the fact that Riley sounded like an old man that was making the laughter bubble up in Jess's throat, it was the appraising stare he was giving Simeon in the mirror.

'Luckily, low fades like the one in the picture are my specialty. So, are we good to go?' Simeon lifted his scissors aloft as he waited for an answer. After a pause like a Roman Emperor determining a gladiator's fate, Riley eventually nodded. Twenty minutes later, it was all over and Riley was still grinning from ear to ear when Jess dropped him off at her dad and Frankie's house. She'd had to leave straight away, to get to the training she and Dexter had been asked to attend as part of their assessment, and she worried she was going to be late. Thankfully, when she got to the meeting room, Dexter and the others were still chatting over teas and coffees.

When Jess got to his side, Dexter kissed her cheek. 'How did the haircut go?'

'Simeon did a great job, just like everyone said he would. Look.' Jess whipped out her phone to show Dexter a photograph she'd taken of Riley after his haircut.

'That looks great. Did he get stressed about having it done?'

'No, he was perfect, but he kept giving Simeon the third degree about how much experience he had.' Jess laughed. 'He was like a middle-aged man, trapped in a kid's body. I don't know where our little boy has gone sometimes.'

'He's growing up fast, that's for sure.' Dexter looked across the room to where a woman was holding a baby, who looked about a year old. 'I can barely remember him being that age.'

'I never even knew him then.' Jess couldn't keep the wistful note out of her voice. Dexter had come into Riley's life when he was only a baby, but he'd already been at school when Jess had met him. Taking Riley to the barbers was the stuff that real parenting was made up of. The day-to-day moments that were all tiny steps towards helping Riley to become an independent adult one day. In the future, he would think back and remember that it was his mum who'd helped him get over his phobia of having a haircut. She wouldn't trade those moments for anything, but that didn't stop her wishing she'd been there in the early days too.

'I wish I could make that happen for you and maybe one day we'll be able—' Dexter's words were cut off as a woman at the front of the room clapped her hands together.

'Thank you all for coming. I'm Sarah Wainwright and I'll be leading the training session this afternoon, along with Sally Fredricks, who's an experienced parent and child foster carer.'

'Thanks Sarah.' Sally, the woman who was holding the baby in her arms, smiled. 'And you'll see that I'm taking the training so seriously that I've even brought along my own prop! My husband is coming to pick Maya up on his way home from work, but it's good to show you the reality of balancing parent and child fostering. Maya's mother left the placement a few months ago, but we're keeping her with us while the court process for her adoption goes through. Maya was due to have supervised contact today, but it was cancelled by her mother at the last minute and it's a pretty good example of how life as a foster carer for parent and child placements can go.'

'How long will you be managing the situation before Maya is adopted?' A man at the front of the room, with a notebook clamped under his arm, asked the question.

'She's already been with us for almost a year, because one side of her birth family are contesting the plans for adoption. But having Maya is by far the easiest part of the whole thing.' Sally jiggled Maya up and down on her hip as she spoke and Jess had to reach out and squeeze Dexter's hand to stop herself from telling everyone in the room that she knew exactly what Sally meant. Caring for Teddy had been as easy as breathing in and out, but giving him away had made her want to stop breathing all together. Suddenly, she wasn't anywhere near as sure as she had been that she could do that all over again, but she had no way of knowing for sure until she tried.

* * *

Meg had been back at home with Tilly and Ed for over a week, but she was still no closer to being able to make the move to live with Johnnie permanently. Tilly had needed the operation in the end and she'd needed a lot of emotional support afterwards. She found it difficult to come to terms with the fact that there was no closure for her, after losing the baby. She'd had a general anaesthetic for the procedure and hadn't witnessed the pregnancy loss in the way that people with a miscarriage often did. She'd confided in Meg that she still felt pregnant and that sometimes it was hard to convince herself that the baby was really gone. Meg couldn't leave her when she was like that, but every time Johnnie asked when she was moving to his, she had to tell him 'not yet' and hear the disappointment in his voice. She missed him every bit as much as he missed her, but it wouldn't be forever.

Tilly had been told by the doctors that waiting three months to try for another baby might help to ensure that she was as ready as possible for another pregnancy, but that it was up to her if she really wanted to try sooner than that. She'd told Meg she had no intention of waiting. Getting pregnant first time around was something that had been partially left in the hands of fate, because Tilly and Ed hadn't had a permanent home of their own. But the miscarriage had made Tilly want a baby even more, and now she wasn't just worried about the endometriosis, she was worried about further miscarriages too. All of that, combined with the fact that she and Ed had a permanent home now, meant Tilly was already going all out to prepare her body for pregnancy.

Books arrived almost every day from Amazon, detailing exactly what she needed to do to optimise her chances of getting pregnant. The latest delivery was a fertility cookbook and Tilly had already given Ed a list of ingredients he needed to stock up on. So far, the promise of Tilly looking after Meg hadn't materialised and she had a feeling that it probably wasn't going to.

'How are you doing Meg? I haven't had the chance to catch up with you since Gwen's leaving do.' Ella was by far the most popular of the health visitors and Meg could see why. She had a way of putting people at ease and making them open up to her, even when they might not have planned to. There was still half an hour of the lunch break left before the patients would start arriving for afternoon appointments, and Meg was more than ready for a break and the excuse to have a catch up.

'I feel huge and exhausted. If I had the energy, I'd put a government petition together to lobby for pregnant women over the age of forty-five to get twice as much maternity leave, because we're at least twice as tired as they are.' Meg grinned, glad she could be honest with someone, instead of having to pretend that this pregnancy always felt like the amazing miracle it was. 'So come on then, make me jealous; how was your trip to Tuscany?'

'Beautiful. Sunshine, good food and even better wine, and I suppose the company wasn't too bad either.' Ella shrugged. 'I mean I can't really complain about my husband when he surprises me with trips like that, can I?'

'Not really. I think you might want to hold on to that one.' Meg hoisted herself out of the chair, just as Hamish came out to reception. 'Are you sure you haven't got a built-in radar? I was about to offer to make Ella a lovely cup of tea and to open those chocolate biscuits I bought, although to be honest they're more chocolate than biscuit.'

'They sound perfect, but we should be the ones making you tea.' Ella moved to take over, but Meg shook her head.

'I need to get up and move every so often, otherwise I seize up like the tin man. I also got this text from Gwen this morning.' Meg passed her phone to Ella, so she and Hamish could see the message.

✉ Message from Gwen

Hope you're keeping well, Meg. Remember to take vitamin D like I told you and make sure you aren't sitting down all day at work, otherwise you'll end up with haemorrhoids the size of your baby's head. Catch up soon xx

'She still never lets us down, does she?' Ella was shaking with laughter, as she handed the phone back to Meg.

'Thank goodness! I think I'm going to have to pop along to the new hospital a few times a week, once Gwen is running the Friends' shop, just so I can get my regular fix of her home spun wisdom. I don't think anyone has ever made me laugh as much as she does.'

'Nadia told me she grew up going to all sort of events at Gwen and Barry's place, and people wouldn't believe it if they heard some of the stories.' Hamish laughed. 'Apparently, when their youngest daughter brought her new boyfriend to a barbeque at their house, everyone was a bit surprised by how short he was. Some of the extended family were ribbing him about it, and Barry told Gwen that he thought it was making their daughter's boyfriend uncomfortable. And guess what Gwen's solution to that was?'

'I dread to think.' Meg could picture the scene all too easily.

'She got up on a garden chair and clinked her glass, as if she was going to make a speech, then told everyone to stop giving their daughter's boyfriend a hard time because the height difference clearly didn't matter to either of them and that everyone was the same size lying down anyway!'

'Oh my God, the poor man. He must have run for the hills.' Meg was laughing, but she couldn't help wishing that all Johnnie had needed to put up with was the sort of well-intentioned foot-in-the-mouth comments Gwen was famous for. With the barbs Tilly had directed at Johnnie since he'd come into Meg's life, it was surprising he hadn't run for the hills too. It must have been even tougher, in a way, that sometimes Tilly was almost affectionate towards him, telling him he made the best curry in the world, or asking his advice about something. Then the next time they met, she could just as easily go out of her way to make sure he knew he'd never be a part of *her* family. Even though Tilly had obviously warmed to Johnnie over the time he and Meg had been together, she could never be certain her daughter would make him feel welcome. It always felt like Tilly could go back to treating him the way she had at the start, for the most unfathomable of reasons. Right now, anything that took Meg's mind off her home life for a few moments was a very welcome distraction. 'Let me just grab those biscuits I promised you, and Hamish can fill us in on a few more of Gwen's classic moments, while we're waiting for the kettle to boil.'

Ella and Hamish were still chatting as Meg walked to the back of the reception area, reaching up to get the biscuits from a high shelf. Suddenly everything seemed to go a bit fuzzy around the edges. The stars started in the corner of her vision, but they quickly spread and everything in front of her seemed to swim out of focus, as if the shelves themselves were moving backwards and forwards. She tried to reach out to stop herself from falling, but all she could do was grab hold of handfuls of air. The thud she made, as she landed on the floor, reverberated up her spine, and she couldn't tell if it was her or Ella who screamed first as she fell.

'Oh my God, Meg, are you okay? Have you hurt yourself?" Hamish was the first to her side, but Ella was right behind him.

'I'm fine, just a bruised bum and a bit of a bruised ego I expect.' Meg was already trying to get up off the floor, but Hamish wasn't taking any chances.

'Let's just check you over first.' He crouched down in front of her. 'Have you got any pain?'

'Just my bum, like I said, and I feel like I've had the wind knocked out of me a bit.'

'There's a good chance you've damaged your coccyx falling the way you did, straight down on to your bottom like that.' Hamish exchanged a look with Ella. 'But what's worrying me more is what might have caused you to fall in the first place.'

'Did Jess mention any issues with your blood pressure at your last check up?' Ella spoke as she moved to stand on the other side of Meg.

'She said it looked perfect.' The hospital had agreed to shared antenatal care for Meg, with routine checks taking place at the unit and some appointments direct with her consultant in between.

'Did you feel dizzy before you fell, or do you think you just slipped?' Hamish looked at the floor, but Meg already knew this wasn't down to her slipping on something that had been spilt. The stars that had swum in front of her eyes were proof of that.

'I just went dizzy when I reached up for the biscuits. Maybe it's the universe trying to tell me that I shouldn't be eating empty calories when I'm already the size of a house.'

'When you're pregnant, biscuits should be available on prescription.' Hamish smiled. 'I think we're probably okay to get you up. Then I can monitor your blood pressure and Ella can take a look at you too. We might need to run a few more tests to check on your blood sugar, to make sure there's no underlying cause of you fainting. But we'll take it slowly, get you on your knees first and then up on to a chair.'

'I'm sure it's nothing. I can just give Jess a call and see if she can fit me in after work.' Meg didn't want Hamish and Ella wasting their limited break looking after her, but they weren't taking no for an answer.

'You need to put your health first and we'll manage reception without you this afternoon, won't we, Hamish?' Ella turned towards him and he nodded.

'Absolutely and one of us will call Jess too, but I think the best thing you can do, once we know everything is okay, is to go home and rest. I'm sure Johnnie will be only too happy to make sure you follow doctor's orders and take it easy for a bit.'

'I know he will.' Meg shut her eyes for a moment, wishing it was as easy as that. But then the baby kicked, reminding her that this wasn't just about her. It was time to move in with Johnnie, for their unborn daughter's sake, if not for Meg's. And Tilly was just going to have to accept it.

20

Hamish had been right about Meg injuring her coccyx. They couldn't be sure whether it was cracked or just badly bruised, but since the treatment for the pain was pretty much the same either way, there was no point exposing the baby to the risk of an X-ray. Instead, Meg was dispatched home with medication and advice on everything – from how to sit to how to sleep. They'd even given her a maternity belt, which was probably the single most unglamorous thing Meg had ever seen. She'd been wearing it for up to three hours a day for over a month, but she still hadn't really got used to it.

'Don't forget you need to take these before you fall asleep.' Johnnie set the pills and a glass of water on the table next to the bed, where Meg was lying on her side with the maternity belt strapped above and below her bump, over the top of a pair of grey cotton pyjamas.

'Thank you.' Meg turned her head to look up at him. She'd been living with him for five weeks now and she didn't think she'd ever been as well cared for in her life. 'I bet you thought that when you finally moved in with another woman that it would all be sexy lingerie and champagne, not maternity belts and stool softeners!'

'Granted, you're the only person in the world who could try and make that sound sexy.' Johnnie laughed. 'But my darling girl, I can promise you this, there's no place on earth I'd rather be, than right here, right now, with you.'

'Me neither.'

'Are you sure about that?' Johnnie slowly got into the bed beside her, clearly not wanting to make any sudden movements that might make her wince in pain. 'Your phone was pinging like crazy earlier and I'm guessing it was Tilly?'

'Uh-huh.' Meg had had to tell her daughter she was going to sleep in the end, because she'd been pushing for an answer about when and where they were going to have Darren's birthday party. Holding a fiftieth party for someone who'd died six months before they'd even celebrated their fortieth probably sounded crazy, but it was what Tilly seemed to want more than anything right now and Meg was trying her best to keep the peace. Just like she always did.

Tilly had cried when Meg had finally told her she'd be moving to Johnnie's. She'd kept trying to insist that she should be the one who took some time off work, instead of Johnnie, to be around more until they were sure Meg was okay. But despite her promises to take care of Meg, none of that had materialised and it wasn't a risk she was willing to take any more. The problem was, Tilly didn't seem to want to take no for an answer. Even when Jess and Ella had both tried to intervene and tell her that Meg needed to be in an environment where she didn't revert to caring for everyone else, Tilly had continued to insist it wouldn't be like that. It had been Ed who'd come to the rescue in the end and reminded Tilly that she needed to be taking it as easy as she could too, so that they could be in the best possible place to start trying for a baby again, as soon as possible. After that, Tilly had reluctantly agreed that maybe it was for the best, but there were still days when she messaged her mother several times an hour. Today had been one of those days.

'How are the plans for the party going?' Johnnie's tone was even. He'd never shown a shred of jealousy about how big a role Darren still played in Meg's life. She wasn't sure she'd have found it easy in his shoes.

'She wants to hold it at the bird sanctuary. Darren and Seth both loved it there, ever since they found that abandoned owlet in the woodland on the road to Port Kara, when Seth was about six. Seth called it Owlbert, and the owners of the sanctuary let him go and visit whenever he wanted. He had all his birthday parties there after that, up until he started secondary school. Even when it wasn't cool to invite his friends to a party at a bird sanctuary any more, he'd still hung out there, volunteering whenever he could. Darren went with him a lot of the time and they even built some of the enclosures. We got quite friendly with the owners in the end.'

'Den and Kerry? They're absolutely brilliant, aren't they?' Johnnie gently stroked the outside of Meg's thigh as he spoke. 'I've lost count of the amount of times they've helped us out with animals that have been brought into the surgery. Den originally set the sanctuary up just for owls, then they started taking in other birds; after that, they set up a cattery to help rehome strays.'

'They're amazing. The sanctuary has held loads of events to raise money for the therapy centre in Port Tremellien too, and even funded some of the courses at Dorton's Adventure Centre in Port Kara for teenagers who are struggling with their mental health. Tilly did one of the courses they funded there about four years after Darren and Seth died.'

'I can see why the place means so much to you both.' Johnnie paused for a moment, his eyebrows knitting together as he looked at her again. 'Do you think Tilly might need some more therapy? Maybe it's just me, but it feels like the miscarriage hasn't just been devastating because she lost the baby, it seems to have raked up a lot of old feelings and she's terrified of losing you too.'

'I think you're right and I have tried suggesting it to her. Jess and Ella both recommended that she go and see a counsellor too. But she's adamant that she's fine, or at least she will be when she's pregnant again.'

'And what if that doesn't happen according to the timeline Tilly has in mind? I'm really worried about both of you, because I know you'll be worrying about her even more than I am. I'm scared it's going to make you ill.'

'I need to be there for her.' Meg put her hand over Johnnie's. 'But I'm not going to let her take over my whole life again, I promise. I know I need to take some time out and we also need to take some time for us, which is why I got you this.' Meg reached over to the bedside drawer and handed Johnnie an envelope.

'What is it?'

'Look inside.'

'The Harbour Hotel.' Johnnie took out a brochure for the seafront hotel in St Ives, where the two of them had spent their first ever night away together.

'I've booked us in for three nights. Just a little break together before the baby arrives. Jess tells me they call it a babymoon, and she's happy to look after the dogs at her place while we're away.'

'That's brilliant!' Johnnie planted a kiss on her lips. 'When are we going?'

'Not until October and I'm afraid I can't promise you it will be like last time.' Meg raised her eyebrows. 'I'm not sure there will be anything in the way of romance with me in this contraption and a huge bump coming between us. I'm not sure even Gwen would have a suggestion about how to get over all of those hurdles.'

'Three whole days with you is all the romance I need.' Johnnie stroked the back of her hand. 'I don't think you've got any idea quite how much I love you, Meg Sawyer, and there's only one thing I'd change about you if I could.'

'Do I even want to ask what that is?' Meg smiled, but despite her bravado she really wasn't sure she wanted to know. Especially if there was nothing she could do to grant his wish.

'It's stupid really, but it's just the fact you're still a Sawyer. I wouldn't even try to take away anything from the life you had with Darren, but I can't help thinking you'll be having our baby, when you've still got Darren's name.' Johnnie shook his head. 'See, I told you it was stupid.'

'No it isn't. I've been thinking about it too and I want the same name as our baby. I know it's old fashioned, but I was going to ask you if you minded if I added your surname to mine and changed it by deed poll.'

'I don't know... That sounds very complicated.' Johnnie turned away from her and she tried to blink back the tears that had imme-diately sprung into her eyes. He clearly didn't want her to share his name after all. 'Especially when I've been wanting to give you this since about a week after our first date.'

Johnnie reached over and took something out of the top drawer of the bedside table, holding it out as he turned back towards her. It was a box. 'This isn't how I'd planned to do it and I can get down on one knee if that helps, but it doesn't matter if I'm kneeling, or lying next to you in bed, I just want you to know you mean every-thing to me. The last two and half years have been amazing, espe-cially this last five weeks, and I won't ever be able to think of anywhere as home again unless you're in it. Which means I need you to marry me, if you think you can put up with that?'

'Oh I think I might just about be able to cope.' Meg didn't even try to stop the tears this time, but for once they were happy tears.

Even when the thought of how Tilly might react started to creep in, she pushed it away again. She wanted to marry Johnnie and she couldn't think of a single thing in the world that could possibly stop her.

21

Jess couldn't remember the last time she'd had the chance to catch up with Ella and Anna for lunch. Life seemed to have become so hectic for all of them just lately. Anna's twins, Kit and Merryn, were now at pre-school, and juggling pick-ups and drop-offs meant that Anna seemed to have less time than ever to do much else other than work. Ella was working part time as a health visitor, but she and Dan had also started a couple of ventures in converted outbuildings at Crooked Cottage Farm. One of them was a therapy craft workshop, which Ella was running in conjunction with Heather, a counsellor based in Port Agnes. It had proved incredibly popular so far and there was already talk of expanding the well-being aspect of the business.

Then there was what Ella called her 'special needs smallhold-ing'. It had all started when some ex-battery hens were left on the doorstep of Johnnie's veterinary practice. Someone had put them there with a note saying that they'd tried to rehome them, but the animals were too traumatised for the new owner to deal with. When Ella had heard about them from Meg, she'd offered to give them a home. After that had come a goat with one eye, called

Nelson, and a three legged cat, called Peg. The animals had their own Instagram account and the #crookedcottagecrew already had a big following. Ella was using it to raise the profile of the craft workshops too and, when income had started to come in from social media, she'd begun to make plans to expand her special needs smallholding.

As for Jess, her whole life – outside of work and caring for Riley – seemed to be consumed with the fostering assessment. The panel was now only a fortnight away and she and Dexter could potentially be matched with their first placement very soon. She'd tried not to worry too much about the doubts that had crept in when they'd gone to the parent and child training, and the last person she'd expected to see when she got to The Cookie Jar café – before Anna and Ella arrived – was Sally, the trainer who'd brought baby Maya along to the session with her.

'Hi Sally, I don't know if you remember me, but I was at the training session you ran at the beginning of last month?'

'Of course I remember. Jess, isn't it?' Sally greeted her with a smile, as the person behind the counter stacked small white cardboard boxes on top of one another. 'I just need to point out that not all of these cakes are for me! We're having a birthday party for Hector, who was one of the first children we fostered. He had his first ever birthday with us, two months after they moved in, but he's six now and it's lovely to see what a great life his mum has made for them both, so we still host his party every year.'

'It must be hard, saying goodbye?' Jess couldn't stop herself from asking the question that had been playing on her mind. She had no idea if Sally would report what she'd said back to her assessing social worker or whether that could raise any doubts about her suitability, but she needed to know what she was letting herself in for.

'It's never been as hard again as it was the first time, because

I've always known what was coming. Even when we have babies for as long as we've had Maya, you can cope if you know they'll never really be yours and you're just taking care of them until they go to their forever home. It's usually much easier once you've met the new parents and seen how desperate they are to welcome the child into their family.' Sally sighed. 'What I find hardest is when the courts decide that the parenting the child is getting is *good enough* and that they should stay with their birth mother or father, when I have serious doubts about whether their parenting is actually *good enough*. It's great when you can help a birth parent upskill to the point where they really can give the child the level of care they need. But that's always a matter of opinion, and the final decision is out of my hands.'

'When I fostered the first time around, I cared for a baby boy whose mother left him on the doorstep of my house.' Jess could picture the moment when she'd first seen Teddy, so clearly. 'I knew I couldn't keep him, but I made the mistake of letting myself fall in love with him anyway and I'm worried I might do that again.'

'I'd be more concerned about you if you weren't.' Sally patted Jess's hand. 'If the parent in placement decides to leave, or if they're just not capable of showing the child enough care, it's going to be down to you to give that baby all the love it needs. But it takes a very special person to be able to love a child that much and still be able to let them go. You've done it before, Jess, so I think you've got it in you to do it again, but I'm not going to stand here and pretend it's easy. Only you know if it is something you can go through more than once.'

'It so hard to know, until you have to do it, though, isn't it?' Jess swallowed hard. Just thinking about the day she'd handed Teddy to his new parents could bring all the raw emotion she'd felt right back to the surface. 'I knew Teddy was going to have an amazing life with his new parents and that they could give him the stability I couldn't offer at the time, even if I'd been allowed to adopt him, but it still broke my heart.'

'I'm guessing something must have mended it? Otherwise you wouldn't be about to start fostering again.'

'It was my husband, Dexter, and our stepson, Riley.' Jess smiled. 'It was Riley who made me realise that, as much as I'd loved Teddy, it didn't come close to what I grew to feel for him. The first time he came to me when he needed comfort, and the first time he called out for me at night, I knew he'd chosen me and that Riley was the child I was always meant to be a mother to. It was the best day of my life when Dexter and I were finally able to adopt him.'

'That's such a lovely story, you've got me all choked up!' Sally blew out her cheeks. 'I think what you've got to do, to cope with looking after babies and then having to give them up, is to keep looking forward. Have it in your mind from day one that you're going to be a *part* of their story, but that you aren't and never will be their mother. The goodbyes might be too hard to do more than a few times, but you'll make such a difference in the lives of the children you help. If you do decide to stop, you'll need to look forward again and decide what's next. I think all of this is harder if you're not sure that your own family is complete; I already had my three and I knew I didn't want any more when I started fostering. But I promise you'll learn a lot about what you want from life and what you want your family to look like from doing this work. Do you think you might want to have more children?'

In any other circumstance, that might have seemed an intrusive question, but Sally was right to ask it. 'We want to adopt again eventually, but we're not ready yet. It's not the right time for Riley and I don't feel like I got the chance to give everything I could to fostering first time around.'

'I think you'll do brilliantly. Just make sure you take enough time between placements to come to terms with saying goodbye.

When you get photos from the new parents and know that you played a part in helping to create that family, it will make saying goodbye the next time a little bit easier. I don't think you ever completely get used to it, but it's a little bit less painful each time.'

'Thank you. It really helps to know I'm not supposed to find it all easy. I was starting to wonder if I'd made a mistake, because I know it'll be difficult to say goodbye each time, but I really do want to play a part in helping to create new families. However small that part may be.' Jess might never have a baby of her own, but suddenly it seemed clear that this was what she was meant to do – just as it had been clear that she was meant to be Riley's mother. She'd be giving someone else that same chance to become a loving parent to a child who desperately needed them. Whether that was the biological parents learning the skills to parent their child, or adoptive parents who'd waited years for that chance. Jess would be helping to create families; keeping that in mind – every step of the way – would make any pain she might suffer more than worth it.

* * *

By the time Sally left the café, with her boxes of goodies for Hector's birthday party, Ella and Anna had already come in and sat down at one of the tables by the window.

'Sorry, I was just talking to a lady who ran some fostering training I went on last month.' Jess leant across to hug Anna and Ella in turn.

'We spotted you, but we didn't want to interrupt you mid-conversation.' Anna passed Jess one of the menus. 'Although I did consider pushing past you to grab the last piece of pistachio cake, but then I realised there was another uncut one on the lowest shelf of the cabinet. I've been thinking about it all week!'

'I can't seem to stop eating at the moment.' Ella's stomach gave a loud growl as she looked at the menu and Jess laughed.

'It sounds like you've got something living in there that needs feeding!' The look that passed between Ella and Anna was fleeting, but Jess didn't miss the way Ella's eyes had widened. 'Have you got something to tell me?'

'Oh God, it wasn't supposed to come out like this.' Ella put the menu down and leant forward in her seat. 'I wanted to tell you after lunch and to explain it all properly, because I knew some of it might be hard for you to hear.'

'If you're going to tell me what I think you're going to tell me, don't you dare let the fact that I can't have a baby steal even a tiny bit of the joy from this moment, because I couldn't be more thrilled.' Jess was already crying, but, despite what Ella might think, they were happy tears. 'Although it's going to be pretty awkward now if you were about to tell me you've just got acid reflux.'

'No, you're right, I'm pregnant.' Ella widened her eyes again, as if she was discovering the news for the first time along with Jess. 'I feel awful that it happened for us so quickly when you've been trying for so long and I wouldn't have mentioned it yet, but I didn't want you to find out in some other way, because I had my booking-in appointment with Anna yesterday.'

'This is something to celebrate. One of my best friends is having a baby and after everything you've been through, Ella, no one deserves good news more.'

'I knew that's what you'd say.' Anna's tone was gentle. 'You're an amazing person, Jess.'

'Hmm, I'm not sure about that, but I hate the idea that people think they need to walk on eggshells around me. And I want to hear all about it.' Jess grinned. 'Well, maybe not *all* about it. I'm not Gwen!'

'We've been thinking about starting a family for over two years now, ever since we got married, trying to decide if having a baby is a good idea. But the MS has been stable for the last year and we started thinking that it was probably now or never. That was what clinched it for me; I was scared about the risks but I knew for certain I didn't want it to be never.' Ella sighed. 'I don't know if I might need more help in the future, but for now I'm managing to keep driving. Changing to an automatic car made all the difference with that. I can't walk as far, or as quickly, as I used to, but the fatigue is the worst thing and I don't think I'd be able to manage working more than part time. I definitely couldn't cope with on-call shifts any more. But in a weird sort of way it feels like I've been training to manage the sleepless nights.'

'That's one way of looking at it!' Jess laughed.

'I kept asking Dan if he thought we were being fair, bringing a child into the world when one of its parents might not always be as active as I am now. I've got a permanent weakness in one of my legs and some days life just wipes me out. But Dan pointed out that no one knows what's around the corner and in some ways we know more than most people about what might be in store. We're so lucky that he's able to take time off when he needs to and we can fit our lives around this baby. We've got so much support and, even if the worst-case scenario developed with the MS, and something happened to Dan as well, it's never going to fall to our child to be my carer. When I realised that, it took all the fear out of it. After I finally got my head around having MS, I was determined not to let it rob me of anything that I didn't need to let go of and having a baby was right at the top of that list. Once we decided to go for it, we thought it would be better if we tried sooner rather than later.'

'And it happened straight away?' Jess kept her tone light. Ella was already worried that hearing about the pregnancy was going to be too much and she didn't want her friend thinking she might be right.

'The second month.' Ella bit her lip. 'I wish with all my heart that it had been as easy as that for you.'

'We all have things that are difficult to deal with, and I wouldn't swap Riley for the chance to become a parent any other way. I might not have given birth to him, but I can see myself in so many of the things he says and does. The way he taps the side of his nose with his pencil when he's trying to work something out, the fact that he loves beans, but can't bear it if they touch anything else on his plate, and even the way he pronounces moustache in the same weird way I do. They're all things he's picked up from me. Hopefully, by the time your baby starts school, we'll have been allowed to adopt a second child and Riley will have a younger sibling who he can pass a lot of things on to as well. I grieved every time the IVF failed, but it also made me count my blessings every time that I already had Riley. I'm going to make the most of all the nappy changing, sleepless nights and weaning that I'll be getting involved with while we're fostering, so that I don't feel I've missed out on any stage of being a mum. But then, when it's right for Riley, we'll start the adoption process again.'

'Whoever that little boy or girl is they're going to be so lucky to have you as their mum.' Anna put an arm around Jess. 'You've been the best godmother to Kit and Merryn too.'

'You have and if you ever want to do some extra nappy changing or other baby stuff, I'll be more than grateful for your help! Who'd have thought when we first met that we'd go through so much together?' Ella raised her eyebrows. 'But you're right Jess, I think life takes you where you're supposed to go. I love being a health visitor, and going part time has meant I've been able to start the smallholding and run the workshops with Heather. I'd never have had the time to do that if I was still working as a midwife, and

I'd never have changed my job or dropped my hours if I hadn't been diagnosed with MS. I might not go as far as saying that I'm glad I have it, because that would be a lie, but I'm grateful for all the things I've been given the opportunity to do since my diagnosis.'

'You two are making me look bad.' Anna laughed. 'Because all I've said I'm grateful for is the fact that there's an untouched pistachio cake on the bottom shelf of the display cabinet, waiting for me to get the biggest slice.'

'Oh, no way! If I'm the only one not getting a baby of my own, I at least deserve the biggest slice of cake.' Jess dropped the perfect wink and looked at her two closest friends. The three of them had supported each other through so much over the last six years and she was so glad she had them in her life. Wherever the road took them next, she just hoped nothing would change their friendship, because it meant the world to her.

* * *

Making the arrangements for Darren's 'birthday party' had proved to be more stressful than they should have been. The second weekend of October was the closest weekend to Darren's birthday, which fell on the Monday, and Meg had made sure she kept it free. When she'd booked the Harbour Hotel in St Ives, it had been for the weekend afterwards, which she hadn't thought for a moment Tilly would want to choose for the party. It had probably been Meg's fault that it all got so tricky. When Tilly had asked her which Saturday she wanted the party to be on, she'd told her that it couldn't be the weekend after Darren's fiftieth as she and Johnnie would be away.

'What are you going away for? You could drive to St Ives and back in a day if you're so desperate to go there.' Tilly had made it sound like the strangest thing in the world for anyone to want to have a short break away, so close to home.

'I just thought it would be nice for us to have a bit of time together before the baby arrives.' If Meg could have taken the words back once she'd seen Tilly's face, she would have done. But it was too late.

'So it's a babymoon? That must be nice for you.' Tilly had said the right things, but her tone of voice and the expression on her face had told a different story. It wasn't long after that that she'd started making little digs about what a shame it was that they couldn't have her dad's birthday party when he would actually have been fifty. And questioning what the point of celebrating was when Darren would still only have been forty-nine. Johnnie had offered to contact the hotel to change the date of their weekend away, but for once Meg had stood firm. She'd loved Darren and nothing would change that, but it was time to prioritise the living. When Tilly had asked for the tenth time if she really wasn't going to move the date, it had taken all she had not to say that it didn't matter when they marked Darren's birthday – a day before, five days after, or not at all – because he could never turn fifty; he wasn't here any more.

In the end, Tilly had finally given up and agreed to hold the party the Saturday before her father's birthday. Meg had left the guest list to her daughter and it had grown much bigger than she'd ever expected. Tilly seemed to have invited people from Darren's past, who neither she nor Meg had spoken to since he'd died. She'd even dug out an old photograph of Darren on his stag do and made it her mission to track down every last person in the picture, as well as inviting as many people as possible from Darren and Meg's wedding. It was almost as though she was trying to prove a point to Johnnie about her parents' shared history. Meg hated the idea that Johnnie might feel hurt by Tilly's attempts to make their relationship look like a mere footnote in the story of her marriage to Darren. But his willingness to take it all in his stride meant it was easy for her to prioritise her daughter's needs, even though she knew she shouldn't. Giving in to Tilly was always easier than standing up to her, but it was no wonder that Tilly had lost respect for her mother somewhere along the line, because Meg had lost respect for herself too.

Thankfully Den and Kerry, who ran the bird sanctuary, along with Den's son, Oliver, had helped make the event as smooth as possible. Tilly had said she wanted to do something more permanent to mark her father's fiftieth, and Meg had talked through the options with Den.

'We could name one of the new enclosures in honour of Darren and Seth. I was thinking we could call it The Sawyers. Half of the other enclosures are only here because of the work Darren and Seth did, so it's the least we can do.' Den had made the suggestion when Meg had gone to the sanctuary to check just how big the event was getting under Tilly's management. She'd arranged for a hog roast in the field behind the main sanctuary building and she'd booked a band to perform on an open air stage she'd hired, which was risky given that predicting the weather was never easy. Especially in the autumn. Tilly had also requested a display with some of the birds of prey and she was planning a speech at the end of the day too.

With a guest list of eighty people, it was nothing like Meg had envisaged. She'd expected it to be Darren's closest family and friends, sharing some cake and reminiscences in the café at the bird sanctuary, talking about how much he and Seth had loved volunteering there. He'd have hated a big party like this and he'd rather have donated the money to the work Den and her family did. But this was for Tilly rather than him, and if it made her feel better, then Meg could live with it. The problem was, Meg wasn't entirely convinced it would make Tilly feel better. She seemed to have thrown herself into this party as a way of coping with the miscarriage, and going so over the top with everything was stopping her from really having to think about what had happened. Meg couldn't help worrying that once the party was over, reality would hit Tilly hard and send her crashing to the ground. The fallout from that was likely to hit all of them.

One thing about the stress of the build-up to the event was that it made the party itself seem like a breeze in comparison. Instead of worrying about things she couldn't control, like the weather, Meg was just glad that the day had finally arrived and that Tilly would have to stop adding extra ideas in and making passive aggressive comments about having to settle for a date she didn't really want. Even more surprisingly, for the first time in a long time, Tilly seemed to be more like her old self. She'd had sweatshirts made for her and Meg, with a picture of the two of them on the front, with Darren and Seth, taken on the last family holiday they'd had before the accident. Johnnie had refused Meg's offer to come along to the party, insisting that this was Darren's day. It was exactly what Tilly would have said too and Meg loved him even more for not just understanding, but always trying to make her life that bit easier. But it made her chest ache to think of Johnnie being side-lined so easily. He was a part of the family now too and the person Meg most wanted to have around. Tilly was going to have to accept that soon, but maybe today wasn't the day to push it.

'Thank you so much for all of this.' Meg caught up with Den, just after the band started their set. There was no one dancing yet, but the hog roast seemed to be going down well with the guests. Although not quite as well as the cider that Oliver was serving from a makeshift bar in one corner of the field, which some of Darren's friends from the building trade had erected the week before. It was one of those bright and unseasonably warm autumn days when you could easily have believed it was still mid-summer.

'It's been lovely to be able to do this for Darren. He was such a big supporter of the sanctuary when I was trying to get it up and running. He was a great guy.' Den gave Meg a level look. 'Although you've definitely got a type. Johnnie's been brilliant too. I had to call him out here, the week before last, to have a look at a couple of cats that had been dropped off to us, but he wouldn't let me pay him anything.'

'I've been really lucky. After being with Darren, I didn't think anyone could ever come close, but somehow I've ended up with the two most amazing men I've ever met.'

'You deserve all the luck in the world.' Den pushed her sunglasses up to hold her fringe away from her face, and pulled out her phone. 'When Johnnie wouldn't take anything for his time, I wanted to do something for you both instead, so I've started making this.'

The picture on Den's phone was of a delicate crocheted blanket, edged with tiny, raised flowers that looked as if they must have taken hours to create. Meg was so touched that someone as busy as Den had taken the time to make this for the baby. 'Oh my goodness, it's so beautiful.'

'I love doing it and I don't think I've ever seen anyone as excited to be having a baby as Johnnie is.' Den smiled again, and Meg was just about to answer, when Ed shot past her, breaking into a run.

'Where's the fire?' She was laughing as she called out to him, but when she saw the look on his face as he turned back towards her, the smile slid off her face. 'What's wrong?'

'It's Tilly, I'm not sure what the problem is, but she called me saying she's up by the gift shop and she was crying so much I could hardly hear her.'

'I'm coming with you.' Meg didn't even wait for a response from

Ed and all she could do was hold up a hand in acknowledgement as Den called after them, 'Let me know if I can do anything to help.'

As kind as Den's offer was, the likelihood was that no one could help. The emotion of the day had probably just got too much for Tilly. As Meg and Ed hurried towards the gift shop, she felt a frisson of guilt that she hadn't experienced a similar wave of emotion yet. She didn't have time to think about all of that right now, though, because her daughter needed her.

* * *

Tilly was sitting on the wall outside the gift shop and café. Her face was pale and tear-stained when she looked up, as Ed and Meg approached.

'I'm bleeding.'

'Have you hurt yourself?' Even as Meg said the words, she realised what Tilly meant. 'Oh sweetheart, I'm sorry.'

It had only been three months since Tilly's miscarriage, so she can't have been very far along this time, but Meg knew that wouldn't make things any easier.

'Maybe we should have waited a bit longer.' Ed's tone was gentle and he tried to reach out for Tilly's hand, but she yanked it away from him.

'When it didn't work last month, you said it was because it was too soon and that we should wait but it's been three months now, so how do you explain it this time?' Tilly sounded like she was blaming Ed, and Meg had to dig her fingernails into the palms of her hands to stop herself from interfering. Her daughter hadn't lost another baby, she hadn't even been pregnant this time, but she'd clearly expected to be and wasn't coping well with the fact that she wasn't.

'Your body might just need a bit longer, baby, that's all. I think we should stop trying for a while and wait until you've had a chance to fully recover.' Ed was still speaking softly and Meg could see he was doing his best not to make things worse, but Tilly seemed determined to direct her anger at him.

'I don't want to wait and if you'd let me test yesterday, I could at least have had a drink to get through today.'

'And if you had been pregnant, it might have been too early for the test to show that up. All I've been asking you to do is to slow down a bit and not put yourself under so much pressure.' Ed was still trying to take hold of her hand, but Tilly flinched every time he got close. 'There's no rush and the most important thing is that you're as strong as you can be before we try again.'

'So this is all my fault!' Tilly jumped off the wall, her eyes flashing as she looked at Ed.

'That's not what he's saying at all, Tilly.' Meg took a step towards her daughter. 'You need to let yourself recover from the miscarriage, physically and emotionally. Rushing ahead will just make things even worse.'

'Like you know one single, fucking thing about what this feels like for me.' Tilly virtually spat the words at Meg, making her recoil. In all the petty arguments and bigger rows the two of them had ever had, Tilly had never once sworn at her like that before. But the venom in her eyes was even harder to take.

'I'm not trying to say I understand, but—'

'Good, because you've got no fucking idea.' Every time she directed the word at Meg it was like a punch in the gut.

'Tilly, don't speak to your mum like that, she's only trying to help and she's only saying exactly what the doctors have too.'

'Oh yeah, because I can't upset the pregnant woman, can I? She didn't even want a baby so why the hell is she still pregnant? Haven't I been through enough shit in my life?'

'Stop it!' The force of the words that had come out of Meg's mouth took her by surprise, but something had finally snapped. 'Do you think you're the only person who's had a tough time? I lost your dad and Seth too, and it crushed me. But I kept getting up, every single day, and pushing the pain down to a point where I could be there for you. I've put you first for the last ten years, but it can't carry on. You've got to stop thinking that the whole world revolves around you and that you're the only person hurting. I tried my best for you, but I don't know what to do any more. I need to look after myself and the baby now. It breaks my heart that you don't get to do that for your baby too, but punishing me isn't going to change that.'

'So that's it, is it? You're done with caring about me and I have to pretend I'm okay with watching you getting closer and closer to having a baby, when I don't know if I'll ever get one? You're making out that I'm so bloody demanding, but I haven't had my dad or my brother since I was thirteen years old, and all I want is a family of my own.'

'Why can't you see that you've already got one?' Meg wrapped her arms protectively around her bump as she spoke. She'd tried talking to Tilly calmly and for once in their lives, she'd even tried giving her a few home truths, but it was as if her daughter hadn't even heard her. Meg had expected her to be shocked that her mother was finally standing up for herself, but she'd barely seemed to notice. It was awful to feel like her daughter had turned into a complete stranger, but she'd never seen her like this before.

'Have I? You've got another family now and in a couple of months you'll have another daughter too. What have I got left, if I don't have a baby of my own?'

'You've got me.' Ed reached out to Tilly again and she finally allowed him to take her into his arms. It was almost impossible now for Meg to remember why she'd ever had doubts about Ed, because if he could stand by Tilly, when she was acting the way she was, he must love her unconditionally, just like Meg did. Although, right now, even she was finding that hard to do.

'I'll ring you later.' Meg silently mouthed the words to Ed, as he looked across at her, still holding Tilly in his arms. She had to get back to the party, before anyone else came looking for them, and pretend that everything was okay. But all she wanted was to get home to Johnnie and for him to tell her that somehow, against all the odds, everything would still work out okay in the end.

22

Ed had ended up ringing Meg and apologising for Tilly's behaviour as if he was the one who was responsible for it, rather than her.

'I don't know what's wrong with her.' He'd sounded exhausted and his voice was strained, although Meg had a feeling he was having to make the whispered phone call while he could. 'It's like ever since she lost the baby, a whole tsunami of emotion has come to the surface. And every month that's gone past, when she hasn't got pregnant again, has made it worse and worse. When I met her, it seemed like she'd learned to live with losing her dad and Seth, but, just lately, it's like it only happened yesterday. She really needs to go back in to counselling, but every time I suggest it, she flies off the handle.'

'Don't give up on her, will you Ed?' Meg couldn't bear the thought that Tilly might push away someone who loved her as much as Ed clearly did. Her daughter needed him more than ever right now, but it would take someone incredible to stick by her side through all of this.

'I'm not going anywhere. I know the girl I fell in love with is still in there somewhere and I want a baby every bit as much as she does. I just don't think now is the right time. I want her to be okay first and not just physically, because if she did end up having another miscarriage...' Ed couldn't finish the sentence, but Meg knew exactly what he was saying. Tilly seemed to think a baby would fix everything, but he was right about the fact that there were other things that needed sorting first.

'I'll have a chat with the girls at the unit and see if any of them can suggest something that might help, but I think if I try to talk to Tilly right now, it's just going to inflame things.' Meg had already picked up the phone to call her daughter a dozen times, but she'd put it down again every time. Meg didn't want to make things worse, but there was more to it than that. She was angry and hurt too, partly about the way Tilly was treating her and Johnnie, but more for the way she was treating her baby sister, before she was even born.

'Deep down she knows how lucky she is to have you; she just can't seem to see it at the moment. But I'm sure she'll apologise in the end.' Ed was such a kind man and, when Meg had told Den how lucky she'd been to have two amazing men in her life, she'd done him a disservice. The universe might never be able to redress the balance, after everything she and Tilly had lost, but sending Johnnie and Ed into their lives was the closest it could ever have hoped to come.

'I hope she realises how lucky she is to have you too.'

'At the moment, I don't think she can even remember why we're together, but I know she loves me and I've got to believe that we can get back to where we were.' Ed sounded so hopeless and all Meg wanted to do was give him a hug.

'If there's anything I can do, you know where I am.'

'Thanks, Meg, that means a lot. I've got to go now; I told Tilly I needed to make a call to my boss to get a few days off work, but if she thinks we're ganging up on her...' For the second time, Ed couldn't finish his sentence, but he didn't have to. Meg could picture the scene all too well. She needed to back off and let Tilly come to her, even if the waiting was tearing her apart.

* * *

Johnnie was making a Thai green curry; the same meal he'd made for Meg the first time he'd ever cooked for her. Usually, just the smell of it cooking made her mouth water and he'd tease her, when she asked how long it would be until dinner was ready, by telling her she'd have to wait at least another two hours. Even now, her stomach was still playing along, rumbling audibly as the aroma filled the air, but she'd barely been able to face food since the one-sided row with Tilly.

'Right, I'm starting to get really worried now Meg.' Johnnie sat down next to her on the sofa. 'You haven't once asked me when dinner is ready. There's a completely untouched tub of cookie dough ice-cream in the fridge, most of your lunch has been scraped into the bin, and I saw you giving Cagney and Lacey your breakfast this morning, when you thought I wasn't looking. I'd be fine if that was just a comment on my admittedly limited culinary skills, but you've barely eaten a thing for the last three days and, every time I look at you, you look like you're about to burst into tears. I'm really worried about you, darling.'

'Are you saying I'm normally so greedy that any indication that I'm eating less has to be a sign of doom?' It was the conversation Meg had been trying to avoid, ever since she'd come home from the owl sanctuary, and she was desperately trying to deflect from the subject by making a joke of it.

When she'd finally got home from Darren's party, she'd needed a hug from Johnnie more than she ever had before. But she hadn't breathed a word to him about what had happened with Tilly. He'd been so understanding of how Tilly could sometimes behave, ever since he'd come into their lives, but when her daughter had said the things she had about their baby, his patience had finally run out. It was understandable, except now she was worried that if she told him about Tilly's latest outburst, his attitude towards Tilly might change forever. Meg had already lost so much and she couldn't bear the thought of there being an irreparable rift within the family she had left. Meg loved Tilly unconditionally and she always would, even when it was hard to like her. She couldn't expect Johnnie to feel the same, though. He was always on Meg's side, but the last thing she wanted was for the people she loved most in the world to end up at war.

'Meg, I know you and this isn't normal; I can't let you just make a joke about this. You can tell me anything, sweetheart, and I promise I'll do everything I can to help. I love you so much, but this is scaring me.'

'It's Tilly.' She looked at him as she spoke. The way he reacted to the first two words she'd said would dictate how much more she told him.

'Is she okay?' He hadn't sighed, or pulled a face, and there was genuine concern in his eyes.

'She's struggling.' Meg blinked a few times in quick succession, determined not to cry. 'She seems determined to try again for a baby, even though it's obvious she's not emotionally ready. It didn't work this month and now she's convinced herself that it's never going to happen.'

'How's Ed coping with it?'

'He can't get through to her either. She thought she was pregnant and, when she found out she wasn't, she lashed out at both of us.' Meg swallowed, but she had to tell him the rest. 'It was like she really hated me. I spoke to Ed afterwards and he was convinced she'd eventually apologise, probably by text knowing Tilly, but there's been nothing. I'm worried that she might be spiralling, and Ed said it's like all the hurt from when we lost Darren and Seth has come back to the surface. But I've got no idea how to help her.'

'I can't pretend to understand and I'd be lying if I said it doesn't make me want to go round there and try to talk some sense into her, when I see what this is doing to you.' Johnnie looked up at the ceiling and let out a long breath. 'But I know Tilly's had a really hard time and that, because you're the best mother anyone could ever want, all you're thinking about is helping her to get through this. You can't do that if you don't look after yourself. I know I probably sound like a broken record, but I'll never forgive myself if anything happens to you or the baby.'

'I am trying.'

'I don't think you can do this by yourself. Maybe it's time to talk to someone who can help you to work things out with Tilly.'

'I think you're right.' Meg looked up at Johnnie and put a hand on his cheek. She and Ed hadn't been able to persuade Tilly to get the professional help she clearly needed yet, but maybe it was time for Meg to go back to see Heather. Even though she'd hoped she'd never feel the need to see her again.

* * *

Meg had cut down her hours at work after the dizzy spell she'd had at the surgery, but she didn't want to just sit at home and stare at the wall all day worrying about Tilly. There were more reception staff at the surgery, to provide cover, so she'd decided to just keep working two days a week at the unit and stop working at the surgery altogether. It also felt like the perfect place to be if there were any concerns about her pregnancy. She was surrounded by people who didn't just know everything there was to know about babies, but who also cared about her too. Which meant it probably shouldn't have been a surprise when Jess picked up on the fact that Meg wasn't her usual self, on her first shift back after Darren's birthday party.

'Do you know when our next appointment is?' Jess put a cup of tea on the reception desk, as she spoke. 'I made you this, by the way; you looked as though you could do with it. Don't worry, it's decaf.'

'Thank you so much.' Meg picked up her phone and checked the calendar app. 'I've got my thirty-four week check with you on Tuesday and I'm due to go and see the consultant the week after that.'

'I'd like to check your blood pressure and run another blood test before then, if that's okay?' Jess smiled, but the note of concern in her voice had been all too evident.

'I've been checking my blood pressure at home and it's been okay.'

'But you're not, are you?'

'I'm just a bit tired that's all.' Meg had been finding it hard to sleep, even before Tilly had stopped speaking to her; now it was almost impossible. But there was no fooling Jess.

'It's not just that. You're really pale, and one thing everyone says about having you on reception is that they feel put at ease because you're always so smiley. I've never seen you like this before. It's as if someone has turned down the dimmer switch. So I want to make sure you aren't anaemic or something. I don't want to wait another week, just in case.'

'Tilly's not speaking to me.' Meg blurted the words out. 'It's really hard, but I'm sorry if it's affecting my work. I probably shouldn't be here when I'm feeling like this, but I can't bear the thought of being stuck at home, thinking about it over and over again.'

'Oh Meg, I didn't mean that; of course you should be here and you're doing a fab job as always. We're just worried about you, that's all.' Jess was around the desk in a flash, giving Meg one of her famous hugs. 'And I'm so sorry about Tilly; that must be really hard for you.'

'We've had hard times before – the hardest – but I've always been able to find a way to help her. Even when I had to break the news to her about Darren and Seth, I still managed to find a way to help her through it. This time, I can't even seem to get close enough to try, and I've got no idea what to do.' Meg was beginning to think she'd never get through another day again without crying, but she'd been there before and things had changed eventually. She had to believe they would this time too. But what made it harder was that, even though Meg knew Tilly was spiralling, she was struggling to forgive her for the things she'd said. Even if Tilly apologised, Meg wasn't sure she could believe it this time. Not when her words had proven so empty in the past.

'Did something happen before she stopped talking to you?' Jess stepped back and when Meg didn't reply immediately, she shook her head again. 'Sorry, you don't have to tell me if you don't want to.'

'No, I do.' Meg pressed her lips together, wondering where to start, but there was no sugar coating it. 'Things got really difficult after Tilly's miscarriage and she said some things that were pretty hard to hear, about it being me who should have lost the baby. But she was devastated and her hormones were all over the place. After that, it was like she became obsessed with getting pregnant again. She seems to think it's her only chance of a family now, because as far as she's concerned I'm moving on with Johnnie and the baby, and forgetting all about her. It's not true, but I can't make her see that.'

'Sometimes the grief after a miscarriage can be so overwhelming that people act in a way you'd never have believed they could, but I can't even imagine how hard that was for you to hear. I doubt very much she really meant anything she said, though.'

'Tilly apologised, and I really hoped she meant it. But then at the party for Darren's fiftieth, her period started. She'd convinced herself that she was pregnant again and, when she realised she wasn't, all the things she really felt came out. She told me I had no right to even speak to her about it, that I didn't understand anything about the possibility of not being able to have a baby, and that she didn't want me around. The look in her eyes... I don't think I'll ever be able to get it out of my mind.'

'That must have been so awful and there's no excuse for her treating you like that, but do you think losing the baby might have triggered other memories for Tilly?' Jess took a deep breath. 'When the IVF failed, it brought back so much for me. Losing Mum, and then Dad disappearing from my life, my marriage breaking up and everything that happened with Teddy. All that stuff was bubbling just below the surface and if I hadn't had the infertility support group to turn to, and my sessions with Heather, I think I'd have been lashing out at everyone too. I couldn't have carried on with this job, because I'd have convinced myself that I was the only person alive who'd had to go through that much. I felt all of those emotions, even though I already had Riley. If Tilly has managed to convince herself that the miscarriage and endometriosis mean she won't be able to have a baby, she'll be feeling like that too. Especially if she thinks you're moving on without her. She really needs to speak to someone else who understands at least part of what she's going through.'

'I think so too and so does Ed, but she's refusing to go back to counselling.'

'Do you think there's any way she might be willing to come to the infertility group? Some of the other members have been diagnosed with endometriosis and sadly we've got more than our share of ladies who've dealt with baby loss, at all stages of pregnancy.'

'She might, but she definitely won't if I'm the one who suggests it. I don't think she's even reading my messages any more.' Meg would have done almost anything if she thought it would help her daughter. As much as it had hurt when Tilly had lashed out, the place of pain her words had come from must have been unbearable.

'We've got our fostering panel next week, but I should have time before then to try and speak to Tilly, if you think that would help? Do you think Ed would be willing to be in on it? Maybe we could arrange to "accidentally" bump into each other? She knows I've heard about her miscarriage and we spoke about the endometriosis when I took you to meet her at the hospital. So, it wouldn't seem odd for me to ask how she's doing if we bumped into each other. If she opens up, even a tiny bit, I could suggest she comes along to the support group.'

'That might just work and I'm sure Ed would be willing to try.' The tension in Meg's spine eased just a fraction, but she was almost scared to pin too much hope on Jess's plan, in case it didn't work out. The fact that her friend wanted to help when she had so many things of her own to deal with made Meg's eyes sting. Jess's kindness in the midst of this awful situation had touched her more than she could ever express. 'Your support means the world to me, especially with everything you've got going on. Thank you so much.'

'It's nothing, but you know I'll do whatever I can to help. Let's get you checked over and then you can try and get in touch with Ed. If we can get Tilly to the group, and she hears from the others how much they've benefitted from counselling, she might eventually be willing to go back to that too. But first things first, we need to look after you.'

Jess's words mirrored Johnnie's pleas for Meg to start looking after herself, and she knew she had to do it, for her unborn baby, if not herself. It was time to step back from the situation with Tilly for a while and let other people see if they could get through to her. But Meg was going to need help doing that and it was time to make the phone call she'd been putting off for far too long.

23

Johnnie had taken to leaving Cagney and Lacey behind on the days when Meg would usually have been at the surgery. They were affectionate dogs and had become Meg's shadow since she'd been living full time at Johnnie's. Cagney, the smaller of the two, would rest her head on Meg's thigh at every given opportunity. Even the slobber the dog left behind was a small price to pay for the affection she so freely gave. Having the dogs with her made Meg go out for a walk every day too and take advantage of the bright autumn days that made it impossible to believe winter wasn't too far away.

Most days, Meg and the dogs would head down the hill from Johnnie's place to the harbour just below. Cagney and Lacey liked nothing better than to trot along the beach, checking whether anything that might have been dropped or washed up would make a little impromptu snack. They didn't mind if it was the remnants of someone's leftover lunch, or half a fish dropped by a passing seagull, because they swallowed what they found so quickly that nothing touched the sides anyway.

Today, Meg had a different destination in mind. She'd taken the dogs along the track behind Johnnie's house that led down towards the other side of Port Agnes, and eventually on to the cemetery at St Jude's.

Meg hadn't been to see Darren and Seth since the fiftieth birthday celebrations. It was ridiculous, given that they'd been gone ten years, but she had no idea how to tell them what had happened between her and Tilly. Talking to them out loud when she visited their grave, was a habit she hadn't even tried to break. It had helped her to process lots of things over the years, almost like someone repeating her own words back to her and allowing her to hear them from a different perspective. But she hadn't wanted to say the things Tilly had said to her out loud, because she didn't even want to think about them, let alone to hear them again. It hurt too much.

The phone call she'd made to her therapist, and the follow up session they'd had to talk things through had both really helped. The advice Heather had given her had echoed much of what Johnnie and Jess had already said, but she'd also given Meg some strategies to help her to start taking more care of herself. One of those things was to acknowledge how much Tilly had hurt her and to allow herself to really feel that, instead of trying to bury it under the concern she had for her daughter. Heather had helped Meg to see that she sometimes used her tendency to try and fix everyone else's problems as a way to ignore her own. When she'd admitted to Heather that she hadn't felt able to visit the boys' graves, she'd suggested it might help if she did. That perhaps what she needed now was to tell Darren and Seth, and let the silence allow her to work out how she really felt about it all.

'I'm sorry I've left things so long.' The English lavender bush that Meg had planted behind the plaque marking the boys' resting place had got bigger every year, but now autumn was well underway it needed pruning. The stalks which had still been heavy with flowers when Meg had last visited in September, had turned brown. And the bees that had buzzed back and forth, like holiday-makers at an all-you-can-eat buffet, were long gone too.

'These last couple of months have been hard, but I can't believe the baby will be here by the end of next month. Given how often she kicks now, I think she's trying to fight her way out already.' Meg smiled. The baby had been moving so much the night before, that Johnnie had been able to feel the movements against his back as they lay in bed. When she'd first gone to see Darren and Seth after discovering she was pregnant, it had felt weird to mention the baby. But they wouldn't have wanted her to mourn their passing forever and she was sure they'd have approved of Johnnie. If only she could have been as sure that Tilly would eventually come to terms with her new life, she might finally stand the chance of getting a proper night's sleep again.

'I hope Tilly is talking to me by the time I have the baby, because this little one is going to need her big sister.' Meg bent down and pulled up some weeds that were growing next to the lavender bush. It was getting much harder to do even simple tasks like that, now that her bump was as big as it was. 'She's really upset with me and I don't know what to do to help her, but I think she's still missing you both more than even she realises.'

As Heather had predicted, silence filled the air; other than the faint sound of a distant helicopter there was nothing. Even though Meg was by no means certain she believed in an afterlife, deep down she'd hoped that somehow, somewhere, Darren might send her a sign of what she could do to help their daughter. Except, this time, there wasn't even a shaft of light to acknowledge her presence, but maybe that was the point.

'I can't fix this, can I? Tilly needs to find a way of fixing it herself.' Meg had been trying so hard to find a solution, but the truth was, unless Tilly wanted one, nothing her mother suggested was going to help. For Meg's own sanity she had to stop trying, at least for now.

* * *

Madeline had been the social worker who'd supported Jess when she'd first fostered Teddy. She was also one of Dexter's best friends. But when her number flashed up on Jess's phone the day before they were due to go to the fostering panel, Jess went straight into panic mode. Even if something had come up on their assessment at the last minute, which meant they couldn't go forward for consideration, it wouldn't be Madeline who called to give them the news. She'd had nothing to do with their assessment, except for providing a reference about Jess's care for Teddy and the way she had handled it when he'd been adopted. Jess was still in touch with his adoptive parents, and she took Riley to meet up with them and Teddy every two or three months. It was time she treasured, and her new social worker had told her that the way she'd coped with Teddy's adoption had been a huge point in her favour, when it came to demonstrating the skills she and Dexter would need as parent and child foster carers. All of which meant that she had no real reason to think Madeline's call would be bad news, but Jess still couldn't stop her mind from automatically going there.

'Hi Madeline, what's up?' Jess held her breath as Madeline seemed to be finishing a conversation with someone who must have been in the room with her.

'Sorry, I was just trying to clarify something with Kelly and I was half expecting to have to leave you a message. I thought you'd be at work. Is Dex there with you?' Madeline's tone was giving nothing away, but the fact that she'd been chatting with their new social worker sent a shiver up Jess's spine. Kelly was supposed to be supporting them at the panel tomorrow, but if she needed to speak to Madeline about Jess and Dexter, that surely didn't bode well. Especially as Madeline had felt the need to check if Dexter was around. She clearly knew Jess was going to need his support if she was about to hear bad news.

'Dexter is at football with Riley. We're taking him out for an early dinner when they get back, then dropping him to his grandparents' house for a sleepover. We wanted tomorrow to be as stress free for everyone as possible, especially as we're the first applicants before panel. Unless you know something we don't?' Jess had barely paused for breath, not wanting to give Madeline the chance to speak first. She needed the social worker to know how much this meant to them.

'Oh God, Jess, I'm sorry, I didn't mean to make you panic. I only asked if Dex was there because there's something I need to ask you and you're going to want to discuss it with one another before you decide. Maybe I should call back later, after you've dropped Riley off?'

'No!' The fervour of Jess's response took even her by surprise, but there was no way she could wait until later to find out what all of this was about.

'Right, well, it's a bit of a weird one and it's going to be a lot to think about, so all I ask is that you consider it.' Madeline cleared her throat. 'We've been informed by social services in Lambeth that Riley's biological dad has fathered another child. The baby's mother, Candice, is in a similar situation to the one that Riley's biological mother was in when she got pregnant. Candice has been through a drug addiction programme, but she's managed to stay clean since she started there just after she found out she was pregnant. At first, she was talking about giving the baby up for adoption, but in the last couple of months of her pregnancy she started wondering whether that really was what she wanted, and whether she could raise the baby herself. She's only eighteen and sadly she's got no family support, because she grew up in care herself. She was in supported lodgings until she gave birth, but she can't go back to the placement she was in before with the baby. Of course, Connor doesn't want to know. Evidently he's still trying to make it as a rock star.'

Madeline's tone when she spoke about Riley's biological dad, Connor, was as derisive as he deserved it to be. Candice was barely more than a child and Connor must be in his mid-thirties by now. Still chasing the dream of being a rock star and still abandoning the children he'd fathered all too easily. He really was a piece of work. He'd walked away from his commitment to Riley and now history was repeating itself, but Jess could only think of one possible reason why that could have anything to do with her and Dexter. 'Poor girl; it sounds like nothing's changed with Connor. She's better off without him. I don't understand what it's got to do with us, though, unless you think Riley should have contact with the baby?'

'Do you think he should?' Madeline had never pulled any punches when it came to asking difficult questions and it seemed nothing had changed on that front either.

'I don't know, I...' Jess hesitated for a moment, but the memories of how often she'd wished she had a sibling, when she'd been in care, were already flooding back. 'Yes, I do.'

'So do I and so does Candice's social worker, Jamie. When he started looking into her and Connor's backgrounds, to find out whether there might be any support for Candice, he discovered that you and Dex had adopted Riley. He got in touch with the team here to ask more and when he found out you were being assessed as parent and child foster carers, I think he thought all his prayers had been answered.' Madeline's words were coming out in a rush and Jess was struggling to process what she was saying, but then Madeline said something that left her in no doubt. 'We want to know if you'd consider taking Candice and her baby as your first placement.'

For a moment Jess was lost for words. Madeline was offering her what she'd wanted for so long, the chance to welcome a baby into their home. But it wasn't that simple, and her mind was already working overtime. There was someone else to consider, someone she would always put first. 'Won't that be difficult for Riley, if he gets to know his sister and then they leave?'

'If things work out and Candice is able to keep the baby, it would be great if she's already built a relationship with you and Dex. That way, the contact between Riley and his little sister can continue, even when they move out to independence. And if things don't work out, you'll be able to build a relationship with the baby's adoptive parents – just like you did with Teddy's – which will also help to establish contact between Riley and his sister later on. Candice has got no real ties to the area she lives in now and Connor has already moved on and stopped all contact with her. So staying with you seems like it could be a really good fit for both her and the baby. The big question is whether it's something you and Dex can envisage taking on. I know it's a lot to ask.'

'What's the baby's name?' It probably wasn't the question that Madeline was expecting, but if Riley had a little sister out there – whatever she and Dexter decided – Jess wanted to know as much about her as possible.

'Candice hasn't decided yet, as the baby was only born last night. She was nearly three weeks early, but all the signs so far are that she's healthy.'

'That's good news.' Jess glanced across at a picture of Riley on the windowsill. Her little boy had a newborn sister out there somewhere and now she and Dexter had the chance to help him get to know her. How could she possibly say no? It should have been easy, but then the image of another baby suddenly swam in front of her eyes. Handing Teddy over to his new family had been the hardest thing she'd ever done, but the only pain Jess had had to bear back then was her own. If Riley's sister was eventually adopted by someone else, there was a chance she'd disappear from Riley's life too. This wasn't just about her and Dexter. If they decided to do this, they'd need to find a way of explaining things to Riley and allowing him to build a relationship with his sister, knowing her stay would only ever be temporary. It seemed like an impossible thing to ask of a little boy of eight, when Jess wasn't even sure she could do it herself. 'I understand why it's important that Riley gets to know his sister, but I still can't help thinking this could be damaging for him.'

'As long as we can be sure that contact is in the best interests of a child, it can be really important in helping them to develop their identity, but you'll need support in how to manage this with Riley and that's part of the reason why you and Dex need to consider this very carefully. But, if it's managed well, it could be a really positive memory for Riley, of sharing this time with his sister, and he can be part of the process of getting to know Candice or the baby's adoptive parents too. It's much more likely to give him and his sister a lasting bond than if they don't spend this time together."

'It's a lot to think about.' Jess's thoughts were already veering all over the place, but the bottom line was this had to be right for Riley.

'I know and I'm sorry to land this all on you right before you go to panel, but Candice and the baby are due to be released from hospital some time tomorrow. Jamie has arranged a temporary placement for them, but I'd be lying if I said you weren't his Plan A for after that.' Madeline breathed out. 'Why don't you and Dex call me back when you've had a chance to have a chat? Any time, it doesn't matter how late; I won't be turning off my phone.'

'Thanks Madeline. One of us will give you a ring later.' Ending the call, all Jess could do was stare at the door and wait for Dexter to get home. It was a huge decision, with Riley right at the centre of it, but Jess was already picturing his little sister's face. The thought of welcoming her into their lives, albeit temporarily, had the potential to be the greatest gift they could ever give their son, but it was also the most terrifying prospect Jess had faced in a long time.

* * *

Jess almost pounced on Dexter as soon as he walked through the door and she had to stop herself from immediately blurting everything out in front of Riley.

'Shall I put the Disney channel on for you for a bit, sweetheart? I've got some popcorn and a glass of milk for you too.' Jess ruffled her son's hair and Dexter gave her a quizzical look. She was usually the one insisting that Riley didn't have a snack this close to dinner, in the hope that he might actually eat what was on his plate, so it was no wonder Dexter looked confused. But she had to do something to keep Riley occupied while she explained everything to her husband. Ten minutes later, and with Riley still deeply engrossed in watching TV, Jess had managed to recount everything Madeline had said. It was almost a relief that Dexter was looking every bit as shocked as she felt.

'Do you think it's a good idea for Riley to get close to his sister and then for her to move on? I know the social worker says Candice is looking for support, but what if she stops us seeing the baby once she's left? That could really hurt Riley.'

'It could, but there are ways of dealing with that and I think it's important that he knows he's got a sister.' Dexter glanced over at their son and then back at Jess. 'But if they're suggesting this, I think there's a good chance they're expecting the baby to move to adoption at some point. Candice is only eighteen and the success rate for parent and child placements at her age is quite low, even without some of the complicating factors she has. I always tried to see the good side in Connor and felt almost sorry for him at times, because he's obviously got his own demons, but my sympathies run out when I think about the trail of destruction he's leaving in his wake. Candice is eighteen for goodness' sake. I bet he sold her the dream too, groomed her by telling her they could make it big together, like he did with Chloe. Now there's another child at the centre of this, well two if you count Candice, because God knows what age she was when all of this started.'

'I know, my heart breaks for her, especially after what Madeline said about Candice having grown up in care too. I know how vulnerable that can make you.' Jess sighed. The scars from her time in care had healed a lot since Dexter and Riley had come into her life, and after she'd reconciled with her father, but it didn't take much to peel back the protective layers and feel the pain again as if it was still fresh. 'If the baby does end up getting adopted, will the new parents *have* to let Riley have contact with his sister, or could they refuse? I just can't bear the thought of him being given this, and then it being taken away again.'

'The courts will probably decide it's in the baby's and Riley's best interests to retain contact if they've built up a relationship while she's with us. And any adopter on the waiting list, who's matched with a baby, is likely to be willing to jump through whatever hoops they're presented with. But the courts might not decide that contact is in the best interests of the children, if we aren't the ones who support Candice and the baby. Especially if Candice is against it, or the baby ends up with other carers who think it might affect the stability of her placement. That shouldn't be our deciding factor, though. I think Riley will cope whatever we choose to do, but I'm more worried about you. You've been through more than enough already, and you don't owe it to anyone to take this on if you don't think it's right for you.'

'I want to do it.' Jess was suddenly more certain than she'd been of almost anything. This baby was her son's little sister and the desire to do the best they could for her, for as long as they could, was almost primal. Candice and the baby had no one, but Jess and Dexter could give them some stability and help them move forward to a more positive future – whatever that might look like. Jess already knew she'd get far too attached to the baby, but as long as the adopters were as good for her as Teddy's had been, she also knew she'd find a way of coping. With Teddy, there'd always been a shred of hope that she might be allowed to keep him, but she knew for certain this time that wouldn't be the case. There were thousands of adopters on the waiting list dreaming of being matched with a baby, and the certainty of knowing this would only ever be temporary was strangely comforting. And, as long as the panel approved them, they'd be welcoming Riley's baby sister and her mother into the house before the end of the month.

24

Meg and the rest of the team had been waiting anxiously on the day of Jess's fostering panel to hear the outcome. When she'd called to let Anna know that not only had they been approved by the panel, but they'd also be starting their first placement, Meg hadn't thought she could respect Jess any more than she already did. But when she heard that she and Dexter would be caring for Riley's baby sister and her mother, she realised she'd been wrong. It had clearly been a whirlwind for Jess and when she'd texted Meg to apologise for not having had the chance to speak to Tilly yet, she'd responded by telling her not to worry and that she completely understood. Meg could hardly expect her friend to take on her problems in the midst of all of this, so it was going to be down to her to keep trying to repair the relationship with her daughter.

✉ Message to Tilly

I love you Tils, but I don't know how to help you and, you're right, I don't know what it feels like to have endometriosis, or to lose a baby. But there are other people who do and there's a great support group in Port

Agnes that Jess set up. I think it might really help. I understand if you
can't face talking to me right now, but please talk to someone. It's
Seth's birthday next week and I know you had lots of ideas for celebrating his twenty-fifth. I'm hoping we can spend a bit of time together
that day, because you and I are the only people in the world who miss
him as much as we do. Look after yourself and I'm here if you need
me xxxx

Meg had tried her version of tough love and backing off to take
care of herself and the baby, but whoever it was who'd coined the
phrase that *you're only as happy as your unhappiest child* had been
spot on. All the taking care of herself in the world wouldn't do
anything for Meg's wellbeing, unless she knew Tilly was okay too.
Every time her phone pinged, she'd get a surge of hope that it was a
reply from Tilly, but it never was. She did get an email from Ed,
though, and the first thing she'd done was to show it to Johnnie.

✉ Email from ed.sommers@bainsvilleholdings.co.uk
Hey Meg,
Hope you, Johnnie and the bump are all doing okay. Tilly showed me
your message and I told her I thought the group was a great idea, but
her reaction was about the same as it's been to everything since the
miscarriage. I'm still hoping she might change her mind, but sadly I
don't think you'll get a response. She accused me of taking your side
and, when I tried telling her we were both on her side, it just seemed to
make things worse. That's why I'm emailing you from work, instead of
texting, because she's started going through my phone.
I'm really sorry and I wish I could get through to her. All she seems to do
right now is spend hours on the internet, looking up stuff that makes her
even more paranoid and now she's booked a private scan to see what's
happening with the endometriosis. I really hope they can give her some
reassurance, because I don't know what will happen if it's bad news.

The trouble is, even if it's good news, there's no way she's in the right state of mind to try for a baby at the moment.

I'm sorry to lay all this on you, but I don't know who else to talk to. I'm just hoping that when we get the scan results, they'll advise her to get some support too and maybe she'll finally listen. If she doesn't, I'm going to make an appointment at the surgery and see if they can suggest anything that might help. I know they can't breach confidentiality, but I'm going to find a way of getting through to her, I promise. It just might take a bit more time.

Take care and I'll be in touch again when there's any news.

Ed

'Do you think I should try going over and speaking to her, face to face?' Meg looked at Johnnie as he handed her phone back after reading Ed's email, but he was already shaking his head.

'I know this is really tough, sweetheart, but I think you've got to wait it out and see what happens when Tilly has been for the scan. You've planted the seed, telling her about the group, and you've made it clear you're here for her whenever she's ready, but she just isn't yet.' Johnnie put his arm around her waist; her bump was getting so big now that he could barely reach all the way around. 'The things she said to you were really hurtful and I'm sure she's going to come to really regret them, but she's not in a place yet to see what she's done wrong and the likelihood is she'd say something like that to you again. In the long run, that's just going to hurt you both more. I think for now, you just need to wait it out.'

'I'm trying, but it's really hard. I just want to fix it for her.' Meg leant her head against Johnnie's chest. 'I can't bear the thought that she might still not be talking to me when the baby arrives. I lost half my family once and I don't want to lose anyone else.'

'I've got a feeling that when the baby comes she won't be able to stay away, and if Ed can use the results from the scan to persuade her to get the help she needs in the meantime, then she'll be in a much better place by then too. Just give it until the baby arrives; they really can work miracles.'

'She's our little miracle already.' Meg closed her eyes and conjured up the image that had got her through the last couple of weeks. She was holding her newborn daughter in her arms with her other daughter by her side, gazing down at her little sister with all the love Meg knew Tilly was capable of. It was all she wanted and she had to believe Johnnie when he said it would eventually happen, because the alternative didn't bear thinking about.

* * *

Jess hadn't been sure what to expect from Candice, but she'd pictured the kind of teenager she'd once been: guarded and resentful of the fact that she was in any kind of care placement at all. Candice, or Candi, as she liked to be called, was nothing like that. She was a sweet girl, clearly desperate for someone to love her and if anything, she could be inappropriately affectionate, especially with Dexter. It meant he and Jess had to be very cautious about her ever being left alone with him. As a social worker, he knew how easily allegations could be made, and neither of them wanted to do anything to put their lives with Riley at any kind of risk, no matter how much they wanted to help Candi and the baby.

It was obvious how easy it must have been for Connor to be able to manipulate someone like Candi. Even now, if his name was brought up, she'd make excuses for why he hadn't been in touch and create elaborate fantasies about how, once he'd finally made it big, he'd come back for her and the baby. The poor little thing still didn't even have a name, because Candi was waiting to hear whether Connor wanted to choose it. But then, suddenly, six days after they'd arrived, Candi made a suggestion.

'Do you think she looks like an Iris?' She was holding the baby in her arms, in the slightly awkward way she did, but she was getting better at the basics every day.

'I think that's a lovely name.' Jess smiled. The baby had the most striking blue eyes and there was no way of knowing yet whether they'd change colour, but Iris seemed somehow fitting.

'It was my nan's name. She was my dad's mum, but he was already in prison by then and I went to live with her when my mum disappeared.' Candi made it all sound so matter of fact and it broke Jess's heart all over again. 'She was really lovely and I wish I could have stayed with her, but then she started to forget things and in the end she didn't even know who I was. I wanted to look after her, but they wouldn't let me. So she went into a home and I went into care. I wish they'd just let us stay together. I wasn't even there when she died last year.'

'That must have been really hard, but I'm sure she'd have been proud of you and I bet she'd have loved the fact that you're thinking of naming the baby after her.' Jess didn't want to put any pressure on Candi, because it was likely to backfire if she did. But naming the baby after her grandmother, instead of waiting for contact from Connor that might never come, seemed like a huge step in the right direction.

'She was a singer like me. She lived in Liverpool growing up and she had all these photos of her performing in a club where loads of really famous people started out. After that, she went and lived in London and carried on trying to make it. You know that old suitcase I've got; it's where I keep all her photos and it's the one thing I've kept with me wherever the social workers have sent me. Nan was mostly a backing singer, but she always told me she was glad she'd given it her best shot before she met my grandad and had my dad. She always told me to follow my dreams before I had a family. Nan said my mum got pregnant with me when my parents were too young to cope with it. I know Nan didn't want the same for me, so I don't think she'd have liked this much.' Candi puffed out her cheeks. 'She'd have loved the baby, but she'd have wanted me to have my own suitcase full of photos first, of all the things I've done. Connor was going to take me to LA with him, but when we found out I was pregnant...'

Candi didn't finish the sentence and it was all Jess could do not to tell her that she was worth a million times what Connor could ever offer her, and that the best thing she could do was to forget him. Instead, she gave Candi's arm a gentle squeeze. 'Just because you've had a baby, it doesn't mean you have to stop singing. It might take a while before you can make any big plans, but Iris could be the reason why you never stop trying to make a good life for the two of you.'

'I feel awful saying this now she's here, but the truth is, if I'd realised I was pregnant sooner, I wouldn't have had her at all. But she was already moving by the time I knew and I just couldn't do it, even though Connor said I should.' Candi gazed down at her daughter, her voice thick with emotion. 'I'm glad I didn't know sooner, but I know I can't keep trying to be a singer if I've got Iris. I don't want to be like my mum was before she disappeared. That's why I was going to put Iris up for adoption straight away, but then the closer it got to her being born, the less sure I was.'

'It's early days yet and you don't have to make any big decisions. You're doing brilliantly with her; you know that, don't you?' Jess shared the reports she wrote for the social workers with Candi every day, so they could go through what had gone well and any concerns Jess was flagging, but Candi really had made huge progress in a very short space of time. Just in this one conversation, she was showing more maturity than most people twice her age were capable of.

'I'm really glad they placed me here; I wish I'd had a mum like you.' Candi leant her head against Jess's for a moment, with the newly named baby Iris cradled between them. Whatever happened, Jess would always be grateful that she'd had the chance to get to know Candi, and Riley's little sister, but she couldn't help wishing they could stay forever.

* * *

'How do I work out how much spaghetti to put in for each person? Do you have to count the strands?' Candi wrinkled her nose as she turned towards Dexter, and Jess couldn't help smiling. Candi had asked to help with cooking from the day she'd arrived and tonight was her first night taking charge. She'd been determined to make Riley's favourite, Bolognese, with Dexter and Jess supervising from the other side of the kitchen. Iris was happily sleeping through the dinner preparations, gently snoring in Dexter's arms and not even stirring when he spoke.

'You can weigh it out, if you like; about sixty grams a person should do it, but you just get to know after a while.'

'Unless you're me.' Jess laughed. 'I still always cook too much.'

'You like the pasta twists more, don't you, Riley?' Candi walked over to where the little boy was busy creating his latest felt-tip masterpiece, and he stopped to look up at her.

'Yes. Mum and Dad always say all pasta tastes the same.' He looked wholly unconvinced by his parents' argument. 'But I don't think it does. Pasta twists fit in my mouth better, which means I can taste them more.'

It was the sort of logic only an eight-year-old could come up with, but Candi was nodding. 'And they're easier to eat, aren't they? I'll cook the twists for me and you then Riley, 'cos I like them best too.'

'Yay!' Riley shot up from his chair and threw his arms around

Candi's waist. It was funny to think how certain Jess and Dexter had been that adopting an older child might make Riley feel displaced, because Candi had stepped into the big sister role almost from the moment they'd met. It was proof that when the right person came along, none of the things you thought were important really mattered.

'It's not going to be long until dinner now, sweetheart. Shall we clear your pens away, so I can lay the table for Candi?' Jess got up from her seat, but Riley was shaking his head.

'I'm nearly done Mum, I just need to colour in Candi's jumper and then I'll be finished.' Riley moved back to his place, holding up the picture as if to prove he was telling the truth. And there they were, the five of them – Mum, Dad, Riley, Candi and Iris – all depicted as colourful stick-like figures, with their names written underneath in Riley's distinctive style. At the top of the page he'd written the words *My Family* and Jess had to blink back the tears as she looked at it.

'That's definitely going on the fridge when you've finished. It's brilliant.' Jess exchanged a look with Dexter that needed no words. They'd finally done it; they'd got the family they'd always wanted. But any day now it would be taken away again, and another piece of Jess's heart would be gone forever too.

* * *

With Candi becoming more and more settled in the placement, Jess had got back in touch with Meg, offering to speak to Tilly as originally planned. To Jess's surprise, Meg had turned her down, explaining the latest with the situation and her decision to wait until the baby had arrived before making contact with Tilly again.

If things had been different, it would probably have been Tilly who'd have arranged a baby shower for her mum. But with that off the cards, Jess had suggested to the other midwives that they plan something for Meg, and everyone had immediately been on board. Ella had taken care of inviting some of Meg's friends from the doctor's surgery and Jess had spoken to Johnnie about who else they should invite. Ella had also offered to host the baby shower at Crooked Cottage Farm, because there was plenty of space for everyone and no close neighbours to hear the uproar there was bound to be with Gwen in charge of the entertainment.

Jess had been planning to take Candi along to the baby shower with her, but in another twist she hadn't seen coming, Candi had made herself an appointment to go to an open day at a college in Truro to find out what courses she could sign up for. Jess had offered to take her, but she'd insisted she wanted to go alone and start proving to everyone, including herself, that she was capable of doing these sorts of things without anyone else's help. She'd raised the fact that she'd need to be capable of this and a whole lot more, if she was going to be able to care for Iris by herself too. Jamie, her social worker, had supported Candi's plans to go alone, which meant Jess had taken baby Iris along to the baby shower, while Dexter took Riley for a horse-riding lesson.

'Oh Jess, she's absolutely beautiful.' Ella greeted her at the door of the farmhouse, her own baby bump just beginning to look more obvious.

'She's making my ovaries ache!' Emily, who was hanging her jacket on the rack in the hallway, looked down at the baby.

'Don't you dare!' Anna suddenly appeared in the hallway, laughing. 'You promised me Keira was having your first baby; I can't lose another of the team, otherwise I think my hair might leave with them.'

'I'm sorry my sabbatical got sprung on you sooner than expected and thanks so much for making it work. You're the best boss in the world.' Jess blew Anna a kiss.

'It was more than worth it for this little one.' Anna touched the baby's foot. 'But we'd better go through before Gwen comes and finds us; she's very keen to get started on the games.'

'Uh oh!' Jess followed everyone through to the sitting room, where Gwen was busy giving Bobby orders about what he needed to do next.

'Right, good, I think that's everyone.' Gwen looked around the room, as Jess found a seat between Toni and Izzy on one of the sofas. 'Bobby's going to bring you all round a glass and you'll see there's an ice cube in it, with a tiny plastic baby frozen inside. This game is going to run while we do some other stuff, but the winner will be the one whose baby emerges from the ice first and you have to claim your prize by telling us your waters have broken. You can help things along by putting the ice in your hands, sticking it under your armpit or anywhere else you don't mind an ice cube going. But what you're not allowed to do is bite it.'

'What's the prize?' Toni looked over her glasses at Gwen. 'If I'm going to consider literally freezing my arse off, I need to know it's worth it.'

'It's a packet of penis pasta.'

'You do know this isn't a hen do, don't you?' Frankie said what everyone was thinking.

'It was left over from my eldest granddaughter's hen do. Her friend accidentally ordered a whole box of twenty packets from Amazon, instead of a single one. We still can't get rid of it, even though I've been giving it to my youngest grandkids and telling them it's rocket ships.'

'Gwen, you're killing me; my pelvic floor is struggling enough as it is!' Meg was almost crying with laughter and it was really nice to see her looking so happy. Jess couldn't remember the last time she'd seen her friend like that, but the Port Agnes midwives were working their magic in the way only they really could.

Glancing down at baby Iris, Jess smiled again. Going back to work at the unit had saved her sanity when she'd had to let Teddy go, and it would get her through when she had to say goodbye to Candi and Iris too. As long as she had family and friends to support her, everything would work out okay in the end. But, for now, she was determined to enjoy having Candi and Iris around and try to stop herself from missing them before they'd even gone.

25

There had been a big part of Meg that had still hoped Tilly would get in touch before Seth's birthday. She and Tilly had never missed celebrating Darren's and Seth's birthdays before. It wasn't always a big event; more often than not, it would be a quiet meal for the two of them, in one of the restaurants Seth and Darren had loved. Or even just a takeaway at home, where they'd look at old pictures and Tilly would laugh at some of the ridiculous haircuts her father had tried out over the years. Not having Tilly there to share Seth's twenty-fifth with her was incredibly hard.

Maybe it was time to start a new tradition and mark the occasion with Johnnie. Whenever she wanted to talk about her memories of Seth and Darren, he let her say as much or as little as she wanted to. On their first date, she'd spent most of the time telling him about them and she'd expected that to be their only date as a result, but he'd listened intently and taken her hand in his for the first time when tears had choked her voice. So, if she couldn't spend Seth's birthday with Tilly, there was only one person she wanted to spend it with.

The fish and chip restaurant on the harbour, next to

Mehenick's Bakery, was run by Anna's husband, Brae, and it had been Seth's restaurant of choice ever since he'd been old enough to give his opinion. Brae hadn't been the one running it back then, but he still remembered Darren and Seth. All of which made it the obvious place to have dinner on Seth's big day.

'What was Seth's usual order?' Rain lashed against the window, as Johnnie spoke. A thunder storm had been threatening for days and it had finally broken, bringing strong winds that had blown in from an Atlantic weather front. The weather might be wild, but Johnnie had a way of making her feel safer than she ever thought she would again after Darren had died. He had the kindest eyes Meg had ever seen and she could tell he genuinely wanted to get to know Seth through her memories of him. It made her love Johnnie all the more.

'When Seth was little, it was always a battered sausage and chips, but then he started to become a proper Cornishman and he loved his sardines.' Meg wrinkled her nose. 'I've never been able to face them.'

'Nothing better than a Cornish sardine.' Johnnie smiled. 'I think Seth and I would have agreed on a lot of things, by the sounds of it.'

'I think you would.' Seth had loved animals every bit as much as Johnnie and, as much as he'd enjoyed helping his dad with building projects, that was where his true passion had been. He'd been in his GCSE year when he'd died and he'd chosen all the science subjects he could, in the hope of either training to be a vet or studying zoology. If Darren had died and Seth hadn't, she was certain her son would have welcomed Johnnie into their lives and she knew he'd have wanted her to be happy. She remembered a conversation she'd had with him, when they'd talked about where he might want to go to university.

'Will you miss me and Tils when we're both at uni?' They'd

been standing in the kitchen, with the sunlight streaming through the window, and she'd caught her breath at how grown up her not-so-little boy suddenly seemed to have become.

'Of course I will, more than you can ever imagine.'

'Do you think it's because you've been a mum since you were really young? It must be weird when you've never really been anything else.'

'It's because I love you, silly.' She'd gone to ruffle his hair, like she had hundreds of times before. But even standing on her tiptoes, it was too much of a stretch.

'Promise me you won't be sad, Mum.' Seth had looked at her with the soulful brown eyes that had always made him look as though he was trying to work out how to solve the world's deepest problems. 'You can miss us a bit, but you should do the stuff that makes you happy when we've left. You've always had to put us first and when we're not here any more you won't have to.'

'And all this time I never knew I was living with Yoda!' Meg had laughed, but he'd kept her fixed with the same serious look until she'd finally nodded. 'I promise I'll do stuff that makes me happy, but you do know that nothing makes me happier than being your mum, don't you?'

'Well, that's a given.' He'd laughed then, and given her one of the brief hugs she'd learned to savour once he'd hit his teens. He probably hadn't thought any more about their conversation after that, but she'd never forgotten his words.

'Would it be weird if I ordered sardines? For Seth.' Johnnie's question brought her back to the present and she shook her head.

'No, I'd like that. As long as you eat them for him, because I couldn't face them before I got pregnant and now... just the thought makes me queasy!' Meg bent down to get a tissue from her bag and caught sight of her phone. It was on silent, but the front screen was full of notifications of missed calls. All of them from the same person. 'Oh God, sorry, but I'm going to have to check my phone. I've had a load of missed calls from Ed.'

'Has he left a message?' The concern in Johnnie's voice was obvious as she looked at her phone.

'There's a voicemail.'

Ed sounded breathless on the recording and the more Meg heard of the message, the harder she was finding it to breathe normally. 'Sorry Meg. I've been trying to get through and I really hope you pick this up before Tilly gets hold of you. The scan showed she's got Asherman's Syndrome. It means she's got scar tissue that bonds the uterus together. They said it's probably from the endo and the D&C. Apparently it's only mild, but they also said it might make getting pregnant even harder and there's a possibility we'll need IVF. Tilly was hysterical on the way home and she didn't seem to have taken in that it's only mild. As far as she's concerned, they might as well have guaranteed she'll never have a baby. She screamed at me to stop the car when we were about half a mile from home. I tried to persuade her to get back in, but she said she was going to find you and she started shouting something about you loving Seth more than her. She seemed even more out of control than she did at Darren's birthday and I'm worried about what she might do. I'm worried about you too. Can you call me when you get this message? Thanks.'

'What did he say?' Johnnie asked and she handed the phone to him.

'You'd better listen for yourself.' She waited until he'd finished and passed the phone back, before she spoke. 'I'm really scared she might do something stupid. She threatened to try it, not long after the accident, and it took two years of counselling before I was certain she wouldn't. But all of this stuff with the baby seems to have taken her right back to that point. I need to call Ed, then we'll have to go and look for her. I can't just sit here and wait.'

'Of course. Have you got any idea where she might go, if she really is looking for you?'

'Well the obvious place would be—' Meg's answer was cut off, as the door to the restaurant flung open and Tilly rushed in. 'She's here.'

Johnnie didn't even have time to respond, before Tilly reached the table. 'What the fuck is *he* doing here? This was Seth's place and it's Seth's birthday. Or have you forgotten that too?'

Ed had been right. Tilly was much more out of control than she'd been at Darren's birthday. Her eyes looked wild and she was screaming rather than speaking. Everyone else in the restaurant was watching them, but that was the least of Meg's worries right now.

'Why don't you sit down, sweetheart, and we can talk properly.'

'Are you joking? Do you think I'd want to sit down with a bitch like you, who can just forget my dad like he was nothing and move in with someone young enough to be your son?' Tilly wasn't letting the facts stand in her way; this was about trying to inflict as much pain on her mother as Tilly was feeling. 'Maybe that's the point. You can't have Seth, so you went and found yourself a replacement. Bit bloody creepy that you're sleeping with him though.'

'Tilly that's enough. I'm not going to sit here and let you speak to your mother like that.' Johnnie's voice was icily calm, but Tilly gave a maniacal laugh in response.

'Like I give a shit what you think!'

'Tilly please.' Meg tried to put a hand out to her daughter, but she batted it away.

'I know you wish it was me who'd died and not Seth. He was always your favourite and you can't even deny it.' Tilly grabbed hold of her mother's wrist. 'But do you know the worst part? It was your fault he died. You should never have let him go with Dad to do a dangerous job like that. You lost your precious son because you're a crap mother.'

Meg couldn't breathe. If Tilly had plunged her hand into her chest, she didn't think it could have hurt any more. The words were choking in her throat as she tried to respond. 'How can you say that? You know I loved you both more than anything and I can't believe you'd—'

'*Loved!*' The look in Tilly's eyes was terrifying now. 'That's it, isn't it? You *loved* us both, past tense. But Seth's dead and I don't matter any more, do I? You stopped giving a shit about me a long time ago.'

'Tilly, for God's sake, stop it.' Johnnie moved to stand, as Meg sat motionless with shock, but Tilly was too quick. Dropping her mother's wrist, she took a step back.

'It's okay, I'll stop. And guess what, Mother, you're finally going to get your wish. I'm going to do what I should have done when Dad and Seth died, and go with them. You can get on with your perfect new life now; I hope it makes you happy!' Darting out of the way as Johnnie tried to get hold of her, Tilly knocked the drinks on the table behind them flying and broke into a run, past the rest of the tables and out of the door.

'Johnnie, you've got to stop her, please.' Tears were streaming down Meg's face as the shock was starting to wear off. She could see Johnnie was torn. 'I'll be fine; just make sure she's okay.'

'I will, I promise.' Johnnie set off after her, turning right out of the door and running in front of the window where Meg was sitting.

'Are you okay, Meg? Can I do something to help?' Suddenly Brae was at the table, as one of the waiting staff attempted to clear up the mess behind them.

'I told Johnnie to go after her, but I need to see what's happening.'

'Are you sure that's a good idea?'

'I can't just sit here.' Meg was already up on her feet. She might not be able to catch up with Tilly and Johnnie at eight months pregnant, but there was no way she could wait around not knowing what was going on.

'In that case, I'm coming with you.' Brae followed her out of the restaurant and Meg felt as if every pair of eyes in the room was boring into her. She didn't care what anyone thought; she had to know that Tilly was safe. Everything else could be sorted out, as long as her daughter didn't do what she was threatening to.

Meg moved as quickly as she could along the edge of the harbour, desperately scanning around to see if she could see Tilly or Johnnie. But she heard the splash, before she saw either of them.

'She's gone in!' someone shouted and the words carried across from the other side of the harbour, before a second splash seemed to echo across the water. Meg was running now, towards where a small group of people were standing on the opposite side of the harbour from the restaurant.

'I'll get the lifebuoy.' A man called out to the people in the water and Meg knew, as soon as she'd heard the second splash, that Johnnie had gone in after Tilly, even before she got close enough to see their faces.

'Please help them.' She was already soaked to the skin by the time she reached the point where Tilly had leapt in and she shivered as the man threw the lifebuoy towards Johnnie. But it wasn't just the cold making her shudder, she was trembling with terror. The two people she loved most in the world were in danger and the fear that history could repeat itself was clawing at her throat. Even as Meg desperately tried to convince herself that it couldn't possibly happen again, her body was telling her otherwise; the way her heart felt as if it was clattering against her ribcage, and the sensation of forgetting how to swallow were all too familiar. It was like she was walking down that hallway again, towards the two police officers standing on her doorstep, waiting to tell her that something terrible had happened. Only this time, the horror was unfolding right in front of her.

'I'm going in too.' Brae had hardly got the words out before he leapt into the water after the others.

'Oh God, please let them all be okay.' Meg's teeth were chattering now and she barely even registered when one of the other bystanders draped a coat over her shoulders. All she could do was watch and keep repeating her plea over and over again.

Johnnie had reached Tilly's side quite quickly, but it was clear she was fighting him. She was screaming something too, but it was lost on the wind.

'I've phoned for an ambulance and Ruth's ringing the lifeboat station.' Jago Mehenick was suddenly at Meg's side and he sounded as if he'd run all the way from the bakery. 'I'm sure we won't need them, though. Johnnie and Brae will have her back up here in no time.'

Meg couldn't bring herself to speak. All she could do was keep her eyes fixed on the water below them. Brae had reached Johnnie and Tilly, bringing the lifebuoy with him and slowly, between the two of them, they began to move Tilly closer towards one of the ladders on the side of the harbour wall, which would be the quickest way of getting her out of the freezing cold water.

'Leave me alone!' Tilly was still screaming, even as they got to the base of the ladder. The lifebuoy floated away as she fought to break free. If Jago hadn't been holding on to Meg, she'd have set off down the ladder and tried to grab hold of her daughter's hand to drag her up the rest of the way herself.

Someone had tied a rope to one of the old metal bollards at the edge of the harbour and had thrown the other end down to Johnnie, who'd managed to loop it around Tilly's waist. The last thing any of them wanted was for her to leap into the water again when she was halfway up the ladder. 'You go up first, Brae, and I'll come up behind Tilly to make sure she doesn't slip.' Johnnie called out the instruction and Brae started climbing the ladder, as Johnnie continued to fight to stop Tilly trying to break away again. When Brae finally reached the top of the ladder, some of the crowd that had gathered started using the rope as a makeshift winch. All the time, Tilly was screaming for them to let her go, her arms and legs flailing out wildly as they made agonizingly slow progress, winching her up the side of the harbour wall.

Meg didn't utter a sound as she watched, but a silent rage was boiling up inside her. She'd been filled with anger at the cruel fate that had taken her husband and son away from her, but it had been a freak accident, something that no one could have anticipated. This was different. Tilly had chosen to put herself in danger, and now she was risking the lives of the people who were trying their best to help her. Meg wanted to scream at the top of her lungs and say things no mother should ever say to her child. She'd been frozen with fear at the thought of losing Tilly, but now a white-hot anger had taken over, and she was too afraid to open her mouth, in case it came out and she never found a way to push it back down again.

Tilly was almost at the top of the ladder, with Johnnie following on just beneath her, when she screamed again, kicking even more violently, her foot making contact with the side of Johnnie's head and sending him toppling backwards. If he'd fallen a few more inches to the right, everything would have been okay, but the sound of his skull making contact with the side of a fishing boat to the left of the steps seemed to reverberate around the entire harbour. It was the most horrific sound Meg had ever heard and it was one she was never going to be able to forget.

26

Even after they'd reached the hospital, the sound of the siren was still ringing in Meg's ears. Johnnie hadn't reacted to the noise it had made on the journey to Truro, or to her desperate pleas to open his eyes and look at her. He hadn't reacted to anything she'd said to him since his head had cracked against the side of the boat.

Brae and Jago had leapt straight into the water, pulling him to safety. A couple of women in the crowd had grabbed hold of Meg's arms when she'd tried to go after them, promising her that it would be okay and that jumping in would just make things worse. But she couldn't lose Johnnie, she couldn't go through that again.

An ambulance had arrived just after Johnnie was pulled out. He'd still been talking at that point, but Meg hadn't been able to get close because the paramedics had said they needed space. Before they could even get Johnnie in the ambulance, he'd started to become very distressed, like he was fighting to get away, and the paramedics had sedated him. It had been even more terrifying to see him lying there motionless. All she'd wanted was some sign that he was still there and that he'd be coming back to her, but there was nothing.

She was back in that moment again, when she'd heard the news about Darren and Seth, powerless and terrified. But in a way this was almost worse. Meg hadn't been there when they'd died, and she'd known they were already gone. She couldn't have watched them die, she'd have screamed and begged them to stay, until she had no voice left. But now she was being forced to watch Johnnie, still here, but not, all at the same time.

Hope was a dangerous thing, but she wasn't letting it go. She'd keep screaming and begging while there was still breath left in her body, but she wouldn't let him die. She couldn't.

Meg didn't take her eyes off him as the paramedics wheeled him through the hospital doors. Seeing the rise and fall of his chest was the only thing stopping her from going completely mad.

'This is Johnnie; he's sustained a blunt force trauma to his skull. He's got a GCS of 9. He's responding to pain stimuli but his speech at the scene became incoherent and this developed into severe agitation, which made it necessary to sedate him. His partner, Meg, came in the ambulance with us.' The words the paramedics exchanged with the A&E team were almost like another language, and when they started listing the checks and medication Johnnie had received, she had no idea what any of it meant. She'd been watching him the whole time they were in the ambulance, waiting for the tiniest twitch of his fingers, or a flicker of his eyelids, and all she could do now was pray that the absence of any sign of life had been down to the sedation.

'We're taking Johnnie straight down for a CT scan.' Meg suddenly realised one of the nurses was speaking to her. She'd just been following the paramedics, in a daze, while they'd continued briefing the hospital team about Johnnie's injuries and his vital signs.

'Is he going to die?' She needed to know, otherwise she wasn't sure she could take another step forward.

'It's too early to know the long-term damage he's sustained as a result of the trauma. The good news is that his heart rate is within the normal range, but his blood pressure is lower than we'd want to see and we don't know yet why he became so agitated or why his speech was affected. We need the CT scan to check the extent of his injuries and then we'll be able to tell you more.' The nurse had such a kind face and Meg wanted to thank her, but she didn't seem able to speak. 'Is there someone we can call to come and sit with you?'

'No.' Meg managed that one word, shaking her head so hard it started to hurt. You were supposed to call family at a time like this, but her daughter had been taken somewhere else in the hospital. She had no idea whether Tilly had any injuries, but she must have been freezing. Meg had caught a brief glimpse of her as she was put into another ambulance, and she'd looked more shocked than anything else. And thank God Brae and Jago had been okay too. Tilly had tried to call out to her, but Meg hadn't responded. She'd been too scared of how she might react if she did, the things she would say that could never be unsaid. And Johnnie had needed her more. Even now, she didn't have the headspace to think about Tilly – what she'd done, or even how she was. She couldn't think about anyone but Johnnie.

'Okay, Meg. You can take a seat in the relatives' room and I'll come and find you as soon as we've got the results. I'll ask someone to get you a drink and just let us know if you change your mind about wanting to call someone.'

'Thank you.' Meg stood there for a moment, watching the nurse with the kind face rush off to catch up with the trolley carrying Johnnie away for his scan. She hadn't said that Johnnie was going to die, but she hadn't said that he wouldn't either.

* * *

✉ Message from Ed

Hoping to God that Johnnie is okay. By the time I got to the hospital, they'd put Tilly in a private side room. She seems fine physically, but she's having a psychiatric assessment. She's horrified about what happened to Johnnie. I'm so sorry.

Meg stared at the message, struggling to work out how she felt, but the reality was she didn't feel anything. She was completely numb and it was a sensation she recognised all too well. It was how her body had coped in the days after Darren and Seth had died, when the initial hysteria had subsided. But she didn't want to repeat a single thing that had happened back then.

She was still staring, unblinking, at the message, when the nurse with the kind face pushed open the door, a younger woman just behind her.

'Is he dead?' Meg shot to her feet, but the nurse shook her head, putting an arm around her shoulders.

'No, he's critical, but stable.' The nurse gestured to the woman behind her. 'This is Doctor Sharma; she'll be able to tell you a little bit more.'

'Hi, Meg, isn't it? Why don't we sit down for a bit?' Dr Sharma sat opposite where Meg had been sitting and waited for her to retake her seat. 'As Zara said, Johnnie is in a stable condition, but the next twenty-four to forty-eight hours will be critical. He started to regain consciousness during the scan, once the medication the paramedics had given him began to wear off, but he became very agitated again and we've had to repeat the sedation. The scan also showed that Johnnie has a blood clot in his brain, so he's going to need to have surgery to relieve the pressure and try to prevent it causing any further damage.'

'But he's going to be okay?' Meg turned from Dr Sharma to Zara, the nurse. Surely a nurse with a face as kind as hers was only ever sent to deliver the good news. But, instead of nodding, she gave an almost imperceptible shrug.

'We just don't know yet and brain surgery is always complex, but he's in the right place with the best possible people looking after him. You're going to need someone to look after you too, though.'

'Can I see him before he has his surgery?' Meg would drop to her knees and beg if she had to.

'He's going to theatre as soon as the on-call surgeon gets here.' Dr Sharma looked at her watch. 'Zara can take you down now, but you need to prepare yourself. There are a lot more tubes and wires than when the paramedics brought him in.'

'I just need to see him.' Meg still hadn't cried, but it felt like her heart was breaking to pieces in her chest. She had to hold it together until she'd seen Johnnie, otherwise they might not let her. And if this was the last time, she needed to make it count.

* * *

Dr Sharma had been right about the amount of equipment Johnnie was now attached to. And when Meg took his hand, she was half expecting it to be icy cold like Darren's had been when she'd seen him for the final time.

'I love you so much.' Meg whispered the words urgently to Johnnie, hoping with every ounce of her that he could hear them. 'I never thought I'd be this happy again and it's all because of you. You're the kindest, most thoughtful person I've ever met and our baby really needs her daddy around, because she's going to love you so much too.'

Meg held her breath, waiting for that longed-for sign that Johnnie could hear what she was saying, but there was still nothing and time was running out before someone would come and wheel him away from her. Maybe for good.

'I need you to know something. Even if you don't make it and you can't come back to me, I'll always be so thankful that I had you in my life for the time I did. You've made me laugh so much and I've had more fun than I ever dreamt I could after what happened. If you can't be here to meet our baby girl, I'll make sure she knows how amazing her daddy was and just how excited you were when we found out she was on the way. I'll miss you every day of my life if you have to leave. But if you come back, even if you can't be the same person you used to be, I promise I'll spend the rest of my life trying to make your days as happy as you've made mine, and to make you feel as loved.'

'I'm really sorry Meg, but we're going to have to take him up now.' Zara suddenly appeared at her side and Meg gave Johnnie's hand a final squeeze, praying that it wouldn't be the last time she ever got to do it.

27

Candi came back from the open day at the college buzzing with excitement and it made Jess smile just watching her.

'They've offered me an interview, Jess. Me! Who'd have thought they'd even consider accepting me on a course like that?' Candi took hold of Jess's arms and danced her around the kitchen.

'They'll be lucky to have you.' When Candi finally stopped spinning her around, Jess gave the young woman a hug. 'You should be so proud of yourself. I am and so is Dexter. Iris is going to be really proud of her mummy too, when she's old enough to understand.'

'I hope so.' Candi's voice took on a far quieter tone at that point and, when Jess pulled away to look at her, she had a serious expression on her face. 'I want all the decisions I make to be the right ones to give her the best possible life. But I couldn't have done this without you and Dexter, and I won't be able to keep doing this without you guys to help me.'

'You won't have to. Even when you and Iris are ready to move on, we'll always be around to support you.' It should have been obvious what the issue was, with Candi's demeanour changing so suddenly – she was scared about being left to cope alone with a baby. But with every day that passed, Jess had become more and more convinced Candi was up to the job. She and Dexter had grown really fond of the young woman too.

Jess's biggest fear had been that she'd get too attached to Iris, but getting so attached to the baby's mother was something she'd never expected. She couldn't have been prouder of Candi for what she'd achieved, but she couldn't deny she was scared of how quickly things were progressing too. Every skill Candi had mastered and every step she'd taken towards being able to parent Iris independently felt like a step further away from Jess's family. She hadn't allowed herself to really think about how empty the house would be without them. Iris was such a tiny little thing, but somehow her presence dominated the whole house and the little world they'd created revolved around her. The first thing Riley did, the moment he got in from school, was go and see his little sister. He'd even learned to use the machine that prepared the bottles and measured out the scoops incredibly carefully, as if using the tiniest bit too much powder could prove disastrous.

'I got so lucky when they placed me and Iris with you.' Candi planted a kiss on Jess's cheek and looked at her wide-eyed. 'Can you look after Iris when I go to the interview next Tuesday? I'm already starting to get butterflies.'

'Of course I can. Or Dexter can have the baby and I can come with you?'

'No, I need to do this by myself, to show everyone that I know what's best for Iris and I'm not afraid to go after it.' Candi pulled her shoulders back, as if to prove she meant business. 'Then, when I come back here for my meeting with Jamie, he'll be able to see for himself all the progress I'm making.'

'Woe betide anyone who tries to stand in your way!' Jess laughed and noted down the date of Candi's interview in the calendar app on her phone, but she had no idea how momentous that day would turn out to be.

* * *

'She just can't seem to settle back down.' Candi had been pacing up and down the hallway outside Jess's bedroom for at least an hour, and Jess had been determined not to interfere. Instead, she'd lain there, wide-eyed, staring into the darkness and listening to Candi's sweet voice as she'd sung her baby daughter a lullaby. In the end, at 4 a.m., Jess hadn't been able to fight the urge to get up any longer. 'I've tried all the usual tricks, but she just seems to want to be held.'

'She might have a bit of wind.' Jess put the back of her hand on Iris's forehead. 'It doesn't feel like she's got a temperature.'

'As long as she's okay.' Candi sighed. 'I just wish she hadn't chosen now to pull an all-nighter. I've got my interview tomorrow and I'm going to look like a zombie at this rate.'

'I'll take her.' Jess hadn't been able to stop herself from making the offer. Maybe she should have encouraged Candi to keep trying and given her a few other strategies that might have helped get Iris off to sleep, but she wanted to take this opportunity. If Candi kept making progress at the rate she was, they could be moved into their own flat before she even started college. There might not be many more chances for Jess to comfort the baby until the little girl fell asleep in her arms. So she wasn't going to miss this one.

'Are you sure? I feel bad asking you to do that, especially as you've got her tomorrow too.' Candi looked genuinely torn.

'You didn't ask me, I offered, and I want to do it. Tomorrow's a big day for you.'

'It is. It's huge.' Candi's shoulders visibly sagged with relief as she passed the baby to Jess. 'You're so good with her. Sometimes I think she prefers you to me.'

'Of course she doesn't.' Jess would rather have died than admit she'd thought the same thing once or twice. It wasn't true, even if a tiny part of her might want it to be. She was just more used to handling babies, that was all, and they were remarkably good at picking up on when someone was a bit unsure. Jess had seen it with new parents time and time again, but the more confident they became, the more settled their babies got too. Candi would get there. 'You just go and get some rest, then you can show the interviewer tomorrow just how amazing you are.'

'Thanks Jess. I knew I could rely on you.' Candi wrapped her arms around Jess and the baby for a moment, and then she was gone.

Even if Iris settled down, Jess knew there was no way they'd be going back to bed. She wouldn't be able to put Iris in the cot without risking waking Candi up, so they headed downstairs. Jess couldn't sing, at least nowhere near as well as Candi did, but that didn't stop her from carrying on where the younger woman had left off. Her mother had sung the same song to her every night, right up until she'd started school, and singing the words to Iris felt like an invisible thread between the past and the present.

'Are you falling asleep just to stop me from singing?' Jess whispered the words, as Iris finally closed her eyes, hardly daring to breathe as she lowered herself down onto the sofa, the baby now fast asleep on her chest.

Jess wanted to drink in every moment; the feel of the baby's weight as she lay on her chest, the little snuffling sounds Iris made, and the warmth of her breath against Jess's neck. This was all she'd ever wanted.

'Mum.' Riley had suddenly appeared in the doorway, his

pyjamas dishevelled, and his hair sticking up on one side the way it always did when he first woke up.

'Come here, darling. Are you okay?' Cradling Iris in one arm, Jess reached the other towards her son. 'Did you have a bad dream?'

'No, but I think the foxes are fighting again.' Riley rubbed his eyes as he walked towards her, snuggling into the crook of her arm as he joined Jess and Iris on the sofa. Just lately, there'd been a couple of foxes who'd got very bold about wandering through the streets of Port Agnes at night. Whether they were fighting or mating, Jess didn't know, but they were certainly loud enough to wake Riley up when they decided that the garden beneath his bedroom window was where they wanted to hang out.

'Why don't you cuddle in closer to me and Iris, sweetheart, then you might be able to get back to sleep. It's very early.'

'Is Iris asleep?' Riley turned towards the baby and gently stroked the side of her head.

'She is now, but she's been fighting it since her last bottle. She doesn't want to miss out on anything.'

'I wanted a brother or sister for ages and ages, but Jackson told me I wasn't going to like it when I got one.' Riley looked thoughtful for a moment. 'But I really love her, Mum, she's so cute and I think she loves me too.'

'Oh, there's no doubt about that, darling.' Holding Riley close to one side and Iris on the other, Jess wondered if it really was possible for a heart to burst. It certainly felt like it. She loved these two little people so much it hurt, and if she could have frozen any moment in time, it would have been this one – right here, right now. With her two babies by her side and the man she adored sleeping soundly above them.

'I wish she could stay with us forever.'

'Me too, darling. But we'll still get to see her all the time, even when she's not here any more, and Iris is really lucky having a mummy like Candi.' The false brightness in Jess's voice made her throat hurt, even though she meant what she said. It didn't stop her wanting this for herself and Dexter, though, and most of all for Riley. Her son had turned out to be an even more amazing big brother than she'd expected him to be.

'But it won't be the same, will it?' Riley had wisdom way beyond his years, and Jess's heart didn't feel as though it was going to burst any more. Now it felt like it was going to break into a million tiny pieces.

'No darling, but—'

'We just need to give her as many cuddles as we can now, 'cos she's going to miss us too when she goes to her new house with Candi.'

Jess hadn't been sure what she'd been about to say to Riley, before he cut her off, but he'd put it perfectly, all by himself. It made her want to freeze time more than ever, but she also knew that the incredible little boy sitting next to her would somehow get her through the agony of Iris leaving.

'How's Johnnie?' Jess rocked baby Iris in one arm, as she put the phone on speaker mode and set it down on the table in front of her. Candi had set off for her interview thirty minutes before and it was the first time Jess had got the chance to call Meg that day. Ever since she'd found out about the accident, she'd been in regular contact with her friend.

When Jess had arrived at the hospital that first night, Meg had been sitting hollow-eyed and silent in the relatives' room. But as soon as she'd spotted Jess, she'd burst into tears. Jess had still been there when they'd come down and told Meg that the operation had been a success, but that Johnnie had been put on a ventilator and needed to go to the critical care ward until they were confident he was ready for them to take him off sedation again.

When one of the lovely nurses had suggested that Meg go home and get some rest, it had taken all of Jess's powers of persuasion and some enforcing of a midwife-knows-best guidance to get her to agree.

After that, from what she could gather, her friend had stayed at Johnnie's bedside every day for as long as the hospital staff would allow her to, before going home to get a few hours' sleep. He seemed to be making progress, but it was Meg she was starting to really worry about.

'They're beginning to reduce his meds, but it could be another forty-eight hours before they'll know how much of a recovery he's made. The scans look promising, but I don't want to let myself hope for too much and it could be a while before we know how much lasting damage there is.'

'It's a good sign that the doctors are positive about the scans and that they want to bring him off sedation. Is there anything I can do to help out? Anna asked me to tell you that Cagney and Lacey are getting on like a house on fire with her dog.' Anna and Brae had picked up the dogs from Johnnie's house on the day of the accident and Jess knew it had been a weight off Meg's mind that his beloved animals were being well looked after.

'I'm so glad the dogs are okay, but there is something you can do.' Meg paused for a moment. 'Can you go and see Tilly for me?'

'Of course, I've got some time today if that works? But it's going to be you who Tilly really wants to see.'

'I'm not ready yet.' Meg's response was emphatic. 'I know she's going to think I've chosen Johnnie over her and the truth is, right now, I have. Tilly's safe and she's being looked after; I know nothing drastic is going to happen to her. I can't be sure of that with Johnnie until he comes round. I've got to put her second and if she's angry with me for that, then it'll just be one more thing we've got to work through. Even though I can't help worrying about her, I'm incredibly angry with her too. She could have killed herself and Johnnie, and I hardly recognise the person she's become. I'm not sure I can be the mother she wants me to be any more. If Tilly expects things to go back to the way they were, and for me to just accept her lashing out, I don't know where we go from here. I'm not putting Johnnie through that again, and I definitely don't want that for the baby.'

'I totally understand, but you *can* get through this, if she's prepared to work at it and you can find it in your heart to forgive her. I never thought Dad and I could get there, but we did in the end and our relationship is better now than it's ever been.' Jess wouldn't have dreamt of being so upfront with Meg if they hadn't already talked about everything that first night at the hospital.

'I hope so, but she's got to accept the help that's being offered to her.' Meg sounded exhausted and Jess wasn't surprised. She knew from the updates her friend had given her, that Tilly had been referred to mental health services and was already receiving treatment at a specialised centre near Redruth. She'd been diagnosed with complex grief and PTSD, which had triggered psychosis. She'd already been unwell when she'd verbally attacked Meg and by the time she'd leapt into the harbour, she'd been plagued by suicidal thoughts. Jess wanted to cry for all of them.

'What do you want me to say, if she asks about you?' Jess wasn't sure she was equipped for this, but she'd promised Meg she'd do whatever she could to help and she wasn't about to break that promise.

'Just tell her I love her and that I want her to do whatever it takes to get well again.' Meg let go of a long breath. 'There's a package at Johnnie's house with stuff to take in for her. It's got a copy of her favourite book; it was one she read again and again as a kid, whenever she needed cheering up. There's also a box of sherbet fountains, which she loves, and some of her favourite perfume. It might make her feel a bit more like herself and less like a patient. Hopefully it won't be too much bother for you to pick up on the way over to her.'

'It's no bother at all. Dexter will be back at eleven and I'll head straight off then.' That should give her enough time to go over and see Tilly before Candi got back from her interview. Candi had said she wanted to go and get a few bits for the baby afterwards and that she'd be gone for most of the day, but Jess didn't want to miss being there to welcome her back when she got home. Whether it was good news or bad, Jess was going to be there to support her. Just like she'd continue to be there to support Meg, too.

* * *

Visiting Tilly had been an exhausting experience and Jess's mind was racing on the journey home. The last thing she'd wanted to do was trigger the incredibly difficult emotions Meg's daughter was trying to process. She hadn't been sure whether to expect Tilly to still be partly detached from reality, but she seemed to be fully aware of what had happened and she was filled with remorse. There was no hint of her being angry with Meg for staying with Johnnie, instead of visiting her. Tilly's greatest fear, besides the prospect of her mother never forgiving her, was clearly the thought of Johnnie dying.

'I lost my phone when I jumped into the water, but I asked to borrow Ed's, because I wanted to try and call Mum. He doesn't think it's a good idea yet and he's probably right. But then we started looking through some old pictures and there are so many from the last couple of years that have Johnnie in them. He was the one who helped us move into our first home and I took a photo of him and Ed trying to get a wardrobe I'd bought off eBay up the narrow flight of stairs to the flat. There were pictures from Christmas, and barbeques in the garden, and the forty-fifth birthday party he organised for Mum. He was even in the background of some of the photos from when I graduated. He came down in his car just so he could chauffeur me and some of my friends to the cocktail bar in Plymouth. He and Mum waited in town until the early hours of the morning and between the two of them they made sure everyone got home safely. He did all of that, even though I'd said I didn't want him at my graduation dinner because he wasn't family.'

Jess had heard the remorse in Tilly's voice, and there was no denying that her actions had been incredibly damaging, but she'd wanted to try and give the younger woman some comfort. 'From what I know of Johnnie, he wouldn't have held that against you.'

'I know, and he hadn't even been with Mum all that long, then, but the truth is, he's been family since day one, and it's taken me all this time to see it. I found myself liking him more and more as I got to know him, but when they told me about the baby... I don't know, it felt like a betrayal of Dad somehow. I always thought of Johnnie as just Mum's boyfriend, not someone who'd be a part of our lives forever. I didn't want Dad or Seth to be forgotten and I thought, if I could push Johnnie away, Mum would choose me and it would be like we had our old family back. The miscarriage just made those feelings even more intense and I completely lost control.'

Tilly clearly had a long way to go to try and escape all her demons, but she was already seeing things completely differently. Jess had met Ed in the corridor, and he'd told her that the doctors were hopeful that, with the right therapy, the outlook was good. In the meantime, she'd been prescribed antipsychotic drugs, which had helped to reduce the anxiety and control the delusional thoughts she'd been having. Tilly no longer believed the whole world was against her, or that everyone, including Meg, was glad she'd miscarried her baby.

There was a good chance she might never have another psychotic episode, if the therapy addressed the issues at the root of everything. The miscarriage, followed by what Tilly had perceived as repeated failures to get pregnant again, had compounded the unresolved trauma from losing her father and brother. The news from the medical team sounded hopeful, but Tilly was clearly terrified that it was already too late to put everything right.

'I thought what I wanted more than anything was to have a baby, but now I'd happily swap the chance to ever do that, just to know for certain that Johnnie was going to recover. I can't lose Mum, Johnnie or their baby. Apart from Ed, they're all I've got and I can't lose any more family.' Tilly had cried almost the whole time Jess was there, even more so when she'd opened the package from her mother.

'She doesn't hate me?' Tilly had looked at Jess.

'Of course she doesn't and I know she's finding it hard not being here with you. Sending you all of this was the next best thing she could do for now.'

'Do you think Johnnie is going to be all right?' Tilly's eyes had searched her face, and Jess had found herself slowly nodding. She needed to believe it, almost as much as Tilly did.

'I'm sure he will.' If it turned out not to be true, Tilly holding on to the hope in the meantime that it would all turn out okay couldn't make things any worse than they already would be. And everyone needed hope.

The sound of Jess's phone ringing suddenly brought her back to the present and she connected it via the hands-free function in her car. It was the one person in the world she most wanted to speak to: her husband.

'I was just about to call you. That was a bit tough; Tilly's in pieces.'

'Candi's missing.' Dexter's words were like icy water dripping down Jess's spine.

'What do you mean she's missing? She went to the interview at the college and then she was going shopping; maybe she's been held up.'

'When she didn't get back in time for the meeting with Jamie, he contacted the college. They couldn't tell us anything, so he rang a friend of his who's in the police. She rang the college and explained it was a welfare check, so they finally agreed to share the information. They've got no record of Candi ever even making an enquiry, let alone an application, and she certainly didn't have an interview today.'

'Maybe I got the name of college wrong.'

'I'm sorry Jess, but I really don't think so. Her passport's gone too.'

'Oh God.' Jess caught her breath. Candi had told them she'd got the passport when Connor had promised her a trip to LA to meet with some record executives. Of course, the trip had never happened and the passport that Candi had struggled so hard to get was still unused – at least until now. 'You don't think she's gone back to Connor do you?'

'That's what Jamie thinks has happened. He said if she has, and she gets back on drugs like Connor, the only hope of her being able to keep Iris is for them to go to a specialist mother and baby unit, where she can go through rehab again.'

'She wouldn't just leave Iris, I'm sure of it.' Nausea was swirling in Jess's stomach, as she pulled the car into a layby. 'She's made so much progress and it's obvious she loves her.'

'I know and I keep looking at the baby and wondering how the hell she could possibly walk away, but Jamie said he's seen it far too many times to think there's any other alternative. I'm really worried about her, Jess.'

'Me too.' The first tear rolled down Jess's cheek, making a dark splash on her trouser leg as it landed in her lap. It was quickly followed by another. 'I just want to know she's okay and then we can take it from there.'

'Are you coming home now?' Dexter sounded just as desperate as she felt and he was the only person she knew who'd understand how she was feeling.

'I'll be there as soon as I can. I love you.'

'I love you too.' As Dexter ended the call, Jess desperately tried to wipe the tears from her eyes. She had to get home to her family and she couldn't allow herself to think about the fact that Candi and Iris might no longer be a part of that, otherwise she'd have no chance of seeing through her tears.

28

Jess had barely slept in the forty-eight hours since Candi's disappearance. When the police had eventually gone to see Connor at his last known address, it had turned out he still lived there and hadn't got any closer to LA than Candi had. Jess and Dexter had fully expected Candi to be with him, but he'd claimed to have no idea where she was and the police couldn't find anyone in the block of flats where he was living who'd seen Candice.

'What's going to happen now, Jamie?' Jess was hoping that Candi's social worker might be able to offer them some words of comfort, but sadly that turned out to be yet another misplaced hope.

'Because Candi is over eighteen now, she's got the right to make her own decisions. The police know she's more vulnerable than other young women her age might be, but they've only got limited resources and there's no evidence that any crime has taken place.'

'So they're just going to stop looking for her?'

'She won't be a priority.'

'And what about Iris?' Jess looked down at the baby in her

arms; the shape of her nose and mouth was so like her mother's. Candi had noticed it too and had beamed when she'd told Jess it was something they'd both got from her grandmother. She still couldn't believe Candi would have walked away from her.

'I need to meet with my manager to discuss it, but if Candi doesn't show up soon, the likelihood is that Iris will be put into a bridging to adoption placement. The process is likely to be quite lengthy if we can't get in touch with Candi to find out whether she wants to surrender her parental rights. We wouldn't expect you to keep Iris placed with you for all of that time, because it would hold you up from starting to support another parent and child.'

'What if we were willing to keep her?' Jess couldn't help holding Iris slightly tighter, even though experience had taught her that the longer Iris was with them, the harder it would be to let her go. The thought was already more than she could stand. Jess had come close to running away with Teddy when she'd realised she wouldn't be allowed to keep him. But she couldn't do that now, no matter how powerful the urge coursing through her veins was. She had Riley and Dexter, and her love for them was the only thing that could get her through this. She loved the little girl in her arms too and the idea of someone taking her away was devastating, but she knew what Jamie was going to say even before he confirmed her worst fears.

'I'm almost certain my manager will want to move her to a specialist bridging placement. We're desperately short of parent and child placements at the moment and she's not going to want you tied up with bridging to adoption for who knows how long. But I promise I'll come back to you as soon as I've had the chance to meet with her.'

'Thank you.' Jess's words sounded empty even to her own ears and the weight in her chest she'd had since Candi's disappearance seemed to have had another twenty kilos added to it by the time she ended the call.

She was just thinking about whether to phone Dexter, when the letterbox rattled and three envelopes landed on the mat.

'Sorry sweetheart.' Jess spoke to Iris, as she bent down awkwardly to pick the letters up, the baby still in her arms. One of the letters was a very official looking brown envelope, the other was from a charity organisation, and the third was hand-written.

Candi had shown Jess a notebook of lyrics she'd written, including a song she'd been working on for Iris, and she recognised the handwriting immediately. Grabbing the envelope, Jess almost ran into the lounge, positioning herself on the sofa so that she could cradle Iris in one arm and still manage to open the letter. Except, once it was in her hand, she was frightened to unfold it. Part of her wanted to wait until Dexter came in, but an even bigger part of her had to know. Even if it was the news she'd been dreading and Candi really had gone for good.

Dear Jess, Dexter and Riley,

I'm writing this letter and I already miss you, even though I haven't even left yet. I miss Iris too and I love her more than I can believe, but I know leaving her behind with you is the best thing I could ever do for her.

You've been like the big sister I never had, Jess, and you've taught me so much since I came to your house. It was like when I was at Nan's, and I felt like part of a family for the first time since she died. I want Iris to have that more than anything. I wish I was ready to be her mummy, but I'm not and I can't expect you to adopt us both!

I've spent ages Googling stuff, and because Riley's her half-brother and you two are foster carers, there's something called kinship care and it means Iris can stay with you. Eventu-

*ally you might even be able to adopt her, if I tell them it's what
I want.*

*I'm sorry I lied to you about college and left without telling
you why, but I didn't want you to try and change my mind. I
know I'm not ready to be Iris's mummy and I want her to have a
dad too, and a brother, because that's something I never had. I
was really at an audition for a job as a back-up singer on a cruise
ship. I couldn't believe it when they offered it to me on the spot.
That's where I'll be by the time you get this letter, probably
halfway to the first stop-off. It's a round the world cruise and I
won't be back for three months. I won't change my mind about
giving Iris up, as long as they let you have her. If they don't, then
I'll do everything I can to stop anyone else from adopting her.*

*I know that because of what you've taught me I could be a
'good enough' mum for Iris, but I don't want that. She deserves
the best and she'll have that with you and Dexter. I'm not ready
to give her everything you can and I want her to have all the
things I never did. You're the only people I want to be her family,
because I know how much you both love her and I know you'll
tell her that I love her too and that's why I did this. I hope I'll get
to visit all of you as often as I can and I can be a sort of big sister
to Iris, just like Jess has been to me.*

*I've written another letter to Jamie explaining all this stuff and
I think he'll be on your side. He might wear some of the worst
outfits I've ever seen, but he's not bad for a social worker and I
should know!*

Give Iris the biggest hug from me.

Lots of love, Candi xxxx

By the time Jess had finished the letter, she could hardly see.
She'd never have believed it was possible to feel so many emotions
in one go – relief that Candi was okay, guilt that she'd had no idea

what the young woman was planning, sadness that Candi saw leaving as her only choice, and immense gratitude that she wanted to entrust the care of her beloved daughter to Jess and Dexter. Even amongst all of that, Jess's most overwhelming emotion was still one of fear. She was terrified that Candi's hopes for her daughter might mean nothing to the people who would ultimately get to make the decision. Even if they listened to what Candi wanted, there was always the chance she might change her mind. Jess felt ashamed for even thinking that way, when her one job had been to give Candi the confidence to parent her own daughter. She wasn't sure she was strong enough to go through all of this again and still end up without a baby in her arms. Whatever Jamie and the other professionals decided, Jess and Dexter had a huge decision of their own to make.

* * *

When Jess had woken up at 2 a.m., to feed Iris, she'd known there was no chance of her getting back to sleep, so she'd gone downstairs. Dexter had followed her down an hour later.

'How are my girls?' Dexter's voice was gentle, but it didn't stop Jess recoiling like she'd been slapped.

'Don't say that. She's not ours.' It hurt, just saying the words, but she knew it was true. As soon as Dexter had got home from work the night before, she'd shown him the letter. Within half an hour, Jamie had rung to tell them he'd had a letter from Candi too. He'd explained that carrying out her wishes was technically possible, but he'd counselled them against assuming it would be that simple. Jamie also told them about several cases he'd been involved in where the biological parent had changed their mind, and reminded them that there was always a chance Connor could come forward.

'She could be ours.' Dexter sat beside Jess on the sofa, laying his hand over where hers met to support Iris's body weight. 'I know this is hard after Teddy, but I feel like it's what we were meant to do. All the failed IVF cycles, all the heartache, I'd go through it all again if Iris is the reason none of that worked. But I know that was harder on you than it was on me, because I didn't have to go through the treatment, and you've had so much more to deal with. So, if you don't want to do this, I'm not going to put any pressure on you.'

'When you and Riley became my family, it made everything that happened with Teddy so much easier to accept. It felt like you were my reward for all the pain I'd gone through, but I can't believe I'll get that lucky twice. When you grow up as the girl who's in care, because her own father didn't want to raise her, you get used to thinking the only luck you'll have is bad luck. I don't know if I can let myself believe that we could have this perfect family. If I do, and she's taken away from us, there'll always be a member of our family missing and an empty space that can't be filled, no matter what we do. If I let myself think, even for a moment, that she might be ours, I'll never be able to give that up.'

'So, what do we do, just let her go?'

'I'm not sure if I can do that either.' Every time Jess thought she knew what to do, another thought entered her head and changed her mind. Candi leaving had felt like a knife in her side, but the thought of letting Iris go was a thousand times worse – like someone was leaning with all their weight and twisting the knife deeper into her body. If she gave Iris up now, the pain of saying goodbye would be excruciating. But if she held on until someone came and snatched her away, Jess was afraid it might actually kill her. Or at least that she might want it to.

'Jamie seemed to think that Iris staying with us would be the best thing for Candi, if she wants to maintain a meaningful relationship with her after she's adopted.' Dexter moved and, right on cue, the baby closed her hand around his little finger. 'I think Iris might be trying to tell us something.'

'What if Candi changes her mind and comes back for Iris when we've grown to love her even more?' Jess couldn't keep trying to hide what she was thinking from Dexter; she had to tell him what she was most afraid of, before the weight of it crushed her. 'I'd feel like the worst person in the world, hoping Candi decides not to be Iris's mum, but that is what I'd be hoping for if we do this. If I'm really honest, it's what part of me is already doing.'

'I think Candi means what she says in her letter.'

'I think she means it too, right now. But Iris isn't even two months old yet. Candi has barely adjusted to parenthood, and she might not even be thinking straight.' Jess wished she could speak to her, to know for sure she was okay.

'Whatever happens in the end, do you think there's anyone else who could take better care of Iris, until we know for sure what Candi wants to do?' Dexter looked into Jess's eyes and she slowly shook her head.

'No, but it's not just our hearts that could be broken. What about Riley?' The thought of him losing his little sister was unbearable. He'd told Jess how much he loved Iris, but he'd shown it too – in the way he looked at her and the little things he did for her, that said so much more than words alone.

'If we don't foster Iris, and pray that we might eventually be allowed to adopt her, Riley is definitely going to lose her. If we take a chance on doing this, he might not. Even if Candi changes her mind, there'll be more chance of Riley having a relationship with Iris than if someone else fosters her in the meantime.' Dexter put a hand under Jess's chin, so she had to look up at him again. 'I'm not going to lie and pretend we haven't got to risk getting hurt, but we can explain things to Riley in a way he understands and make him part of it, every step of the way.'

'It's already too late to stop ourselves getting hurt if she goes, isn't it?' Jess had known a long time ago that it was too late for her, but any hope she'd had of protecting her husband and son was gone now too.

'It is, but whatever happens, we've still got each other and Riley, and at least we'll know we've done our best for Iris and Candi.'

'Our best is all we can do.' Jess looked down at the baby sleeping in her arms and offered up a silent prayer, to whoever might be listening, that things would work out in the best possible way for Iris. Even if Jess and Dexter had to pay the price.

* * *

The doctors seemed delighted with Johnnie's progress. He'd started to say a few words less than twenty-four hours after they'd reduced his sedation and by the second day his speech was almost back to normal, although he still seemed to get tired really easily. Meg's parents had offered to come over from France when they'd heard about Johnnie and Tilly, but she'd played the situation down, asking them to wait until Johnnie was home before they made the trip. His sister was on a holiday of a lifetime with her family in Florida and Meg had made the difficult decision not to call her. There was nothing she could do and there'd been no point in Meg worrying her until she knew what the outcome was likely to be. Now that the doctors were confident that Johnnie would make a complete recovery, she'd call his sister and let her know.

'Is Tilly okay?' It had been one of the first things Johnnie had said and Meg couldn't have loved him more at that moment. Despite everything she'd put him through, the relief on his face when Meg had assured him that Tilly was doing well had been palpable. She was still too afraid to leave him for any length of time and she'd found a room in a hotel close to the hospital. Ella and Anna had brought over some clothes for her, and Jess was still being an incredible source of support, even with everything she had going on. When she'd told Meg about Candi's letter, her voice had been shaking and Meg had wished there was something she could do to repay Jess for all that she'd done for her. But there was nothing she could do, except listen and be there for Jess if things fell apart. And for now, she couldn't bear to be any further from Johnnie's side than she had to be, until he was finally allowed home.

'We're going ahead with the plan to move Johnnie out of critical care and on to a ward. If his scans look like we're expecting them to, we can begin to make a plan for the remainder of his recovery and his eventual discharge. He's making excellent progress.' One of the nurses, who'd been involved in much of Johnnie's care since his operation, smiled at her warmly and Meg did her best to mirror him, but a pain like a metal band tightening across her abdomen almost took her breath away. The nurse's expression changed as he looked at her. 'Are you okay?'

'Just a bit of cramp in my back from sitting around so much and sleeping in a strange bed at the hotel.' Meg forced a smile as the tightening gradually eased off. 'I think I might stretch my legs while Johnnie's having his scan; will he be taken straight down to the new ward?'

'That's the plan, but I've got your number, so I can text you once they've called to confirm.'

'Thank you so much for everything, Troy.'

'It's an absolute pleasure. Seeing patients like Johnnie making the kind of recovery he has is what I came into nursing for. If I don't see you again, good luck with the baby and I hope you manage to walk off the cramp. If not, it might be time for you to go home and have a proper rest. Johnnie will be absolutely fine if you leave him for a day, I promise.'

'I'm sure I can walk it off.' Even as Meg said the words, she knew it was a lie. She recognised this pain. She'd been through it twice before.

29

Jess was tempted to spend every moment of every day holding Iris in her arms, in case the chance to do it was suddenly whipped away again. But she needed to give herself some space away from the baby, if there was any hope of her holding things together until the social workers made a decision. When Dexter said he was planning to go and see his sister on her birthday, Jess had suggested he take Iris with him, so that she could check on Meg and see whether she needed anything. When Meg had requested her hospital bag for delivery 'just in case', Jess hadn't been able to resist teasing her.

'Do you know something I don't? I thought the consultant was reviewing you next week to discuss whether to go straight for a caesarean?'

'I'm not even going to discuss booking a C-section until Johnnie is well enough to be there. I've still got time to decide and I'd like to see if I can have a natural birth. I know they're not keen after I had a C-section with Tilly, and a retained placenta with Seth, but if nature decides to take its course before I see the consultant, I want to be ready.'

'Okay. I'm leaving now, so I'll grab your bag, then head straight over. Is it in your bedroom?'

'Uh-huh.' Meg's response came out as almost a grunt.

'Are you sure you're okay? You sound a bit strange.' There was no response and for a moment all she could hear was the sound of laboured breathing, and her own voice. 'Meg, are you there? Are you okay? Meg? Meg!'

Jess was really starting to panic, when her friend finally replied, 'Sorry, I just had this weird pain. I think it's the start of a water infection. I've been putting off having a wee longer than I should every time I've needed to go, because I didn't want to keep leaving Johnnie. Sorry, that was probably more information than you wanted.'

'No, it isn't, and I want you to promise me you'll ask at the hospital if anyone there can prescribe you something. And if you haven't done it by the time I arrive, I'm going to march you straight down to the pharmacy myself. The last thing you need, if you do go into labour, is a water infection.'

'Yes, Miss!' Meg laughed. 'I can't thank you enough for everything you've done for me and I'll see you when you get here.'

* * *

It was nearly an hour and a half later by the time Jess got to the hospital and, when she'd texted to see where Meg was, she'd told her that Johnnie had been moved to another ward and that they were hoping to get him home by the end of the week. Even having heard all that before she got to the ward, Jess was still surprised to see Johnnie sitting up in bed when she finally tracked them down.

'I know I look like I've gone ten rounds with Tyson Fury, but you should see the other guy.' Johnnie smiled as she came into the room.

'You look pretty amazing considering what you've been through.' Jess wished she could say the same for Meg, but her friend looked completely exhausted and she grimaced as she got up from her chair.

'You're a star for bringing that in.' Meg was still pulling a face as she reached over to take the bag from Jess.

'No heavy lifting for you at this stage of the game.' Jess set the bag down underneath the end of the bed. 'And I'm guessing the same goes for you?'

'They've given me a whole list of things I can't do. No working or driving until the surgeon signs me off. No strenuous activity of any kind, including housework, so I'll need to organise some help to make sure it doesn't all fall to Meg. And there'll be no champagne to wet the baby's head either.' Johnnie still looked pretty cheerful, despite the list of restrictions he'd been given. 'But the good news is they're finally going to let me get up tomorrow, so I can start to build my strength back up. I've even been promised a shower. If I do all of that, they think I'll be able to go home in a couple of days. I'm just so grateful that I didn't miss the baby being born and I'm even more grateful that I'm here at all.'

'Not as grateful as I am.' Meg was still on her feet. 'Why don't you take my seat, Jess? I need to stand up for a bit. I keep getting cramps in my back from sitting around all the time.'

'That could be the infection spreading up to your kidneys. Did you speak to the doctor?'

Johnnie cut in before Meg could even answer. 'What infection? Are you okay?'

'I'm fine. It's just a bit of a water infection, and I spoke to my consultant's secretary about it. They're going to send a prescription down to the pharmacy. But that's not why my back's hurting; it's cramp. I need to stretch it out, that's all.' Meg moved to the end of the bed and bent forward, screwing her face up as she stretched her back out.

'I keep telling her she should go home and rest.' Johnnie sighed. 'But I might need you to kidnap her for me, Jess.'

'If she hasn't agreed to go home by tonight, I'll happily oblige.' Jess glanced at Meg, who still looked really uncomfortable. 'But I won't stay long now; I know you must both be exhausted.'

Meg finally stood up straight again, the cramping she'd had clearly easing off. 'Johnnie keeps drifting off to sleep in the middle of our conversations, but I'm sure you've got far more interesting things to say than I have. How's everything going? Is there any more news from Candi?'

'Jamie is doing everything he can to try and speak to her. The letter on its own might not be enough. If she really wants us to care for Iris on a long-term basis, they need to make sure she understands the implications and that no one is coercing her.'

'Can she change her mind about that further down the line?' Johnnie's speech seemed entirely normal, but even the bruising couldn't hide how tired he was.

'Even if she tells them she wants to give up parental responsibility for Iris, it would be at least a year before they'd allow us to adopt her. Candi can change her mind at any point and rightly so.' Jess knew only too well, from her experiences with her father, that it was possible for someone to become a good parent in the future, even if that person hadn't been ready for it before.

'That's a long time for you guys to be in limbo.' Johnnie didn't seem to be having any problems grasping the situation, but it was Meg who seemed to be struggling to follow the conversation and she was gripping the end of the bed so hard her knuckles had gone white. She was arching her back and this didn't look like cramp to Jess, not after over a decade of midwifery.

'Are you sure you're okay, Meg?' Jess took a step closer to her friend, who nodded.

'I'm fine, honestly. My body is just trying to remind me why forty-six-year-olds aren't supposed to get pregnant.'

'You're not too old for anything, you're perfect, and when I woke up and found you sitting at the side of my bed, I...' Johnnie suddenly did a yawn so wide it looked capable of dislocating his jaw.

'Are you trying to say that you woke up, saw me sitting there, and wished you could just go back to sleep?' Meg managed a smile for the first time since Jess had arrived. But then suddenly she arched her back again and grimaced. Jess would have bet everything she owned that this wasn't a water infection.

'Maybe we should let you get some rest and I can take Meg off for a cuppa and a slice of cake.' Jess turned to Johnnie, who didn't seem to have any idea that his partner was almost certainly in early labour, and there was clearly a reason why Meg didn't want him to know.

'Good idea. They said I'd be really tired for a while and I'm rubbish company for Meg at the moment.'

'Come on then, Meg, let's go and see what delights the hospital restaurant has got to offer us.' Jess wanted to get her friend on her own to see if she could find out why she was trying to deny that she was in labour, because she had no idea what Meg could possibly be hoping to achieve.

* * *

'It's just twinges in my back and some Braxton Hicks, that's all.' Meg was trying as hard as she could not to show how much the tightenings across her abdomen were hurting, but when she'd had to stop, halfway down the corridor from Johnnie's ward, to lean against the wall, she knew the game was up. She should have realised she couldn't fool a midwife, especially when the pains were now so powerful that she couldn't even speak until they eased off.

'Meg, even Riley wouldn't believe that line. How long have you been having contractions?'

'They were only mild to start with, but they've been getting worse since just before you got here.' Meg bit her lip; she'd been trying so hard to hold on. If she could just wait until tomorrow, when Johnnie's consultant had said he could try getting out of bed, maybe they'd let him come up to the labour ward, even if it was just for the last few minutes. But the baby couldn't come yet; Johnnie wasn't ready. He'd already said how grateful he was not to have missed the birth of his daughter, but now it looked like he was going to miss it anyway.

'Why didn't you say something?'

'I didn't want it to be true. I thought if I could just wait until tomorrow, Johnnie might be able to be there, at least for a little bit.'

'Oh sweetheart, I'm so sorry, but it doesn't matter how hard you try to hold on, I'm afraid babies don't wait for anyone.'

'Labour can easily last for over twenty-four hours, though, can't it?' Meg desperately wanted to believe she could hold out, but the pain was getting worse with every contraction.

'It can, but that's not what we really want for you or the baby. You've done brilliantly and it's been great that you haven't had the high blood pressure or diabetes your consultant was worried might be a risk. But the reason she offered you a planned C-section wasn't just because of complications with your previous deliveries. It's much more common for women over forty-five to have a significant loss of blood during labour, so she won't want to see you labouring for too long and I can't let you risk that either. The most important thing is that the baby makes it here safely and that you're okay too. You know that's all Johnnie's really going to care about.'

'I do, but I just wanted to wait a bit longer so that—' Meg was mid-way through her sentence when something that usually only happened in TV dramas suddenly happened right there, halfway down the hospital corridor. The splash of her waters hitting the floor made a woman walking towards her stop in surprise, as the young girl with her pointed in Meg's direction.

'Mummy, why has that lady just wet herself?'

The little girl's mother shushed her, ushering her along the corridor as quickly as possible and all Meg could do was laugh. If she didn't, there was a very good chance she might cry.

'It seems like my daughter's determined to make an entrance on her own terms.'

'And to get her Auntie Jess's shoes soaking wet in the process.' Jess was laughing too. 'Right, I'm going to get you a wheelchair and track down a clean-up crew for aisle twelve.'

'Will you come with me to the labour ward?' If Meg couldn't have Johnnie, there was only one person she wanted with her.

'Just try stopping me. Don't move, I'll be right back.'

'I'm not going anywhere.' Meg gritted her teeth and watched her friend hurrying down the corridor as another contraction took hold. Jess was right, babies didn't wait for anyone and there was nothing Meg could do to slow this labour down, no matter how much she wanted to. The moment she'd been waiting for was finally here, but none of it was as she'd envisaged, and she was scared. When Seth and Tilly had been born, the nerves had been tempered by excitement, and Darren had been there with her, every step of the way. They were the greatest moments of his life, that's what he'd told her afterwards, and it broke her heart that Johnnie wasn't going to be there to see his daughter born. But she was coming right now, and the only thing left for Meg to do was pray that everything would be okay.

30

Jess's work at the hospital meant that she was allowed to oversee the delivery itself, rather than just be Meg's birthing partner. The consultant had been informed and had confirmed she was happy for Meg to try for a natural delivery, but if there were any signs of either the baby or Meg struggling, she'd need to be taken straight for an emergency C-section.

'You're doing amazingly, Meg. You're at nine centimetres now.' Jess had just completed her latest examination and as relieved as Meg was that things were progressing so quickly, part of her still wished they wouldn't. There was no point in hoping that things would slow down though, because that would only end up in a C-section, and Johnnie wouldn't be present for that either. At least Meg stood the chance of being up and about quite quickly if she had a vaginal delivery and she could take the baby to meet her father as soon as possible.

'You don't see many people getting this far without pain relief.' Trish, the maternity care assistant who'd been supporting Jess with the delivery, smiled. 'If someone had offered me a C-section with my two, I'd have snatched their hand off.'

'I don't want to forget any of this, because it's definitely the last time I'll be doing it.' Meg had thought the same thing when she'd had Tilly, but now it was a guarantee. If Johnnie couldn't be at the birth, she needed to have enough memories of it for both of them.

'Given how quickly you've progressed from seven to nine centimetres dilated, I'd say we're less than twenty minutes away from the second stage.' Jess looked at Meg for a moment, before turning towards Trish. 'I'm just going to have a quick chat with Nancy about coming in when Meg's ready to push, so that we can keep a really close eye on things. I'll only be a few minutes. Will you be okay?'

'I've been doing this job since before you were born, I'd imagine. We'll be fine, won't we Meg? Two golden oldies together.' Trish laughed and Meg couldn't help joining in – it was almost like having Gwen there – but then another contraction took hold and all she could think about was breathing through the pain. They were coming thick and fast now, and despite Jess keeping her promise that she wouldn't be too long, Meg had experienced three more contractions by the time her friend came back into the room and she was starting to feel a lot of pressure to push.

'I think I need to start pushing.' Meg wasn't sure she'd be able to control the urge, even if Jess told her not to.

'I'm just going to examine you again sweetheart. I'll be as gentle as I can.'

'You'll have to be quick; I'm only getting about a minute between contractions now.'

'Okay, we'll start after the next one, but if you feel another contraction coming on once I start the examination, let me know.'

'I'm getting one now.' Meg screwed up her face and waited for the contraction to pass. 'I'm ready.'

Jess carried out the examination as quickly and as gently as she'd promised, but she still only made it just in time for the next contraction. 'Go with it, Meg. You're at ten centimetres now, so if you want to push, just listen to your body.'

Meg didn't answer. Instead, she dropped her chin to her chest and pushed. Jess had asked her earlier if she wanted to try another position, and she knew that lying on her back wasn't ideal, but it was what felt most comfortable.

Jess continued her encouragement as the contractions kept coming, but Meg barely heard what her friend was saying. She was more exhausted than she could ever remember being and she couldn't stop herself from crying. It wasn't the pain, or even the crippling tiredness. It was the memories of the two babies she'd had before – one she'd lost forever and one she wasn't sure she'd ever really get back. All she wanted was Johnnie, telling her it would all be okay somehow, but he wasn't there.

'Trish can you go and get Nancy, please? Tell her it's time.' The urgency of Jess's words brought Meg back to the moment and then Trish said something that made her go cold.

'The baby's heartbeat is starting to drop a little bit.'

'I know, and I'm not sure if we can wait much longer, but Nancy needs to know what's going on.'

'Is something wrong with the baby?' Waves of panic were washing over Meg and she tried to get up, but Jess put a hand on her leg.

'It's okay, I promise. She's just getting tired and you are too. I want to speak to Nancy first, but I think it's time for us to do something. You're so close, they might want to try forceps if the baby starts to crown soon, but we'll need a doctor either way. I don't think we can wait much longer, but Nancy asked me to call her first if we needed help. I'm not going to let anything happen to you or the baby, but I'd rather we intervened as soon as possible if we're going to have to.'

'I want Johnnie here!'

'I know you do sweetheart, but the most important thing right now is you and the baby. So I need you to focus all your energy on that.'

'I'm not sure I can stop myself from pushing if I get another contraction.' Meg didn't know if the doctors would want her to stop trying, if they decided to do a C-section. She was about to find out, though, because she could already feel the next contraction building.

'You don't need to stop. Just keep listening to your body and let us worry about the rest.'

'I've put the call in.' Nancy came into the room just ahead of Trish, as Meg's latest contraction began to ease.

'To both of them?' Jess's shoulders visibly relaxed as Nancy nodded.

'They're on their way.'

'I can see the top of the baby's head, but she's not crowning yet.' If Jess was panicking, she wasn't giving anything away, even though some of this was clearly new territory to her. 'I've only done episiotomies when the baby is already crowning.'

'Her heartrate is a little bit slow, but I think we're okay for now. If the doctor wants to go for an instrumental delivery, they're going to want to do an episiotomy anyway. Let's hold fire for now unless anything changes.' Nancy exchanged a look with Jess. 'We've got time to wait for them to arrive.'

Meg was trying not to read too much into the fact that more than one doctor was on their way, but that couldn't be a good sign. She didn't have much time to panic, though, because another contraction was already starting and this one was the most powerful so far.

'The baby's head is crowning. Well done, Meg, that's it, keep bearing down.' Jess sounded like a personal trainer. 'Go on, that's it, give it everything you've got.'

Meg screwed up her face again, with her eyes half-shut, only dimly aware of more people coming into the room. At that point she didn't care if the whole hospital passed by the end of her bed. As long as she could get the baby out safely, nothing else mattered.

'Oh my God, Meg, I can see her head.' It was the last voice she'd expected to hear and for a moment she was convinced she was dreaming, even when she opened her eyes and saw Johnnie, in a wheelchair just behind Jess. When she realised it was really him, warmth flooded her body and the tears filling her eyes were tears of happiness.

'I'm going to make a little cut now, Meg, just to help baby out as quickly as possible.' Nancy's tone was gentle. 'The doctor is on the way, but we might make it by ourselves with the next push if we give you a helping hand.'

'You can do whatever you need to, but I can already feel another contraction coming.' After that, Meg couldn't speak, all she could do was go with what her body was telling her to do and the rest of the world was just a blur. She wasn't even sure, until she spoke to Jess afterwards, whether Nancy had given her the episiotomy. But by the time the obstetrician arrived, the baby's head was fully out.

'One more good push to get the shoulders out, sweetheart, and the rest of the baby should follow.' Jess was still encouraging Meg every step of the way and, with the next contraction, she pushed as if her whole life depended on it.

'Oh Meg, oh darling, you've done it. She's here.' Johnnie was sobbing and someone was pushing his wheelchair closer to the edge of the bed, as Jess lifted the baby on to Meg's chest for skin-to-skin contact. 'I love you so much. You were amazing, and she's beautiful, just like you.'

'How did you get here?' Every word Meg said was a mammoth effort and it still felt like she was in a dream.

'Jess called in some favours and one of the other midwives persuaded a doctor to bring me up here, but they said I could only stay ten minutes. I can't believe I managed to see her being born. I'm the luckiest man in the world.' Johnnie was half laughing and half crying now, but all Meg could do was nod. He was right about their daughter being beautiful and about it being nothing short of a miracle that he'd been there for her birth. And for the first time in a long time she was starting to feel like one of the luckiest people in the world too, but she was too exhausted to tell him that. It didn't matter, though, because he'd survived to see their daughter's arrival and she had the rest of her life to tell him just how grateful she was that he had.

31

'You look done in.' Dexter was rocking Iris in his arms as Jess came into the lounge, fresh from a shower. She'd changed out of the borrowed midwifery scrubs at the hospital, but she didn't want to risk being around the baby until she'd made certain there was no chance of having brought any germs home with her. Iris was far too precious for that.

'It turned out to be quite the day.' Jess couldn't help smiling when she pictured Meg and Johnnie in the moments after their daughter was born. He wasn't allowed to stay long and he probably wouldn't have made it there at all if Nancy's new boyfriend hadn't happened to be one of his doctors. Jess had clamped the umbilical sooner than they usually would, but she'd needed to put her hands over Johnnie's to help him cut through it. He was still weaker than he was prepared to admit. But cutting the cord early meant that Johnnie had been able to hold his baby daughter for a few precious seconds, before she'd needed to be checked over and he'd been taken back down to his ward. Jess had expected Meg to get upset at that point, but she'd been too exhausted to do much more than lie with her daughter in her arms, once the checks had been done.

The baby, who still had no name, had been perfect and within minutes she'd been rooting around for her first feed.

Jess had stayed with Meg until she was taken to the postnatal ward and thankfully there'd been no issues with the placenta this time, which had made it all as straightforward as it could possibly be. Nancy had put Meg in a corner bay by the window and when the baby had finally been settled in the crib beside her, she'd reached out and touched Jess's arm.

'Thank you for what you did today. You gave us a miracle.' Meg had looked as though she was in that blissful kind of exhaustion, with a smile on her face even though her eyes were half closed.

'You made your own miracle. She's so beautiful, Meg.'

'She really is.'

'You need to get some rest now, but just ring me if you need anything.' New mothers were normally sent home the same day, but Nancy had agreed with Jess that Meg needed an overnight stay at the very least, probably a bit longer. What she'd been through in the lead up to the baby's birth was what had really taken it out of her. And, if she was going home alone, she needed to be strong enough. Once he was back, things would still fall mostly to Meg for quite some time and she'd need to care for Johnnie too. Although, if the determination to get better meant anything, he seemed capable of setting a record recovery time.

'You've been more than a friend to me these last few months, you've been like a sister, and if there's any justice in the world, you're owed a miracle of your own.' Meg had closed her eyes after that and her words about Jess being like a sister had echoed Candi's almost eerily. Jess didn't know if she believed in signs, but at that moment all she'd wanted to do was get back to Iris, Dexter and Riley, and cling on to the promise of her own miracle while it lasted.

'I think Iris wants a cuddle with her...' The sound of Dexter's voice made her jump, bringing her back to the present, but she didn't miss the fact that he'd stopped short. He didn't know how to describe who Jess was to the baby, and she didn't either. But she was more certain now than ever of who she wanted to be.

'I've been looking forward to this all day.' Jess lifted Iris out of Dexter's arms and held her close, breathing in the smell of baby lotion and listening to the little snuffles she always made when she was drifting off to sleep.

'I promised Riley I'd finish building the Knight's Castle with him. At least that way there might be a few less Lego pieces for us to step on in the middle of the night.' Dexter laughed. 'But I'll make you a drink first; I've already got a curry in the slow cooker, so all you need to do is sit down and cuddle Iris.'

'I think I can cope with that.' Jess looked at him, catching her breath unexpectedly as their eyes locked. He'd been her first miracle. After Dom had broken her, Dexter had given her the strength to put herself back together and find a way to be happier than she'd ever been. 'Thank you.'

'For the curry? You haven't tasted it yet.' Dexter laughed again, but she shook her head.

'Thank you for loving me and for never once making me feel like you were giving something up because of me, when the fertility treatment didn't work. You could have a baby tomorrow if you wanted one, but I haven't felt even a moment's doubt that you'd choose that. I really love you, you know.'

'Should I be worried that it sounds like you've only just realised that?' Dexter shook his head, putting his arms around her and the baby. 'I loved you from almost the first moment I met you, and I promise I don't care one little bit that we aren't going to have a child that's genetically ours. When you think about it, the person you're supposed to love most in the world, before you ever have kids, is someone who used to be a stranger, someone who you might never have met if things had taken a different turn. But fate puts them in your path and you choose to build a life together. That kind of love can do amazing things. We get to experience that with our children too, getting to know these incredible little people that fate has put in our path. They'll grow up knowing we've chosen to love them, not because of a sense of duty or a genetic link, but because of who they are. How many people get to experience something like that in their lives?'

'We really are lucky.' Jess leant into him, fighting the urge to ask him for the hundredth time whether he really thought they'd be allowed to keep Iris with them. Fate had brought her Dexter and Riley, and after a gift like that, anything was possible.

'We are. But right now I'm going to get you that drink, because you need to sit down, before you fall down.' Dexter smiled again. 'There's nothing more relaxing than watching Iris sleep, but I can put her down for her nap if you'd rather go and have a lie down.'

'I'll have a cuddle and a cup of tea first, then put her down for a nap so I can come and see the progress you and Riley have made on that castle.' Jess sank down onto the sofa with the baby in her arms, shifting as the mobile phone in her back pocket dug into her. Pulling it out, she saw the alert. She'd put her phone on silent in the hospital and forgotten to turn the volume on again. There were three missed calls, all from Candi's social worker. She could see Dexter's mobile on the other side of the room, plugged in and charging. She got up as quickly as she could, the baby giving a little squeak in protest at being disturbed from her comfortable position.

'Sorry darling, but I need to check something.' Jess whispered the words as she crossed the room, snatching up Dexter's phone. He often put his phone on silent when he wasn't at work, or covering the on-call service, and today was no exception. As a social worker, it was the only way he could carve out some proper family time, but he probably didn't do it as often as he should, because he was the sort of person who always put others first.

There were four missed calls from Jamie on Dexter's mobile. Clearing the notifications and deleting the voicemail message, having only listened as far as 'Hi it's Jamie', Jess breathed out. She couldn't stop Dexter from talking to Jamie forever and she couldn't keep ignoring his calls either. But if this turned out to be their last night as a family of four, Jess didn't want anything to spoil it for Dexter and Riley. They could face reality tomorrow, but for now she wanted to hold on to the hope that sometimes miracles really did happen.

* * *

Meg had no idea how Johnnie had managed to persuade the physiotherapist to let him practice his walking on the postnatal ward, but when she looked up and saw him walking from his wheelchair to the bay where her bed was, with his physio hovering next to him, tears filled her eyes. And, for once, they were the happy kind.

'You'll be running a marathon by Christmas at this rate!' The physio smiled, pulling out the chair next to Meg's bed for Johnnie to sit on.

'I think I might have better things to do, like spending every moment I can with these two.' Johnnie turned to Meg. 'This is Katya, my wonderful physio, who kindly gave in to my nagging when I asked if I could do some of my exercise up here. It seems like the perfect place for a short walk to me.'

'I've heard so much about you already, Meg.' Katya smiled again and it looked as though it was probably her default expression, which must have helped motivate her patients. 'But to be honest, I only let Johnnie persuade me to come up here because he saved my cat when she got hit by a car.'

'I should probably have admitted that any of the vets at the practice could have done the same thing, but I needed to wangle a visit to see how my two favourite people are doing.'

'We're really good.' Meg wanted to say so much more, but with Katya there it wasn't the time. Although it turned out physiotherapy wasn't Katya's only talent, and she'd either picked up on that fact that Meg might want to be alone with Johnnie for a bit, or she was genuinely addicted to the terrible coffee from the hospital vending machine.

'I'm going to grab a coffee while I'm down here, because I might not get my break later. Especially if I'm trekking all over the hospital with this one. Would either of you like one?' Katya caught Meg's eye for a moment and gave an almost imperceptible nod.

'No, but thank you so much.' Meg hoped Katya could tell that her thanks weren't just for the offer of a drink.

'I think the coffee in this place is designed to make patients determined to leave as soon as possible.' Johnnie pulled a face, as Katya shrugged.

'You found us out so quickly! Right, I'm off to treat myself, if you can call it that, but I'll be back in about ten minutes to ferry his majesty back down to the ward.'

'Thanks, see you in a bit.' Johnnie turned back towards Meg, as Katya disappeared. 'She's only doing all of this because I promised her free check-ups for her cat and a year's supply of worming treatment.'

'You always did know the way to a woman's heart!' It was so nice to see Johnnie laughing and like his old self, despite the nagging worries that still wouldn't leave the pit of Meg's stomach.

'I hope so, because I can't wait to marry you. And even though this might be the most unromantic place in the world, and there's absolutely no chance of me being able to get down on one knee, if I hadn't already proposed, I'd be asking you right now and trying to persuade the hospital chaplain to make it official before you could change your mind.'

'I won't be changing my mind, I just wish—'

'That Tilly was here?' There wasn't a trace of bitterness in Johnnie's voice, despite what he'd been through, and she didn't have to ask if he'd forgiven Tilly, because it was written all over his face. 'She'll come when she can. And she's going to fall completely in love with her little sister when she does; how could she not?'

Meg desperately wanted to believe he was right, but the last time she'd seen Tilly, before she'd jumped into the water, she'd said things it was hard to imagine she could ever take back. 'What I do know is that this little girl of ours needs to have a name.'

'I have had another idea, but I don't know what you're going to think of it.' They'd been toing and froing on names ever since they'd discovered they were having a girl, but there'd been nothing that both of them had really loved.

'Go on, but if you suggest Mildred again, even as a joke, you're not getting any say in what I pick!' It felt so good to laugh with Johnnie again and even if he did end up suggesting something they were never going to choose, she was just glad he was there to say it.

'One of the paramedics who brought me in, came in to see me down on the ward this morning, because she wanted to know how I was doing. After she'd gone, the nurse told me that it was her decision to sedate me at the scene, and that she'd probably saved my life by minimising the swelling in my brain. Her name's Hattie. I don't know, I just really liked the name, and it would have a special significance too. It's part of our story and it's why I was here to see her being born.'

'Hattie.' Meg said the name out loud and looked across at her little girl. 'I really like it, and naming her after someone who did something so amazing makes me love it even more. Do you know what it means?'

'No, but I'm sure Google will.'

Meg picked up her phone from the unit at the side of her bed and less than a minute later they had their answer. 'It means ruler of the home.'

Johnnie laughed again. 'I've got a feeling that might turn out to be right! So what do you think?'

'It really suits her.'

'And I was thinking Jesse for her middle name.'

For a second, Meg could hardly breathe, but then she managed to speak. 'That was Seth's middle name.'

'I know and I also know it means gift. I thought about suggesting it a while back, and I also looked for a female version of the name Seth, only there isn't one. You probably know all of this already, but I found out that Seth was the name of Adam and Eve's third son, and that the Bible says he was sent by God to heal the family's heartbreak after the death of Abel. It's not a religious thing for me, but I don't know, it feels like Hattie has been sent to do that too and giving her Seth's middle name just feels right. It's got to be up to you though.'

'It's perfect.' Any hope Meg might have had of her tears being a thing of the past had gone out of the window. Making Hattie's middle name Jesse would give her a link to her brother that would stay with her for life. And if she turned out to be anything like the other person who shared that name – Jess – then she really would be a gift to the world.

32

Jess had tried to block the thought of the missed calls from Jamie out of her head, but it was no good. A night of tossing and turning, and Dexter asking her what was wrong, hadn't made it go away. She needed to face up to the news, whatever it was.

'Jamie's been trying to get hold of us.' It was 5 a.m. when Dexter asked for the third time if she was okay. 'We both had missed calls and he left you a voice mail, but I deleted it because I wanted us to have one more night with Iris.'

The baby was asleep in the cot at the foot of their bed. It had been a relief when she'd woken for a feed at 2 a.m., because at least it had given Jess something else to think about for a little while.

'You don't know that it's bad news.'

'I know. And the worst thing is, the calls could be about Candi needing our help and I've been ignoring them. I'm a terrible person and I don't deserve Iris.'

'Jess, you're the furthest from being a terrible person than anyone I've ever met.' Dexter pulled her into his arms. 'But you're not going to get any rest until you know why Jamie was calling. Did you delete the messages from your phone too?'

'No, but I'm not even sure if Jamie left me a voicemail. I didn't want to look.'

'Shall I go and get it?'

'Okay, but promise you won't listen until you get back up here.'

'I promise.' Jess felt as though she was holding her breath for the entire time Dexter was gone, but the moment he came back into the room she was half tempted to tell him to go away again.

'Do you think it'll wake Iris up, if we play the message?' Dexter slid back into the bed next to Jess, the mobile phone that felt like it was going to determine their whole future clasped in his hand.

'I don't think so.' It didn't matter even if it did, because if the baby was about to be taken away from them, Jess didn't want to waste a moment with her.

'Right, here we go then.' Dexter put the phone on loudspeaker and the voicemail system announced that Jess had one new message; two seconds later, Jamie's voice filled the room.

'Hi Jess. It's Jamie. I've been trying to get hold of you and Dexter all afternoon, but I'm not having a lot of luck.' Jess still felt as though she was barely breathing and she was straining to listen as closely as she could, trying to work out if there was a tone in Jamie's voice that might give anything away. But she didn't have to wait long to discover why he was calling. 'I wanted to let you know that I finally managed to track Candi down to talk to her in person, over video call at least.'

Jess's heartbeat was thudding in her ears and her fingers were itching to press the button that could delete the message in a split second. But it was no good, she couldn't run from this, whatever the outcome. 'She was very clear about what she wants to happen with Iris's care and she reiterated everything she said in the letter. She's agreed to meet with me to make it official when she's back from this trip, but she's already signed up for the next one, so she'll only be back in the UK for two weeks. I think it's highly likely, given that you're already registered foster carers and that you have an established relationship with Iris, not to mention having adopted her brother, that we can get an agreement for kinship care. If nothing changes with Candi, we can also discuss a plan for you to apply to adopt Iris once she's been with you for at least a year. I just need to know from you guys whether it's what you want. If you can give me a call as soon as you get this message please, we can take it from there.'

'Oh my God.' Jess was sure she was about to have a heart attack. Her pulse wasn't just thudding in her ears now, she could feel it in her entire body.

'It's amazing!' Dexter flicked on the bedside light and turned back to look at her. 'We're going to be parents to that incredible little girl over there and I'm sorry if this wakes her up, but I think she needs to be part of it.'

'Mmm.' Jess suddenly felt really weird, like the world was moving in slow motion. She didn't know if it was shock, or disbelief, but she was struggling to process what was happening. She wanted to be Iris's mum more than anything in the world, but she'd spent the last twelve hours preparing for the worst, to try and stop herself from falling apart completely when the little girl was taken away. She hadn't even let herself imagine this outcome.

'Are you okay? You've gone really pale.' Dexter's voice was immediately filled with concern, but Jess was determined not to spoil this moment, even if it meant physically shaking off the shock that seemed to have taken away her ability to speak.

'I can't believe it.' Her voice was wobbly when she finally got the words out. 'She's really going to be ours.'

Jess couldn't have explained it if she'd tried, but somehow she knew for certain in that moment that Candi wasn't going to change her mind. There wouldn't be any risk of Jess's heart being broken into a million pieces, if she allowed herself to truly be Iris's mum, because Candi had given away the most amazing gift and she'd chosen them to receive it.

'I think Iris was always meant to be ours, even before we met her.' Dexter kissed Jess and then pulled away again to look at her. 'I knew it almost from the moment I saw her, just like I did with you.'

'I never had you down as someone who thought life was all mapped out in the stars, but I really think you might be right.' Jess smiled, as Iris finally began to stir. 'Now The question is, who's going to see to our daughter, now that you've woken her up?'

'Rock, paper, scissors?' Dexter laughed.

'I thought you'd be racing me to get to her?' Jess raised a questioning eyebrow and he shook his head, still smiling.

'We've got our whole lives to be there for our little girl, but I think I should let you take this one. There's no one she wants more than her mummy when she wakes up in the night.'

'And that's me.' Jess had to blink three times to make sure she really was awake; things like this didn't happen to her, but when she scooped Iris into her arms she could finally let herself believe this was real. Happiness didn't even come close to describing what she was feeling, but she'd seen the look of pure bliss on new mothers' faces a thousand times. So, even without a mirror, she knew exactly how she looked at that moment. She had everything she'd ever wanted at last, and all the hard times she'd been through were already much harder to recall. Dexter, Riley and Iris were her present and her future, and the past had finally been put where it belonged.

* * *

Meg had been thrilled when the hospital staff had told her that she, Johnnie and Hattie could all be discharged, but then she'd suddenly realised she had no idea how they were getting home.

She'd left her car at Johnnie's place, before the accident, and the car seat they'd bought was still in the spare room at his place too. When Jess had called to tell her about Iris, she'd offered to come down and pick them up, but there was no way Meg was going to drag Jess away from her brand new family while the news had been sinking in.

Her parents were on the way over from their home in France to meet their new granddaughter, but they wouldn't be arriving until much later. There were plenty of other friends she could call, but most of them would be working. She was sitting in the chair beside her bed, just about to ask one of the nurses if they could wait to be discharged until the end of the day, so she could ask Ella or Hamish to pick up the car seat and drive over, when Johnnie suddenly appeared. His walking was picking up pace every time she saw him, but there was no sign of Katya and she had no idea who'd brought him up from his ward.

'I've sorted out transport for us to get home.' Johnnie sat on the edge of her bed, before she could get up from the chair, and took hold of her hand. 'Ed called the ward and asked if he could speak to me. When I said we were being discharged today, he insisted on picking up the car seat and driving us all home.'

'Is he here already?' Meg craned her neck, but there was no sign of Ed.

'They both are. They brought me over in the wheelchair and I just walked the last bit from outside the ward. But they're still waiting out there, because Tilly is scared you won't want to see her.' Johnnie's swallow was audible. 'There's room in Ed's car for all of us, but she said she's happy to go back in a taxi if you aren't ready to face her.'

'Of course I want to see her. I'll go and get her.' Meg went to get up, but Johnnie put a hand out to stop her.

'I'll do it and I can wait with Ed until you've had a chance to talk to her. I think you need a bit of time alone with both your daughters.'

'You're only supposed to be walking short distances.' Meg was worried about Johnnie, but she had to admit that at least part of her was also terrified of facing Tilly alone. The last thing she wanted to do was say something that might make things even more difficult between them, or to send Tilly spiralling backwards.

'Katya told me to push myself a bit more every time.' Johnnie knew her far too well and he squeezed her hand again as he stood up. 'It's going to be okay, once you see each other again, and it'll get much easier from here on out.'

'I really hope so.' Meg lifted Hattie out of the cot beside her and tried desperately to work out the right thing to say when Tilly came in. But, in the end, when she saw her elder daughter again for the first time, all she could do was go with her instinct.

'I've really missed you, Tils, and so has your sister.'

'Oh Mum, she's perfect and I'm so sorry for what I did.' Tilly wasn't even trying to wipe away the tears that were streaming down her face. 'I wish I could take back everything I said and did. I never thought I'd get to be someone's sister again and now I'm scared that I've thrown the chance away.'

'Of course you haven't. You weren't well when all of that happened and I knew it wasn't really you.'

'But even before that I've been selfish, thinking I was the only one who found it hard, but when I lost the baby... I can't even imagine what it was like for you losing Seth.'

'It was unbearable for both of us, but I'd never have got through it without you. You were what kept me going and now we've got Hattie. She's going to need her big sister when her mum and dad are driving her crazy, or she wants someone to go on the rollercoasters with her. I'll be almost sixty by the time she's a teenager.'

'And if I know you, you'll be the first in the queue for the roller-coaster if that's what Hattie wants to do. She doesn't know it yet, but she's got the best mum in the world.'

Meg's eyes were stinging and there was a lump in her throat the size of a cricket ball, so she knew the tears were going to come no matter how Tilly responded to what she was about to ask.

'Do you want to hold her?'

'Can I?' Tilly was crying too, as Meg placed Hattie in her sister's arms. 'I've got something for her. It's in my right-hand jacket pocket; can you get it out for me?'

Meg reached into the pocket as Tilly had instructed, her hand making contact with something soft. When she pulled it out, a fresh crop of tears welled up in her eyes and slid silently down her cheeks.

'It's Owlbert II, do you remember?' Tilly looked at her mother. 'It was Seth's favourite when he was little. He gave it to me when he started secondary school, but I think he only parted with it because he was worried his mates might see it when they came over and laugh. He made me promise to look after it forever, but I know he'd have wanted his little sister to have it now.'

'Oh Tilly, that's so lovely.' Meg was still crying, but as hard as it was to think about the boy she'd lost, these tears were the good kind too. There'd been a time when she thought she was going to lose her daughter as well as her son, and now she had both daughters by her side. She could never forget the past and she didn't want to, because there'd been far more happy times than sad ones before tragedy had struck. But she could finally look forward, knowing that they had the chance to make memories as a family again, and that was the greatest gift she could ever have been given.

EPILOGUE

Hattie's first birthday couldn't have been held anywhere other than the bird sanctuary. Den and her family had pulled off their usual magic, organising activities for the older children and even letting them meet Owlbert III, a magnificent bird who'd been rescued in the spring and named after Seth's original fledging.

Meg had organised a picnic that had been laid out along the row of trestle tables set up inside the new barn that had been built over the summer. There was a bouncy castle in one corner for the bigger kids, including Anna's and Toni's children, and it was one of those autumn days that seemed to have forgotten that summer was supposed to be long gone.

Ella and Dan's baby boy, Gryffyn, who was seven months old, was entertaining everyone with his belly laugh every time he spotted one of the birds. Izzy and Noah's son, Isaac, was a month older and was possibly the most contented baby in the world, happy to go to almost anyone for a cuddle. If Meg hadn't already had Hattie, Isaac would have been in danger of making her seriously broody.

It was wonderful to see Jess finally getting the chance to experience every aspect of motherhood too. Hattie and Iris were similar in so many ways, confident and funny, pulling silly faces to make sure they were never less than the centre of attention.

'I think you need to put those two on the stage! That's a double act in the making if ever I saw one.' Nadia came over to where Meg and Jess were standing watching their girls sitting on the playmat together, with Hamish by her side.

'I know, double trouble, but I think they're going to be the best of friends.' Meg smiled. 'If I'm looking after Iris, when Jess is at work, people are always asking me if they're twins, even though they look nothing alike.'

'It's so lovely they've got each other to grow up with.' Nadia glanced at Hamish. 'Our girls were really close before we even got together.'

'And after the wedding, Remi and Daisy will finally get to be sisters officially. Frankie and Guy have been great at helping out with the wedding plans too.' Hamish put an arm around Nadia. 'But I wasn't expecting to beat you and Johnnie to the altar, Meg.'

'Tilly and Ed have got their wedding at Christmas, so we thought we'd wait until next year.'

'It sounds like she's doing really well.' As Tilly's doctor, Hamish knew what she'd been through, and he'd been incredible in making sure she got access to the right therapy.

'She's doing great and she's been so supportive with Hattie. She's decided to concentrate on being a big sister for now, but she knows she can join the infertility support group if and when she decides she's ready to try for a baby again. Jess has really helped her with working through her feelings about that.'

'I'm really impressed you've been able to keep taking the lead with the group, Jess. What with starting at the new hospital too.

You're putting the rest of us to shame.' Meg had to agree with every word Nadia had said; Jess really was amazing. She was working three shifts a week at the hospital, as well as running the support group that continued to grow in size and remit. But she was also as hands-on with Iris as she could possibly be. Jess had gone back to work after nine months' adoption leave and had made the leap from the unit to the new hospital straight away.

'I couldn't have done it without Meg looking after Iris when Dexter and I are both at work. She's like the big sister everyone needs in their lives.' Jess gave her friend a gentle nudge. 'And being at the hospital, I get to benefit from Gwen's wisdom whenever she's volunteering in the Friends' shop. But I can't ever really imagine stopping the support group. It got me through some really tough times and watching how strong other women can be never ceases to amaze me. I'm just hoping that Keira is the next to graduate, now that Leo and Jemima are expecting their second baby.'

'Are Nicole and James still considering trying again?' Nadia raised her eyebrows.

'I think they've decided to count themselves lucky and stop now. After what they went through with Gracie I suppose there's always a bit of a gap that nothing can quite fill. You can never replace a child and that's always going to hurt, but I think it can teach you to appreciate everything you have got, in a way that other people never quite get to experience.' Jess reached out and touched Meg's arm, a unique understanding passing between them. They'd both been through losses that had bonded them from the start, long before they'd ever imagined they'd been bringing up their daughters as closely as they were.

'We're lucky because there always seems to be something to celebrate these days and the next big thing is going to be Iris's family day, when the adoption is finalised.' Meg was almost as excited about the day Jess's family became official, as her best friend was. 'Riley has got a few ideas of his own about how to mark the occasion, but he's sworn me to secrecy. I'm not even allowed to tell his mum.'

'I knew you two were cooking something up. As hard as that boy tries to keep a secret, his face always gives him away. I'm just so glad that Candi's going to be home in time. She texted me this morning to say she's bought the girls dresses from a shop in Madeira; she said the embroidery on them is beautiful.'

'She spoils them both so much.' Meg loved how much a part of Jess's family Candi was, and describing her next visit as *coming home* was spot on. Candi always brought gifts back for both girls and she'd told Meg how happy it made her to see Iris growing up side by side with her little best friend.

'Right, you lot.' Dexter suddenly came up behind them. 'Johnnie's told me I need to round everyone up so he can bring Hattie's birthday cake out. I did try to warn him that coming between the team from the Port Agnes Midwifery Unit might be more than my life's worth. I've already had to rope Bobby in to help me get the others over to the right place. Anyone would think you lot never see each other. I've never known a team of people get on so well, but then you guys have always been more like a family.'

'We have and even though we don't all work in the same place any more, I don't think that's ever really going to change. Do you, Meg?'

'No, family is family. And even though I joined later than anyone else, I've never felt so much like I've found where I was meant to be.'

'I think we can all drink to that. But Johnnie's right, we need to sing happy birthday to Hattie first. We didn't spend all that time on the karaoke for nothing.' Jess set off towards the table where the rest of the team were gathered, with Iris in her arms, and Meg followed on behind with Hattie. Life was taking her friends in different directions, but she had a feeling they'd find their way back together at every chance they got and she was looking forward to the next time already.

ACKNOWLEDGMENTS

I can't believe that this is the eighth and final novel, at least for now, in the *Cornish Midwives*' series. I have been overwhelmed by how readers have taken the series to their hearts and it has changed my life. After more than twenty-five years, I've said goodbye to teaching to write full-time. The messages I receive from readers, telling me how much the books have meant to them, have exceeded even my wildest dreams – which says a lot for a writer with far too vivid an imagination! As I always say, there are no words to express my gratitude to the wonderful readers who've chosen my books. Every reader who has bought a copy in whatever format, and everyone who has taken the time to leave a review, has helped make so many of my writing dreams come true. Thank you.

Sadly, I am not a midwife or doctor, but as always, I have done my best to ensure that the medical details are as accurate as possible and if you are one of the UK's wonderful midwives, maternity care assistants or doctors, I hope you'll forgive any details which draw on poetic licence to fit the plot. I'm very lucky my good friend, Beverley Hills, is a brilliant midwife. Bev has been a source of support and advice in relation to the midwifery storylines throughout the series.

There are some characters in *Happy Ever After for the Cornish Midwife* named after very special people. One of my lovely readers, Debbie Sleigh, won a competition to name a character. Debbie chose to combine the name of her sons Simeon and Tobi. I couldn't just settle for one character, so the brothers running the barber's shop are named in honour of Debbie's sons. Some wonderful friends of mine, Toni and Allan Jones, lost their daughter Nicky Kirby to ovarian cancer. Gwen's dance teacher in *Mistletoe and Magic* is named after Nicky, who was a huge fan of *Strictly*. In this latest novel, Nicky makes a reappearance, offering sage advice to Meg, and Nicky's real-life sister, Laura, just had to make an appearance too. I also owe Toni a huge thank you for casting an expert eye over the manuscript during my final read through, as I am so bad at spotting my own mistakes! Finally, my good friend, Kerry, also sadly lost her lovely sister, Den. The two of them and Den's son, Oliver, appear in this novel, running a sanctuary for owls, one of the many things Den loved. The novel is about sisterhood of all kinds and is jointly dedicated to Den and my sister, Sam.

There are so many people I need to thank for their support throughout this series, including the book bloggers who are part of the wonderful tours organised by Rachel Gilbey. I want to say a particularly big thank you to Scott from @bookconvos, Jan Dunham, Meena Kumari, Beverley Hopper, Tegan Martyn, Anne Williams, Ian Wilfred, Debbie Blackman, Jane Hunt, @thishannahreads, Isabella Tartaruga, Mandy Eatwell, @jaffareadstoo, @wendyreadsbooks, @bookishlaurenh, @jenlovesreading, @Annarella, @BookishJottings, @Jo_bee, Kirsty Oughton, @kelmason_, @TheWollyGeek, @bookslifethings, @Tiziana_L and @Ginger_bookgeek.

My thanks as ever go to the team at Boldwood Books for making my dreams come true, especially my amazing editor, Emily Ruston and my brilliant copy editor and proofreader, Candida Bradford, without whom this series wouldn't exist. I'm really grateful to Nia, Claire, Jenna, Ben and the rest of the team for their amazing work behind the scenes, and to Amanda for having the vision to set up such a wonderful organisation.

As ever, I can't sign off without thanking my writing tribe, The

Write Romantics, and all the other authors who I'm lucky enough to call friends. I'm also hugely grateful to the community of readers who join me on my Facebook page and make me smile every day. They also gave me some input for the things they wanted to see happen, including giving Ella and Jess their longed-for babies. Christine Spiers even shared an incident with an oyster that made it into the book! Thank you all.

Finally, as it will forever do, my biggest thanks goes to my husband, children and grandchildren. This is for you and always will be.

MORE FROM JO BARTLETT

We hope you enjoyed reading *Happy Ever After for the Cornish Midwife*. If you did, please leave a review.

If you'd like to gift a copy, this book is also available as an ebook, large print, hardback, digital audio download and audiobook CD.

Sign up to Jo Bartlett's mailing list for news, competitions and updates on future books.

http://bit.ly/JoBartlettNewsletter

Why not explore Seabreeze Farm, another wonderful, heartwarming series from Jo Bartlett...

ABOUT THE AUTHOR

Jo Bartlett is the bestselling author of over twenty women's fiction titles. She fits her writing in between her two day jobs as an educational consultant and university lecturer and lives with her family and three dogs on the Kent coast.

Follow Jo on social media:

 twitter.com/J_B_Writer
 facebook.com/JoBartlettAuthor
 instagram.com/jo_bartlett123

Boldwood

Boldwood Books is an award-winning fiction publishing company seeking out the best stories from around the world.

Find out more at www.boldwoodbooks.com

Join our reader community for brilliant books, competitions and offers!

Follow us
@BoldwoodBooks
@BookandTonic

Sign up to our weekly deals newsletter

https://bit.ly/BoldwoodBNewsletter